Praise for Renee Ryan

A Touch of Scarlet

"Renee Ryan's second book in her Gilded Promises series, with its emotional depth and wonderful sense of time and place, is another thoroughly engaging and sigh-worthy read."

— Winnie Griggs, award-winning author of inspirational historical romance

Journey's End

"Utterly charming and not to be forgotten, *Journey's End* is Gilded Age delight."

— Victoria Alexander, #1 *New York Times* bestselling author

"Powerful and inspiring. *Journey's End* is a wonderfully rich and rewarding book."

— Gerri Russell, bestselling author of *Flirting with Felicity*

"Renee Ryan's heart-tugging story set in New York's Gilded Age kept me turning the pages well past my bedtime!"

— Winnie Griggs, award-winning author of inspirational historical romance

"Ryan's written a touching story of family, forgiveness, and a forever sort of love."

— Holly Jacobs, award-winning author of *These Three Words*

Dangerous Allies

"Ryan outdoes herself with this latest offering—a mix of romance, intrigue, and spies. She writes her characters with strong feelings and heart."

—Patsy Glans, RT Book Reviews

Finally a Bride

"I absolutely love books where the two main characters previously had a relationship that ended badly. Watching them work through past issues and forge a new, stronger relationship is so enjoyable. Garrett and Molly are great characters . . . Watching them open up their hearts and seeing them learn to trust each other was so sweet. *Finally a Bride* was such a great book and I definitely recommend it to fans of Christian romantic fiction (5 stars)."

—*Britt Reads Fiction*

Once an Heiress

ALSO BY RENEE RYAN

Gilded Promises historical romance series

Journey's End

A Touch of Scarlet

Charity House historical romance series

The Marshal Takes a Bride

Hannah's Beau

Loving Bella

The Lawman Claims His Bride

Charity House Courtship

The Outlaw's Redemption

Finally a Bride

His Most Suitable Bride

The Marriage Agreement

World War II historical series

Dangerous Allies

Courting the Enemy

Village Green contemporary romance series

Claiming the Doctor's Heart

The Doctor's Christmas Wish

Stand-alone works

Heartland Wedding
Homecoming Hero
Mistaken Bride
"New Year's Date" in *A Recipe for Romance*
Wagon Train Proposal
"Yuletide Lawman" in *A Western Christmas*
Stand-In Rancher Daddy

Published as Renee Halverson

Extreme Measures

RENEE RYAN

Once an Heiress

A GILDED PROMISES NOVEL

Waterfall
PRESS

Published by Waterfall Press, Grand Haven, MI

www.brilliancepublishing.com

Amazon, the Amazon logo, and Waterfall Press are trademarks of Amazon.com, Inc., or its affiliates.

ISBN-13: 9781542046350
ISBN-10: 1542046351

Cover design by Kirk DouPonce, DogEared Design

Printed in the United States of America

To Dee Halverson, for being a loving and supportive mother-in-law. Thank you for sharing your son with me.

It was meet that we should make merry, and be glad: for this thy brother was dead, and is alive again; and was lost, and is found.

Luke 15:32

Chapter One

New York City, Herald Square, 1901

Gigi Wentworth pulled the bulky, oversized cloak tightly around her shoulders and stepped into the early-morning foot traffic. A cold gray mist snaked around the hem of her skirt. The frigid air was a stark reminder that winter would have the city fully in its grip before long.

Wrapped inside the heavy black wool, Gigi took comfort in her shrouded anonymity. No one would recognize her in the ugly garment. They would certainly never suspect she was the missing daughter from one of the wealthiest families in America.

That was, of course, the point.

For nearly a year, Gigi had put forth great effort to create an ordinary, forgettable persona.

Reaching up, she stuffed an errant strand of faded blonde hair beneath the hood of her cloak.

She increased her pace, quickly rounding the corner of Thirty-Fourth Street and Sixth Avenue. With no small amount of relief, she spotted the three perfectly round, golden spheres suspended above a weathered awning up ahead. The time-honored symbol beckoned her forward, giving her a glimmer of hope that soon she would be able to go home. *Soon,* she vowed silently.

Home.

The word brought a bittersweet mixture of pleasure and apprehension. A year was a long time to be away from the people she loved. Would her family welcome her return?

Not if you arrive without the pearls.

Certainty took hold. The trials of the past eleven months were almost at an end. One final task lay before her.

Gigi had scraped and saved for this moment, hiding her true identity in a quiet life of servitude. Not by choice. No. She'd been driven by something far more powerful. Shame.

Shame for what she'd done. For the people she'd hurt. For the pretty lies she'd clung to with willful obstinacy.

Gigi drew to a stop outside Ryerson's Pawnbroker Sale Store.

This was not the first time she'd visited the pawnshop in Herald Square. Assuming everything went according to plan, it would be her last.

Heart pounding wildly against her ribs, she looked over her shoulder. The eerie sense that she was being followed had her looking right, left, back to the right. No one paid her any attention. Nerves, she told herself. Nothing more.

She twisted the brass doorknob and all but stumbled into the building. She held perfectly still, waiting until her eyes adjusted to the darkened interior. Once her vision cleared, she scanned her surroundings. She was alone.

Not for long.

A skeleton-thin, dark-haired young man materialized from behind a red velvet curtain. Dressed in an ill-fitting suit that hung awkwardly on his skinny frame, he greeted Gigi with a head-to-toe inspection. On the trip back up, his gaze landed on the velvet satchel tucked beneath her arm.

"You have merchandise to sell?"

Gigi shook her head. "To redeem."

His gaze dropped to the satchel once again. "I assume you have a claim ticket."

Hand shaking, she dug into one of the cloak's pockets and clutched the item in question. A sense of calm enveloped her. The sensation lasted only a moment.

Icy sweat broke out on her forehead. Something about this shop clerk, with his haughty smile and superior attitude, made her uneasy. He hadn't even had the decency to introduce himself. "I would prefer to conduct my business with Mr. Ryerson."

"Your name?"

"I am Gi—" She swallowed, then began again in the flat Midwestern accent she'd adopted months ago. "My name is Sally Smith. Mr. Ryerson will know who I am and why I have come."

To his credit, the clerk didn't show any signs of questioning the veracity of her statement. He did, however, take his time giving her another rude head-to-toe assessment.

At last, he nodded. "Wait here, please."

Spine ramrod straight, he disappeared behind the red velvet curtain. Gigi took the opportunity to pace along the collection of display cases.

She ran her fingertip over the beveled glass, studying the treasures relinquished by desperate people for a fraction of their original value. There were a few exceptional items, though not many, and nothing like the pearls she'd forfeited.

As if to mock her attempt at calm, past folded over present, dragging her mind back to that awful day. The morning had dawned gray and dreary, much like this one. She'd been beyond desperate, nearly destitute, facing the real possibility of jail. There'd been few options left at her disposal.

You could have gone home and admitted your sin.

She could have, and been promptly turned away. Her father had made that clear. Harcourt Wentworth was not an easy man, or a forgiving one. He'd given Gigi an ultimatum. Abandon her friendship with Nathanial Dixon or suffer the consequences. She could not have both the man and her inheritance.

Gigi had been naïve, believing surely—surely—her father would change his mind. *Surely*, once she and Nathanial were married all would be forgiven. The faulty rationale had made sense at the time. And so she'd slipped out of Harvest House in the dead of night to be with the man she loved.

Had it only been eleven months ago that she'd stolen away with Nathanial? Though barely twenty-two years old, she'd lived three lifetimes since, each far different than the one she'd created in her dreams. With no small help from Nathanial.

"We'll be married," he'd whispered in her ear. "I'll make you my wife and keep you by my side for all eternity."

Gigi had made him say the words again and again. He'd been happy to oblige. She'd given him everything of herself, only to receive false promises spun by his silver tongue.

"We'll spend our days reading Shakespeare and Byron."

It had sounded so wonderful, so delightful and idyllic.

"We'll while away our nights at the theater. Then we'll come home and play Bach or Beethoven on the piano. Mozart, if we're feeling especially passionate."

She'd blushed then, caught up in the romantic picture he'd painted of their future together.

A future that would never be hers; she knew that now, had discovered the truth mere days after running away with him. Gigi slammed her eyes shut at the memory.

Humiliation flooded through her, hotter than any emotion she'd ever felt before meeting Nathanial Dixon. All her life, she'd longed for such a suitor. Handsome to the point of beautiful, blessed with tousled, sandy-blond hair, piercing gray eyes, and a gift with words. He'd known exactly what to say to win her heart.

The scoundrel had devastated her good sense with poetry and piano duets and secret, not-quite-innocent assignations in the dark. Gigi had happily followed Nathanial through his web of lies, straight to New York City. Straight to her ruin.

A heavy price to pay for love.

Nathanial had taken her money, but he hadn't known about the pearls. Keeping them hidden until her wedding day had been Gigi's one smart move among the dozens of missteps she'd taken.

Sighing, she forced open her eyes. Only to discover the clerk had returned and was looking at her with a smirking expression. "Mr. Ryerson will see you now."

Gigi managed a regal nod. "Thank you."

"Follow me." He turned on his heel.

Gigi blinked, her mind racing, her heart bursting. *This is it.* The words swept through her mind. *At last, at last!*

Heart in her throat, she hurried after the clerk. He led her behind the curtain, into an open office area where a series of large, high-top desks sat in a neat row. All three were teeming with stacks of papers, books, and ledgers. There was a sense of respectability in the organized clutter, as if important business took place in this room and there was no time for something so inane as properly filing away papers.

Peering around her stiff-backed escort, Gigi spotted Mr. Ryerson sitting behind the center desk. Even though he had his head bent over a thick ledger, she recognized him immediately.

She could never forget the way he held his writing instrument in a white-knuckled grip as he made furious notations across the page beneath his hand. The constant, even ticking of a wall clock beat in stark contrast to the pawnbroker's manic scribbling. Gigi silently ticked off the seconds in her head until Mr. Ryerson acknowledged her.

He was close to her father's age, perhaps a shade older. He'd discarded his suit jacket. The knot of his necktie hung loose and slightly off-center. His shirtsleeves were rolled up, revealing a pair of beefy forearms.

When he failed to greet her, Gigi cleared her throat.

The pawnbroker lifted his head. Bored indifference played across his fleshy face. He studied her with an unwavering stare but made no attempt to gain his feet. After several endless seconds, he dismissed the clerk with a curt "Leave us."

A final look in Gigi's direction and the young man quit the room.

"Miss Smith," the pawnbroker began once they were alone. "Your appearance this morning is . . . unexpected."

She said nothing.

What could she say? Of course her appearance was unexpected. She'd come about a month ahead of the deadline he'd given her. "I wish to redeem my property."

True. Yet not completely accurate.

"Ah, well then. Let's proceed." The pawnbroker reached out a hand, swept it in the general direction of the area in front of his desk.

Gigi stepped forward, then paused, not sure if he was motioning her to take the empty seat or simply to come closer. She took the seat.

Wanting this transaction over as quickly as possible, she didn't remove her gloves or her hat or the suffocating cloak.

She placed the satchel on her lap and waited. When Mr. Ryerson remained silent, she reached inside the bag and pulled out a small stack of bills arranged in order of denomination, least to greatest.

Chin lifted, she set the entire pile on the desk. "That should cover the cost of my pearls."

No, not her pearls. Her great-grandmother's pearls, a family heirloom worn by generations of Wentworth women on their wedding day. Gigi couldn't go home without them.

6

Mr. Ryerson stared at the stack of money for a long moment, considering. Familiar with the tactic—her father was a master at pausing for intimidating effect—Gigi once again made the next move. She retrieved the claim ticket from her pocket, then placed it on top of the money.

After setting aside the slip of parchment paper, the pawnbroker took his time counting the bills. "Where did you manage to come by this much money a month ahead of schedule?"

Granting him her most pleasant smile, Gigi called forth all the charm she'd once been lauded for among the gentlemen of her acquaintance. "Does it matter?"

A series of creaks and groans was his initial answer as he leaned back in his chair and tented his fingers beneath his chin. "To be perfectly candid, yes, it does matter. Quite a lot. I cannot accept payment acquired by unlawful means."

She resisted the urge to sigh. Mr. Ryerson hadn't been this skeptical during their first meeting, or so unfriendly. "I earned every bit of that money with hard, honest work."

"Is that right?" His tone suggested disbelief.

Hating that he questioned her integrity, especially when he hadn't done so before, Gigi chose her words carefully. "I found a position as a lady's maid."

Actually, after settling her debt with the Waldorf-Astoria, she'd worked for three separate women in various private homes. Her current place of employment—the third—was much smaller than the others but no less grand.

Each of her employers had needed Gigi as much as Gigi had needed them. She'd grown to care for the women, connected in something resembling friendship and yet . . . somehow . . . not.

She became aware of a painful hollowness inside. When she spoke, her voice was hoarse with pent-up emotion. "I have been fortunate in my choice of employers."

They'd treated her kindly and had paid her well, nearly twice the wages she'd received at the Waldorf-Astoria.

Mr. Ryerson's lips pressed into a hard, thin line. "I see."

Gigi feared he saw things far too accurately. He probably thought she lacked a strong moral fiber. He would be half right. She'd committed more than her share of sins. And although she hadn't stolen the pearls, she had taken them without permission.

She went stiff at the thought. Nathanial hadn't been the only guilty party in their brief time together. Gigi had allowed the line between right and wrong to blur.

She had much to atone for when she met her Maker.

The pawnbroker consulted his ledger. He flipped one page, another, then at least ten more until, finally, he halted. Gigi clasped her hands tightly together in her lap and held her breath as he slowly ran his finger down a long, narrow column.

A wistful ache gathered in her throat. So close. She was so very close. After what she'd done, she could endure ridicule, material loss, even physical pain. But to fail here, now, when she'd come this far, *that* she could not accept.

"You are short fifty dollars."

Short? Fifty dollars? That couldn't be right. She'd counted the money herself, several times. Twenty times. A hundred.

"But . . ." What sort of game was this man playing? "That is the exact amount you gave me for the pearls."

She indicated the stack of money with a jerk of her chin. The sum hadn't been enough to cover the hotel bill Nathanial had left her to pay, but it had been enough to keep Gigi out of jail. Thankfully, the hotel manager had taken pity on her and allowed her to work off the rest of her debt.

"Miss Smith, you are clearly uneducated in the ways of commerce. The additional fifty dollars is interest."

The man was a crook. Gigi nearly said as much but knew better than to risk his ire. Hands sweating inside her gloves, she appealed to the sense of fairness he'd shown her eleven months ago. "That wasn't our deal."

For a moment, Mr. Ryerson refused to meet her gaze. "Perhaps not. However, I have an interested buyer who is willing to pay three times what I'm charging you, interest included."

It was still a fraction of their worth. "The pearls are my property."

"At the moment, they belong to me." He picked up the claim ticket to punctuate his point, flipping the thick paper through his fingers. "As I said, you are fifty dollars short."

Cheat. Scoundrel. Thief!

The words echoed in her mind. Here sat yet another man attempting to take advantage of her. But she voiced none of her indignation. What would be the point? They both knew Mr. Ryerson held all the power. Men always held the power.

She contained her outrage behind a bland smile. "Perhaps, Mr. Ryerson, you could explain something for me?"

Politeness itself now that he had the upper hand, he inclined his head. "I will do my best."

"How does this supposed buyer know of the pearls' existence?" It was a fair question. When she'd made the initial sale, the pawnbroker had promised to keep the necklace locked away in a secure place and only put the pearls on display if Gigi failed to meet the terms of their agreement.

"The man in question is looking for a gift for his wife and is on a tight deadline. He wants a piece of jewelry of the finest quality. As you are aware, Miss"—he hesitated—"Smith, your pearls are of the very finest quality."

"I still have a month." She was grasping, she knew, but he owed her the time. Somehow, someway, Gigi would get the fifty dollars. She wasn't completely without resources. She had connections now, though she preferred not to use them. She'd gotten herself into this mess. She must be the one to get herself out. Atonement would come no other way.

"I will honor the terms of our agreement, plus the interest I quoted," Mr. Ryerson said magnanimously. The brute. "But I will not give you one day past your original deadline."

The crushing disappointment eased a bit. "I would like to see the pearls, if you please."

With no small amount of reluctance, he retrieved the necklace from the safe behind him and set it on the desk.

Gigi studied the collection of four individual strands fastened together with three platinum braces covered with diamonds. Knowing better than to trust this man, Gigi counted the pearls on each strand—forty-two, forty-six, forty-nine, and fifty-four. She still carried the numbers in her head.

Not trusting herself to look away from the Wentworth family heirloom, she asked, "The price you just quoted, the extra fifty dollars, you will honor that as well?"

"I will, indeed." The words lacked sincerity.

She ran her fingertip along the shortest of the four strands, then looked up. "You vow not to charge additional interest when I come back in a month?"

He nodded. Again, not quite meeting her eyes. The gesture gave Gigi a bad feeling, one she knew better than to ignore.

"I want your promise in writing."

He had the audacity to look taken aback by the request.

Refusing to relent, she kept her gaze fastened on his face. "I'll wait while you draw up the document."

* * *

With the promissory note in her possession, Gigi exited the pawnshop, her mood gloomy. She'd underestimated the depths of Mr. Ryerson's greed.

She should have known not to trust the man. He was, after all, in the business of trading on other people's misfortunes. Nevertheless. Changing the terms of their agreement was reprehensible, and one more betrayal to add to all the others Gigi had endured since arriving in New York.

Helplessness consumed her. To come so close . . .

The suffocating blow of her failure was nearly too much to bear. But bear it she would. She had options. Not many, but some. She would redeem the pearls. And then she would go home.

As Gigi entered her place of employment, a three-story town house on Riverside Drive, an icy calmness settled over her. Fifty dollars was not so very much money.

It's a fortune for someone in your situation.

Gigi's footsteps grew heavy, making her ascent up the back stairwell a Herculean task. Time was running out. Her sister's wedding was six short weeks away. Annie must wear their great-grandmother's pearls. It was her right as a Wentworth.

What if Gigi was turned away? What if her family didn't welcome her home? The prospect of total banishment was too horrible to contemplate. And so she shoved the terrifying thought out of her head.

Stepping inside her tiny room on the top floor of the town house, Gigi discarded the heavy cloak. Working quickly, she secured a white apron over the black dress she wore six days a week. She then coiled her hair atop her head, smoothing and tugging until the brittle blonde ends concealed the majority of the darker roots.

The addition of an oversized mobcap, a tug on the uniform's sleeves and, at last, Sally Smith stared back at her from the mirror.

Satisfied the transformation was complete, Gigi left her room. By the time she arrived on the second-floor landing, her thoughts were focused solely on serving another woman facing the scandal Gigi herself had managed to avoid.

Sophie Cappelletti had not been as successful as Gigi at keeping her secrets. Now, with all of society's eyes on her, the twenty-one-year-old had to face the consequences of her actions.

Determined to guide the young woman through the difficult days ahead, Gigi gave a brief knock before entering Sophie's bedchamber. She found the young woman dressed and sitting at a table near the window. Weak light filtered through the clouds floating past, casting flickering shadows over Sophie's bent head.

Gigi shut the door behind her with a soft click. "Good morning, Sophie."

"Good morning, Sally."

Sally. Would Gigi ever get used to the fake name?

"Well?" Sophie stood, then smoothed a hand over the line of pleats that had taken Gigi half a day to press. "What do you think about my choice of attire for the luncheon?"

Sophie's light Italian accent was heavier this morning.

Hearing the anxious note in the question, Gigi took a moment to study the gown. The plain, pale-green muslin did nothing to enhance Sophie's arresting features. The conservative cut was also wrong.

The young woman's exotic beauty called for vibrant colors and bold, modern designs. She had the kind of loveliness reminiscent of another era. Hiding behind a starched, unflattering dress was a choice Gigi could not support.

"It simply won't do. Not for a luncheon at the Waldorf-Astoria." As soon as the words had left her mouth, Gigi winced. She hadn't meant to be so blunt with her opinion.

Frowning, the young woman looked down at the gown. "The dress *is* rather boring. But considering the stakes, I thought boring was the correct approach."

"Not today." Gigi took the young woman's hands and squeezed gently. "You have been invited to dine with Mrs. Genevieve Burrows and a collection of her closest friends, some of whom are the most influential women in New York society. You must look your very best."

"I don't want to attract unnecessary attention." Sophie jerked her hands free. "I am not my mother."

"No, you are not." Esmeralda Cappelletti was the most revered opera singer in the world. She was also flamboyant and dramatic to the core. She enjoyed attracting attention—the good, the bad, and everything in between.

"I won't be compared to her."

Some things could not be helped.

"Comparison is inevitable." The daughter would always be weighed against the mother, especially now that the world knew who Sophie's father was. "You demanded Warren Griffin acknowledge you in front of New York's social elite. You cannot continue to hide from what you've done."

Was she speaking to Sophie, Gigi wondered, or to herself?

"I can try."

If only it were that simple. If only youthful mistakes could be erased with determination alone.

"You must present an aura of confidence. It is the only way to earn society's respect." Perhaps with respect acceptance would come. It was Gigi's greatest wish for the young woman she'd come to think of as a friend.

Sighing, Sophie lowered herself into a chair facing her dressing table. Picking up a hairbrush, Gigi moved in behind the girl. With a skill honed from endless hours of practice on her own hair, she worked the dark curls into a modern style she'd come across in a recent edition of *Harper's Bazar*.

"At the moment, you are somewhat of a novelty," she said. "This luncheon is your opportunity to make a proper impression before the newness wears off and the whispers turn ugly."

"Oh, Sally." Sophie's doelike amber eyes filled with tears. "The society pages have branded me the Daughter of Scandal. How much uglier can it get?"

Much uglier, Gigi thought.

She understood how these matters worked. Though Gigi had avoided scandal, it was only because of the well-crafted lie her family had told in the wake of her disappearance. Even after eleven months, the Boston gossip columns still speculated over the veracity of the Wentworths' claim that Gigi was studying music abroad. Every day, she teetered on the edge of disaster. One wrong move on her part and the ruse would be over. Her sisters' chance at happiness would be at risk.

Gigi had ruined her own life. She would not ruin theirs.

"What if I make a mistake this afternoon?" Sophie asked, her voice shaking with obvious concern. "What if I say something inappropriate, or eat with the wrong fork, or drink from someone else's water glass?"

In that, at least, Gigi could alleviate the young woman's concerns. "We have practiced for weeks. You are ready."

Sophie looked prepared to argue. Gigi didn't give her the chance. "Your half sister and her mother-in-law are hosting the luncheon. You cannot ask for a more influential pair in your corner."

"Penelope and Mrs. Burrows have been very kind."

Sophie's half brother, Lucian Griffin, and his wife, Elizabeth, had also aligned themselves with the young woman. She was not alone in her scandal.

Unlike you.

Gigi caught Sophie's gaze in the mirror and, smiling softly, gave her the same advice she'd given her previous employer. "I have found that taking the first step makes the next one easier, and the one after that easier still."

It was good advice, Gigi thought. Words of wisdom she herself should take to heart. All she had to do was keep trudging toward her goal, one step at a time. Or rather, one *dollar* at a time.

Of course, she would have to keep her identity secret a little while longer. How hard could it be? She'd been Sally Smith for eleven months. Certainly, she could continue the deception for one more.

Chapter Two

She was here. Christopher Nolan Fitzpatrick could practically feel her presence. It had taken him considerable time and money, two private investigators, and several wrong turns, but Fitz's search was over. He'd found Gigi Wentworth.

According to the current investigator's report, she'd changed her name—one of the many reasons the trail had gone cold—and was now working as a lady's maid in Esmeralda Cappelletti's household. A lady's maid! In an opera singer's home.

How far the spoiled heiress has fallen, Fitz thought wryly, his eyes narrowing as they roamed over the interior of the Summer Garden Theater.

Gigi was nowhere in sight. But she was here. Fitz was certain of it. The tensing of his shoulders, the uncomfortable roil in his gut, and the inability to breathe easily were nothing new. Fitz always had this visceral response whenever Gigi was near. His reaction to the woman was the source of his greatest frustration.

He managed most areas of his life with decisiveness and precision. Not so where Gigi was concerned.

If only she'd stayed hidden.

But, of course, she hadn't.

Fitz consulted his pocket watch for the third time in as many minutes. He would have preferred to leave this particular errand to one of his subordinates. Unfortunately, the stakes were too high, and the need for privacy too great, to trust anyone but himself.

And so here he stood, loitering in the wings of a New York theater, waiting for the troublesome woman to show her face.

A theater wasn't a bad place to hide, Fitz admitted to himself. A bit obvious, but Gigi had always been a bit obvious. She embraced drama as though it were as vital to her existence as air. This place was so filled with drama that Fitz's skin crawled.

He crossed his arms over his chest, felt the perfectly cut wool of his jacket move smoothly with the gesture.

Someone whispered his name loudly enough for him to hear. Fitz glanced to his left. A pack of young women huddled closely together. Heads bent, they spoke in rapid, hushed whispers.

Occasional pauses accompanied their swift glances in his direction. Fitz welcomed their interest like a cold rush of biting air on bare skin. He tried to ignore their conversation, but the acoustics in the theater were top-notch.

"I hear he plans to purchase the theater from Mr. Everett."

Giggles followed this statement. More glances were tossed in Fitz's direction. Fitz blew out a slow hiss of air. He'd never liked being the center of attention.

"I do so hope the rumor is true," one of them said in a stage whisper—Fitz finally understood the odd term—and then added, "He's very handsome."

Another pause, longer than the first. More glances and giggles, accompanied this time with heartfelt sighs.

Fitz shifted his stance and put his back to the lot of them.

There, he thought, problem solved. Or . . . not.

The whispers grew louder. "I'd be more than willing to assist Mr. Everett with the negotiations. I can be quite persuasive."

Fitz shook his head. The female interest in him wasn't new, nor would it last. He was not a man ladies sought for light company, not once they got to know him. He was distant. Reserved. Some would say broody. Others would say callous and unfeeling.

It wasn't that Fitz didn't have feelings. Of course he did. He simply didn't make outward displays. He was gifted with numbers not words. He preferred to read contracts and study ledgers. He had little acquaintance with literature, philosophy, or art.

On more than one occasion, Gigi had called him boring and unimaginative. She had not been wrong, especially when compared to her.

Gigi Wentworth was Fitz's complete opposite in every way. Where he thought through every action, she leapt in without a second glance. He followed the rules. She pushed the boundaries. She was engaging, romantic, and full of smiles.

Fitz was . . . none of those things.

Men had always been drawn to Gigi, Fitz included. But she'd never crossed a line. Not until Nathanial Dixon. From the beginning, Fitz hadn't trusted the man. He'd tried to warn Gigi. His advice had gone unheard.

At least her family had been able to keep her scandalous behavior secret. Fitz wasn't especially pleased with his role in their duplicity, but deception had been necessary. Her reputation was safe, for now.

For how long?

If Fitz's hired man had been able to locate her, surely someone else could as well. A reporter, perhaps, especially now that her sister's wedding was nearly upon them and the Wentworths were once again in the news.

Another round of giggles sent Fitz on the move.

Where was Gigi?

Fitz wanted this business over.

His gaze scanned the theater quickly, restlessly, ignoring the men, focusing solely on the women. He willed himself to be patient. More hushed whispers wafted over him, the speculation about his presence growing more absurd.

Whose fault is that?

He could set the record straight, tell them he had no plans to buy the theater. But then he'd have no cause to be milling around backstage on a Monday afternoon less than two weeks before opening night of Esmeralda Cappelletti's return to the American stage.

Allowing Mr. Everett to believe he was interested in purchasing the theater hadn't been Fitz's finest moment.

Although the stage was abuzz with activity, rehearsal wouldn't get under way until Esmeralda graced them with her presence. Like most divas with her level of international acclaim, the opera singer operated on her own schedule, caring not that her whims inconvenienced others.

No wonder Gigi felt at home in the diva's household.

As Fitz waited along with the rest of the cast and crew, he, too, felt their frustration. His hands slid into his pockets.

Patience, he told himself. Gigi would show herself soon enough.

There'd been a time when he'd despaired of ever finding her. She'd left Boston in the middle of the night. Not alone. No, not alone.

She was alone now.

The investigator's report had been clear on that point. It had been unclear on many others. For instance . . .

What had led Gigi to change her name? Why had she become a lady's maid? Just how far had she fallen? And, most important of all, *where* was Nathanial Dixon?

Gigi had arrived at the Waldorf-Astoria with the man. They'd lived extravagantly. Both had vanished a few days later. Gigi had been located two weeks ago.

Dixon was still missing.

The conclusion was obvious enough. The scoundrel had abandoned her.

Fitz's gut roiled. He'd warned Gigi about the man. Fitz hated being proved right. Hated more that Gigi had suffered at Dixon's hands.

The specifics of her disgrace are not your concern.

No, Fitz's goal was simple. Though he feared his task would not be easy. His attention moved to the stage. Gigi could be anyone she wished in this false world, where nothing was as it seemed and donning disguises was an everyday affair.

"Mr. Fitzpatrick." A sultry female voice interrupted his thoughts. Fitz turned away from the stage to face the incomparable Esmeralda Cappelletti.

He'd met the singer two evenings ago, at a party thrown specifically for Fitz by Mr. Everett. In an attempt to woo him, or rather his money, the theater owner had encouraged Esmeralda to use her charms to persuade him to invest.

Of average height, the diva was fashionably curvy. Her eyes were nearly black as coal, and her ebony hair spilled in wave upon wave down her back. There was no denying she was alluring.

Fitz remained unmoved.

Only one woman had ever captured his interest. The thought brought a slice of mind-numbing regret. So many things he would do differently, given the chance. Then again, nothing would come from entertaining such a notion.

So he smiled at Esmeralda. She reached out to him.

Knowing his role in this particular drama, Fitz took the outstretched hand and swept a brief kiss across the knuckles gloved in fine kid leather. "Miss Cappelletti." He released her hand. "Always a pleasure."

"I should think we are beyond such formal address." Eyes locked with his, she curled her slim fingers around his forearm. "You must call me Esmeralda. And I shall call you Christopher."

"My friends and family call me Fitz."

"Then I shall call you Fitz."

He inclined his head. "I insist you do."

Her smile turned beguiling. The opera singer was very good at making a man feel special. Gigi had been blessed with the same gift.

"Tell me, Fitz. Have you come to watch today's rehearsal?"

"Among other reasons." He did not expand.

Esmeralda possessed an awe-inspiring presence. Her exotic heritage could be Italian, as she claimed. Fitz suspected she was possibly Spanish but probably Mexican. Her age was indeterminate, anywhere from twenty-eight to forty years old. Since she had a twenty-one-year-old daughter, Fitz was leaning heavily toward the upper end of that range.

"What is your first impression of the Summer Garden?" Esmeralda asked, her distinctive Italian accent thicker than before. "You approve, yes?"

Fitz swept his gaze over the stage's riggings, past the row of dancers warming up, and beyond the other players in various poses. The entire scene was too loud, too messy, too chaotic. In sum, everything Fitz avoided in his well-ordered life.

The burdens he carried were too heavy for disorder.

And yet, this glimpse of what it took to produce an opera utterly fascinated him. The way all the various working parts, seemingly unrelated and hectic, eventually came together and created something orderly was similar to what he did as an investment banker. "I approve."

Clearly pleased with his answer, Esmeralda slipped her arm through his. "You must allow me to show you around."

Esmeralda had an entire opera company waiting on her. "Another time. I'm afraid Mr. Everett is waiting for me to review the accounting books with him."

"You would prefer numbers to my company?" From her stilted tone it was obvious she'd taken offense.

"I am a financier," he said simply. "Numbers are my business."

It was exactly the wrong thing to say, Fitz realized a moment too late. A tantrum built in the diva's eyes. The private investigator had done his research here as well. Upsetting Esmeralda was never a wise move.

Fitz switched tactics. "Perhaps you would escort me to the office while pointing out various areas of interest along the way."

After a moment of quiet contemplation, Esmeralda performed a very Gallic shrug. "That would be acceptable. Come. We go now."

Lips pressed into a pretty pout, she began the abbreviated tour. They wove through the labyrinth of rigging and freshly painted set pieces. Esmeralda chattered and pointed and generally entertained Fitz with her candid observations. What he found most amusing was how the thickness of her accent came and went with her enthusiasm.

Fitz found he rather liked the singer, which came as a surprise. Perhaps it was her hard-driven will to excel in her profession. A trait they shared.

A movement to his left caught his attention. He snapped his head in that direction in time to see a cloaked figure moving along the far wall.

The shadowy form moved with soft, elegant steps, floating along like a tender snowflake, slowly, smoothly, and yet coolly controlled.

Fitz's heart kicked an extra-hard beat.

That flowing, almost poetic grace could only belong to one woman. Georgina Catherine Wentworth, the missing daughter of the wealthiest family in Boston.

Fitz let out a slow, imperceptible hiss of relief. His search was over.

Now came the tricky part.

* * *

Gigi stuck to the shadows out of pure survival instinct. Disaster had struck in the form of a man.

Disaster always came in the form of a man.

Of all the people to come looking for her, why did it have to be . . . him? Gigi continued moving, deliberately and carefully. She didn't dare glance in his direction for fear he would catch a glimpse of her face. Oh, but the urge was strong.

Don't look, Gigi told herself.

Do. Not. Look.

She looked.

Her feet dragged to a halt.

Her breath clogged in her throat. Her heart slammed against her ribs. It *was* him. Christopher Fitzpatrick. Fitz. Once a friend, turned villain. No. Not quite a villain, but certainly an antagonist in her story.

Fitz was exactly as she remembered. The far-too-serious boy with the shy manner and kind smile who'd grown into an even more serious man, the one her father had expected her to marry—insisted upon actually. An impossible demand. Fitz was everything Gigi was not. Principled. Driven. Someone who knew his purpose in life.

Gigi had always felt a little on edge in his presence. Fitz had been the only person to make her feel that way. She averted her gaze.

It was no use. Fitz's image remained branded on her mind. She knew every facet of that strong, coldly handsome face. She knew the full breadth of those wide, muscular shoulders, the intense green eyes that were the same rich color as the velvet curtains of the theater. His hair, a shade nearly as black as a raven's feather, was expertly cut. Gigi expected no less.

Fitz was always the picture of perfection, a man who never took a misstep, never showed any sign of human frailty. She couldn't help but feel a little inferior in his company and had grown to dislike him because of that.

Why was he here? Why now?

Alarm stole through her limbs as a thought took hold. Her worry turned into sheer panic. Had something happened to someone in her family?

No, Gigi would have discovered something that awful in the Boston newspapers. She read them daily, always looking for news of her sisters, her mother, even her father.

Fingers fumbling for purchase, Gigi adjusted the mobcap on her head and melted deeper into the shadows. Casting a discreet glance from beneath her eyelashes, she watched in stunned fascination as Fitz disentangled himself from Esmeralda's hold on his arm.

He took a step in Gigi's direction.

His eyes were unreadable from this distance. She held her breath and prayed for . . . what? What did she want? More time? A moment of inspiration? A deep hole in the floor to sink into?

Fitz took another step toward her, then stopped abruptly when Esmeralda called out to him. He was forced to turn his back on Gigi.

This was her chance to slip away from the theater. It would not be easy. Fitz stood halfway between her and the backstage door. She would have to be careful. Stealthy.

As she edged behind a rack of costumes, one thought kept spinning around in her head. The charade was over. All because of the appearance of a single man. Not just any man.

Gigi stole another glance in his direction, felt her heart drop to her toes. He looked so very austere.

Some things never change.

He'd interfered in her life once before, to disastrous ends. And now, here he was again, when she was so close, a mere fifty dollars away from redemption.

Bitterness raced through her veins. Gigi glanced toward the exit again, back to Fitz, back to the exit. He continued to stand between her and the door.

No way out. Yet.

Perhaps if she kept out of sight until he left the theater. Surely, there was a nook or hidden alcove where Gigi could wait out the next hour or so without being seen.

Inching to her right, she glanced around the ornate theater, ablaze in light. The expert woodwork, elaborate chandeliers, and vibrant frescoes were too well lit.

A string of angry Italian came hot and fast over the sound of the orchestra. All other conversations halted. The musicians quit tuning their instruments. Gigi did not need fluency in Italian to recognize Esmeralda's obvious displeasure.

The diva marched out on stage and began waving her arms while flinging out demands. No stranger to her mercurial moods, Maestro Grimaldi ascended from the orchestra pit and smoothed the singer's ruffled feathers with softly spoken words meant only for her ears.

Almost immediately, Esmeralda's mood grew less violent, her demands less vitriolic. A good sign. Rehearsal would begin soon.

Not soon enough.

Gigi took a step toward the backstage door. She looked to her left, to her right, back to her left. Her gaze brushed over Fitz. He still barred her way to the exit, his attention divided between the stage and . . . her.

Resentment flared. How Gigi hated skulking about.

With an impatient huff, she moved to a spot within the folds of the velvet curtain.

The opening notes of the prelude sounded from the orchestra pit, pulling Fitz's gaze in that direction. The music besieged Gigi, urging her to forget his presence, begging her to stare in wide-eyed wonder at the stage, to sigh in pleasure and allow her mind to drift, to dream.

There'd been a time when she would have given in to the impulse. That sort of behavior belonged to another woman, from another place and time. Gigi was Sally Smith now. Her life was that of a servant to a young woman in need of her guidance.

Poor Sophie. She had looked so ill at ease when her half sister had arrived at the town house. Despite her half-sister Penelope's attempts to make light conversation, Sophie had still appeared nervous.

The young woman had suffered a great deal for what she'd done in a smaller theater much like this one. At least her half siblings had forgiven her. Today's luncheon was a solid step toward others forgiving her impulsive act as well.

Sighing, Gigi returned her attention to the stage.

Composed now, Esmeralda launched into the first verse of "Habanera," the most famous aria from *Carmen*. Once upon a time, the operetta had been Gigi's favorite.

No more. The lead character had no idea the pain she would soon suffer because of love. Gigi knew. Oh, how she knew.

She closed her eyes and counted to ten.

The strains of the aria flowed over her. Esmeralda was an unrivaled talent. She conquered the descending chromatic scale with practiced skill. What a joy it would be to sway to the music, Gigi thought, to indulge her senses in the lovely, perfectly pitched notes.

Gigi forced open her eyes.

Arms outstretched, Esmeralda glided across the stage, her voice expertly dipping through the verses.

"*L'amour est un oiseau rebelle*," love is a rebellious bird, "*Que nul ne peut apprivoiser*," that none can tame.

The heart-wrenching melody washed over Gigi, each note more superb than the last.

Fitz's attention remained riveted on Esmeralda. *Now or never.* Gigi set out, moving quickly through the shadows. Whispers followed her, their content impossible to ignore.

"Who is he?" someone asked.

Gigi couldn't fault the young women's curiosity. Men with the kind of wealth and power Fitz possessed rarely lurked backstage during rehearsals.

"I hear he's planning to buy the Summer Garden."

Gigi found that hard to believe. Fitz and his cousin Connor were corporate financiers known for their ruthless business tactics. They stopped at nothing, acquiring large companies, then dismantling them for profit. No, Fitz wasn't here to buy the theater.

He'd come for Gigi.

Renewed panic clogged her throat. She gritted her teeth and continued toward the backstage door. *Almost there.*

"They say he hails from Boston."

They would be right.

Fitz's family was one of the most established and respectable in Massachusetts. Gigi's family was wealthier but lacked the same level of prestige among the Boston elite. Harcourt Wentworth's greatest wish was to see one of his daughters married to a member of the Fitzpatrick clan.

"His name is Christopher Fitzpatrick."

"He looks like a Christopher."

Did he? He'd always been Fitz to Gigi, once a friend, a *good* friend, who'd become a stranger nearly overnight. She hadn't understood the change in him, why he'd grown distant. She—

"Sally." A hand closed over Gigi's arm, making her jerk in surprise. "*Sally!* Didn't you hear me calling you?"

Gigi gave a little jerk. "No, I . . ." She pulled in a shaky breath of air. "You startled me."

"I know, dear." With an apologetic grimace, the older woman patted Gigi's arm. "You were caught up in the music again."

Gigi opened her mouth to protest, then decided it was as good an excuse as any. "I suppose I was."

Mentally shaking herself, she forced a smile for the theater's premier wardrobe mistress.

Mrs. Llewellyn smiled back, adding another pat to Gigi's arm. This time, Gigi's smile was almost, nearly real.

The wardrobe mistress wore her mousy brown hair in an ordinary bun at the nape of her neck. She had sparkling hazel eyes, features that had aged quite well due to a set of high cheekbones, and an inner beauty that radiated out of her like a sunbeam splitting through a dingy cloud.

"Have you heard the news?" Before Gigi could respond, Mrs. Llewellyn continued, "The theater may be changing hands soon."

Hoping to end the conversation before it started, Gigi made a non-committal sound deep in her throat. The wardrobe mistress had given her part-time work as a finisher, paying her a fair wage for the detail work. She would never wish to insult Mrs. Llewellyn. But, oh, Gigi really—*really, really*—didn't want to discuss the latest theater gossip.

Clearly undeterred by her lack of enthusiasm, the older woman peered around Gigi's shoulder. "I tend to believe the rumors. Mr. Fitzpatrick spent most of the morning looking around the theater. He seems to be awfully—"

"Calculating?" Gigi suggested.

"Oh, no, dear." Mrs. Llewellyn gave a little laugh. "I was going to say focused."

Focused. Yes, Fitz was definitely that, more so in recent years since he and his cousin had taken over their family's investment firm. The gossips claimed the "power duo" would stop at nothing to close a deal. There was even talk that they had pushed Fitz's father out of the company for their own greedy purpose.

A shiver navigated up Gigi's spine. She knew all about men who sought their fortune by violating another's trust.

"He's turned quite a few of the girls' heads. There's a wager as to which one will gain his attention first."

Despite having every reason not to care, Gigi felt something move through her chest, something she couldn't quite define. If Fitz were another man, and she another woman, she would call the sensation jealousy.

Ridiculous. Fitz was the last man Gigi wanted for herself.

From what she'd gleaned in the society pages, he'd remained unattached since her departure from Boston. Not that she'd been looking for information about him.

"Oh, my." Mrs. Llewellyn straightened, her hand reaching up to smooth her hair. "I believe he's coming our way."

Gigi chanced a glance over her shoulder. Her heart dipped to her toes. Fitz was, indeed, striding toward them. And he was looking straight at her.

Their gazes met, locked. Held.

Gigi nearly choked on her own breath.

Floodgates of emotion burst open, giving her no time to brace for the impact. Sensation after sensation rolled over her. Dread, fear, guilt. There was something else in the storm of feelings running through her, something truly terrible, a scorching pain in her heart. *Fitz knows what I've done. He knows the source of my shame.*

Did he also know she'd taken the pearls? Surely her father hadn't brought Fitz into his confidence.

Run. The word echoed in her head.

As if sensing her desire to flee, he picked up his pace, determination in every strike of his heels to hard wood. Gigi pivoted toward the exit.

He moved directly in her path, his face devoid of emotion. She knew that look, had seen it once before. Unwavering purpose emanated off him, securing Gigi in place as if she were a small woodland creature caught in a cobra's trance. Air tightened in her lungs.

Seconds ticked by, pounding in perfect rhythm with her accelerated heartbeats. Her hand flew to her throat. She took several hard swallows.

It's over.

All the evasion, all the half-truths and attempts at subterfuge had been for naught.

The question remained. Had Fitz come to fetch her home? Or was he here to prevent Gigi from returning?

Chapter Three

Fitz calculated he had four, maybe five, seconds to close the distance between himself and Gigi before she made a break for the exit. He'd lost her once. He wouldn't let her get away again.

As he continued holding her stare, moving purposefully toward her, something inside Fitz shifted, softened, and then resettled in a way that made him regret what he'd come here to do.

He swallowed back the uncomfortable sensation and kept striding in Gigi's direction.

Moving closer, ever closer, he took in the straight spine, the square shoulders, the soft quiver of her chin before she firmed it. She was afraid. Of him? Or that her lies and deceit had come to an end?

He would find out soon enough.

With grim determination, Fitz kept his gaze locked with Gigi's, willing her to understand he wasn't here to hurt her. He didn't want explanations or details of her ruin, and he certainly didn't want an apology. What he wanted was far more tangible.

Hoping to ease her fears, he splayed his hands at his sides in a nonthreatening manner.

Her eyes widened. She looked at him the way a rabbit stared at a hawk swooping in for the kill. Evidently, he was to be cast in the role of villain yet again.

So be it.

Jaw tight, Fitz looked pointedly to the exit, then back to Gigi and gave a slow shake of his head. *Try it,* he silently challenged. *See how far you get.*

That impertinent chin lifted a fraction higher.

There she was. Same stubborn girl he'd always known. The spoiled heiress who took what she wanted, whether it belonged to her or not.

For months, Fitz had searched for her. He'd redoubled his efforts the morning after the official announcement of his cousin Connor's engagement to Gigi's sister. Fitz owed Connor a debt that could never be repaid.

That didn't mean he wouldn't try. Gigi held the key to Fitz's success.

He came to a stop at a respectable distance from her, only then realizing the wardrobe mistress stood with her.

Patience, he told himself. He would get Gigi alone soon enough.

"Good day, ladies." He divided a smile between the two women, his eyes lingering on Gigi a shade longer than polite.

Her flinch was nearly imperceptible, one he would have missed if he hadn't been looking closely. When she didn't quite meet his gaze, he felt oddly vindicated. Though she hid her reaction behind a benign smile, Fitz knew Gigi was nervous in his company. Good. He liked knowing he wasn't alone in his struggle to remain indifferent.

Affecting a bland expression of his own, he gave her a short nod. Her shoulders grew unnaturally stiff. Fitz knew he was the cause of her tension, and he told himself he didn't care. He wasn't here to smooth away her anxiety.

He opened his mouth to speak, not sure what he meant to say. Mrs. Llewellyn broke the silence first. "Mr. Fitzpatrick, are you enjoying the rehearsal?"

Adopting a relaxed demeanor he didn't quite feel, Fitz gave the older woman a short nod. "I am, very much."

He was surprised to discover he meant every word. He rarely attended the theater. There simply wasn't time, especially of late. Now that he'd seen behind the curtain, so to speak, he regretted skipping so many performances. Watching Esmeralda and the other cast members had kindled his interest. He found himself fascinated and somehow transported momentarily from the weight of his burdens.

Most who knew him would find this surprising, Gigi included. How many times had she accused him of lacking imagination? Too many to count.

"I find the process of putting together a production utterly captivating," he admitted. "I had no idea how much went into preparing for opening night."

Mrs. Llewellyn beamed at him. "Then it was fortunate you accepted Mr. Everett's invitation to look around the theater this afternoon."

For the next few minutes, the wardrobe mistress engaged Fitz in a conversation about what he found most intriguing (the staging) and the least (the creative arguments).

He glanced in Gigi's direction, this time taking in the changes. He hardly recognized the woman she'd become. The high cheekbones and alabaster skin were the same. Her eyes were still a pale blue, the color of rain clouds shot through with threads of silver. But the pretty frocks were gone, as were the ready smiles and charming manner. And what had she done to her glorious, lush hair? She must have tried to bleach out the rich auburn that had once gleamed a pretty shade of red in the sun. The stringy, faded yellow ends were nearly colorless and clashed with her skin tone.

The drab black dress she wore now only added to the impression that she'd endured great suffering. The light had left her. Fitz detected the sadness. The wistfulness. As though she wanted for something so far out of reach she could no longer feel joy. Fury slithered through Fitz's calm, making him burn with guilt and unexpected resolve. Nathanial Dixon would answer for what he'd done, once the investigator located the cad.

Mrs. Llewellyn paused. Fitz took advantage of the moment and addressed Gigi directly. "I don't believe we've met."

She opened her mouth, looking a little disconcerted, as if she'd expected him to reveal her identity right then and there. He was far savvier than that.

"Oh, where are my manners?" Mrs. Llewellyn's hands fluttered at her face. "This is Miss Sally Smith. Sally, this is Mr. Christopher Fitzpatrick of Boston."

Sally Smith. Fitz couldn't stop himself from grimacing. The most sought-after debutante in Boston was masquerading as Sally Smith. Why that name?

The report had been unclear on that point.

The report had been unclear on many points, leaving Fitz with more questions than answers. Fitz would unravel the mystery of Gigi's new life eventually.

For now, he schooled his features into a bland, nonthreatening expression. Unfortunately, his composure evaporated the moment Gigi's gaze met his.

His heart slammed against his ribs; his breath hitched in his lungs. Even with the dramatic changes to her appearance, Gigi still held the power to make him a tongue-tied schoolboy.

He cleared his throat, twice. "A pleasure, Miss . . . Smith. I am—"

"Silenzio!" Esmeralda clapped her hands over her ears and howled, "I cannot hear the music with all the chatter offstage."

Duly chastised, Fitz closed his mouth.

Nose in the air as if she'd just gotten a whiff of something unpleasant, Mrs. Llewellyn snapped her back ramrod straight. "That's my cue to get back to work."

"I'll join you," Gigi said.

Mrs. Llewellyn lifted a hand. "No, dear, I'm not ready for you yet. I must take inventory of the costumes before I put you to work."

"Oh, I . . ." Gigi's gaze tracked to Fitz, then quickly away. "I can help you with that."

"You will only be in my way. Stay." The wardrobe mistress took Gigi's shoulders and turned her in the direction of the stage. "Watch Esmeralda's rehearsal. I know you have a fondness for the music."

Gigi made a soft sound of protest in her throat, barely audible, but Fitz caught it. And so, it appeared, had Mrs. Llewellyn. "You don't enjoy the music?"

Fitz waited to hear how Gigi would answer. The fact that she'd attempted to flee with the wardrobe mistress didn't surprise him. No, what threw him off guard was the way she spoke in that bland Midwestern accent.

The changes in her appearance were disturbing enough, but to conceal her lovely, melodic voice in such an odd manner was, quite frankly, dumbfounding.

"No," Gigi finally replied.

Mrs. Llewellyn lifted a skeptical eyebrow.

"That is to say . . ." Still speaking in that ludicrous voice, Gigi blessed the other woman with a sweet, sweet smile, all politeness and easygoing manner, a small glimpse of the woman she'd once been. "I do, just not this particular aria. It makes me sad."

With the faintest trace of amusement, the older woman patted Gigi's arm in a motherly gesture. "That is rather the point, dear. Stay, enjoy. I will send for you when I'm ready for your assistance."

Having issued her command, Mrs. Llewellyn set out toward her part of the theater.

Gigi attempted another, less subtle escape. She stepped back, practically falling over her own two feet in her haste to get away from Fitz.

"Oh, no you don't." He moved directly in her path and took her hand. "You're not going anywhere."

"I have nothing to say to you."

"Ah, but I have much to say to you."

She tugged her hand. Fitz held on tight.

He didn't know what he meant to do or what he planned to say. All he knew was that he didn't want to let Gigi go.

Not yet.

* * *

Gigi reached the end of her endurance, all because Fitz had her hand wrapped inside his. This was the first time in nearly a year that she'd seen him. So much had occurred in the months since. Yet he'd reached for her with such ease. There'd been no hesitation, no pretense.

The unexpected familiarity of the gesture put her immediately on guard. Fitz had never been this forward with her, or this calm and casual. He was up to something.

Of course he was up to something. The man had not earned his ruthless reputation without reason.

She yanked her hand again.

He pulled her a step closer, looking as if he had much to say, none of which she cared to hear. Unless he had news of her family.

Blinking hard as her throat cinched closed, Gigi struggled to contain her conflicting emotions. Fitz's touch felt so . . . so . . . safe. That had never been the case before, at least not since they were children. There had been nothing easy between them as adults.

Time seemed to slow as past overlaid present. Fitz looked as uneasy as Gigi felt. Yet, still, he held on to her hand.

"Please," she said, the word barely a whisper. "Please," she repeated more fervently. "Let me go."

His eyes narrowed, and she knew better than to look away from the portrait of upright perfection he made. He was tall and inflexible, with a handsome face and an air of complete assurance. A man confident about his place in the world. A man who *owned* his place in the world.

Why wasn't he speaking?

Why wasn't she?

"Say what you've come to say and then leave me in peace."

"You wish to do this here?" He made a point of looking around them, his gaze pausing over a group of dancers who watched them intently and made no attempt to hide their curiosity. "Now?"

Gigi shrugged one shoulder, remaining silent in an attempt to gain some bit of advantage over him. On the surface, Fitz's words were calm and controlled. Yet she heard the warning in them. The man might not prefer an audience for this conversation, but he wouldn't let a few nosy dancers deter him from his goal.

Whatever goal that might be.

"Let me go," she hissed.

"Not yet."

Feeling trapped and needing to lash out, she did what any wise woman would do in her circumstances. She went on the offensive. "We both know why you're here."

His eyebrows lifted in silent challenge. "Do we?"

"You have no interest in buying this theater."

His brows moved a shade higher. "Don't I?"

"You are here for me." She held his gaze, daring him to object. When he continued staring at her with that unreadable expression, she issued her own challenge. "Tell me I'm wrong."

"You're not wrong." He leaned in then and raked her with one long look, taking in her face and plain black dress.

Gigi had never felt more unworthy. Or confused. "What do you want from me?"

One side of his mouth twitched in what she imagined was displeasure, perhaps disdain. "You have to ask?"

Her shoulders bunched in irritation. He was toying with her, drawing out this moment for some cruel purpose.

"Give it your best guess," he said. "Contemplate the possibilities long and hard before you respond."

Fitz wouldn't relent until he got what he'd come for. He never accepted defeat. In that, he was just like Gigi's father. Too much. The two had plotted out her future as if she were just another one of their business deals. That cold, impersonal lack of consideration had left her vulnerable. Easy prey for Nathanial to swoop in and win her affection, and . . .

Gigi wasn't being fair to Fitz. Or her father.

Her decision to run away with Nathanial had been hers. It was no one's fault but her own that she'd been desperate for romance. She'd wanted—needed—to be treasured and admired and, yes, loved.

Marriages in her world provided none of those things. Gigi had been full of romantic illusions. She'd wanted something grander than an arranged marriage. That stubborn desperation had made her the ideal target for a fortune hunter.

She'd been such a fool, believing God had brought Nathanial into her life at just the right time for the Lord's perfect purpose. How utterly fanciful. Gigi had left all she knew, all the people she loved, for empty promises whispered under the moon and stars.

Fitz had been right to warn her about Nathanial. So why wasn't he demanding an explanation?

Because they had a captive audience, leaning in, straining to hear their exchange. Fitz was not the sort of man to indulge in unnecessary drama. Then why did he still hold her hand cupped in his?

Surely he would say something, anything to put a halt to this endless moment.

Gigi searched for words to fill the void, but nothing came to mind. She and Fitz hadn't spoken directly to one another since the night he'd confronted her about Nathanial. All she could do now was force herself to breathe. Even that simple task proved nearly impossible.

At last, he let go of her hand and stepped back.

The lack of contact left her feeling oddly alone. She turned to go. He stopped her with a hand on her arm. "Try to run from me," he warned. "Give it your best effort, but know that I'll find you again."

She glanced down at his hand on her arm, back up to his face. "Is that a threat?"

"A promise." His green gaze swept over her as he spoke, his features still unreadable.

The embroidered waistcoat he wore highlighted the unusual color of his eyes. Why had she never noticed how the irises were rimmed with a thin band of gold?

Gigi wondered at the direction of her thoughts. At the same moment, Fitz's glance flicked to a spot just over her right shoulder. Only then did she become aware the music had stopped.

"Fitz, darling, I fear your attention has wavered." Stepping beside them, Esmeralda gave Gigi a sidelong glance, frowned, then returned her full attention to Fitz. "You will come with me now. I wish for you to hear my rendition of *Carmen*'s signature aria."

The husky command was followed by a short pause as the diva turned to glance at Gigi. Her eyes were not quite hard, but neither were they soft. "The crimson satin gown I wear in the final act has acquired a stain at the hem. I require it gone before my next fitting."

Though stain removal was not her forte, or her job as Sophie's maid—and since Mrs. Llewellyn didn't need her assistance—Gigi couldn't think of anything she'd rather do more. "I'll see to the matter at once."

"Yes. Well, then. Off you go." Esmeralda made a shooing motion with her hands.

Happy to oblige, Gigi spun in the direction of the wardrobe closet. In her haste, she moved too quickly, and her skirts tangled around her ankles. She stumbled back a step.

Fitz's hands clasped her shoulders from behind as he supported her against him. "Easy now," he whispered in her ear. "I've got you."

Gigi should have been frightened by the underlying meaning in his declaration. Instead, his low voice steadied her and brought to mind a time when life had been simpler, a time when she and Fitz had been friends.

A time when her head had been filled with nothing more complicated than a stain on the hem of one of her own dresses. She closed her eyes a moment, only briefly, and reveled in the feeling of security that washed through her.

So much had changed. She'd done things that couldn't be taken back. Gigi had lost the woman she'd once been and barely recognized the woman she was now. What was real and what was fantasy?

I've got you.

Did Fitz know how terrifying those words sounded? He was so stable, so predictable, so . . . familiar. There'd been a season in her life when she'd scorned him for his steadfast ways. She'd accused him of being boring, as if that were the greatest crime a man could commit.

How ridiculous she'd been. How silly and naïve and utterly horrid.

"Sally, are you unwell?" The suspicion in the diva's voice nearly, but not quite, matched the concern in her eyes.

Gigi pulled herself together.

"I'm perfectly well, thank you." Readjusting her collar, Gigi stepped away from Fitz, away from the burst of emotions and memories and impossible wave of hope that had no place in her new, pragmatic life. "I merely lost my balance."

Esmeralda tilted her head at a curious angle. "It was fortunate Mr. Fitzpatrick was here to catch you."

Gigi gave a humming response that could be interpreted as agreement.

Fitz gave an equally dispassionate response. They shared an awkward glance and then, as if they'd practiced the move, looked away from each other.

Eyes widening, as though suddenly realizing the oddity of their familiar manner, Esmeralda looked from one to the other and back again. Her gaze filled with questions.

Gigi willed the diva to keep them to herself, at least until Fitz was out of earshot.

Of all the people Gigi had met in New York, Esmeralda asked the most pointed questions about Gigi's past, never quite believing her answers. No wonder, that. The woman made her living inside a character, taking on a role that had little to do with reality. Of course she would recognize that Gigi wasn't who she pretended to be.

"I believe you wanted me to listen to your rehearsal?" Fitz spoke to Esmeralda with the sort of gentle patience he'd used with Gigi all those years ago. "I find myself quite enamored with your talent."

"You are a man of discerning taste."

He cast a brief glance in Gigi's direction. "Some in my acquaintance would disagree."

Esmeralda sniffed delicately, the sound almost musical. "Then they aren't worth knowing."

"Indeed." A small smile played across his lips as he offered his arm to the singer. "Shall we?"

"But of course." Adopting a queenly posture, Esmeralda allowed Fitz to escort her back to center stage.

Neither acknowledged Gigi again.

Relief weakening her knees, Gigi went to do Esmeralda's bidding. She hurried her steps. The more distance between her and Fitz, the better. But the drama unfolding onstage had her pausing in the wings a moment longer. The story of two young lovers desperate to be together, doing what they must to avoid discovery, hit too close to home.

Gigi couldn't help but look back at Fitz. Distance and dim lighting couldn't hide the way he pressed his lips in a flat line, or how his gaze bore into her.

Her first instinct was to run. From Fitz, from the theater, from New York and the life she'd created for herself out of necessity and shame. So much shame. Unfortunately, Esmeralda paid her too well. If Gigi was to redeem her great-grandmother's pearls, she had to endure her circumstances a while longer.

At last, Fitz turned away and focused on Esmeralda. Gigi should have been thankful. But as she watched him give his undivided attention to the beautiful singer, the sensation running through her blood felt like . . .

God help her, the sensation felt like longing.

Chapter Four

As Fitz exited the theater, a touch of shock wound through his determination. His encounter with Gigi had left him unsettled. He felt restless and uneasy, and no closer to securing the item he'd come to retrieve.

Pulling out his watch, he checked the time. Not yet four o'clock. He could meet with the private investigator before heading back to his hotel to change for dinner with Esmeralda and her daughter.

Fitz allowed himself a small smile of satisfaction. An evening with the opera singer—in her private residence—would afford him the opportunity to seek out Gigi once again. He would end their business tonight, once he figured out how best to approach the matter.

Gigi had changed considerably. He'd hardly recognized her. But there was no reason for him to grieve. She'd made her choices.

And so had he, some harder than others.

Wishing for a different outcome to their story belonged to his younger self. He'd made initial contact with the woman. The hardest part was over.

Yet the image of Gigi's vulnerability slammed into Fitz's mind, shaking his concentration. He took a hard breath. What did it matter that, for a brief moment, he'd encountered the friend from his childhood?

What did it matter that, with her pulled up against him, he'd felt her pain as if it were his own? *Let it go, Fitz.*

Let her *go. Your loyalty lies elsewhere.*

A man dressed in a wrinkled suit beneath a frayed overcoat approached him from the alleyway on his left. Hat pulled low over his eyes, he advanced on Fitz with hardened tenacity as he shouldered his way through the crowded sidewalk.

Fitz greeted the private investigator with a short nod. "Mr. Offutt, what news do you have for me?"

"I have a few answers to the problem that presented itself this morning." He pushed his hat back, revealing a face like a mountain terrain, all rough lines and recessed planes. "I trust now is a good time."

"Let's walk up the block." Fitz took off without checking to see if the other man followed him. He always thought best on the move.

The investigator fell into step beside him. "I went back to Herald Square as you requested."

The man had been following Gigi for well over a week, ever since he'd sent word to Fitz that he'd found her. Apparently, she'd become a creature of habit, which had made Mr. Offutt's job easy. Her days were filled with mundane tasks as expected of a woman in service. Her one indulgence was a solitary walk every morning just after dawn.

This morning had been no different. However, she'd chosen a different route. Because of her switch in routine, Mr. Offutt had lost her in the crowds near Herald Square.

"Were you able to discover anything?" Fitz asked.

Retrieving a small notepad from an inside pocket of his jacket, the investigator proceeded to run through the list of shops and restaurants in Herald Square.

Fitz listened, his mind working through several scenarios. Gigi could have disappeared into any of those businesses. The question was whether she'd gone on an errand for herself or her employer. Or had she gone to meet someone?

Nathanial Dixon, perhaps?

The latter possibility was unbearable in a way Fitz refused to acknowledge on any conscious level. By all accounts, Dixon was out of Gigi's life. Mr. Offutt had been adamant.

What if Dixon isn't out of her life?

It didn't matter one way or another, Fitz told himself. Still, doubt prowled through his attempt not to care.

With considerable effort, he returned his attention to the investigator's report.

Pausing mid-sentence, Mr. Offutt flipped the page and placed a finger on the final item scribbled there. "A millinery is also in the area, but it wasn't open at that hour, so she couldn't have gone in there."

Fitz gave the man a skeletal grin. He was paying far too much for information he could gather on his own. "Of the dozen or so businesses you just mentioned, which do you believe she ducked into this morning?"

The man shut the notebook, tapped the binding with an agitated finger. "From my calculations, considering her walking speed, she could have gone into one of two shops."

Fitz waited.

"A delicatessen or a haberdashery. However, the delicatessen is more likely."

Despite the chill in the air, sweat trickled between Fitz's shoulder blades. "What makes you say that?"

"The haberdashery specializes in men's wares, and she wasn't carrying any packages when I caught up with her again."

Who had Gigi gone to meet? It could have been any number of people besides Dixon.

"I couldn't get any information out of the waitresses or cashier at the delicatessen, nothing conclusive, at any rate."

Fitz made a mental note to visit the restaurant himself. Although the private investigator didn't exactly instill confidence, the employees' tight-lipped refusal to answer his questions didn't make sense. Were they being difficult, or did they simply not remember Gigi? "Let me see your list of businesses again."

The investigator flipped back two pages, then gave Fitz the book. Fitz scanned the page, pausing at *Ryerson's Pawnbroker Sale Store*.

Surely, she wouldn't have . . .

Fitz dismissed the thought before it had a chance to take root. Gigi had made any number of bad decisions in the year she'd run off with Dixon. But she wasn't a bad person. She would never sell off something that didn't belong to her. If she had, she wouldn't have needed to take on a life of service.

Unless there was more to the story than the private investigator had uncovered.

What have you been up to, Gigi?

Frowning, Fitz handed back the book.

"You want me to continue following her?"

"Yes." Fitz's response came immediately. He'd seen Gigi's fear this afternoon and recognized her internal struggle to stand her ground or flee.

She'd run once before. She could easily do so again.

"I'll return to the theater and wait for her there."

"Very good."

They parted ways at the street corner. Fitz watched the investigator retrace his steps before heading in the opposite direction, his mind in turmoil.

Fitz was a man who dealt in facts. He refused to let his thoughts wander to supposition and unfounded concerns.

He'd found Gigi. That was enough for now.

It had to be enough.

* * *

After completing the exhaustive process of removing the stain from Esmeralda's costume, Gigi returned to the town house on Riverside Drive. Twice, she feared she was being followed. But each time she scanned the area, nothing seemed out of place.

Her anxious state, bordering on panic, was the same numbing sensation that had lurked in the shadows of her mind all day. She was hardly aware of moving, of entering the house, of mounting the back stairs, of passing the second-floor landing. But suddenly she was in her room, gasping for a decent breath of air that had nothing to do with exertion.

Turning in a fast, hard circle, Gigi searched frantically for a solution to her predicament. *Run.* The word permeated every thought, attacking every attempt she made to calm her rioting nerves.

Run.

She couldn't.

She could. She must.

What other choice did she have? If Fitz had uncovered her whereabouts, others could as well. The name change, the disguise, becoming a servant, none of it had been enough.

Gigi had fooled herself into thinking she could outrun her past. She'd been naïve to hope she could return home and pretend she'd been studying music in Vienna as her family claimed. There were men and women of her acquaintance—mostly women—who would gleefully pick away at the story until the shameful details were revealed. Gigi didn't fear the consequences to her own reputation. But her younger sisters, Annabeth and Mariah, must be allowed to make their own way in the world without the taint of Gigi's scandal rubbing off on them.

Run.

Cruel pain burst inside her chest and leaked into her limbs. She'd confronted one blow after another since she'd climbed out of bed this morning. A matter of hours, a mere half day, and Gigi's calm, boring life had been thrown into chaos. Every instinct told her to . . .

Run.

Where was her suitcase? She spun in another, faster circle, her eyes darting around the room, landing on the tiny four-drawer dresser, the end table, the bed.

The bed.

She dropped to her knees, groped around until her hand connected with a small leather case. Closing her fingers around the cold metal handle, she gave a hard yank, dragging it close before scrambling to her feet.

She didn't know where she would go, just away from this house, this city, this demi-existence she'd built for herself out of lies.

Somewhere in her mind, Gigi knew she wasn't thinking rationally. Running would do her no good.

Try to run from me. Give it your best effort, but know that I'll find you again.

Fitz had never been a man to make empty promises. That knowledge didn't stop Gigi from setting the small piece of battered luggage atop the mattress and flinging open the lid. She went to her dresser, pulled out its top drawer, and began tossing items haphazardly toward the bed. She was halfway through the second drawer when a knock sounded on her door.

Gigi's hands stilled.

"Sally?" Another, more urgent knock. "I know you're in there. I can hear you moving around."

Gigi's heart raced, then nearly beat out of her chest when the doorknob rattled. "Please, Sally. Let me in."

There was something off in the muffled voice that gave Gigi pause.

"Just a minute, Sophie." She quickly shut the half-filled suitcase and stuffed it back under her bed. Next, she hurried to the dresser and closed the open drawer with a fast sweep of her hand. "Enter."

Sophie's perfectly coiffed head poked into the room. "I'm home."

The obviousness of the statement nearly had Gigi smiling, until she noted the lost look in the young woman's eyes. All thoughts of running were abandoned. Sophie needed her, as evidenced by her dejected manner and red-rimmed eyes.

"Oh, dear." Gigi joined her friend in the hallway and took in the pinched expression. "The luncheon went badly."

"Actually . . ." Sophie crossed her arms in front of her waist and sighed. "The entire afternoon went without a hitch."

"Then why the miserable tone?"

The young woman opened her mouth, snapped it shut, opened it again, shivered. "Can we talk somewhere besides this drafty hallway?"

"Of course." Gigi took Sophie's arm and led her toward the stairwell. "We'll go to your room, and I'll stoke the fire. Once you feel warmer," *and steadier,* "you'll tell me about the luncheon."

With a distant look in her eyes, as though lost in deep contemplation, Sophie allowed Gigi to guide her to her room. Neither spoke as they entered the young woman's personal domain, which took up most of the second floor.

Esmeralda spared no expense when it came to providing for her daughter's comfort. The dressing and bathing rooms flanked the main bedchamber, which contained an enormous bed with a polished headboard and columns supporting a green-and-gold silk canopy. As a final nod to style, the wallpaper in all three rooms featured flowers and birds in a variety of complementary colors.

"Sit here," Gigi told her friend.

While Sophie settled on an overstuffed chair facing the hearth, Gigi saw to the fire. With quick, efficient moves, she stacked several pieces of dry wood in a crisscross pattern over the remnants of the previous fire. A few pokes with the fire iron and the new load ignited.

Satisfied, Gigi brushed her hands together. Soot had taken up permanent residence beneath her fingernails. Callouses showed on her palms, and a thin white scar ran across the knuckles of her right hand.

The old Gigi would have been appalled by the physical reminders of how far she'd fallen from grace and how, with her selfish choices, she'd become a liar, a fraud, and a woman completely unworthy of the world she'd left. Most days, she still was horrified. But in rare moments like this, when she looked at her hands, she saw each imperfection as a badge of honor.

She'd learned to survive on her own, without the help of a man, her family, or anyone but herself. She knew the value of hard work, as well as the joy of a job well done.

Perhaps that wasn't a bad thing. Perhaps there were blessings to be found in her adversity. Something to think about when she was alone.

"Now then"—she turned to Sophie—"that should warm you right up."

She positioned the screen in front of the snapping fire, then sat on the footstool beside Sophie's chair. They each stared at the flames in silence.

After a moment, Gigi shifted her position. The light bounced off Sophie's troubled features, making her look heartbreakingly young.

Gigi hurt for her friend. She felt a connection to the young woman that went beyond servant and employer. In Sophie, Gigi saw herself.

"Tell me what happened at the luncheon."

Sophie stared into the fire for several more seconds. The flames painted an orange glow across her features, highlighting her misery. "They *loved* me."

"And that's a problem because . . . ?" Gigi prompted.

"It was all an act and not very well played, either." Sophie slammed her fist on the chair's arm. "The ladies were only pretending to be interested in what I had to say. I could see the impatient glee in their eyes as they said their farewells. I know they're tucked safely in their homes right now gossiping about me. The little nobody, that Daughter of Scandal, who thinks she can become one of them."

Unfortunately, Sophie was probably right.

"Surely not *all* the ladies are saying terrible things about you."

"Perhaps not all of them," Sophie admitted, albeit reluctantly. "Not Penelope. She's the kindest, most genuine woman I know. I'm honored to call her my sister."

"What about Mrs. Burrows?" Gigi asked. "Do you doubt her sincerity?"

Sophie smiled, and for that one moment, she looked a little less wretched. "She seems to like me well enough."

"The others will come around."

"Will they?" Sophie let out a strangled sob. "Will they come around?"

I hope so.

But Gigi couldn't be sure. New York society was notoriously conservative and a bit cruel in its exclusivity. Even with the support of Penelope and Mrs. Burrows, Sophie had a rough road ahead of her. The Daughter of Scandal was attempting to navigate the treacherous waters of one of the most elite circles in America, something even women of legitimate birth scarcely accomplished.

It was all so morbidly unfair. Sophie didn't deserve the censure she received for what her parents had done.

Gigi reached out again. This time, she laid a hand on Sophie's knee. "Give it time. Even the most influential grande dame of society will soften toward you eventually."

Sophie's snort of laughter lacked all signs of humor. "You seem to know a lot about the inner workings of society."

Catching the suspicion in the other woman's tone, Gigi sat back and schooled her features into an innocent stare. "I have lived in some of the finest homes in America."

It wasn't a lie. Her father owned eight houses in four states, each grander than the last.

"That may be true." With eyes far wiser than her twenty-one years would suggest, Sophie leaned forward. "Yet it doesn't explain how you know the difference between a teaspoon and a dessert spoon."

Sophie made a valid observation. Ladies' maids knew how to put together a breakfast tray and tea service. But they were too busy with their other chores to work in the kitchens and dining rooms. Gigi should not know how to properly set a table.

"My training was extensive." Again, not a lie. Her mother had drilled proper etiquette into Gigi as a child.

"Sally?" Something came and went in Sophie's eyes, something kind yet also shrewd. "We are friends, yes?"

Gigi nodded, not sure how the conversation had turned so completely back on her.

"As my friend, won't you please tell me your secret?"

"I don't have a secret." She spoke quickly. Too quickly.

Sophie wasn't fooled. Her eyes narrowed ever so slightly. "I have heard the way you play the piano. No domestic servant gets that sort of *extensive* training."

Gigi's breath backed up in her lungs. Sophie's suspicions weren't new, and yet there was something different in them today, a knowledge that surpassed simple curiosity.

"The way you carry yourself has a certain *je ne sais quoi.*"

"Would you believe I trained on the stage?"

"I would not."

Bottom lip caught between her teeth, Gigi turned her attention to the fire. She needed to stop Sophie from continuing, as she'd done every other time the young woman had pressed for information about Gigi's background.

Why couldn't she stop her friend?

"You have tutored me in the elaborate set of rules governing a young lady's behavior in the upper classes. That sort of knowledge is handed down from mother to daughter, not lady to maid. Much less from a maid to her lady."

Finally, Gigi found her voice. "My tutor was a woman of high standards. She demanded I behave with proper comportment."

Sophie continued as if Gigi hadn't spoken. "Even more telling, you're terrible at stain removal, making tea and tonics, and you don't know the first thing about polishing silver. Sally, my dear, sweet friend, you are no more a servant than *I* am a debutante."

Finished having her say, Sophie raised her eyebrows, a silent dare in the gesture.

Tears came, instant and unwelcome. Gigi was suddenly so very exhausted. She felt her control slipping with each beat of her heart. She was so very weary of hiding her identity, of pretending she was someone she was not.

Perhaps it was the devastating events of the day. The disappointment she'd endured at the pawnshop coupled with the sudden appearance of Christopher Fitzpatrick. But the last shreds of her resistance dissolved. "How long have you suspected?"

Sophie gave her a triumphant grin. "From the very first moment we met."

"That long?"

"That long."

All Gigi could do was stare at Sophie in stunned disbelief. The young woman was far too perceptive. It was remarkable, really, and yet . . .

Was it?

Esmeralda had raised Sophie in a world of make-believe, where slipping into disguises and fake personas was a way of life. Like her mother, the young woman would know how to look past the surface and see the truth beneath the lie.

"I have spent much of my life in theaters and opera houses," Sophie said, the words putting a fine point on Gigi's thoughts. "There is no deception I have not witnessed, no charade I have not been a party to. I know a disguise when I see one. And I know when someone is lying to me."

Gigi had once thought the theater a magnificent world of hopes and dreams, a wonderland of wish fulfillment. She'd envied Sophie her childhood. Now, she saw the flaw in her thinking. Sophie had experienced her share of difficulties, and Gigi had been yet another person to deceive her. "I'm sorry, Sophie."

"Don't apologize. I find your situation rather fascinating. I have made up all sorts of romantic tales about your past."

Romantic? No. Tragic, sorrowful—a cautionary tale, at best. The transgressions Gigi had committed in the name of love could not be undone. Whether the truth came out or not, she would always be a woman of questionable morality, one who'd put her passionate desires ahead of all else.

"I have always loved a good secret-identity story. I'm especially partial to *The Prince and the Pauper*."

Gigi had liked that tale once, long before she'd been forced to live out the charade.

"Are you like the prince?" Sophie asked. "Are you pretending to be a pauper to find out how the other half lives?"

"There is nothing romantic about my tale." And there would be no happy ending.

"I'm sorry." Sophie touched her arm. "Will you tell me your name? Your *real* name?"

Consumed by a need to keep her sordid details private, Gigi reluctantly shook her head.

"Please. You can trust me. I am very good at keeping secrets." Sophie made a face. "Unless, of course, they're my own."

The commiseration in Sophie's voice was Gigi's undoing. She stared at her friend for a long moment, counting her own heartbeats as a battle waged within. One beat. Two. Three.

By the fourth, she gave up the fight. "My name is Georgina."

"Georgina." Sophie cocked her head to one side. "Georgina," she repeated, enunciating each syllable.

"Gigi for short."

"Gigi. Yes, the name suits you. I like it." Sophie reached out and touched the mobcap atop Gigi's head. "Is red your natural color?"

Gigi's hand went to her head as an enormous wave of embarrassment coursed through her. Had she fooled no one? She'd tried to hide the roots of her hair beneath oversized mobcaps, but the task had grown more difficult in recent months. Had others noticed she'd dyed the strands so many times the ends were breaking off at an alarming rate?

"Not to worry." Sophie leaned in close, much the same way schoolgirls did when sharing a confidence. "Those ridiculous hats hide most of your handiwork. I doubt anyone else has noticed, except perhaps my mother. But she probably thinks you're practicing different styles and color on yourself. If she hasn't mentioned anything to you yet, she probably won't."

Gigi could only pray Sophie was right. She needed this job, at least for another month.

"Well? Are you going to answer my question?"

"What question?"

Sophie straightened. "Is red your natural color?"

"Yes."

Sophie gently removed the cap and studied Gigi as if attempting to decode a riddle. "I wager it's stunning when all grown out."

Gigi had once considered the red tresses, quite literally, her crowning glory. One of her suitors had penned poems in his attempt to describe the flaming color.

How frivolous her life had been.

"Please, Sophie, you cannot tell anyone what I've told you."

"Have no fear." Sophie took her hands, the gesture reminiscent of when Gigi had taken hers earlier that morning. "This will be our little secret . . . *Sally*."

Gigi swallowed around a knot in her throat. Her eyes stung, and she was very close to tears. "Thank you."

"When you are ready, I trust you will share your tale with me."

Not if, *when*. Gigi didn't trust herself to speak.

The clock struck the bottom of the hour. Sophie frowned.

"Oh, drat, look at the time. Mother has invited a *special* guest to dine with us this evening." Her frown deepened. "I'm to be my most charming."

A tingle of dread swept across Gigi's lungs. "Did your mother tell you the name of this special guest?"

"Perhaps. I don't remember." Sophie gave a delicate shrug. "I think he's from Philadelphia. Or . . . maybe Washington."

Gigi felt her shoulders relax.

"No. Boston. He's from Boston."

Of. Course.

"He's someone very important. I am not only to be on my best behavior, but I am to look my most ravishing." Sophie made a face. "Mother's words, not mine."

Gigi took a deep, purifying breath. "Then we had better get you changed."

Chapter Five

An hour later, Gigi circled Sophie, taking in her appearance with an objective eye. The young woman did indeed, as Esmeralda had requested, look ravishing in a blue silk gown the color of lightning trapped in a bottle. Gigi smoothed out a final wrinkle and declared, "You are ready."

After a slight roll of her shoulders, Sophie nodded her agreement. Consulting the clock on the mantelpiece, she sighed, clearly reluctant to spend an evening with her mother and a man she didn't know. "I believe I will read awhile before I head downstairs."

"I'll leave you to it."

Gigi exited the room. Out in the hall, she leaned back against the door and released a short sigh. All she wanted to do was sit in her tiny room, stare at a blank wall, and review the disturbing events of the day. She needed perspective. Much had changed in her life.

Everything had changed.

She caught her mind wandering to Fitz. She tried not to worry. How could she not? With his appearance came too many contingencies she couldn't control.

Why had he come? Why not send one of his employees? He had masses of them.

Fear swept through her. Gigi shoved it down with a hard swallow. She was not yet defeated. Unless Fitz had sent word to her family that she was living in New York. She'd gone to great lengths to keep her location secret, while also letting them know she was alive and well. One word from Fitz and she would be forced to go home before she was ready.

How would she explain the missing pearls?

She pushed away from the wall, her steps slow and heavy. Gigi hadn't felt such helplessness since the day Nathanial had abandoned her on what was supposed to have been their wedding day.

Dark crept over the edges of her vision, threatening to pull her back to that terrible morning. She rubbed frantically at her temple as if the gesture could banish the memory. It came anyway. And with it, the full force of her disgrace.

Back in her room, she searched for her Bible and opened it to Philippians. Just as she found the verse she was looking for, a knock sounded on her door.

Will this day never end?

Setting aside the Bible, Gigi called out, "Come in."

Lottie Flannigan entered the room, hands braided at her waist, feet shuffling. "Herself wants to see you."

The young kitchen maid didn't need to explain further. Gigi knew exactly who had summoned her.

"Thank you, Lottie. I'll be there directly." When the girl hesitated, Gigi reached out and touched her arm. "I'll only be a moment. I need to straighten my clothing."

This explanation seemed to satisfy the girl. Esmeralda expected her domestic help to be properly groomed at all times.

Gigi shut the door and fought to stay calm. This was a bad time for doubt, but she couldn't help herself. Esmeralda rarely called Gigi to a private meeting.

Had Fitz said something to her? Had he revealed their connection?

Heart in her throat, pulse beating wildly through her veins, Gigi went to the lone mirror in her room and winced at her reflection. Nothing could mask the ravages of the day. Tension showed in the fine lines around her mouth and eyes.

Gigi blamed Fitz.

Nothing had prepared her for his touch, or her reaction to his hands clasping her shoulders and pulling her close. She'd been in his arms only briefly, a mere handful of seconds. Yet, for the first time in eleven months, she'd felt comforted. Safe.

Had Fitz's brief display of kindness been an illusion or part of some cruel game he was playing? Ruthless and hard, Gigi could handle. But a man who made her feel safe in his arms?

How did she fight against that?

She spun away from the mirror. There had been a fleeting moment when she'd stared into Fitz's eyes and seen an aching loneliness that called to her, one human to another, two lost souls searching for their place in the world.

That couldn't be right. She'd misread the moment and . . .

Esmeralda was waiting for her.

Gigi hurried down the back stairwell. She bypassed the kitchen as she made her way down a darkened corridor that ran along the southern perimeter of the first floor. A few more twists and turns, then, finally, she stopped just inside the parlor where Esmeralda entertained her guests.

Drawing in a soothing pull of air, Gigi waited for the diva to speak.

Esmeralda had positioned herself next to the hearth. Light from the fire turned her beaded gown into a shimmering gold. She stood with the attitude of a woman whose high opinion of herself far outweighed her place in society. That haughty stance, along with her unrivaled talent, had helped her rise to the top of her profession. Though she was a coveted addition to any guest list, she would never be fully accepted into polite society.

"You wanted to see me?"

"I wish to know how my daughter's luncheon went with Mrs. Burrows and the other women."

"I believe it went as well as can be expected," Gigi replied with stiff courtesy, choosing her next words carefully. "You will have to ask Sophie for a more detailed report."

Esmeralda let out a long, dramatic sigh that had a musical quality. Even in her frustration, the singer had impressive voice control. "I knew it was too much to hope you would respond candidly."

She wanted candor? Gigi would give her candor. "You hired me to serve as your daughter's maid. I was not aware you wished for me to spy on her as well."

For a long moment, silence was Esmeralda's only response. Then, miraculously, her gaze softened. "Your loyalty to Sophie does you credit."

Gigi blinked. Had Esmeralda just given her a compliment for standing up to her? Not many dared to do so, and far fewer survived the experience, which only managed to highlight how distraught Gigi truly was over the events of the day. She'd been patently unwise to challenge the woman who paid her salary. "I apologize if I overstepped my bounds."

"Think nothing of it." With one quick slash of her wrist, Esmeralda dismissed Gigi's concern. But then the diva suddenly looked weary and strangely vulnerable. "We share the same goal. I wish only for my daughter to find her place in the world."

Gigi nodded. "That is my wish as well. To guide Sophie during this awkward time of transition."

"No." Esmeralda shifted her pose, her dark eyes flickering with annoyance. "You are to help my daughter understand the pitfalls of living among the upper crust of society."

"I am merely a lady's maid."

"You are far more." Esmeralda slanted her lips in a slow, meaningful smile. "You, my dear girl, are a fraud."

Gigi's heart turned bleak. She blinked several times, but nothing could stop the black, ragged edges of despair moving through her. The sensation stole her ability to breathe.

"I have caught you by surprise. Well, no matter." Esmeralda lifted a silk-clad shoulder. "Your story is quite sad, I'm sure. You have made a terrible error in judgment that has sent you into hiding."

Gigi realized she was clenching her fists and made a grand effort to relax her fingers.

The habit of denial was hard to break.

"I am not in hiding." Even to her own ears, the lie fell flat.

"Don't look so tragic, dear." Esmeralda drew close enough to rest a hand on Gigi's arm. "You will get no judgment from me." It was a kind thing to say, more so coming from Esmeralda. "Let me give you a piece of advice."

"I really would rather you didn't," Gigi muttered.

"You must not despair over your past. You are terribly young." The singer lifted her hand away from Gigi's arm. "Youth is easily deceived."

A familiar ache tugged at Gigi's heart. Her mouth opened, but nothing came out. If only she could blame her behavior on youth. She'd acted with willful disobedience and no thought to her family. She'd made choices out of a selfish desire to have what she wanted, when she wanted it.

She'd loved Nathanial, or as much as a *youthful* heart could love another. But now, the memory of that love brought a metallic, bitter taste to her tongue.

"I do not need to know your story to know you have suffered at the hands of a man."

Gigi had suffered because of Nathanial, yes, but she had only herself to blame for her misery. For some reason, it was important to her that Esmeralda understand that. "I was fooled by a fantasy of my own making."

"That is precisely why I want you to protect Sophie from a youthful indiscretion. My own have harmed her enough."

There was a frantic note in Esmeralda's voice. She clearly loved her daughter.

To see this side of the diva was unexpected, humbling, and a cold reminder that Gigi's actions could harm the people she loved as well.

"You understand what I am asking of you?"

"Yes." Gigi would not abandon Sophie at her greatest hour of need.

"I have invited Mr. Fitzpatrick to dine with Sophie and me this evening."

Gigi felt her hands ball into fists again. She flexed her fingers, once, twice, relaxed them, flexed again.

"He hails from Boston." Esmeralda smiled. Or maybe she didn't. Gigi wasn't sure what that twist of her lips meant. "I would very much like to see Sophie settle away from her father and half siblings. Boston would be a lovely city for her to make a home and start a family."

Heat crawled up Gigi's neck. "I understand perfectly."

"I knew that you would. You may go now."

Happy to flee the room, Gigi turned to leave. She made it halfway across when Esmeralda's butler appeared in the doorway, barring her exit.

Irving was ancient, somewhere between eighty and a hundred, and had been one of the most accomplished actors on the British stage half a century ago. Proving his talent was still without rival, he stood tall and dignified, his stance embodying the very essence of the upper-crust, snooty butler. "Mr. Fitzpatrick has arrived."

"Thank you, Irving." Esmeralda sat in a red leather wingback chair, then arranged her skirts around her legs with practiced ease. "Please send him in."

Irving performed a bow worthy of the greatest butlers ever trained. "Very good, madam."

The same moment he left the room, the clock chimed the top of the hour.

Of course Fitz would arrive on time, Gigi thought, frantically searching for another way out of the parlor. There was no escape. She shifted to a spot near the bookshelves.

Unfortunately, the move proved useless. Fitz entered and, as if he'd expected to find her there, immediately caught sight of her.

Trying not to sigh, she shut her eyes, battled a wave of emotion, then snapped them open again. Fitz was already on the move, striding across the patterned rug at a steady pace. He headed straight for her, his moss-green eyes unreadable in the dim light.

Gigi retreated to the shadows, her gaze never leaving Fitz's face. He looked every bit the successful financier. His jaw was free of stubble, indicating he'd recently shaved. He wore elegant evening attire, perfectly appropriate for a dinner with the most celebrated opera singer in the world and her daughter. The pristine white of his starched linen shirt stood in stark contrast to the black wool of his tailored coat and vest.

An unwelcome jolt of longing crawled through Gigi, landing somewhere in the vicinity of her heart. Something flickered in his eyes as well, something personal, just for her. The questions were there, too, questions about the past eleven months she was unprepared to answer.

Panic reared, morphed into a far more complicated mix of emotions. Fury. Foolishness. Irritation. *Shame.*

Her need to escape this room, *this man*, intensified. But her feet refused to move. Why wouldn't her feet move?

Glancing in the same direction as Fitz, Esmeralda sighed dramatically. "Sally, please inform my daughter our guest has arrived."

"Yes, ma'am." Gigi scurried out of the room as fast as her feet could carry her.

* * *

Fitz watched Gigi's retreating back, unable to stop staring. Even in her maid's uniform, she was a stunning woman. The exotic curve of her lips, the attractive tilt of her head, the regal bearing that had always been a part of her were still there. Hidden, but not gone.

If Fitz was honest with himself, he'd admit that she still called to him, even now, when he knew the risk. The unlikelihood anything would come of the attraction.

He had one goal and would not be distracted by a pretty face. Wanting the business with Gigi over and done with, he took a step toward the empty doorway.

An obstruction impeded his exit.

Looking down, Fitz spotted an enormous ball of black-and-white fur squatting at his feet, belly protruding.

The animal looked like a cat. He—she—*it?*—swished the fluffy plume of a tail, crouched low, danced on its hindquarters, and then . . .

It launched its massive body into the air with surprising alacrity. Fitz staggered back, arms instinctively wrapping around the large animal. He turned to Esmeralda with a question on his lips.

She made the introductions before he could voice his query. "That's my dear, sweet Othello."

"He's spoiled beyond measure."

This last statement came from somewhere behind Fitz.

Shifting the heavy load in his arms, he glanced over his shoulder. Sophie Cappelletti stood framed in the doorway.

Once again, Esmeralda performed the introductions.

"It's a pleasure to meet you, Miss Cappelletti."

"You may call her Sophie," Esmeralda told him.

Fitz divided a smile between the two women.

Sophie was a younger version of her mother, nearly a perfect copy, except where Esmeralda's eyes were dark brown, Sophie's were pale amber. Fitz wasn't especially moved by the dark beauty, but he suspected most men were.

Taking his cue, he set the animal on the ground. Othello waddled over to his mistress.

"My sweet boy doesn't usually like men." Esmeralda set the cat on her lap and looked from Fitz to her daughter. Fitz to her daughter. Fitz. To. Her. Daughter. "You should be flattered, Mr. Fitzpatrick."

His smile tightened. "Should I?"

"Othello is an excellent judge of character."

Fitz responded to this piece of absurdity with a bland smile.

With her self-importance firmly in place, Esmeralda invited him to sit on the settee beside her daughter. An awkward pause passed. Then they began a stilted conversation about the weather.

Only a part of his mind was on the conversation. The rest focused on Gigi. She was still in New York, which was a good thing. She hadn't run.

Yet.

Unpleasant emotions edged through him. Impatience, frustration, a need to settle matters between them quickly and decisively. Fitz wouldn't leave this house until he retrieved what Gigi had taken.

He had to get through dinner first.

Fitz suffered more small talk about upcoming soirees and the latest fashions. Despite the inane talk, he knew most men would consider dining with these two beautiful women a rare blessing. Fitz did not.

His mind remained elsewhere, reviewing the exact moment when his gaze had connected with Gigi's. His reaction had been that of a schoolboy. Fitz didn't want to be attracted to her. And he certainly didn't want to feel sympathy for her plight. She'd made her choices, including the one that could be deemed a criminal act if her father decided to press charges.

A memory of her panicked expression flashed in his mind.

She had to know why he was here.

Would his appearance chase her away before he could take back what she'd stolen?

Let her run, Fitz thought grimly. She wouldn't get far. He would find her again. And again, until he had what he wanted.

"Are you enjoying your time in New York, Mr. Fitzpatrick?"

Fitz shifted his attention to Esmeralda's daughter.

She wore a blue-and-silver gown that complemented her coloring. Though she wasn't as shiny or glittering as her mother, there was something rather likable about the young woman. She had an honest innocence about her that couldn't be faked.

As she smiled into his eyes, Fitz realized she didn't look any more interested in him than he was in her. Her expression was pleasantly polite, not too bright, not too dim.

"I am enjoying my stay very much." He met her honey-brown eyes. He'd seen that unusual color before.

Where? Fitz couldn't remember. The connection was there, in the back of his mind, but he couldn't retrieve it.

"Which attractions have you seen?"

"None," he admitted, then amended his answer slightly. "Other than the Summer Garden and my hotel."

Sophie laughed softly. "I don't recall you mentioning where you are staying."

"The Waldorf-Astoria." He'd chosen his lodgings because of Gigi. The famous hotel was the last place she'd been seen before her disappearance. Fitz had asked discreet questions of the hotel staff but he'd met with tight-lipped silence thus far.

Much the same as the reaction he was getting from Sophie Cappelletti. He wondered at that. When she failed to say anything in turn, he added, "The hotel's décor is unparalleled."

"Yes, it is." Sophie's gaze dropped to her lap, and she said nothing more. Seconds turned into a minute, and still she kept her silence.

Clearly, Fitz had upset the young woman. He couldn't think what he'd done to make her uncomfortable. This was why he hated these types of affairs. Having no idea how to restore the harmony, other than to wait for Sophie to speak again, he leaned back on the settee and turned his attention to Esmeralda.

Fitz caught the sly look in the singer's eyes. She was in for a large disappointment if she thought to match him with her daughter.

True, Sophie was attractive and charming, and Fitz had no doubt she would make some man a suitable match. Fitz was not that man. Marriage was not in his future. Even if he were in the market for a wife, Sophie Cappelletti would not be his first choice.

He preferred women with red hair, even if they dyed their glorious tresses a tarnished yellow-gold in a ridiculous attempt to hide their identity.

Gigi's face materialized in his mind. Fitz banished the image. He had not sought her out to woo her.

Sophie broke her silence at last. "It was unseasonably warm today."

And they were back to the weather. Would this evening never end?

Fitz caught Esmeralda's eye roll before responding. "I fear it won't last. The air smelled of snow when I alighted from my hired carriage."

"There is to be a ball at your hotel this weekend, hosted by Genevieve and Hugh Burrows." Sophie's brows rose. "Are you acquainted with the Burrows family?"

"I have conducted business with Hugh and his son."

"You know Simon?"

Fitz nodded, wondering at Sophie's sudden animation. If he remembered correctly, Simon had recently married.

Esmeralda made an unladylike snort. "Do not speak of that family in my presence."

"But Simon married Penelope. And Mrs. Burrows is sponsoring me in society. She has been very kind and—"

"Do not make the mistake of thinking that woman's kindness is for you." Esmeralda stroked her cat's fur. "Your connection to her daughter-in-law is the only reason she tolerates you."

Sophie's eyes widened, looking as if her mother had slapped her.

Seeing a war brewing between mother and daughter, Fitz interjected himself into the conversation. "I am acquainted with Simon's wife, though only in passing. I am friends with her brother."

"You are friends with Luke?"

"We attended Harvard together." His friend owned a fledgling automobile company. Rumor had it his main partner was looking to sell his interest. Discussing the opportunity was one of the reasons Fitz had chosen to come to New York personally.

"Oh, how wonderful." Sophie leaned forward. "Was he as witty and charming back then as he is now?"

Again, Fitz wondered at the young woman's reaction. Then he remembered hearing a rumor connecting Sophie to his friend and the man's sister. But he wasn't one to listen to gossip and couldn't dredge up the specifics.

"Were you very great friends with Luke at school?"

"We rowed together on the eight-man crew team."

"How interesting. Were you any good?"

Fitz smiled. "We won our share of races."

As Sophie pumped him for information, Esmeralda grew quiet and distant. It was the opera singer's uncharacteristic silence that sparked Fitz's memory.

Luke's father was a legendary patron of the opera. He also had a passion for opera singers, mezzo-sopranos in particular.

The puzzle pieces fell into place, and Fitz knew where he'd seen eyes similar to Sophie's. Luke Griffin bore the same unusual shade, as did his sister, Penelope. *And* Warren Griffin.

Was Sophie the product of a forbidden liaison between Luke's father and Esmeralda?

How did one broach such a subject?

One did *not* broach such a subject. Fitz might not be very adept at negotiating social gatherings, but he knew not to question a young lady's parentage.

Esmeralda said his name, her tone full of impatience.

Fitz turned his head in her direction and found her eyes narrowed in obvious displeasure. He raised a brow.

With little grace, and zero tact, she turned the conversation in a new direction. "Was Mr. Everett able to sway you to invest in the Summer Garden? Do not keep us in suspense. What is your decision?"

Fitz couldn't fault the woman's straightforward approach. "Mr. Everett has made a strong case."

It wasn't a fabrication. The theater owner had presented a picture of a lucrative endeavor, backing up his claim with receipts from the previous three years.

"Has he convinced you, then?" This from Sophie, asked with all politeness.

Fitz turned a smile her way. "Not quite."

"Then let me add my arguments to his," Esmeralda offered.

The conversation segued into a lengthy discussion as to why the singer considered the Summer Garden Theater a worthy investment. She mentioned everything from supporting the arts to enjoying the best seats in the house.

She finished her one-sided speech with, "I have performed in theaters across the world, and there is no rival to the Summer Garden."

A bold statement. "I will take that under advisement."

"That is all I ask." Clearly satisfied she'd made her case, Esmeralda launched into another litany. This one cataloguing the many reasons she was considered the most celebrated diva of her day. "The critics claim my phrasing is nothing short of awe inspiring."

Fitz rifled through what he'd read in the papers about Esmeralda and came up with what he hoped was an appropriate response. "Yours is a magnificent instrument, unrivaled in all the world."

He must have chosen his praise well, because the diva inclined her head as if accepting the compliment as her rightful due. "Most singers my age are on the decline. But my talent keeps increasing."

This time, Fitz didn't need to recall a newspaper clipping to know what to say. "You are remarkable, indeed."

"Hard work is the key element in my success. Flawless performances are about careful preparation."

Now that she had center stage, so to speak, Esmeralda carried on. And on and on and on.

Two exhausting hours later, after an excellent meal and a promise to dine with the ladies sometime soon, Fitz stood in the entryway, waiting for the butler to deliver his overcoat and top hat.

He turned in a slow circle, taking in the sweeping staircase, high ceilings, and massive mirrors that caught and reflected light from the chandelier. The colors were too bold for his taste, bordering on the garish.

Where did the servants disappear to when not working?

Fitz was trying to work out how best to locate Gigi when the butler appeared with his overcoat folded over his arm and top hat in hand. "Thank you, Irving."

"Good evening, sir." The butler attempted to escort Fitz to the door.

Fitz dug in his heels. "May I ask—"

"I am not at liberty to discuss such things."

Seconds later, Fitz found himself outside Esmeralda's town house, staring up at the three-story building with what he assumed was a bemused expression.

He huddled deeper in his coat. There was a hard chill in the air. The evening had been long and tedious, and Fitz had failed to accomplish his goal.

A weight settled in his stomach. He could not fail. He owed his cousin too much to return to Boston empty-handed.

He let out a slow, frustrated breath.

"Esmeralda has that effect on men."

Fitz went still for the span of a heartbeat. The sound of footsteps echoed from the shadows on his left.

Triumph swept through him. He wouldn't have to seek out Gigi after all.

She'd come to him.

Chapter Six

Fitz couldn't see Gigi yet, but he could hear her heels striking the stone steps that led to a basement door below Esmeralda's town house. He squinted into the inky night, finally spotting the dark figure moving toward him.

His shoulders shifted, flexed, and then went still again as a shadow elongated, then morphed into a familiar cloaked shape.

"Good evening, Gigi."

"My name is Sally." She stepped into the circle of light cast by the streetlamp. "I am Sally Smith now."

Insulted that she spoke in that ridiculous accent even when they were alone, Fitz said nothing, letting the stony silence stretch between them in the hope of intimidating her.

"So." A sigh leaked out of her. "You're determined to extract your pound of flesh."

It was his due. Her scandalous behavior had complicated his life in ways she couldn't possibly understand. He was responsible for keeping too many secrets that weren't his own, including hers.

And there she stood, glaring at him as though he were the villain in this farce.

You certainly aren't the hero.

He growled at the thought, knowing it was true. He wasn't without blame in Gigi's fall from grace. He'd played his role.

Gigi lifted her head, revealing her face from beneath the hood of her cloak. For a moment, Fitz could only stare. Even narrowed to slits of insolence, her eyes were glorious in the glow of the streetlamp. Expressive and filled with irritation and fear.

"Why are you here, Fitz?"

Despite the cold, he was suddenly over-warm and oddly out of breath and feeling as defiant as she looked. It appeared this second meeting was to be filled with antagonism.

"I was invited to dine with Esmeralda and her daughter." Though still not properly in control of his respiration, he added, "The three of us had a lovely evening."

"You know that's not what I meant." Her lips quivered, then firmed. "Why have you come to New York?"

"You know why."

Her sullen gaze dropped to the ground, then whipped back up with lightning speed. She stood in the same pose as she had at the theater—straight spine, square shoulders, and lifted chin. There was a new strength in her that he couldn't help but admire.

"Let's walk," he said.

He expected her to argue, but she agreed without complaint. "All right."

As they fell into step, matching each other's rhythm, Fitz was reminded of another time, a lifetime ago, it seemed, when he and Gigi had been friends. They'd been children, really. Life had been easy for them then.

Now, they each carried a heavy weight. Fitz studied her out of the corner of his eye.

He'd never seen that look of hopelessness in Gigi. She'd always been lighthearted and happy, a winsome girl free with her affections, living every day as if she hadn't a care in the world.

"What happened to you? What led to your . . ." He nearly said *ruin* but caught himself in time. No need to create more hostility between them. "What led to you becoming a lady's maid?"

"You don't really want to know."

No, he didn't want to hear the details, because then he would have to accept his responsibility for her downfall. He'd nearly convinced himself that he didn't care that he'd hurt her. But he did. He cared a great deal.

A breath-stealing numbness took hold of him. "Where is Nathanial Dixon now?"

Her head snapped to his. The anger he'd seen earlier had changed to something else. Annoyance. No, something far more powerful. Disgrace? Fitz felt the impact of the emotion as if it were his own.

"I don't know where Nathanial is." She said the words on a strangled sob. "He left a long time ago."

Fitz cursed softly. The sound was lost on the wind. He stopped walking.

She did the same, though with obvious reluctance.

"When did you last see Dixon?"

Her hands went wide, as if to say, *Isn't it obvious?*

"When, Gigi?" He knew his voice was too rough. Knew he was pushing her too hard. Any minute she would bolt like a frightened doe.

"I haven't seen or heard from Nathanial since the week we came here."

Fitz felt as though he'd been punched in the gut. Dixon had abandoned Gigi almost immediately upon arriving in New York. The scoundrel had left a pampered young woman to fend for herself in an unfamiliar city. If he stood before him now, Fitz would rectify the situation quickly. He would right the wrong and force the man to the altar, one way or another.

A vision flashed, Gigi in a beaded wedding gown, skin like porcelain, flaming red tresses cascading down her back. There was a time when Fitz would have claimed her for his own bride. Their union would have merged their two powerful families.

One problem. Gigi hadn't wanted him.

She'd been wise not to. Their union could have had a disastrous ending, at least for Gigi. She could have been trapped in a lifetime of servitude, a different kind than the one she lived now but just as suffocating. She couldn't have known that at the time. Fitz himself hadn't known, which begged the question . . .

"Why didn't you return to Boston after Dixon left?"

"I couldn't go home." The words were rife with pain and no small amount of regret.

Perhaps Dixon had ruined more than her reputation. Had the rat taken her innocence along with her dignity?

Fitz didn't want to know. He didn't *need* to know. Gigi had run off with the man and shared a hotel room for at least three days. No matter what had actually occurred between them, in the eyes of society, she was a fallen woman.

Even knowing this, Fitz still asked, "Why, Gigi? Why couldn't you go home?"

Her lips twisted in a dejected smile. Her silky lashes lowered to conceal her thoughts. "My father told me if I continued seeing Nathanial, he would disown me."

Fitz had no ready reply. He didn't doubt the veracity of her claim. Harcourt Wentworth was a good man, but a hard one as well.

"You are his daughter. Surely he would have forgiven you, especially once Nathanial was no longer in your life."

"The situation was not that simple."

Fitz wondered what he was missing. Gigi wasn't just sad. She was despairing, as if all was lost. Was the loss of her virtue the only reason for her state, or was there more to her tale? He wasn't supposed to feel sympathy for Gigi's plight, yet his gut roiled with the emotion.

In silent agreement, they resumed walking at a companionable pace, falling into an awkward silence as they approached the street corner. The evening air was scented with the promise of snow, thick and wet, the kind that stuck to tree branches and turned the world white. Even now, big, slow-moving flakes floated softly around them, creating a surreal, almost wistful feel to the moment. Another lie to add to all the others swirling between them. There was nothing soft about this moment. Nothing calm or wistful.

They paused at the street corner, where Fitz asked the one question he dreaded most. "Do you still love him?"

Gigi jerked at the words. Tears filled her eyes, along with fury. She'd looked at him like this when he'd confronted her about her growing attachment to the fortune hunter. Fitz had feared the worst that night, that Gigi was falling prey to the well-crafted lies.

"I have to get back." She spun on her heel. "Before my absence is noticed."

Fitz matched his gait to hers.

"I can find him for you," he offered. "I can make him marry you."

Her steps faltered, then halted altogether. "Please don't do that."

Though she'd uttered the words softly, Fitz heard the conviction in them and was surprised at the sense of relief that swept through him. "Will you run again, now that I've found you?"

Her answer would determine his next move.

She resumed walking but moved too quickly and stumbled over the hem of her heavy cloak.

Fitz reached out and took her elbow. Once her balance was restored, she yanked free of his touch and set off in the direction of Esmeralda's town house.

"Will you run?" he repeated, easily matching his strides with hers.

"That is none of your business."

"Oh, but it is." Fitz was finished stalling. "I have come for the pearls."

She pulled to an abrupt stop. "What did you say?"

Words formed in his head, disappeared, and then reformed in a new order. He'd made a promise to himself, one he would fulfill this very night. No more dancing around the matter. "I want the pearls you stole."

Gigi went utterly still. Fear lived in her eyes. But when she spoke, it was in her real voice. "I didn't steal them."

Fitz didn't know why he was disappointed. Deep down, he'd known she would deny the accusation. "Then you had Dixon steal them for you."

She muttered something under her breath, presumably not for him to hear, but it sounded suspiciously like "Maybe I should run after all."

Staring into her panicked expression, he felt the remaining scraps of his patience slip. Fitz let exasperation fill him and turn his heart hard to her situation.

"I don't care what you do after you hand over the pearls. But I'm not leaving New York without the necklace. That, Gigi, is a promise."

"My name is Sally." She pushed out the words through gritted teeth, her silver-blue eyes turning the same dull gray as the clouds covering the moon. "I am Sally Smith."

Enough. *Enough.*

Fitz pulled her into a side alley that housed more shadow than light. "You can change your name. You can dye your hair and speak in whatever outlandish accent you choose. But you will always be Gigi Wentworth, daughter of Harcourt and Alma, sister to Annabeth and Mariah."

He let five humming seconds of silence drop between them.

"You can pretend to be a humble servant. What you cannot do is evade the truth any longer." He held her gaze for another two full seconds. "You are a thief, and I have come to retrieve the property you stole."

Her expression shifted, no longer filled with vulnerability or fear, but with rebellion.

To behold her now, no one would believe this was the woman who had once allowed romantic sensibilities to rule her every decision.

"Listen to me, Fitz. No matter how many threats you make, I will never give you the pearls."

"You will."

"They don't belong to you."

"Perhaps not, but neither do they belong to you." He leaned over her, using his superior height as a weapon in their verbal battle. "You will give the pearls to me, tonight, or—"

"Or what? What will you do, Fitz?"

"Or . . ." He let his lips curve into a ruthless smile. "I shall involve the police."

* * *

Gigi stared into the eyes of a man she'd known all her life yet hardly recognized now. Fitz had always been intense and, if she was honest with herself, put her on edge whenever they shared the same air. But in all their time as friends, then awkward acquaintances, then opposing forces, he'd never frightened her.

Until now.

How was she supposed to hand over something she didn't have?

You are a thief.

Fitz would never understand what had possessed her to sell the pearls. She'd made a grave error in her assessment of the man. She'd underestimated his cold-bloodedness. Or perhaps he'd never been the dull, self-righteous prig she'd dismissed so easily only a year ago.

Perhaps, despite the odds, the rumors about him were true.

As she held his gaze, she saw something flash there, something not quite civil.

A shiver traveled through her limbs, one Gigi chalked up to the chill in the air and the snowflakes falling lazily from the sky, mocking her effort to remain calm.

Lying to herself had become a nasty habit, she realized. Nevertheless, as she yanked the edges of her cloak tightly around her, Gigi turned her back on Fitz and said in her calmest voice, with no affectation or false accent, "We're done here."

"Not by half."

He moved in front of her, using his body to bar her from exiting the alleyway.

When had Fitz become so intimidating?

Gigi shut her eyes, tried to calm her erratic heartbeat. She told herself that this was Fitz. He'd once been a friend.

He wasn't a friend anymore. How dare he involve himself in a family matter.

He'll be family soon, once his cousin marries Annie.

His inserting himself in the situation suddenly made sense. He was here on an errand for his cousin. But that didn't mean he had the right to insult her. Who was he to judge?

The man deserved a crushing set-down. When Gigi opened her eyes to deliver it, she discovered he'd moved to stand beside her. He was too close. She could smell the scent of sandalwood and bergamot.

Another shiver worked its way down her back. This one came with something more than fear. Something that didn't bear considering. Surely, she didn't find him . . .

No. Not worth considering.

Gigi had a plan. Christopher Nolan Fitzpatrick would not prevent her from atoning for her sins.

Realistically, his very presence made him an obstacle. He knew her name, her background, her secret shame. One word to the wrong person and he could derail her efforts to make matters right.

"You have no cause to interfere in this matter." She hated the desperation in her voice. "I would have thought you learned your lesson."

Her verbal jab had the desired effect. His flinch was small but noticeable and very, very gratifying. Gigi was feeling rather smug until he leaned over her and said, "Where are the pearls, Gigi?"

"In a safe place." *For now.*

But for how long?

What if Mr. Ryerson sold the pearls before her deadline? Gigi could practically hear time running out for her.

Should she tell Fitz the truth? Would he loan her the fifty dollars she needed to redeem the pearls? Or would he buy them back himself and steal her only chance for penance?

Gigi tried to think past the welter of emotion growing inside her. Did she dare trust Fitz? "Give me the pearls, Gigi." His face had changed somehow, becoming inflexible.

The stern man staring back at her hadn't always been there. Oh, Fitz had often been quiet and somewhat distant, but the tough exterior had only revealed itself *after* he and his cousin had taken over his family's investment firm. Looking at him now, she could believe him capable of anything. This was not a man she could trust.

"I don't have them on me." It was all she was willing to tell him.

"I'll wait while you go inside and get them."

Though she'd purposely meant to mislead him, she hadn't expected him to call her bluff. "I'm afraid I can't do that."

"Why not?"

The question came out harsh and unforgiving. She refused to cower. "They aren't in the town house."

"Where are they?"

"As I said before, the necklace is in a safe place."

Eyes narrowed, Fitz stared long and hard at her.

Gigi held his gaze without flinching. They might have been two furious armies, neither willing to give quarter, both wanting possession of the same piece of land.

"Did Dixon take them with him when he left you?"

"No." She struggled for the right words to convince Fitz she spoke the truth. "I . . . He never even knew about the pearls."

"I find that hard to believe."

"It's true." She hated how defensive she sounded and felt her lips curl in a self-deprecating sneer. What she'd thought would be the best day of her life had been her worst. She'd planned to wear the necklace on her wedding day, as all the Wentworth women had for generations. She'd wanted to surprise him. Instead, it was she who got the surprise.

Fitz had asked if she still loved Nathanial. How could she love such a man? She'd sacrificed her entire world for his, only to find herself abandoned in a strange city with no money or skills to speak of. Her only hope of survival had been the pearls.

If Nathanial showed up, contrite and apologetic, would she want him back in her life? In the early weeks after he'd disappeared, to her utter mortification, Gigi had hoped he would come looking for her, that he would find her and beg for her forgiveness.

He was supposed to marry me.

The disgrace came again, scorching and hopeless, and with it, the tears. Gigi furiously blinked them away. She would not cry in front of Fitz. She would not cry for herself. And she definitely wouldn't cry for Nathanial.

Nathanial.

He was supposed to be my prince.

We were supposed to live happily ever after.

Yes, well, life was no fairy tale. The prince really was a toad, and the princess was never meant to live happily ever after.

If Gigi still believed that God heard her prayers, she would pray now for guidance, for help, for comfort. But her Heavenly Father had turned His back on her in the same way her earthly father had done.

"What now?" she asked Fitz, feeling as beaten as she sounded. She was tired of running, of lying about who she was, of hoping atonement was a mere fifty dollars away.

"It appears we are at a stalemate."

"Then I'll bid you good night."

"Not so fast." His hand shot out and took hold of her arm. His grip was firm but not painful. "I will give you two days to retrieve the pearls from their 'safe' place. Then you will surrender them to me."

"Just like that?"

"Just like that." He tightened his grip ever so slightly. "You do this, Gigi, you give me the pearls and I'll keep your identity secret. I will leave you to live out the rest of your life as Sally Smith."

How she hated his calmness, his control of the situation. "How very fair-minded of you."

"Gigi." Sympathy flared in his eyes, and she'd never disliked him more than in that moment. "Though you may find this hard to believe, I have come in the spirit of friendship."

"You expect me to believe you're on a mission of goodwill?"

"Choose to believe whatever you like." His obvious frustration sounded in his voice. "Connor wants Annie to wear your great-grandmother's pearls on their wedding day. I am here to make that happen."

"Why send you?" Above the whirling and clicking of the blood rushing in her ears, Gigi managed to say, "Why didn't Connor come himself?"

Fitz rubbed a hand over his face, a small chip in his calm exterior exposed. "It's complicated. Suffice it to say, I owe my cousin a great debt, and this is one small step in repaying him."

"What if I refuse to give up the pearls?"

There was a short, taut silence as he contemplated the question.

"What if . . ." She swallowed. "What if I wish to return the necklace myself?"

Fitz took one—two—*three* furious breaths. "Nothing must be allowed to jeopardize the wedding."

"I agree."

"Then give me the pearls and stay hidden, at least until after the occasion."

He spoke as if he had all the power. *He does have all the power.*

No, not all.

Gigi could end this now. She could return to Boston tomorrow. Tonight. This very moment. She could confess her sins and ask for forgiveness.

What of your promise to Esmeralda? What of Sophie?

Gigi was trapped, more now than even this morning. Anger swept through like a violent thunderstorm, fast and fierce and unforgiving. She wasn't aware of moving, but suddenly she launched herself at Fitz. "How dare you interfere in my life again!"

He easily caught her wrists. "Calm yourself."

The cold voice of sanity cut through her torment. She breathed in sobbing gasps, desperate and fearful she would never earn her freedom. Afraid that forgiveness would never be hers if she didn't return the pearls on her own.

Fitz held her steady, staring hard into her eyes. His hold didn't hurt but was strong enough to keep her hands from making contact with his far-too-handsome face. In the darkened alley, he should look menacing. Instead, he looked as weary as Gigi felt. As if he were fatigued by his own impossible burdens.

Carefully, deliberately, he lowered her hands to her sides. He gentled his hold, then released her completely.

"The marriage between Connor and Annie will happen, Gigi. The wedding must go off without a hitch, not a single whiff of scandal.

And . . ." He held her in place with a look. "Your sister will wear your great-grandmother's pearls."

Somehow the quiet conviction in Fitz's voice reached Gigi as nothing else could have, and she found herself nodding in agreement. "Is Annie happy?"

"I believe so, yes."

"You're not just saying that?" Annie could have been forced to take Gigi's place, the sacrificial lamb for her father's desire to align with Fitz's family and her mother's wish to climb several more rungs on the social ladder. "My sister truly wants to marry your cousin? She is not being forced into marriage as I would have been had we . . ."

She left the rest unspoken.

Fitz had no problem stating the obvious. "You mean, if we had become engaged."

"Yes."

His chest rose and fell in a soundless sigh. "Your sister is pleased with the way things have turned out."

"And your cousin? Is he also pleased?"

"He claims theirs is a love match."

A love match. Gigi's remaining shreds of resistance faded but then returned full force when Fitz said, "The pearls, Gigi. You have two days to produce them."

She felt her face drain of color. "I need more time."

"You have forty-eight hours. Not a moment longer."

Having made his pronouncement, he stalked off. He didn't look back, not once. Gigi decided to be relieved. Fitz had given her two days to produce the pearls. She would use the time to figure out a way to get rid of him.

How? She didn't know. It would require careful planning. But she would free herself of him eventually.

She predicted a long, sleepless night ahead.

Chapter Seven

Fitz's throat tightened. He brutally swallowed the burning ache, composed himself, and strode across the street. He waited until he heard Gigi enter Esmeralda's town house before turning back around.

Stuffing his hands in his pockets, he stared up at the three-story structure. A man used to getting what he wanted, and wise enough to reject what he couldn't achieve quickly, he found himself in uncharted territory.

His heart pounded with antipathy. Gigi's resistance to giving up the pearls wasn't a surprise, precisely. The woman had always been difficult. It was, however, a complication he could do without.

One of the previously darkened windows on the third floor came alive with flickering light. Gigi lived in the servants' quarters, Fitz concluded. The thought sat about as well as her inability to be reasonable had earlier, which was to say not at all.

There was more to her story, something she wasn't telling him about the pearls. She'd seemed genuine in her desire to return the necklace. And yet, Fitz sensed a secret there. He knew all about keeping secrets.

Maybe he was overthinking the situation.

Frowning, he rocked back on his heels and pulled in a deep breath of the frigid night air. He caught a wisp of stale cigar smoke mere seconds before a murky figure stepped out of the shadows and joined him on the sidewalk.

"You want me to keep following her?"

"Yes." Fitz didn't take his eyes off the third-floor window. "She could run again."

Gigi could be packing her belongings even now.

"She won't get far." The confidence in the detective's voice was why Fitz was paying the man a small fortune.

Fitz swiveled slightly to his left. The investigator's eyes glinted black in the dark night. Mr. Offutt had come highly recommended and proven competent, except for the mistake he'd made this morning when he'd lost Gigi in the crowds on Thirty-Fourth Street.

They discussed their next meeting time and place. And then Fitz waved down a carriage for hire to take him back to his hotel.

Thirty minutes later, he entered the Waldorf-Astoria and retrieved his key from the front desk.

The evening clerk, an older gentleman with a receding hairline and a perfectly trimmed beard, was dressed in an impeccable blue suit and a silver brocade waistcoat. His nameplate identified him as Marvin Kapinsky.

"Good evening, Mr. Fitzpatrick."

Fitz returned the greeting, his mind back in the alley with Gigi. She'd mentioned her father's ultimatum as the reason for staying in New York. No ultimatum would keep her from going home. She loved her sisters too much.

So why not return home the moment Dixon had abandoned her in this very hotel? Fitz would find out why, in time.

Regrettably, time was something he didn't have.

"A telegram arrived after you left earlier." The clerk set the slip of paper on the counter and then wished Fitz a good night.

Fitz shot the telegram a cursory glance, noted the name of the sender. The muscles in his back instantly tensed. Connor wouldn't have contacted him unless it was important.

It could be nothing more than checking in.

Fitz's gut said otherwise.

Fitz always trusted his gut.

A headache beat behind his eyes. He ignored the pounding as he stepped out of the elevator and onto the seventh floor.

In his room, Fitz sat at the writing desk and read the telegram.

Your father left his house before dawn. Showed up at the office hours later. Took entire staff out to lunch at the Parker House Hotel. Situation under control.

Fitz's heart sank. So much said in a spattering of sentences. So much left unsaid. His father had escaped his nurse this morning and wandered the streets of Boston for hours, alone. He'd then shown up at the office and played the benevolent boss.

Lowering his head, Fitz read the last sentence again. *Situation under control.* Translation: *Your secret is still safe.*

Once again, Connor had proven his loyalty to the family and protected them from scandal. Fitz had only to recollect how the press pilloried members of society for something far less than a business titan's erratic behavior.

Time was running out. He had to find a cure.

Fitz ran a hand over his face. No doubt today's incident had left his mother in a frantic state. He would write back in the morning and recommend his cousin hire an additional nurse for their father's care. One clearly wasn't enough.

Finding trained workers that could keep their mouths shut was costing the family a fortune. Fitz would find a way to cover the expense.

And his father's bad investments. The company had been teetering on the edge of ruin for a while, thanks to Calvin Fitzpatrick's loss of sound judgment. Had Fitz not insisted on reviewing the ledgers, the situation would have become dire, perhaps even irreversible. Immediately upon discovering that the firm was on the brink of bankruptcy, Fitz and Connor had taken control of the company.

Although they'd made remarkable progress, it would take years to restore the business to its former glory. Fitz had settled his father's debts, paid off the bad mortgages, and reorganized the accounting system.

The investment firm was solvent again, but not yet thriving. Connor's marriage to Annie Wentworth would go a long way to putting them at the top again. Her inheritance would provide the necessary income to expand.

Even without Annie's inheritance, Fitz would bring the firm back to greatness. The source of his larger concern was his father. The man's unpredictable behavior was getting worse.

Unable to sit still, Fitz stood abruptly and paced along the perimeter of the room. Few knew of Calvin Fitzpatrick's condition. Connor had aided Fitz in keeping his father's illness from becoming public knowledge. So many secrets, he thought, feeling the weight of them like a millstone around his neck.

An image of Gigi flashed in his mind.

The woman he'd encountered today was so far removed from the vibrant young girl he'd once adored from afar. He didn't know quite how to process the changes. Even the name she'd chosen spoke to her situation.

Sally Smith was plain, unassuming, practically invisible. Gigi Wentworth had been charming, sparkling, a woman who turned heads and—

Fitz experienced a pang of guilt. He'd seen the sadness in Gigi's eyes when he'd mentioned Nathanial. The wistfulness. As though she wished for his return, regardless of what she'd said.

Fitz knew about wishing for what he could never have.

He knew about pining for someone who could never be his.

Lips pressed in a hard line, he pivoted on his heel and retraced his steps around the room. If Gigi refused to give him the pearls, he would have to rethink this strategy.

He must gain Gigi's trust. Therein lay the problem. She'd never trusted him, and time was working against him. Originally, Fitz had thought to return to Boston in a few days, a week at most. He could tell her family where she was and let her father handle matters from there. But the last time Fitz had interfered in her life, he'd caused more harm than good.

By his third pass around the room, his headache had settled into a dull throb. An improvement, yet Fitz couldn't shake his foul mood. He picked up the telegram, read the typed words again, let out a slow hiss. *Situation under control.*

For how long?

Fitz crumpled the piece of paper in his hand, then tossed it in the fire. He shut his eyes and searched his pounding, churning mind for answers. Answers, he resolved, that would come in time. He needed another week.

Perhaps two. Three at the very most. Far more time than he'd arranged to be gone. It couldn't be helped. Connor would have to understand. Fitz sat at the writing desk and composed a response to his cousin.

* * *

When Gigi awakened the next morning, her mood was as dark as the sky. Mechanically, she rose from her bed and proceeded to braid and coil her hair with an efficiency born of habit. The previous evening's encounter with Fitz had been frightening, but the man hadn't broken her will.

Two days, indeed.

He could stay in New York a week, a month, *a year*, and she wouldn't give him the pearls. She'd had the courage and fortitude to create a new life for herself on her own. She would figure out a way to send Fitz back to Boston empty-handed. He could not—*would not*—be the one to return the necklace she'd taken.

You mean the necklace you stole.

Borrowed. She'd always intended to return it.

Blinking through the pre-dawn gloom, she stared up at the ceiling. The plaster was peeling in places, its repair evidently not a priority.

Sighing, Gigi lowered her gaze. She'd tossed and turned all night and still hadn't been able to decipher Fitz's motivation. What did he have to gain by playing the hero in this little farce of theirs? What sort of debt did he owe his cousin?

As she laced up her ankle boots, Gigi reviewed their conversation and the man's threat to bring the police into the matter. She very much doubted he would go that far.

Her mind stuck on something else he'd said. *The wedding must go off without a hitch.*

Why would that be a concern?

If Annie and Connor's union was a love match, as Fitz claimed, nothing could keep them apart. Not even scandal.

Gigi had seen the power of true love. Both of her previous employers had found their soul mates in the midst of scandal and were living happily ever after. Though it hadn't turned out so well for Gigi, she knew love could, and often did, conquer all. She wasn't so jaded to think otherwise.

What if Annie *wanted* Gigi at her wedding? They'd been close once upon a time, as close as any sisters could be. They'd laughed and shared confidences. Some had been silly, some serious. They'd dreamed of the future and of meeting their everlasting love.

Then Nathanial had shown up at a party hosted by a friend of a friend. Gigi had been instantly smitten and would hear nothing against him. She'd shut out her sisters, her friends, and anyone who didn't approve of her attraction to the handsome charmer. Annie hadn't been as vocal as the others, but she'd urged Gigi to be cautious. Gigi had happily taken leave of her senses. She'd seen the beauty in her love for Nathanial, not the danger.

Did Annie hold her selfishness against her?

Gigi would only know when she returned to Boston.

And when she returned, Annie should be the one to decide if she wanted Gigi to be a part of the wedding celebration.

If she was turned away . . .

No, she refused to let her mind spin in that direction. One step at a time. First, she had to send Fitz back to Boston. But not before extracting his promise not to tell her family where she was. Gigi must make restitution on her own.

She finished dressing, then stepped out of her room and hurried down the back stairwell. She followed her nose to the one place she felt truly comfortable in this house.

The noise level increased as she conquered each step. By the time she reached the first floor, the scent of bacon frying and bread baking restored the appetite she'd lost the day before. The growling of her stomach reminded her she'd missed dinner last night. Knowing Fitz was in this house had made the thought of eating distasteful.

Not so, now.

Unlike the rest of the town house at this early hour, the kitchen was a hive of activity. The room was well lit, warm, and welcoming. Gigi attributed the latter to the staff's laughter. Heat and pleasant aromas drew her forward.

She paused in the doorway, a smile on her lips. *I'll miss these people when I'm gone.*

Swiping at her eyes, she took in the familiar scene.

A wooden table sat in the center of the room, with two identical tea services waiting to be prepared and then taken up to the bedchambers where the ladies of the house still slumbered. A smaller table off to her right was filled with Gigi's fellow servants. They were already digging into a hearty breakfast of bacon, eggs, a medley of fruit, and thick pieces of toast loaded with butter and jam.

Gigi's mouth watered.

The cook, a large man whose girth practically equaled his height, barked at Gigi to stop dawdling in the doorway and sit at the table. He then turned to his assistant, Lottie, and gave the reed-thin blonde a succession of curt orders. The girl scurried back and forth from the pantry to the table.

The housekeeper looked up from her plate and motioned Gigi to sit. "Eat, dear, before the eggs get cold."

Gigi took the chair directly across from the plump woman with the twinkling eyes and ready smile. "Good morning, Mrs. Garrison."

"Good morning, Sally."

They were joined at the table by the butler, Irving, the gardener and his assistant, Esmeralda's lady's maid, and the two additional house-maids. All but Lottie were on the wrong side of fifty. Every one of them had once worked in the theater, but the roles had shriveled up with each passing year, the curse of making a living on the stage.

Even Lottie had been a child actress. Her cuteness had matured into something not quite womanly and several steps from attractive, and thus she'd found herself out of work by the ripe old age of thirteen.

Of all the homes where Gigi had served in the past year, this one had her favorite staff. They were open and friendly, and told marvel-ous stories about their days on the stage—*treading the boards*, as they called it. Gigi suspected most of their outrageous stories were more fiction than fact, at the very least heavily embellished. She didn't mind. Listening to their tales of life in the theater was the one indulgence she allowed herself.

Well, that and the Boston newspapers she read from cover to cover whenever she had a free moment. Something that would be far more precious now that she had to earn fifty extra dollars in only a few weeks.

As she filled her plate and began eating, Gigi listened to the chatter floating around the table. They were gossiping, of course, about Esmeralda, their favorite topic. Gigi felt a smile tug at her lips until she realized the speculation wasn't about Esmeralda after all but rather the surprise dinner guest from the night before.

Gigi's appetite took a dramatic turn for the worse. She thought she might be sick. Setting aside her fork, she silently mourned the waste of all that lovely food on her plate.

"Do you think he's pursuing Sophie?"

Perfect. Even the servants were playing matchmaker. The roiling in Gigi's stomach took on a life of its own.

She couldn't imagine Fitz and Sophie together. Although maybe if she squinted her eyes very tightly and thought it through very, very carefully, she *could* envision them as a couple.

Fitz would provide Sophie the one thing she desired most, respectability. Sophie would bring light into Fitz's austere existence. Where Fitz was hard, Sophie was soft. Her gentle nature would temper his arrogance. His steadiness would bring her stability.

They would produce beautiful babies.

The thought of Fitz and Sophie building a family together brought an odd reaction, a strange sort of unwholesome desire to rip every hair out of her friend's beautiful head. The ugliness of her reaction to something that hadn't yet happened brought heat crawling up Gigi's neck.

"It must be Sophie he's wanting," the gardener's assistant said. "He's far too young for Esmeralda."

"Right," one of the housemaids said in a sarcastic British accent. "As if the age difference has ever stopped a young man from pursuing the mistress."

Agreement sounded from nearly everyone in the kitchen, save for Cookie, who was too busy sending Lottie back and forth from the pantry to the stove.

There was a pause, and then, "But *who is he?*"

Another pause fell over the table, and Gigi could see each of them waiting for one of the others to supply something of substance about Fitz.

The silence lengthened.

"Surely, he has a name?" the housekeeper asked the room in general. "Does no one here know it?"

"Christopher Nolan Fitzpatrick."

All eyes turned to Gigi. There was another beat of silence, during which the entire staff seemed to stop and wait, and then the interrogation began in earnest.

"Have you met him?" Followed by, "Is he as handsome as Lottie claims?" This had both housemaids wondering out loud and saying simultaneously, "Does he have designs on our Sophie?"

Gigi held up a hand to still the flow of inquiries. She answered them in order. "Yes, I met him at the theater yesterday," she told Mrs. Garrison. To the gardener's assistant, Gigi said, "He's quite handsome," because, well, Fitz *was* attractive, if a woman went for dark hair, intense green eyes the color of fresh ivy after a spring rain, and the strong, broody, silent type. Lastly, she said, "I have no idea if he's pursuing Sophie."

The hitch in Gigi's throat could be explained away by her need to respond briskly to the rapid-fire questions.

"I believe he is in negotiations to purchase the Summer Garden Theater," she added with no additional prompting.

"He's rich?"

As Midas. "I believe so."

"And respectable?" Lottie asked, setting another tray of toast on the table.

Gigi thought about her answer. "Very."

"A handsome, wealthy, respectable man is wooing our Sophie?" Mrs. Garrison asked the rhetorical question with a wistful note in her voice. "How absolutely . . . wonderful."

Gigi agreed that Sophie deserved a good man. The problem was Gigi couldn't say for certain if Fitz *was* a good man. On paper, yes. In reality, she simply didn't know. Respectable didn't necessarily equal moral. In truth, Fitz had always been a mystery to Gigi. And now, he was being as secretive as ever, making threats and demands without offering a hint as to his real motives.

More questions came at her. She answered them as best she could, evading when a truthful answer would reveal a stronger connection to Fitz than a single meeting would warrant.

At last, the conversation turned to the current production of *Carmen* and the dubious talent of half the cast. None of whom were as gifted as those sitting at the table had been in their day.

Seizing her opportunity for escape, Gigi went to work filling the tray with Sophie's preferred breakfast items. She added that morning's edition of the *New York Times* and headed up the back stairs.

Once she was alone with only her thoughts for company, a sense of desperation nagged at her ability to remain calm. *You have two days.*

She'd spent much of the night trying to come up with a plan. The obvious answer was to tell Fitz the truth about the pearls and ask for his help.

If only she could trust him.

What am I going to do, Father God?

Silence met the question, just like all the other times she'd sought guidance from the Lord. Gigi was alone, as she'd been for eleven long months.

She cleared her mind of Fitz and his preposterous two-day deadline. Gigi would figure out what to do. She always did.

Chapter Eight

Gigi found Sophie as she usually did at this hour. An early riser, the young woman sat at the table near the window, drenched in the golden, rosy tint of dawn. Esmeralda's treasured cat, Othello, slumbered in a sunbeam at Sophie's feet.

Gigi moved to the table and set down the tray of pastries, coffee, and two soft-boiled eggs in pretty enameled cups of blue-and-gold porcelain, Esmeralda's signature colors.

"Good morning, Sophie." Gigi handed the young woman the *New York Times* and then poured the Earl Grey tea she preferred in a cup. "I trust you slept well."

"Not a wink."

"Oh, dear." Gigi studied Sophie more closely, noting the light dusting of purple shadows beneath her red-rimmed eyes. Alarm had her asking, "Do you want to talk about it?"

"Not especially." The words were spoken without conviction.

"If you're sure . . ."

"Oh, Sally. It's just . . . No." She shook her head decisively. "There is nothing I wish to discuss at present."

Hands slightly shaking, Sophie spread the newspaper out on the table and pretended grave interest in the front page.

At the obvious dismissal, Gigi went about tidying the room.

Out of the corner of her eye, she saw Sophie pick up her spoon and give one of the eggs a hard whack. With a look of distaste, Sophie sighed heavily and then selected a pastry off the tray. As she took a bite, she bent down and absently stroked the cat's sleek fur. Othello's rumbling purr overwhelmed all other sounds in the room.

Gigi picked up a blanket off Sophie's bed and began folding it into a meticulous square, her mind only half on the task.

Clearly, something had upset her friend. Gigi was determining how to broach the subject when Sophie broke her silence. "I understand you met Mr. Fitzpatrick at the theater yesterday."

Gigi's hands froze mid-fold. Of course Sophie wanted to discuss Fitz. He seemed to be the favorite topic of the entire household this morning.

"I did meet him, briefly."

"What did you think?"

Gigi ignored the pit forming in her stomach, schooled her features into a bland expression, and answered with as much enthusiasm as she could muster. "I found him to be very . . . polite."

"Polite." Sophie gave a hum of agreement, petting the cat with lazy strokes. "That he is. He hails from Boston. Did you know that?"

"I recall you mentioning that."

"His family is one of the most respectable in the city. Have you heard of them?"

Remembering that she'd told Sophie her real name and had indicated she came from wealth, she saw there was no use lying. "Yes."

"And Mr. Fitzpatrick? Have you heard of him?"

"Yes."

"But you do not *know* him?"

Did anyone ever really know another person? Gigi had thought she'd known Nathanial. How wrong she'd been there.

After her encounters with Fitz, Gigi suspected he was as much a stranger as Nathanial had proven himself to be. Thus, it was with complete honesty that she said, "I do not know him."

"Hmm." Sophie lifted the cat into her lap and stroked her hand down the long, silky fur.

"Did Mr. Fitzpatrick upset you last evening? Did he say something"—*about me?*—"that caused you to lose sleep?"

"No, he was a delightful guest." She nibbled on her bottom lip, a striking young woman lost in contemplation. "He's really rather perfect. Although, now that I think about it, I found him a bit distant and not fully present."

Distant. Not fully present. Gigi had once accused Fitz of those very things. He hadn't been distant last night. Edgy, restless, demanding, and arrogant. But, no, not distant.

"I had a hard time deciphering his true feelings about any of the topics we discussed," Sophie continued.

Fitz had made himself clear enough to Gigi in the darkened alleyway. Issuing orders and threats. *I shall involve the police.*

"Mama thinks he would be a good match for me."

A sudden rush of emotion had Gigi picking frantically at the fringe on the blanket in her hands. It was hard not to like Sophie. She was sweet and gracious and deserved better than a match manipulated by her mother.

"You don't like Mr. Fitzpatrick?" Gigi asked.

"I don't know him well enough to like or dislike him."

Gigi set down the blanket, picked up another one. "What do you think of him as a potential suitor?"

"I think . . ." Sophie sat back in her chair and cuddled the cat close. "We would be a terrible match. He is too perfectly polite, too perfectly gentlemanly, and too perfectly . . . perfect."

There'd been nothing perfect about Fitz in the alleyway. Except for his being perfectly awful. No, that wasn't entirely true. He'd shown a moment of genuine sympathy and vowed to find Nathanial for her.

"Marriage to a man like Mr. Fitzpatrick would mean instant acceptance and respectability," Gigi ventured.

"In Boston society, perhaps that is true. But what of New York?"

Sophie posed a valid question. "Marrying a man like Fitz—Mr. Fitzpatrick would certainly be an excellent start."

"Not enough, I fear. Not nearly enough." As if sensing Sophie's gloomy mood, Othello cracked open an eye and studied Gigi through the narrow slit. He gave her a dismissive sniff and returned to his nap, chin resting lightly on his front paws.

Gigi tried not to feel offended. But, really—weighed, measured, and found wanting by a cat? Not the greatest of humiliations, but still.

"I am supposed to accompany my mother to the theater today," Sophie said. "She claims we will go shopping at Bergdorf Goodman after her rehearsal, but I know that's not the reason."

"No?"

"It's because she wishes to throw me in Mr. Fitzpatrick's path as much as possible." Sophie set the cat on the floor and stood, eyes miserable. "I must prepare."

"You're already dressed."

Sophie smoothed a hand down her skirt. "I am not happy with the color."

"That shade of green does wonders for your coloring."

"Precisely."

Baffled, Gigi joined her friend in the closet. Standing shoulder to shoulder, they eyed the contents together. Sophie reached out and closed her hand over a hideous gray gown Gigi had attempted to toss out on several occasions.

"Not that one," Gigi urged. "Your mother will object."

Sophie gave her a sly grin. "Precisely."

"But the color is unflattering, and the cut of the dress is too large."

"Precisely."

"You . . . oh." Understanding dawned. "You don't wish to attract Mr. Fitzpatrick's attention."

"Precisely."

The young woman looked rather pleased with herself. Gigi was rather pleased with Sophie as well, for reasons she refused to contemplate. "What if he isn't a man swayed by fashion?"

"All men are swayed by fashion, even the ones who think they are immune. It is all part of the mating game." In that moment, Sophie sounded very much like her mother. "The key is to know the rules and use them to your advantage."

Now she even *looked* like Esmeralda with her haughty pose and the nonchalant sweep of her hand.

"I thought you didn't care to play that particular game."

"Oh, I care. I care a great deal. I merely object to having my mother set the rules."

Gigi took the gray dress and followed Sophie out of the closet. "I don't understand what has brought on this sudden need to rebel."

"It's quite simple, really. I have been at the mercy of my mother's decisions all my life. I have followed her rules to the letter. And now that I am on the brink of creating a new life for myself, she wishes to stall my efforts by throwing a man in the mix. A man of her choice, not mine."

Gigi laid the dress on the bed and went to help Sophie out of the pretty green gown. She should have known Sophie would eventually test her boundaries. The young woman had a strong will and harbored great anger toward her mother. Rebellion was inevitable. But one step would lead to another.

And then several more. Gigi had lived out the scenario herself. She'd then seen the pattern repeated with her previous employer. Elizabeth St. James—now Elizabeth Griffin—had rebelled against her mother's strict rules. The young woman had avoided scandal only because a good man—Luke Griffin—had come into her life.

Sophie was stepping out on her own and, because of that, Gigi feared the outcome. Youthful mistakes were regretted for a lifetime. "I urge you to think carefully about how you proceed."

Something in her voice must have gotten through to the young woman, because Sophie's bold expression settled into one of uncertainty. "It's only a dress."

Elizabeth's rebellion had started with a dress.

"You are close to earning a spot in New York society. I would hate for you to take a misstep merely because you wish to upset your mother."

"Yes, well." Sophie stepped into the gray dress. "I know what I'm doing."

Something in the way the woman made this casual remark put Gigi immediately on guard. "If your mother didn't like Mr. Fitzpatrick, would you be this determined to avoid his attention?"

The question gave the girl pause. She straightened one of the sleeves, plucking at the thin ivory lace. "Rest assured, I am certain Mr. Fitzpatrick is not the man for me. It's important to let him know this from the onset of our acquaintance."

"You are resolved on this route?"

"Absolutely." Sophie spun around. "I have a request."

Not liking the calculating look she saw in her friend's eyes, Gigi's heart took a fast lurch.

"I cannot be alone with Mr. Fitzpatrick. I want you to make sure that doesn't happen."

"Me?" Gigi gaped at the woman. "You wish for me to—" She swallowed back a gasp of dismay. "Distract him?"

"You don't have to look so appalled. I'm not asking you to accost the poor man. I'm simply requesting you chat him up, keep him company, or maybe show him around the theater."

"I'm sure he's already had a tour."

"Then take him up to the roof garden, unless I'm up there. Then find some other out-of-the-way spot."

The suggestion rendered Gigi speechless. She couldn't take Fitz up to the roof garden or anywhere intimate. He would no doubt use the occasion to ask her about the pearls.

"I should warn you." Sophie tugged on an errant curl that Gigi had yet to pile atop her head with the others. "Now that Mama has it in her mind to throw Mr. Fitzpatrick and me together, your task will not be an easy one."

Gigi breathed in sharply, the only outward sign of her distress. Fitz had been adamant last night in the alleyway that he wouldn't rest until he had her great-grandmother's pearls in his possession. She'd hoped to avoid him while she thought up a plan to dissuade him of the notion.

"Did you hear what I said?"

Gigi started, realizing that Sophie had continued talking while she'd been fighting off panic. "Er . . . no."

"I asked if you understood what I'm asking of you."

A sigh slid out of her. "I understand perfectly."

"Very good." The girl looked at her far-from-stellar reflection and gave one quick, firm nod. "Mother wishes to leave within the hour."

"I'll be ready." Back in her room, Gigi packed a small satchel. She tossed in random items—a small sewing kit, a clean hairbrush, hat pins, an assortment of ribbons, and a book. The last item was one of Sophie's favorite novels by Jane Austen. Gigi included the tome in case rehearsals went long and Sophie grew bored.

That task complete, Gigi sat on her bed and looked around her tiny room. So much smaller and plainer than the one she'd inhabited at Harvest House. But she had a bed, clothing to wear, the promise of three meals a day, and a roof over her head. Really, what more did she need?

Freedom.

There was no such thing. Not for a woman with a past like hers. And though Gigi had once lived with a strong faith, gifted with the surety of her Heavenly Father's love, now she felt no connection to her Lord. She felt nothing. Knew nothing.

Believed nothing.

Eyeing her reflection in the mirror, she contemplated the woman blinking back at her. Sally Smith was as plain as her servants' quarters.

Othello shoved into the room and wound around her ankles, a black-and-white, pudgy ribbon of fur. Welcoming the company, Gigi reached down and scratched the cat's belly. The need to escape smothered all other thought. She would leave this house, change her name again, find another job, do charity work, get her hands dirty, and maybe own a fat cat. She would spoil him—of course—mercilessly. The two of them would live out their days in quiet solitude, far from society, far from the glittering balls and nosy reporters and gossip and . . .

Gigi would never see her sisters again.

No, she thought, a friendless, cheerless, solitary existence was not what she wanted. She wanted to be restored to her family. And . . . and . . . she wanted to go home.

She *would* go home.

Fitz could make his demands. He could threaten, cajole, or use any manner of persuasion. Gigi would never relent.

After sparing Othello one last scratch behind his ears, she picked up her tote bag and went to meet Sophie in the foyer.

* * *

Gigi arrived at the theater with Sophie and Esmeralda. They entered through the backstage door at a leisurely pace set by the opera singer.

Stepping into a wall of noise and light, Gigi took in the swarm of activity. Four men stood in a semicircle, hunched over a set of drawings. They argued over one of the designs, two of them convinced the arch should be painted green, the other two confident the color was supposed to be brown.

Esmeralda breezed past them without a single look in their direction. Likewise, she ignored the half-dozen women in matching bright-blue dancer costumes, her destination clear.

Fitz stood statue still. Enveloped in the golden glow cast by warm stage lighting, he stood separate and alone, watching the activity with an expression that betrayed his implacable resolve.

Of course the odious man would have already arrived at the theater. Fitz was nothing if not predictable. The music director walked up to him. Mr. Lawrence was a slight man of indeterminate years. He had a clever face and dark-blond hair that stuck out in every direction.

For his part, Fitz looked, as Sophie had claimed, quite naturally . . . perfect. He was dressed in business attire that fit him so well that Gigi had no doubt he still employed the best tailor in Boston.

He looked over at her.

Gigi looked right back.

Something odd dipped in her stomach. The sensation wasn't altogether awful. She quickly lowered her head. When she lifted her gaze again, Fitz had shifted his attention to Esmeralda.

"Ah, Fitz. There you are. Just the man I wished to see." As if she'd been searching for him all morning, Esmeralda lifted her hand in a queenly summons.

Even from this position, Gigi could read his exasperated expression before he smoothed it away with a benign smile. He crossed the distance with ground-eating strides. "Good day, ladies."

Sophie immediately stiffened at the greeting. She took hold of Gigi's arm and squeezed. Hard. Esmeralda carried the bulk of the conversation, saying something about how fortuitous it was running into Fitz so soon after their evening together.

Fortuitous for whom, Gigi wondered. Certainly not for her, or for Sophie, if her death grip on Gigi's arm was anything to go by.

Esmeralda placed a gloved hand on Fitz's bicep.

Seizing her chance to flee, Sophie mumbled a quick, garbled farewell and took herself away, dragging Gigi with her. Despite her earlier request that Gigi distract Fitz, the young woman practically heaved Gigi through the maze of hallways.

They ascended an alarmingly steep, twisting stairwell made of rickety wrought iron.

"I didn't even know these steps existed," Gigi said, gasping for breath.

"Shh," Sophie ordered. "Someone will hear you."

They reached the top. Sophie threw open the door and stepped into a beam of sunlight. She motioned for Gigi to follow.

Gigi did as requested, momentarily blinded by the blast of sunshine. She attempted to regain her vision with several fast blinks. The task was made more difficult as an image of Fitz's freshly shaved face and still-damp hair intruded.

His eyebrows had been drawn together in concentration, his mouth a flat line of grim determination. He'd looked like a man on a mission.

Shivering in the wind, Gigi washed out her lungs with several gasps of fresh air. When that failed to calm her, she put a hand on her forehead and shoved her hair back. At last, her surroundings came into view.

Sophie had brought them up to the roof garden.

Gigi had only been up here once, via a less precarious, carpeted staircase situated in the auditorium. The garden's architecture was very pretty. Tables and chairs were scattered throughout, not haphazardly but in an arrangement that created an artistic and inviting atmosphere. Tiny, intimate islands of seating and large potted plants placed at strategic spots brought cohesion to the overall design.

Despite the chilly temperature and the light dusting of snow, it was a perfect hiding place for a woman wishing to avoid a certain man. Gigi let out a relieved sigh.

"You know you have to go back down there." Sophie must have caught Gigi's startled expression, for she added in a soft voice, "You promised to distract Mr. Fitzpatrick, remember?"

Of course, this was a hiding place for Sophie, not Gigi.

"Ah, yes. Right." Gigi cleared her throat. "I'll head back down now."

She turned to go, then remembered the item she'd stuffed in her bag and spun back around. "I brought this for you."

Digging inside the satchel, she retrieved the copy of *Persuasion*, Sophie's favorite Jane Austen novel.

Gratitude filled the young woman's eyes as she reached out a gloved hand. "You have thought of everything."

Not everything. Gigi still had to come up with a plan to send Fitz packing once and for all. "I'll let you know when the coast is clear."

This time, when she turned to go, she kept walking. She picked her way carefully—*very carefully*—down the rickety stairwell and arrived on terra firma with slightly shaky legs. She took in one breath, two, a third. Equilibrium restored, she took one final pull of air, and went in search of Fitz.

She passed a group of young women. She nodded a greeting, which they promptly returned. Nearer the stage, Gigi caught sight of Maestro Grimaldi whipping his arms about as he conducted the musicians and singers through a practice run of the famous "Toreador" aria from the second act of *Carmen*.

Unable to stop herself, Gigi closed her eyes a moment and let the bass-baritone couplet in F-minor roll over her. Though the song described a bullfight, the time signature was in common time, which brought a sense of order to the music that Gigi found comforting.

It was moments such as these, when she was treated to a performance by some of the best musicians and singers in the world, that she missed her studies most. If only she'd taken her training more seriously, maybe then she'd have been immune to Nathanial's advances.

Fitz wouldn't have felt compelled to interfere. And her father wouldn't have disowned her.

Remembering her duty, she blinked open her eyes. Fitz was no longer in the wings watching the orchestra.

Where was he?

With Esmeralda, probably.

Except the diva was onstage with the others. Thinking through her options, Gigi came up with a plan that would satisfy her promise to Sophie. She would guard the stairwell to the roof garden.

As soon as the thought materialized, she discarded it. There was more than one entrance to the roof. She would have to locate Fitz after all.

Perhaps he was in the business office with Mr. Everett, talking about, well, business.

One way to find out.

Gigi rapped on the door and was told to enter. She pushed into the room. It was a small one, cluttered with stacks of paper on every available piece of furniture. The air was drafty, as there was no working fireplace or stove to ward off the chill.

Mr. Everett sat behind the lone desk facing the door. She couldn't see his face or his caterpillar eyebrows. Head down, the theater owner wielded a brass letter opener with focused intent, ripping open envelopes with swift, efficient swipes.

A glance to her left, then her right, and Gigi determined the man was alone.

"Miss Smith." He greeted Gigi with a suspiciously cheerful smile. "What can I do for you this fine morning?"

"I was actually looking for Mr. Fitzpatrick."

"You just missed him."

The faint spicy fragrance of Fitz's scent lingered in the air, telling her that she had, indeed, just missed him by mere minutes.

Well, drat.

Gigi glanced around the office again, tugging her bottom lip between her teeth. "Do you happen to know where he went?"

"He took himself off to the wardrobe room." That explained why they hadn't crossed paths.

"I see you are busy." Gigi glanced at the stack of unopened letters waiting for the owner's attention. "I won't keep you from your work."

Yet instead of leaving, Gigi realized this was her chance to earn a bit of money. She squared her shoulders. "Mr. Everett? May I impose on you a moment longer?"

He gave her a slow smile, his good mood all but radiating off him. "Of course."

"I am in need of a job."

The man's eyebrows drew together into one thick black line. "You are already employed."

"I meant something in the evenings. Perhaps I could sort the mail, or organize your desk. The clutter is quite out of hand and—"

"My desk is precisely the way I like it. *Organizing*, as you put it, would only cause confusion." He spoke kindly with no real censure in his voice, which gave Gigi the daring to continue.

"Oh, well then, maybe I could . . ." *Think, Gigi. Think of something you can do.* "Perhaps I could clean the theater? I'm rather proficient at polishing brass and mirrors."

She'd performed similar work at the Waldorf-Astoria.

"I already have a cleaning crew."

"I'm a hard worker," she ventured. "There must be something that needs an extra pair of hands." She wiggled her fingers to punctuate the point.

The theater owner tossed down the letter opener and sat back, tapping his fingers against the table for a minute before saying, "I'm afraid nothing comes to mind."

Gigi folded her lips, then met Mr. Everett's kind eyes. "I can paint the sets, take tickets, hand out programs once the show opens."

"I'm sorry, Miss Smith." He gave a slow shake of his head. "I already have people performing those tasks."

The apology was in his eyes, as was the pity. How many times had Gigi seen that look since Nathanial had abandoned her?

Too many times to count, each one more humiliating than the last, but what did pride matter? She'd learned long ago that pride couldn't fill her belly. And it certainly wouldn't buy back her great-grandmother's pearls.

"Right. Anyway." Her hands fluttered, then gripped at her waist. She would not regret approaching him for work. "I'll be off, then."

She turned.

"Miss Smith."

Gigi glanced over her shoulder.

"If anything comes up, I'll let you know."

"Thank you." She left the office, closing the door behind her with a soft click.

How will I ever earn fifty dollars?

Hopelessness filled her. She nearly wobbled, but forced her knees to lock. For several seconds, she counted every heartbeat as she'd once counted the steps of a waltz. One. Two. Three.

I will not be defeated.

One. Two. Three.

No man was going to keep her from her goal. Not a shady pawn-broker, not a contrite theater owner, and especially not a handsome suitor from her past harboring his own secretive agenda.

As if the thought alone could summon up the man, Fitz stepped out of the wardrobe room. He didn't see Gigi. His frustration showed in his stiff strides, in the striking, almost brutally handsome face that held a forbidding scowl.

The breath backed up in her lungs.

Furious at the visceral reaction, Gigi shoved at her hair, nearly dislodging the mobcap from her head. No. Oh, no, no. Fitz was not allowed to have power over her. Gigi wouldn't allow it.

She would not.

With the faintest trace of trepidation shadowing her resolve, she straightened the mobcap and went to meet the man head-on.

Chapter Nine

Fitz saw Gigi bearing down on him. His footsteps slowed, then stopped altogether. His mind raced. What had caused that look to come across her face? He'd never seen her quite so intense.

Caught in the moment, he couldn't help but notice how the lines of her black dress swung in soft waves around her ankles as she marched across the divide between them.

Her eyes, that mesmerizing silver-blue, so beautiful, so enthralling, held her determination. His guard instantly went up. Fitz was staring at a stranger. No longer Gigi Wentworth, but not meek Sally Smith, either.

Whoever this new, severe woman was, he was intrigued. He saw strength when he looked into her eyes, an expression more truthful than words.

Perhaps that part of her hadn't existed before.

The horror of what she'd been through struck him anew. What must she have suffered in those early days after Dixon had abandoned her? Believing her father had forbidden her return, she'd been forced to fend for herself in a large, unknown city. She must have been terrified.

The burst of anger Fitz felt, anger on Gigi's behalf, had his footsteps striking faster, harder. Overwhelmed by the enormity of what she'd endured, he ached for what Gigi had lost. Her family and friends, her dignity and romantic ideals. Even her name was no longer hers.

In that moment, Fitz felt a little less sure of his reasons for taking the pearls from her. He could repay Connor another way.

Fitz fought against a surge of guilt. Gigi had made her choices out of selfishness, then desperation. The consequences of her actions were hers to bear, not his. Fitz's loyalty belonged to his family. It didn't matter if Gigi regretted her actions. It didn't matter that she wanted to restore her relationships with her family. It didn't matter—couldn't matter— that he'd once considered her a friend.

And yet, in that instant, when Fitz's gaze connected with Gigi's, his sole ambition pointed to a single goal. Ease her suffering.

She drew closer.

Time seemed to stand still. A silent message passed between them, something his heart understood but his head couldn't quite grasp.

He'd never felt this connected to Gigi before, or this concerned over what was about to come out of her mouth. And yet, this was the most real, unaffected moment they'd shared since childhood.

For several long seconds, Fitz stayed where he was, drawing in air, willing his mind to remember where his loyalty lay.

Gigi came to a halt directly in front of him. Her eyes were desolate behind the thick lashes. Fitz knew whatever she said next, he wasn't going to like it.

He gave her a curt nod in greeting, careful not to use her real name in public.

She returned the gesture, her eyes locked with his. She had a beautiful, dramatic face that no disguise or poorly dyed hair could hide.

"I want you to know," she began, looking over her shoulder and then back again. "I am not one of your employees."

Despite the seriousness of her tone, Fitz felt his lips twitch in amusement. "That certainly needed clearing up."

She made a face. "I will not allow you to bully me into giving you my great-grandmother's pearls."

He said nothing.

"I have reasons for wanting to return them myself."

Fitz studied her face. The strength and sorrow that shifted across her features made his heart burn with regret. He could never erase her loss of innocence. Did she distrust her own judgment? Did she question every man's motives?

Of course she did.

That was no way to live.

"I *must* be the one to return the pearls." Despite her proud conviction, her entire bearing was a study in misery.

Inside Fitz's chest, his breath stalled and his heart began to throb harder. "I am not here to harm you." It was important she understand that. "I mean it."

He put a hand on her arm, felt a shock of sensation rush through him. She felt it, too. Fitz knew she did by the way her eyes widened and her breath quickened.

"We are in agreement, then?"

He angled his head, a silent question in his response to the one she'd just asked of him.

She gave him a soft, sad smile that managed to reach inside his heart and squeeze. "Annie must wear the necklace at her wedding to Connor. And you will let me be the one to give it to her."

Fitz was torn. He'd thought of nothing but the pearls since awaking this morning. But he had a good idea why Gigi wanted to be the one to return the necklace. She wanted absolution.

He wanted to give it to her. Yet he couldn't make himself say the words. Gigi couldn't know how much he owed his cousin. Connor had kept his father's condition secret and had asked for nothing in return.

When Connor had mentioned the Wentworth wedding tradition centered on the pearls, and his desire to see Annie wear the heirloom on their wedding day, Fitz had redoubled his efforts to find Gigi. He'd hired a second private investigator when the first had failed. For the most part, Mr. Offutt had proven himself better than the man before him.

But if Fitz himself returned the pearls, Gigi would have nothing but her promises to prove she'd changed. Fitz would be the hero and Gigi the villain. There was no joy in the knowledge. No triumph.

He stared into her startling blue eyes, knowing he couldn't hurt her like that. "You may be the one to return them."

The lines of strain around her mouth seemed to smooth out right before his eyes. "Thank you."

Emotion scraped through the words. Her gratitude made him stand a little taller, as if he had the power to conquer any obstacle, slay any dragon.

Fitz fought to contain thoughts of what might have been had he been a little less rigid and she a little less frivolous. But he couldn't change who he was or the fact that she hadn't wanted him. Their time had come and gone. He found himself caught between yearning and frustration.

The reflex to drag her into his arms came fast, strong, and too powerful to deny. He reached for her.

"Mr. Fitzpatrick." Mr. Everett sauntered over to their tense little group of two. "Would now be a good time to review the accounts payable? I have arranged them in order of importance."

Fitz couldn't fault the man's persistence. The owner was quite determined to push the sale. Out of the corner of his eye, Fitz noticed Gigi melting away.

A moment later, she seamlessly joined a group of women dressed in blue costumes and engaged in their conversation as if she'd been there all along.

Unable to think of a handy excuse, Fitz followed the theater owner into his office. After producing a large stack of receipts, Mr. Everett left him to make his review in peace.

A half hour later, Fitz found his concentration wavering for the tenth—or was it the eleventh?—time. His mind returned to the most recent telegram from his cousin that had arrived this morning. Connor had ended the message in the same way as the one before: *Situation under control.*

Fitz would repay Connor for his loyalty to the family. In the meantime, something had to be done about his father. Fitz now had the names of three specialists in New York willing to meet with him. He was still waiting to hear from the fourth. Maybe one of the doctors would have answers.

With no reason to rush back to Boston, Fitz would use his extended stay to investigate potential new investments.

Giving up all pretense of work, Fitz set down the pencil and rubbed at his eyes. His father was getting worse by the day. The strong-willed, fair-minded man of his youth was gone. If his father wasn't watched closely, he wandered off. Sometimes he was gone for an hour, sometimes longer. He would show up at the racetrack, the park, and, worst of all, the office. The latter required careful handling to avoid talk getting out.

The worst part was that Calvin Fitzpatrick never remembered where he'd been or why he'd gone out in the first place.

Fitz wanted his father back. The one who'd taught him how to toss a ball and balance accounting books.

Music drifted through the seams of the office door. Fitz dropped his hands and listened. He didn't know the song, but that didn't stop his mind from returning to Gigi. The young girl she'd been, the one who'd loved the theater and the opera, was as much a memory as the loving father Fitz had lost to mental illness.

He reached for his pencil, plucked it free from the desk, and began twirling it between his fingers. He longed for simpler times, for relief from his many burdens. He wanted to go back to the days when his life had added up as neatly as the line items listed on the ledger beneath his palm.

After an hour of sitting through tedious calculations, Fitz's brain throbbed. He needed a break, a distraction. The obvious solution was playing out on the stage beyond the shut door.

Decision made, Fitz left the office. He looked out over the auditorium. Pools of gray shadows concealed the plush velvet seats. The entire area beyond the stage was empty, save for a lone man polishing the brass rails. His movements were slow and rhythmic, as if he'd subconsciously timed them to the music.

Fitz shut his eyes a moment. He recognized the opening notes of "Habanera," the lead mezzo-soprano's famous aria.

He hated *Carmen*. The tragic operetta was absolutely the worst tale of love and deception ever composed. The convoluted story was Gigi's all-time favorite and—ironically—the source of their first argument. He'd been forced to attend the theater with his family, around the time his father had begun showing signs of instability, but no one wanted to acknowledge the problem, not even Fitz. At the party afterward, Gigi had gushed over the music.

Happy for the diversion, Fitz had vehemently disagreed with her, saying the story was overly dramatic. She'd called him boring and accused him of possessing the imagination of dry toast.

His thoughts leapt to the end of their verbal tussle, straight to the remarkable conclusion of their disagreement.

Fitz had pulled Gigi into his arms and pressed his lips to hers. He'd only wanted to shut her up. That's what he told himself, anyway. Much to his surprise, she'd clung to him and kissed him in return.

The glorious moment had been short and never repeated. Their relationship had grown tense from that day on, full of awkward pauses and uncomfortable silences.

Lost in the memory, Fitz changed direction. Instead of watching Esmeralda take center stage, he allowed his feet to take him to the wardrobe room.

Mrs. Llewellyn had told him she'd hired Gigi in a part-time capacity as a finisher, whatever that was. Fitz deduced her duties had something to do with sewing. The pay had to be minuscule. Fitz wondered why Gigi had agreed to such menial work. Out of the goodness of her heart or for another reason?

She was becoming somewhat of a mystery.

Fitz hated mysteries. He told himself he was only seeking her out to solve the puzzle of this latest hole in her story. But he knew that wasn't entirely true. He wanted to know all of Gigi's secrets, even the ugly ones. He wanted to know what she was hiding.

What did it matter?

She'd promised to return the pearls. His business with her was complete. He should return to the theater office, back to the familiarity of receipts and ledgers and numbers that always added up.

Fitz kept walking.

He made it halfway to the wardrobe room when a movement caught his eye. Gigi stood in the wings, her eyes on the stage. Fitz watched her a moment, saw her wince. He couldn't blame her reaction. One of Esmeralda's understudies was butchering the opening aria.

Even Fitz could tell the difference between Esmeralda's vocal adroitness and the screeching coming from the stage. He'd nearly reached the end of his endurance, yet the heavyset woman continued shrieking out her heart's most hidden desires for love and passion.

The singer's overuse of the dramatic was nothing short of criminal. Her command of the lyrics was questionable at best. She kept stumbling over the French word *l'amour*, pronouncing it "la-mare."

In Fitz's estimation, the only saving grace was that he wasn't alone in his misery. Some of the cast actually gave in to the impulse and slapped their palms over their ears.

Two dreadful stanzas later, the director called a halt to the magnificent torture.

Esmeralda took her place, all but shoving the woman out of her way, muttering something under her breath that Fitz was glad he couldn't hear. No doubt a few curses were included in the angry spurt of English mixed with Italian.

The music began again, and Fitz felt the shift in the theater's atmosphere almost immediately. Esmeralda's approach to the song was restrained and elegant.

Glancing at Gigi, he caught the sigh sweeping out of her, noted how her eyes were two pools of watery emotion. Esmeralda's masterful performance obviously stirred her.

Fitz wasn't sure why he did it. He couldn't fathom what had gotten into him, but he moved to stand beside her. She smelled of soap, lavender, and mint. Fitz would always equate those particular scents with Gigi. He reached out and took her hand.

She turned her head and, clearly caught up in the moment, gave him a soggy smile. His chest moved soundlessly as he breathed his way to composure.

That look, it brought all sorts of inconvenient emotions to the surface. Tenderness, longing, a need to protect. Not for the first time that day, Fitz wanted to drag Gigi into his arms, fight off the men in the world who would hurt her.

He didn't have the right. He'd never had the right.

Her delicate perfection, now in disguise, was not for him. *She* was not for him. She'd never been for him.

And so he'd stood by and watched helplessly as she'd run away with a fortune hunter. He'd let her turn her back on everything she knew, her family, her friends, *him*, because Fitz had known she didn't want him.

Even now, when he would like nothing more than to find Nathanial Dixon and make the man better acquainted with his fist, Fitz accepted the truth. No matter what he did, he would never win Gigi's heart. He wouldn't even try.

The life he had to offer her would only bring her more pain.

She may have cared for him, once, as a friend. But Fitz had never accepted the status of second best, not in business and especially not in a woman's heart. *You mean, not in Gigi's heart.*

After she'd run away, the original private investigator's report had arrived and Fitz's suspicions had been confirmed. Nathanial Dixon was not the man he seemed. He was not from a wealthy English family. He was a con man from Philadelphia who'd targeted Gigi for her inheritance.

Gigi had not been his first mark. Nor, Fitz doubted, his last. As soon as the report had landed on his desk, Fitz had begun to look back and wonder if he'd been wrong about Gigi's affections for Dixon. If he'd stayed out of their relationship, would she have grown tired of the man?

They would never know.

Still, she'd run away and had done . . . who knew what. She'd made her choice. And that choice had not been Fitz.

She'd dodged a lifetime of regret and didn't even know it.

He must keep that in mind or he would never be able to maintain the necessary distance between himself and Gigi. Distance. Yes, he needed distance.

Then why are you still holding her hand?

And why was she clutching his in return?

Esmeralda's performance came to an end. A pause, a moment of poised silence, a collective sigh of appreciation, and then . . .

Gigi jerked her hand from his. Eyes wide, mouth agape, she stared at him.

He liked that he'd put that flustered expression on her face. "Something wrong, Miss . . . Smith?"

A furious blush colored her cheeks.

"Do you feel faint?"

Her answering scowl was answer enough.

"No? Well, then it must be another reason." He leaned over her. "The lovely music perhaps? It was really quite wonderful, wasn't it?"

She found her voice at last. "You hate *Carmen*."

"And you adore it."

"Not anymore."

"I remember a time when you were quite passionate in your praise."

Back ramrod straight, she glared at him. "I have to go."

Eyebrows cocked, Fitz stepped closer. "I wonder . . ."

"Mrs. Llewellyn is expecting me."

"I wonder," he repeated, moving directly into her path, "if you recall the other time we came to blows over this operetta?"

Her eyes instantly narrowed, telling Fitz all he needed to know. She remembered their argument as well as he did.

They were in dangerous territory now, and neither seemed capable of walking away. As they settled into their silent standoff, Fitz noticed that Gigi wasn't calling him boring or unimaginative.

Mind stuck somewhere between past and present, he stepped closer still. He moved his head a fraction closer to hers, and—

Common sense returned.

He shifted his stance and looked toward center stage. A groan shot past his lips. Perfect. Just perfect.

The afternoon had only needed this.

Esmeralda had spotted him. The look of displeasure on the diva's face was similar to the expression Gigi wore on her delicate features. Fitz had that way with women. Some men charmed them. He was unnaturally talented at frustrating them.

Giving up Gigi as a lost cause, he swung around to smile at Esmeralda.

The diva stood in the halo of light pouring over her. "Fitz, darling, come here, please."

Fitz answered Esmeralda's call without a single glance in Gigi's direction. All right, he looked. Once. Briefly.

Briefly was all it took. The image of her frowning displeasure would stay with him for hours to come.

* * *

Gigi told herself she didn't care that Fitz had obeyed Esmeralda's summons. She knew what the diva was about. Of course she knew, but Esmeralda would find her machinations wasted. Sophie had no interest in Fitz.

Did Fitz share Sophie's disinterest?

It didn't matter. He'd given up on the pearls. Gigi had won.

Where was her sense of satisfaction, then, her glee?

With a strange sinking sensation in her stomach, Gigi stepped into the wardrobe room. "What can I do to help?"

Mrs. Llewellyn glanced up from her sewing. "At the moment, nothing."

"Please, there must be a chore you can think of." Her voice sounded raspy and desperate. She swallowed and began again. "I need something to do with my hands."

The wardrobe mistress looked around the room, her eyes searching and then landing on a bucket.

Gigi inwardly cringed. *You asked,* she reminded herself.

Placing a smile on her face, she said in the most philosophical voice she could muster, "I have a sudden passion for sorting buttons."

"How fortuitous."

"Indeed."

Gigi sat on the ground and tucked her legs under her skirt. As she settled into the tedious task given her, she reviewed her recent encounter with Fitz through the brutal objectivity of time and hard-won experience. There'd been a moment, several, actually, when she'd been caught up in the romance of the music.

But she should know better than to be swept away by music and sentiment. Had she learned nothing from her time with Nathanial? Apparently, parts of her former self were alive and well in the woman she'd become.

The weight of her mortification should be heavier. Fitz had come looking for her not because he'd missed her or regretted his behavior of the past. No, he'd come for a necklace. For all intents and purposes, Fitz was her enemy.

So how could she have clutched onto his hand as if her life had depended upon it? Could she have been more foolish?

Gigi blamed her loss of sense on the music. Esmeralda's extraordinary talent had captured her imagination. How could Gigi not have been moved, especially after Tasha's horrible squawking moments before Esmeralda had taken the stage?

Trepidation lifted ice from her belly and deposited it into her lungs.

There was no room for nostalgia in her life. If only Fitz hadn't reminded her of that time, years ago, when they'd argued over *Carmen*. He'd been so passionate in his hatred of the dramatic story, his face full of masculine opinion and *emotion*. Gigi had been drawn to him like a moth to flame. His had been her first kiss.

She'd never told him that part.

She never would, either. He would never believe her; his opinion of her was that low.

Eyeing the bucket of buttons with dread, she reached in and pulled out a handful. She was ten minutes into sorting them by size, color, and shape when the door opened and one of the dancers entered the room. She would have tumbled over Gigi if she hadn't moved out of the way just in time.

"Oh, Sally. I apologize. I didn't see you sitting there on the floor."

"No harm done." She added a little hum in her throat to underscore her sincerity. Then, with the speed of a seasoned jacks player, she swept up the pile of yellow buttons inches from the dancer's toes.

"What is it, Jessica?" Mrs. Llewellyn asked from her perch on the other side of the room, her eyes scrutinizing the costume the girl wore. "Did you rip your skirt?"

"No. I. Actually, I . . ." The dancer's gaze chased about the room, landing nowhere in particular. "I was looking for Mr. Everett."

"Well, clearly, he's not here."

"I see that now." Seeming in no hurry to leave, the dancer stared down at her curled fingers, studying the nails as if the answer to a complicated problem resided there. "Do you happen to know where he is?"

"I am not in the habit of monitoring the theater owner's whereabouts. He is somewhere beyond this room."

Though Mrs. Llewellyn pointed this out gently, Jessica visibly cringed. "I didn't mean any offense."

"Was there anything else?"

"Not particularly." Jessica lifted her thumb to her lips and began chewing in earnest. "I'll search for him elsewhere."

She gave Gigi a pitiful nod before exiting the room with a slow, defeated shuffle of her feet.

Knowing it was none of her business yet hating to see such dejection, Gigi followed the dancer out into the darkened hallway.

"Jessica," she called after the girl, who'd picked up her pace considerably once she'd left the wardrobe room. "Wait. Please. Slow down. I wish to speak with you a moment."

The dancer swung around, her eyes glittering with unshed tears.

Gigi didn't know the dancer well, but she knew desperation when she saw it. "Is there something I can help you with?"

The girl's large hazel eyes rounded. "You want to help me?"

"I'd like to try."

Jessica lowered her head and took two, three breaths. "But you don't even know me."

"I know you are a gifted dancer employed by the opera company." Gigi put a hint of encouragement in her voice. "I also know that you are a hard worker. No matter how many run-throughs the director requests, you perform each step with as much passion as if it were the first. You try very hard to arrive on time, though you don't always succeed, and that upsets you a great deal."

For a long moment, Jessica eyed Gigi. There was enough light to see her grin. "You are very observant."

Gigi tried not to sigh. She hadn't always been aware of others or their individual needs. Her world had been very small and privileged, centered solely on her own wants. She'd attended church every Sunday, but there had been no real Christian charity in her heart beyond a sort of nebulous sense of right and wrong.

"Tell me what's happened to upset you."

Tears slipped from the girl's eyes before she frantically swiped at them with the back of her hand. "You—you truly want to know?"

Gigi clutched the girl's sleeve, then dropped her hand almost as soon as she made contact. "I do, truly."

"It's my neighbor, Mrs. Toscanini."

"Is she ill?"

"No. Well, yes." Now that she'd begun, the words tumbled out in a garbled rush of air. "She fell and broke her ankle a week ago, and because of her injury, she can't get up and down the stairs no more, I mean, anymore, which is perfectly understandable but also upsetting. I presented my concerns, but she promised her ankle wouldn't become a problem."

Gigi waited as the girl drew in a big gulp of air.

"Now she claims her ankle *is* a problem. She watches Fern, you see, and I'm not convinced she's the best choice, but what am I supposed to do? She's the only help I have, not that it matters, anyways, because now she can't keep her anymore and I have no one else to turn to."

Jessica paused to take another breath. This time, Gigi took advantage of the chance to interject a question. "Who is Fern?"

"Fern is my daughter. I told you that." Her brows pulled together. "I . . . didn't I?"

Actually, she hadn't. But Gigi decided saying so would only upset the girl further. She studied Jessica, wondering her age. She couldn't be more than seventeen, maybe sixteen. She didn't wear a wedding band. Nor had she mentioned the child's father. There was an unpleasant story there, Gigi thought. "How old is your daughter?"

"She's three and a very good child. She hardly ever cries or fusses."

As Jessica extolled her daughter's virtues, Gigi heard the love in the dancer's voice, a love so profound Gigi felt a jolt of something like longing. She'd always seen herself having a houseful of children.

When Jessica wound down, Gigi offered up a solution. "Why don't you bring Fern to the theater until you can find someone to watch her?"

Jessica glanced over her shoulder, frowned when her gaze landed on Esmeralda. "I can't."

"Of course you can." The words did nothing to erase the stricken look on the girl's face, so Gigi asked, "Why ever not?"

Looking back at the stage, she sighed heavily. "Esmeralda wouldn't like it."

"Leave Esmeralda to me."

Chewing on her fingernail again, the dancer looked at Gigi as if she'd lost her mind. Perhaps she had. Jessica was absolutely, completely correct. Esmeralda would not want a child running around the theater untended. Ironic, really, since she'd raised her own daughter backstage in countless theaters across Europe.

"Suppose I did bring Fern to the theater, what would I do with her while I'm rehearsing?"

"I'll watch her." The words flew out of Gigi's mouth without pause, and she realized she actually wanted to care for the child. Sophie rarely needed her during the day. Gigi could make it work if she used the evenings to complete her other duties, mostly seeing to Sophie's clothing.

"You . . ." Jessica cocked her head. "You mean it?"

Gigi nodded.

"I could pay you."

Gigi started to wave off the offer but then remembered the pearls. Even if she saved every penny Esmeralda paid her as a domestic, and sorted every button in the state of New York, Gigi would still fall short of the money she needed to redeem the necklace.

As much as she would like to serve Jessica out of the goodness of her heart, she simply couldn't. "How much do you pay Mrs. Toscanini?"

"Three dollars a week."

That seemed an outrageous sum. Gigi did a quick mental calculation and came up with a number that would help get her to her goal without robbing Jessica of her hard-earned money. "I'll do it for two."

After working out the particulars, the young dancer thanked Gigi, then ducked around the corner and went back to work.

Gigi returned to the wardrobe room. It was with a lighter heart and a sense of hope that she tackled the intensely mind-numbing job of sorting buttons.

Chapter Ten

Several hours later, Gigi was once again tucked safely in the warmth of the town house on Riverside Drive. Standing beside Sophie in the young woman's enormous closet, she studied the contents with the critical eye of someone who'd once prided herself in her own wardrobe.

Esmeralda had spared no expense on her daughter's attire. Despite her negative remarks about New York society, the mother wanted her only daughter to achieve success in her father's exclusive, privileged world.

Beauty was not enough to win approval. Sophie must learn to put on airs without seeming as though she were doing so. It all started with choosing the right gown. As the young woman hesitated in indecision, Gigi fought the reflex to choose Sophie's gown for tonight's dinner party at her half sister's home.

Sophie skimmed her fingertips down the skirt of a pale-pink silk dress with intricate embroidery on the bodice. It was a good choice, but not the best one. Gigi resisted the urge to say as much. She couldn't continue picking out the young woman's clothing. At some point, Sophie had to learn to dress appropriately for all occasions without Gigi's help.

"Well?" Gigi asked patiently. "Which one is it to be?"

"I don't know."

Gigi turned her head to look at the young woman. There was enough light in the spacious closet to illuminate Sophie's apprehensive expression. Clearly, Gigi's work with her was not yet complete. "Would you like me to pick?"

"Yes, please."

She reached for a gown the color of the midnight sky under a full moon.

"You think I should wear that one?" Sophie's voice held unmistakable skepticism. "It's not too . . . understated?"

"Tonight, understated is exactly the right approach. You want to present the picture of innocence."

Dress in hand, Gigi indicated that the young woman should follow her back into the bedchamber.

Once Sophie had stepped into the gown and moved to the full-length mirror, Gigi took her place behind her and began the laborious process of securing the long row of buttons at her back.

Sophie was silent as Gigi worked her way from top to bottom. With each button she secured, Sophie's confidence returned.

"Tell me, Gigi"—she faltered only briefly—"I can call you Gigi when we're alone, can't I?"

Gigi nodded. In truth, it was somewhat of a relief to hear her name on someone else's lips, or rather someone other than Fitz. It made her connection with the disturbing man seem less intimate.

"What sent you into hiding?"

Gigi's hands stilled.

"Or should I ask who?"

Gigi was too busy searching for a response—and too confused by the events of the past two days—to notice that Sophie had moved away from the mirror and was leading Gigi to a chair.

"I can't count the times you have listened to me. Let me do the same for you." She pressed on Gigi's shoulders until she sat, then

Sophie kneeled before her. "Tell me what happened to make you go into service."

Gigi felt a prick of unease. She ignored it and, with a strangled laugh, glanced about the room. "I needed the job."

"That doesn't answer my question."

Even if Gigi trusted herself to speak, there were too many sordid details to unpack in a single conversation. Would Sophie judge her? She judged her mother for her affair with Warren Griffin.

It's not the same. Nathanial hadn't been married, as far as Gigi knew, and her time with him hadn't produced a child. *It could have ended that way.*

Nathanial had pushed for intimacy. Gigi's desire to give him everything he wanted had overruled her good sense. She'd let her emotions guide her actions. Love, or what she'd thought was love, had made her uninhibited. No, it had made her reckless.

Perhaps that was why she'd been sympathetic to young Jessica's plight this afternoon. Gigi could have found herself abandoned with a child.

She glanced over Sophie's shoulder and connected her gaze with her own reflection. What Gigi saw wasn't good, or wholesome, or forgivable. What she saw was a woman who'd paid the ultimate price for love, only to have her trust destroyed and her character spoiled.

Sophie, on the other hand, may have been brought into the world by disreputable, unconventional means, but that didn't make her any less upright. She was a faithful Christian woman who lived a blameless life.

"I asked you a question, Gigi," Sophie said as gently as if speaking to an injured child.

Gigi didn't want her pity. She knew the young woman meant well, but Gigi was fearful of relaxing her guard.

Her past was not something she wanted to revisit. The gullible belief that she was the most important thing in a man's eyes had been her disgrace. How foolish she'd been, falling for Nathanial's false promises. He'd only wanted her money. Once he'd come to understand that her father had disowned her, he'd fled.

"My story is nothing you haven't heard before, certainly nothing original. It's a tale as old and clichéd as one of your mother's operas."

Sophie's eyes widened. "I just had a terrible thought. Are you alone in the world? Are you without family?"

Her previous employer had asked a similar question. At the time, Gigi had evaded in such a way as to give the impression that she was, indeed, alone in the world. It was a lie she couldn't tell anymore. "No, I have family."

"Then why not go home?"

You can never go home, an ugly voice in her head whispered. *You have gone far past the point of forgiveness. You deserve censure not redemption.*

She shoved the disturbing thought aside. "I can't."

"Why not?"

"I was disowned." The truth shamed her.

"Oh, my dear, dear friend. How completely awful." Standing, Sophie pulled Gigi to her feet and wrapped her arms around her.

Gigi accepted the comforting embrace, resisting the urge to cling. Tears pricked at the back of her eyes. Her loneliness fought a hard battle with her embarrassment.

"Will you tell me what happened?" Sophie set Gigi away from her. "Will you tell me what terrible deed put you at odds with your own family?"

"You wouldn't understand."

"You might be surprised." Alert, watching, gaze filling with sympathy, Sophie softened her voice to a near whisper. "You'll find no judgment from me, no condemnation. You can tell me anything."

"I . . . wouldn't know where to start." Layer upon layer of misery and remorse rushed like a river through her blood. "It's complicated."

"Most tales such as these are."

Gigi had a sudden, deep driving desire to share her story with Sophie. But honesty required a level of vulnerability that no longer came naturally.

"You're going to be late." Gigi knew her voice was too sharp, too defensive. She struggled to lighten it. "We'll talk another time, when you aren't rushing off to a dinner party."

"The cause was a man, wasn't it?"

Gigi took one long breath. "Yes."

The cost of confession was so great that the burning in her eyes became excruciating. She stiffened her spine, refusing the release of a single tear.

"In whatever way he betrayed you—"

"I didn't say he betrayed me."

"You didn't have to."

As if sensing her distress, Othello rubbed against Gigi's shin, a big, fat furry band of feline acceptance. Gigi picked him up and hugged the animal close, burying her nose in the thick, silky fur. He rewarded her with a rumbling purr.

"Whoever he was, he didn't deserve you."

Gigi's hands tightened ever so slightly around the cat. "That's very kind of you to say."

"It's the truth." Sophie reached out and stroked Othello's fur. "Whatever the dreadful man talked you into doing, I want you to remember that there is no sin too great for God's forgiveness."

Gigi lifted her head, felt the burn of tears in her throat, and dropped her face back to the cat's neck. "That's a rather liberal interpretation of Scripture."

"Although I chose to paraphrase, the meaning behind my words is no less accurate."

The cat squirmed for release. Gigi set him carefully on the floor. "Let's finish getting you dressed."

"Changing the subject, are we?"

"We are, yes, most definitely we are." She attempted a laugh.

"Gigi, my dear, sweet friend. Pretending to be someone you're not isn't the answer. I should know better than most."

Tears starred the edges of Gigi's vision.

"Be truthful with yourself," Sophie said. "Only then can true healing begin. This is advice I plan to apply to my own life. I suggest you join me in the endeavor. Now . . ." She turned to face the mirror. "Let's get me dressed. I have a good feeling about tonight."

Fingers slightly shaking, Gigi went back to work on the endless row of buttons.

"There is a man out there for each of us," Sophie said, her eyes fervent and young, so young. "The most mundane details of our lives will matter to them, and they will stand by us, no matter what we face."

Gigi sighed, wishing the spark of hope had not just ignited in her heart.

"My time for love has come and gone." Gigi's voice hitched over the words. "Please, don't try to correct me on this. I . . ."

Give her a reason. Any will do, even the truth.

"I am too far from redemption to earn a good man's love. But that doesn't have to be the case for you, Sophie." She thought of the promise she'd made Esmeralda. "I am here to help you avoid making the same mistakes I have."

Sophie held Gigi's gaze in the mirror, studying her face longer than was comfortable, her eyes searching, boring in as if she could read the very secrets of Gigi's soul. "No one is so far from righteousness that God can't redeem them."

Gigi felt an odd sensation that was part confusion, part longing. "I'm not sure that applies to me."

"God's grace is available to all."

"Even your mother?"

"Yes." Although her voice never wavered, a trace of impatience played across Sophie's face. "God's grace is available even for my mother."

* * *

Early the next morning, Fitz went to meet with the first doctor on his list of specialists. Dr. Trent, the one he'd been waiting to hear from, had finally responded late the previous afternoon with a brief message requesting to meet at his office before nine. Fitz had collected the names of all four doctors from extensive research. One of them had to have the answers he was looking for.

As he made his way through the morning foot traffic, he tried to banish Gigi from his mind, but that odd moment when they'd held hands wouldn't disappear.

Even before then, Fitz had been aware of nothing but her, so lost in the moment that he'd given in to her request about the pearls with hardly a fight. His resolve had melted as if it were raining and he were a malleable pile of mushy spring snow.

Ever since the investigator had informed him of Gigi's location, Fitz had told himself he only wanted to retrieve the pearls she'd stolen from her family. He'd told himself he was here for Connor. Now, Fitz admitted the truth. He'd come to New York for Gigi, not only to ensure she was well, but also to see her again.

She'd changed.

His feelings for her hadn't.

Fitz knew that now, accepted it, lamented over it. He had enough to worry about without having to fight off the memory of leaning toward Gigi, moving closer, ever closer. Her eyes had been frightened yet combative, like a wild animal uncertain whether to flee or fight. What might they have done if they'd been alone?

He shouldn't want to know. But he did.

Frustrating him further, Fitz couldn't stop thinking about the first, and only, time he'd kissed her those years ago. The connection had been brief, barely a meeting of lips, and yet Fitz hadn't been able to replace the image with another. He'd kissed other women. None had left him that stirred.

None had made him yearn.

He looked to the heavens, seeking guidance or perhaps a reprieve from his troubling thoughts. He found neither.

Puffs of cottony white were in constant motion, floating against the pristine blue of the sky.

Enormously preoccupied with the memory of Gigi's lips pressed to his, Fitz nearly missed the three-story brownstone on the East Side of Manhattan. The bottom level had been converted into an exclusive medical clinic, his destination.

Almost immediately upon giving his name, he was escorted past the reception area and left to wait in a small, unassuming office that could have belonged to an attorney, a businessman, or any number of low-level clerks.

Fitz didn't know what he'd expected, but this wasn't it. The dark furniture, with its bold, masculine lines, was functional and sturdy but lacking all signs of craftsmanship.

A fire snapped in the hearth, giving the room a pleasant, smoky odor. The atmosphere was too warm, too inviting. Shouldn't a place where illness and death loomed be more somber?

The sound of approaching footsteps reverberated off the walls like hammers on nails. A second later, the door opened with a long creaking groan, and in walked a man carrying a small medical bag in one hand and some sort of intense-looking apparatus in the other. He was young, close to Fitz's age, with dark hair and grave, aristocratic features.

He wore what Fitz thought of as the quintessential doctor's uniform of black pants, a crisp white linen shirt, and a serious expression. Fitz had seen that same look on his father's physician far too often in the past two years. The most memorable was on the night Calvin Fitzpatrick had nearly drowned himself in Boston Harbor after forgetting he didn't know how to swim.

"I'm Dr. Trent." The man set down both objects he'd carried in the room with him, then reached out. "And you must be Mr. Fitzpatrick."

Fitz shook the offered hand.

"Please. Have a seat." Dr. Trent waved toward a matching pair of nondescript hardbacked chairs facing a large mahogany desk.

Fitz lowered himself into the one on his right.

The doctor divested himself of the bag and instrument, then, instead of rounding the desk, took the empty chair next to Fitz.

He wasted no time getting to the point of the visit. "I've had a chance to review your father's medical history. His physician in Boston has been very thorough."

Appreciating the doctor's direct approach, Fitz pressed his palms on his thighs. "Do you have a diagnosis?"

"Before I give you my thoughts, I'd like you to tell me about your father's condition in your own words. When did you first notice changes in his behavior?"

"I don't know, precisely. The shift began small, in ways we didn't notice at first. But two years ago, he started acting in ways we couldn't dismiss as we had before."

"How so?"

"He misplaced items, forgot names, lost his ability to recall details of past events."

"Go on."

"I didn't think the problem was serious until he began having difficulty remembering names of people that have been in his life for years, some since childhood. He'd always been better with faces, so I didn't think there was anything to worry about initially, but then"—Fitz lifted a wool-encased shoulder—"his personality changed."

"How so?"

"He would get agitated when he couldn't recall names or common words, mostly nouns. It was especially noticeable at the office, probably because I worked alongside him every day. He would review a contract, then be unable to repeat the important points he'd just read minutes before."

"What about his sense of time? Any problems with that?"

Fitz shoved at the hair on his forehead, forcing himself to relay the facts with the same matter-of-fact tone he adopted for board meetings.

His father was important to him. Fitz had always admired the man. He couldn't remember a time when he didn't want to turn out exactly like him. It was as if Fitz was losing his father, little by little. Calvin was disappearing, still living and breathing, but not the same man. Fitz didn't know how to put his silent anguish into words.

He had to try.

"Some days, it's as if he's right there, standing in front of me. The same intelligent, savvy businessman I've always known. But then, seemingly in the blink of an eye, he's gone. It's like he's gotten lost in his own mind." Fitz rubbed a hand over his face, the stubble scratching against his palm. "I'm not making sense, am I?"

The sharp planes of the doctor's face softened. "You're making perfect sense."

Fitz feathered his fingers through his hair.

"We knew something was wrong when he lost his ability to make sound decisions. In the past two years, he's made a string of bad investments. He hid the worst of his mistakes. I didn't discover the magnitude of the situation until it was nearly too late to save the company."

"Did you confront your father once you realized what he'd done?"

Fitz shut his eyes, the events of that spectacularly bad day turning his breath cold in his chest. "He became angry and accusatory. He claimed my cousin and I were trying to force him out of the company."

The doctor nodded. "Anything else?"

"He's become increasingly paranoid of late." There was no other word for it. "He often accuses my mother and the household staff of stealing."

Fitz laid out the details of a terrible argument over a timepiece that had sent his mother into hysterical tears. He then went on to explain his father's refusal to bathe and his mercurial moods, ending with the increasing bouts of depression.

"Does he wander off and get lost?"

"Far too often."

Now that the most concerning topic had been broached, Fitz unloaded the bulk of his worries. He told the doctor of the time his father had wandered off and ended up at the racetrack. He'd bet and lost a fortune on a horse with fifty-to-one odds.

"He calls me Declan," Fitz said, shaking his head. "Declan is his younger brother who died twenty years ago." He stared at the doctor. "Well? Is my father . . . is he going mad?"

"I can't know for certain without a thorough examination of the patient. But what you've described could be a brain disease that's most often found in patients of a certain age."

Fitz's pent-up frustration came out in a ragged sigh. "Can anything be done to reverse the effects?"

"The science is incomplete. The experts disagree on the best approach."

Disappointment seeped into every bone of Fitz's body. *Ask the question,* he told himself. "If he does have this brain disease, is it hereditary?"

A long, excruciating silence followed. "The research is inconclusive at this time. Did either of your father's parents show similar degeneration as they aged?"

"They both died young, in a boating accident."

"Ah."

Fitz shifted in his chair, stretched out his legs, pulled them back in. No amount of repositioning his body brought him comfort.

"Let's deal with what we know," Dr. Trent suggested. "Rather than what we don't."

"That seems a logical approach."

The doctor leaned forward and rested his forearms on his knees. "Eventually, patients with your father's symptoms require full-time care. Simple daily activities such as dressing, feeding himself, even walking, will become too much for him to carry out on his own."

The breath in Fitz's lungs turned cold enough to freeze into icicles. He thought of his mother, of the pain she'd suffered already and what she would have to endure if her husband's disease progressed to what the doctor had described.

Mary Fitzpatrick had aged considerably since his father had taken ill. How much more could she withstand before her own health suffered?

Fitz wanted to howl in fury. He'd come into this building with a sense of tempered hope. Dr. Trent's calm, detached summation of the possible disease his father had contracted dashed that hope to pieces.

"Thank you for your candor." Having nothing else to ask, Fitz stood. "I won't take up any more of your time."

Dr. Trent joined him at the door and shook Fitz's hand. "I urge you not to despair. There may be another reason for the symptoms you described. I won't know for certain until I've had a chance to examine your father."

"I understand," Fitz said, making no promises.

He still had three other experts to consult. Perhaps one of them would have better news. He wanted to cling to that chance. But as he exited the doctor's office, the pang in his heart was grief, not hope.

Chapter Eleven

After turning his back on the clinic, Fitz was too agitated to sit inside a closed carriage. Nor did he want to be alone with his thoughts, and so he covered the ten blocks to the Summer Garden Theater on foot. Moving at a good clip, he was propelled by a need to escape Dr. Trent's diagnosis.

A cold mist hung on the air, mimicking the gloom in Fitz's heart. He hunched his shoulders against the wind and rounded the street corner, putting the doctor's visit in the back of his mind.

At the edge of the next block, he caught sight of his reflection in the shop window on his right. It was only the dimmest of impressions but enough to send waves of shock quivering through him.

Fitz saw his father in the blurry image. The likeness went beyond the physical, Fitz knew, in ways that couldn't be seen or easily measured. They were both hardworking, dedicated to the firm and its employees, loyal to a fault, and loved nothing more than family and a balanced ledger.

Dr. Trent had confirmed the secret fear that had haunted Fitz for months. The same illness that was ravaging his father quite possibly lay dormant in Fitz, waiting to appear as he aged.

The doctor maintained the research was inconclusive. Fitz found no comfort in the claim. He saw what the disease was doing to his mother. Her grief and helplessness were killing her as surely as the illness was destroying his father. If Fitz ever married, it stood to reason that he would be condemning his wife to the same fate.

Fitz would never ask a woman to marry him, knowing he might have to live out his twilight years trapped inside his own mind, unable to remember the simplest things or take care of his personal needs.

And what of children? If the disease was hereditary, Fitz could pass it on to them.

The risk was too great.

He must never marry, or father children. The realization was the worst kind of blow. Fitz had always wanted a family of his own.

He stared down at his hands, his head full of the burdens he carried. His mother had insisted he keep his father's condition a secret. At the time, Fitz had been all too willing. Mary Fitzpatrick didn't need to contend with outside speculation and cruel gossip on top of the other hardships she endured.

Now, Fitz wondered at the cost of his silence. He'd never felt more alone, a situation that would grow more severe as he aged. There'd been a time when he'd dreamed of a different kind of future, one that included a wife and children. He would have taught them how to appreciate the arts, something his own education had lacked. He would have taught them the intricacies of commerce, as his father had taught him.

That dream was a distant memory now.

According to Dr. Trent, Calvin Fitzpatrick's illness would continue to drain the family's resources. The future required Fitz to do what he'd been trained to do—find promising investments and turn lucrative profits.

Luke Griffin's automotive company was the most *promising* of the investments Fitz had his eye on, or so it seemed on paper. He would know more after their meeting.

Fitz conquered the remaining blocks and entered the theater through the backstage door. He listened a moment to the music.

Though fluent in French, he didn't need to understand the language to know that Esmeralda was singing about unrequited love. Her voice was full of pain and lost hope. Each note sung in her dynamic voice was gut-wrenching, raw, and very real. The words wrapped around Fitz, digging deep in his heart and twisting.

Watching Gigi fall for Nathanial Dixon had been excruciating. Learning of her ruin had been even worse. Fitz didn't know if he still loved her. But he knew he still cared and regretted his role in her shame.

He could do nothing about the past, but perhaps he could change the future. He would help Gigi find redemption.

The task loomed large, but Fitz was undeterred. He always got what he wanted. *Almost always,* he amended, a self-deprecating smile slanting across his lips. He'd never won Gigi's heart.

Now, he never would. She deserved better than a life trapped with a man who would one day succumb to a brain disease.

"You look deep in thought."

Fitz relaxed his shoulders deliberately, muscle by muscle. He liked the stage manager. Will McClain, a tall, bespectacled man with baggy features and kind eyes, had been in the theater's employ for over thirty years.

"I blame my mood on Esmeralda's performance."

Will nodded a head full of thick white hair. "She's certainly one of the greatest talents ever to play the Summer Garden, if not the best, which is saying something."

Fitz looked to the stage. Esmeralda sat on a chaise longue, her voice now filled with fatigue. Her eyes drooped, nearly shut before she fumbled them open again to stare at the young tenor playing Carmen's lover, Don José. The longing in her eyes looked genuine.

Paul Dupree, the singer playing the male lead, grazed his hand over hers, the move casual yet somehow proprietary, indicating intimate knowledge.

A slow smile curved Esmeralda's mouth.

The scene was expertly executed, a triumph of acting and singing. Fitz felt as though he was eavesdropping on a private moment. The audience was in for a show opening night.

"How are the negotiations going between you and Mr. Everett?" Will asked.

Fitz didn't pretend to misunderstand. He did, however, give a cautious answer. "He insists the value of the theater is worth the price he is asking. He is embellishing, of course."

The stage manager's expression turned shrewd. "You have no intention of buying the Summer Garden, do you?"

Had Will asked the question a week ago, perhaps even a day ago, Fitz would have silently agreed, though he wouldn't have admitted the truth aloud. Today, he found himself captivated, not only by the theater with its ornate décor, roof garden, and public café, but by the people that worked to put on a production.

Fitz assured himself sentiment had nothing to do with his interest in the Summer Garden. But as he watched the drama unfolding on the stage, he finally understood why Gigi loved the theater.

This world suited her, nearly as much as the world she'd lost. A world Fitz vowed he would restore her to, no matter the cost to him personally.

"I find," he said, "the more time I spend in this building, the more intrigued I become."

"Not exactly an answer."

No, but it was all Fitz was willing to give. "What can you tell me about the theater that I don't know already?"

"I'd rather show you." Will took Fitz on a tour, his fifth, yet far different than all the others before.

The stage manager led Fitz up into the rafters, where he pointed out the rigging, lighting, and various other technical aspects of the building itself.

"We're far superior to most theaters in Manhattan or Brooklyn. In fact, the Summer Garden was one of the first to put in electrical lighting and indoor plumbing."

They toured the roof garden next, then wound their way down a rickety spiral staircase and into the café. When they returned to the spot where they began, Will spoke again. "It's more than the building that makes the Summer Garden special. We're a family."

Family, the word on Fitz's mind all morning. "How do you mean?"

"Most of the crew have been with the theater for at least ten years. Same goes for many of the dancers and bit players, the ones who live and work in the city. Take Jessica over there." He pointed to a young woman in a blue sparkling costume. "She's performed in every show for the past three years. Bridget, Matilda, and Celeste have as well."

Will went on to list the wardrobe mistress and set designer as long-time employees of the theater. "Mrs. Llewellyn started the same week I did."

By the time Fitz left the stage manager to his duties, he had a better idea how the theater worked. What had seemed a frivolous, risky investment at first had turned into something far more promising.

Was he really considering buying the Summer Garden? He did a quick mental dance over the possibility and focused on the more pressing problem of restoring Gigi to her family.

The sooner he spoke to her, the better.

He found her buried beneath a pile of costumes in the wardrobe room, head bent in concentration. The picture she made was so different from any he would have attributed to the spoiled heiress of the past, and yet it was somehow right.

She sat curtained in shadows. Bottom lip tugged between her teeth, she wielded a needle and thread as if she'd been born to the task. The room was cold, the low light bouncing off the sequins and sparkles of a mountain of costumes strewn on an overstuffed sofa, several tables, and Gigi's lap.

Fitz shut the door with a soundless click and moved deeper into the tiny room, no bigger than an oversized closet. Gigi had twisted her hair into a complicated braid. She'd always had lovely hair, a deep red that showed hints of gold in the sun. Even tucked beneath the mobcap, the blonde strands looked out of place, dull, and lifeless.

Fitz lowered his gaze. He found himself riveted by Gigi's pretty, graceful hands laboring over a seemingly tedious task. Those long, elegant fingers used to glide across the piano keys and create the most beautiful music he'd ever heard.

Gigi's talent had been unrivaled among her peers. All young society ladies were expected to play, but Gigi had excelled.

Fitz had spent many evenings in the drawing room of Harvest House watching her at the piano. He'd admired her talent and beauty, mostly from afar, while Nathanial Dixon had swooped in with his phony British accent and fake title. He'd used Gigi's love of music to worm his way into her heart.

The two of them had played duets. Except, now that he thought about it, Fitz realized they'd only ever played the same song. They never finished because Dixon would say something low, meant only for Gigi's ears, and she would become too flustered to continue.

All part of the man's ruse, Fitz thought furiously.

He should have protected Gigi better. She'd wanted romance, soft words, and love. Fitz hadn't known how to give her those things, not then and surely not now.

He felt the familiar race of his pulse. Regret and longing nagged at him.

Her hands moved with competence and grace, the task far more menial than playing a piece of music written by Mozart or Bach. She'd once had her own maid to attend to her clothing. Now, she took care

142

of another woman's wardrobe and sewed tiny sequins onto inferior material.

And yet . . .

She didn't look unhappy. She looked oddly peaceful.

Fitz drew close enough to realize her scent was cleaner today, fresher, more . . . honest.

Ironic, when she was living a lie.

A lie you've helped perpetuate.

The leaden feeling returned to Fitz's stomach.

He'd watched her in silence long enough. When he spoke, his voice sounded like he'd gargled gravel. "Gigi."

The eyes that met his were wary, vulnerable. For some reason that made matters seem worse.

"I am Sally now. Why can you not remember that?" She sounded matter-of-fact, but a tremor moved through the words. "Gigi no longer exists."

This was the exact opening Fitz had hoped for. "You don't need to be distressed. I have no plans to expose you."

"So you say." Gigi sighed in cautious relief. "You promised you wouldn't tell my family where I am, but you didn't say whether they know what I've . . ." She paused, lifted her chin. "Do they know I am a . . . a—"

"Lady's maid?"

She nodded.

"No, they don't know anything about where you live or what you do. They don't know if you're safe or even alive."

Setting aside the costume, she gained her feet slowly, carefully. "They know I am well."

"How?" Fitz moved closer. "How do they know you are well?"

"I send a letter home monthly, by way of a carrier who keeps my location and situation secret."

Fitz had a thousand questions, primarily, "Who is this carrier, and how does she"—*or he?*—"deliver your letters?"

Gigi seemed to consider her answer carefully. "I met Sister Mary the afternoon I was supposed to marry Nathanial. She was very kind to me and insisted I keep in touch. I did, and we continue to meet whenever she's in the city."

"Which, I gather, isn't often?"

Gigi shook her head. "She trains traveling nurses at a mission near the Bowery, and does the same in Philadelphia, Washington, DC, and Richmond, Virginia."

But not Boston, Fitz noticed. "That still doesn't explain how she manages to get your letters to your family."

"She mails them from various locations in each city, though never New York."

Fitz had additional questions, too many to count. But he sensed Gigi had already told him more than she'd planned. If he pushed her too hard, she might end the conversation altogether.

Still, he couldn't stop himself from asking, "Do you ever wish for a reply?"

"Never." She said the word with something perilously close to a sob. "I fear any confirmation that my father hasn't forgiven me."

Fitz's heart constricted at the raw emotion smoldering in Gigi's eyes. His breathing shallow, he asked, "Have you told him that Nathanial is no longer in your life?"

"I keep the letters short. I give no specifics. I merely say that I am happy and well."

"Why not tell them the truth about Nathanial? Surely your father would have let you come home once he knew the scoundrel was gone."

Her sad eyes rolled up to his. "The situation is more complicated than that."

So she'd claimed the other night in the alleyway. "Your father is not as unforgiving as you seem to believe."

Tight-lipped and frowning, she glanced away from him.

Again, Fitz wondered what she wasn't telling him. "Why can't you go home?"

Her face filled with unspeakable pain. "What does my father think happened to me?"

This, Fitz could answer without a single fabrication. "He fears the worst."

"And my mother?"

"She hopes for the best. Your sisters, nearly as romantic as you ever were, seem to believe you are happily married and living out a real-life fairy tale."

Her lips twisted. "And what about you, Fitz? What do you think happened between Nathanial and me?"

He flexed his hands into fists. "I am in agreement with your father."

Her face somehow shifted, no longer filled with curiosity or fear but an odd sort of defiance. "You must be feeling very smug."

Smug? She thought he was happy with the knowledge of her downfall? It was shocking how sorrowful he could feel about something that had happened to a woman who'd all but spurned him.

Gigi had been caught in Nathanial Dixon's evil snare. The rat had hurt and humiliated her, and had put Fitz in a position to do the same, because it was time to stop dancing around the truth. "Let's get one thing straight, *Gigi*."

She opened her mouth to speak, no doubt to correct him on her name.

Fitz talked right over her. "Despite all the warnings, ultimatums, and threats, you chose to run off with a fortune hunter. It doesn't matter what happened in that hotel room. For all intents and purposes, you are a"—he paused for emphasis—"fallen woman."

* * *

Fallen woman. Gigi felt her face drain of color. *Fallen woman.* The words reverberated in her head. Fitz knew . . .

Somehow he knew that she and Nathanial had . . .

Without the sacred vow of marriage . . .

Gigi shuddered at the implacable expression on Fitz's face. He was right, of course. She was a fallen woman and no amount of atonement could erase her dishonor.

Her skin seemed to prickle and burn white-hot, as if she'd tumbled into a frigid lake.

"You claim it doesn't matter what happened in that hotel room." Aware she sounded angry and scared, she took several soothing breaths. "But we both know it does."

He was silent, which worried her a little. A lot. The only movement was the ticking of a muscle in his neck. After several seconds passed, Gigi thought the conversation was over. Fitz would now leave the room. And New York. And forget he'd ever found her.

But then he spoke. "I don't care what you did or did not do with Dixon."

"Of course you care." She couldn't let the issue drop. How Fitz viewed her shouldn't matter. But it did, and she knew why. If he, of all people, could see her as the woman she used to be, without the taint of her transgressions, then maybe she could learn to do so as well. "You once thought me worthy enough to consider marrying me."

"Your father and I had an agreement, one that was never properly secured beyond a few vague promises." He moved a step closer. "We are not pledged to one another, nor have we ever been, and thus I do not care if Dixon or any other man ruined you."

He was too calm, too composed. Gigi searched his gaze. A mistake. His eyes locked with hers, and she saw the turmoil there. Her heartbeat went wild, thudding uneven and heavy against her ribs. Fitz did care but was insisting otherwise. What she didn't understand was why.

The rebellious part of her wanted to push him.

"We are to be related by marriage, Fitz. My secret disgrace, if revealed, will reflect on you and your family."

As soon as the words left her mouth, she understood why he was here. Why he was *really* here. He hadn't come for the pearls. That had only been an excuse. No, he was here to determine the depths of her scandalous act, and then keep the news from getting out.

It made sense. If the truth of her wantonness became public, the scandal would rub off on Fitz's family.

Perhaps it already had.

With the promise of a potential engagement between her and Fitz, there would have been speculation from his peers when she'd suddenly disappeared. There would have been questions from his business associates. "Did you help my father draft the lie about my studying music in Vienna?"

"No, but I remained silent about the truth." And that made him complicit.

More to the point, her return would bring questions about their future together. "You don't want me to go home."

"On the contrary, I want to make your return go as smoothly as possible."

"I wish I could believe you." He'd covered up her sins as surely as if he'd constructed the lie that now prevented her from returning home.

The lie that also protected her reputation.

She didn't deserve that kind of consideration, even if it was also to Fitz's mutual benefit. Gigi hadn't thought of anyone but herself the night of her flight. But Fitz had been forced to think of her since. By remaining silent, he shared in her deceit.

"Does my father truly not know where I am?"

One side of Fitz's mouth tilted at a wry angle. "He does not."

"You didn't tell him you found me?"

Fitz broke eye contact, and his hands found his pockets. "I already interfered in your life once, for which I am greatly sorry."

He was apologizing to her?

That threw her back a step. Since the beginning, Gigi had been assigning ugly intent to Fitz's motives. Yet here he stood, taking the moral high ground.

"Had I not inserted myself into the matter," Fitz continued, "you might not have left home."

How wrong he was. As much as she'd wanted to blame him—as much as she *had* faulted him—Fitz's meddling hadn't pushed Gigi into Nathanial's arms. She'd have left with him anyway. That's just how enamored she'd been with the scoundrel. How gullible and naïve.

"You tried to warn me," she admitted, reminding herself of that fact, too, and feeling even more wretched than before. When Fitz had confronted her about Nathanial nearly a year ago, he'd started out with tact, but when that hadn't worked, he'd resorted to shock, then cold, hard bluntness. She'd been so outraged at the time. But looking back on it now, Gigi couldn't deny that his intentions had been honorable. When hers had been anything but. "I refused to hear your concerns."

Fitz did not press the issue. He simply stared at her in that patient way of his.

Gigi swallowed. Fitz's silence said more than actual words. She'd never understood him, and was even more confused by his behavior now. Had he displayed a hint of fury or censure or any number of reactions, she would have bolted.

Taking care to keep as great a distance between them as possible in such a small space, Gigi glanced at the ceiling, the costume-draped wall, anything to avoid Fitz's gaze. The man she'd all but jilted. She closed her eyes, reeling from a powerful onslaught of emotion. Guilt, humiliation, confusion, and the ever-present self-loathing.

The sound of material rustling told her Fitz had shifted his stance. She opened her eyes and found him still watching her, waiting calmly for her to speak again. Not a single piece of his hair was out of place. The hand-tailored suit he wore cost more than her yearly salary, five times more than the money she needed to buy back her great-grand-mother's pearls.

She couldn't bring herself to look away. She was too intensely aware of his presence. How had she missed the way Fitz commanded a room? Always, he lived decisively in his skin. The hand-tailored clothing nothing but expensive drapery.

"Why?" she asked. "Why didn't you come after me sooner? Why now?"

His lips pressed into a flat line, the only indication he wasn't as calm as he'd appeared. "It's taken me this long to find you. You are very good at hiding. I had to hire two private investigators."

Her pulse danced. Fitz had hired men, as in plural, to find her. The confession should have infuriated her. Instead, she felt something in her simply let go.

All this time, he'd been searching for her. Eleven months and countless deceptions.

She'd changed her name, taken different jobs, never staying in any position longer than a few months. Each of her previous employers had thought it their idea that she'd moved on to a position they'd hand-picked just for her, when Gigi had maneuvered the situation herself.

She'd made sure no one recognized her. If anyone had, the story her family had made up would have been scrutinized. All it would have taken was one slipup and the truth would have been revealed.

Gigi was suddenly tired. She didn't want to keep hiding and worrying and being afraid of exposure. For months, she'd donned a disguise and had lost herself in the process.

And still, Fitz had hunted for her. For reasons she couldn't fully comprehend. He spoke plainly and seemed sincere, yet Gigi sensed he wasn't being completely authentic. He was holding a portion of himself back.

Of course he was holding back. She'd treated him callously, thinking only of her own happiness. Instead of demanding the explanations he deserved, Fitz was . . . *apologizing*.

Her face burned.

Pain burst inside her heart and leaked all the way to her soul. Her mouth shook, but no words came out. She stood closer and closer to Fitz but was not aware of moving. Perhaps because she hadn't moved. Fitz had been the one to close the distance between them.

"Gigi—"

"My name is Sally. Sally Smith."

His hands clasped her shoulders gently, tentatively, as if he understood he needed to handle her with care. Did he know how much his consideration stung? Much more harshly than a slap in the face would have.

"You are Gigi Wentworth," he whispered, lowering his hands and stepping back.

"Not anymore."

His expression filled with compassion. "So you say. But I still see her in you. I hear her in your voice whenever we are alone."

So he'd caught that. No matter how hard Gigi tried, she couldn't seem to flatten out her vowels in his presence.

"I also see Sally Smith, a woman you created out of desperation. The real you is somewhere in between the two."

He couldn't be more right. Or more wrong.

The old Gigi was no longer inside her. Nathanial had destroyed that part of her, as surely as if he'd buried a knife in her heart and twisted. She couldn't bear Fitz championing her. What had she done but cause trouble for him? She'd hurt him terribly, simply because he'd not been exciting enough for her.

"I'm sorry," she said. The words were so inadequate. That didn't make them any less true.

"You have nothing to be sorry for, Gigi." Fitz's voice was soft and kind. So kind her throat clogged.

Fitz was proving himself a good man. Deep down, Gigi had always known this about him. She might have even reconciled herself to the prospect of marrying him if he'd been a little less formal and set in his ways. His lack of imagination and inability to live in the moment had scared her. She'd feared never living up to his standard of perfection and thus had convinced herself they would never suit. The rumors about him and his cousin had sealed his doom.

But there had been other signs.

Gigi had watched her best friend, Verity, suffer in a cold, loveless marriage arranged by her parents. Her friend had become a shell of her former self and had wanted more for her own future. She'd wanted passion and adventure.

Be careful what you wish for, Gigi.

Fitz had said that to her, on more than one occasion. He'd meant to caution her. She'd taken his words as a challenge. She'd pushed him to be the man she wanted instead of appreciating the man he was.

Their one kiss had been . . . it had been . . .

Lovely.

Unexpected.

And so very frightening.

Made worse because Fitz had maintained his distance from that point forward, never letting down his guard again. Just when Gigi had given up on ever restoring their friendship, Nathanial Dixon had arrived on the scene, as if he'd calculated the timing down to the minute. With very little effort, he'd won Gigi's affection and promised such a false sense of freedom.

Ever since her foolish act, she'd dreamed of going home and starting over. She often awoke sweat-soaked and cold from nightmares of being turned away. The instinct of self-preservation had kept her from making the short trip from New York to Boston. That, and the pearls.

She was so close. And yet, so very far away.

"Come home with me, Gigi."

"I can't."

"You can." Fitz reached out his hand. "I'll stand with you when you face your father."

Gigi tried to think past the flurry of emotions swirling in her stomach, making her dizzy and sick. Whatever motivated Fitz to make such an offer, she knew it wasn't simple kindness. He never did anything without thinking through every step, every outcome.

You are a fallen woman.

How he must despise her.

Then why not say the words? Why offer to stand by her?

"What if I'm turned away?"

"Then you'll know you tried."

She waited for more. He simply stood there, unblinking, seeming to stare straight into her soul. In that moment, she knew Fitz would never consider marrying her again.

Why did that hurt so much?

Fitz deserved more than a woman like her. They suited even less now than when she'd been Gigi Wentworth, the spoiled, most-sought-after, silly debutante. Her hand went to her lips.

His gaze followed the movement. A heartbeat later, he took a step closer.

As if wading through water, she mimicked the move.

He made to take another step, froze a half second, then continued forward until nothing separated them. His hands went around her waist. Her fingers went to his shoulders, flexing once, twice, then relaxing into the thick wool of his coat.

He was going to kiss her. Again.

There had to be a prayer to prevent this sort of disaster.

At the moment, Gigi couldn't think of one. She couldn't think at all. Fitz held her closer still, and reaction took over.

Something spread through her, something that made her feel reckless and far too much like the daring young debutante she'd once been.

Christopher Fitzpatrick was the very last man with the power to make Gigi feel reckless and daring. Besides, she was Sally Smith now. Sally was never reckless or daring. She was about control. Rigid control.

She shifted out of Fitz's reach.

The door burst open a second later.

"Ah, Sally, there you are." Sophie breezed into the room, an envelope fluttering in her hand, a cloud of jasmine and innocence following in her wake. "I need your advice. I have been invited to a ball and, oh—"

Sophie's feet ground to a halt.

"Mr. Fitzpatrick, I didn't see you there." She looked from Gigi to Fitz, her brows pulled together in confusion. "I was told you left the building."

"Your maid was explaining why such a massive amount of costumes is necessary to put on a production."

"Oh, well, yes." Sophie's expression relaxed. "I suppose that would seem daunting to someone new to the theater."

"Now that I have the information I need, I will wish you both a good day."

He exited the room with the kind of smooth sophistication that had been bred into him from childhood. The man was not especially personable or charming, or even likable. He was intense and . . . Gigi sighed. He'd nearly kissed her.

Sophie stared at the door Fitz had just walked through, her brow still furrowed. "I can't quite put my finger on it, but I believe that man is not what he seems."

The young woman had no idea how close to the truth she'd come.

As if something had only just occurred to her, Sophie spun to stare at Gigi, eyes wide. "You know him."

The statement had Gigi rubbing at her temple, where the beginnings of a headache pounded. "Mrs. Llewellyn introduced us days ago."

Sophie's suspicion morphed into certainty. "You *know* him."

Gigi wished it wasn't true. Suddenly, the minuscule, airless wardrobe room felt infinitely smaller.

"And . . ." Sophie gave her a saucy wink. "You like him."

Gigi didn't like Fitz. She tolerated him. She'd . . . nearly kissed him.

Well, she thought in furious despair, maybe she did like Fitz. But only a very little.

Chapter Twelve

Fitz was a man who rarely confronted defeat. He set a goal and strategized the best plan of attack. He then destroyed every obstacle until success was his. It was a good way to go through life, safe and effective.

Just shy of a week after his arrival in New York, Fitz was in a state of complete frustration. He hadn't accomplished a single goal he'd set for himself. He'd yet to find a cure for his father's condition, though he'd spoken to three more specialists. And three of the five investments he'd been considering had proven unworthy of his time.

Most disturbing of all, he had no idea what to do about Gigi. He should have known better than to come for her himself. But now that he was here, he would not—could not—leave without her. Gigi deserved a chance to make amends with her family, and Fitz would see that she got it. It didn't matter that she was proving difficult. He'd endured tougher barriers than her stubborn resistance.

Fitz was a man who dealt in facts. Thus, as he exited the Waldorf-Astoria and turned toward the Harvard Club, he faced them.

He'd nearly kissed Gigi.

She'd nearly kissed him back.

A freezing rain, razor-thin and sharp as needles, sliced through the air. Frigid water dripped off the bill of his hat and occasionally slipped under his collar. It was a miserable day, matched only by Fitz's dismal mood. He was feeling helpless.

He hated feeling helpless.

He moved quickly through the driving rain and focused on what he could control: his upcoming meeting with Lucian Griffin, an old school chum from his days at Harvard.

Luke's automobile company was a young business, barely operational, but Fitz had done his research. The potential for expansion and large profits was there. Within the hour, Fitz would know if he wanted to make an offer for part of the company.

Ice crunched beneath his feet as he rounded the street corner. The Harvard Club loomed one block ahead on his right. A sense of homesickness filled him, as if he'd been dropped into a slice of Cambridge, Massachusetts, in the middle of New York City.

People hurried past him, rushing about their business, their breaths pluming in frozen puffs around their heads. Horses whinnied, dogs barked, a motorcar coughed and spit to life.

Drawing in a long pull of air, Fitz breathed in the scent of rain mixed with ice and snow. The cold, wet, dreary weather sparked a renewed sense of urgency. He wanted to make this deal, not only for the company but also for his father. The more solvent the firm became, the less likely word of the bad investments would get out.

Fitz would like to think he and his cousin could keep his father's medical condition a secret indefinitely. But the truth always had a way of coming out.

The truth shall set you free.

Not in Fitz's experience.

He stopped in front of the club. Some of the most powerful businessmen in the country had attended Harvard, men who were building America and turning her great. Back in his prime, Fitz's father had been one of them. He'd been a sharp investor, financing large corporations that had significantly influenced the nation's economy.

Fitz would restore his father's legacy.

His plan was simple. Broker a deal with Luke that would bring them into the future. Like Fitz, his former classmate was a man who understood the benefit of a calculated risk.

As Fitz stepped beneath the awning of the most exclusive club in the city, resolve spread through him.

The doorman greeted him with a smile. The short, barrel-chested man wore livery in the Harvard colors of crimson and gold.

Fitz stated his business. "I'm Christopher Fitzpatrick. I have an appointment with Lucian Griffin."

Proving he knew his job well, the doorman nodded. "Mr. Griffin is waiting for you in the billiards room on the third floor. You'll find a stairwell at the back of the building that will take you there without delay."

Instructions given, he pulled open the gold-plated door and stepped aside for Fitz to pass.

One hand on the rich oak bannister, Fitz climbed the long flight of stairs that led to the main gathering area. The smell of expensive tobacco and freshly polished wood mingled with the scent of leather, books, and old money.

Fitz checked his coat, hat, and gloves with the smiling, elderly attendant dressed in livery the same colors as the doorman's uniform.

Making his way through the cavernous hall, Fitz took in the high ceilings and dark wood-paneled walls, then glanced at the men scattered throughout the room. A few looked familiar. Not surprising since election for membership to any of the Harvard Clubs across the country was limited to graduates of the prestigious university and tenured faculty.

Fitz took the back stairwell to the third floor and made his way to the billiards room, using his ear as his guide. Determination took hold.

He wanted to make this deal, but only if the company proved as profitable as his research led him to believe.

He paused at the threshold. The billiards room was awash in light and conversation.

Fitz stepped forward, wavered. Luke wasn't alone. Another man was at the far end of the table, lining up a shot. Fitz knew him. Knew him well and considered him a friend.

Fitz stepped fully into the room.

Luke immediately set out toward him. "Fitz, my good man." Luke's hand clasped his shoulder, strength and assurance in his grip. "You're looking well."

Returning the greeting, Fitz shook his friend's hand. Luke hadn't changed much since their days at Harvard. He was Fitz's height, with much the same lean-muscled build. He had sandy-blond hair and amber-colored eyes that were more gold than brown, and was still as fit as he'd been in college. Luke had been the strongest rower on their eight-man boat.

"You remember Jackson Montgomery." Luke indicated the other man in the room with a nod.

Fitz shook Jackson's hand. Back at school, he and the other man had shared a similar intensity and drive for excellence. Jackson appeared more at peace than he'd been at Harvard. Dressed impeccably in a dark navy-blue suit and crisp linen shirt, the man was clean-shaven, his black-as-midnight hair perfectly cropped. The easy smile on his face was new and matched the one on Luke's.

Both men had recently married. Fitz remembered reading about their weddings in the Harvard newsletter. There was a bit of scandal surrounding both, though he couldn't remember what.

"We're nearly through with our game," Luke told him.

Fitz waved the men back to the table. "By all means, finish."

Jackson took his turn. Luke jeered as he lined up his shot. He called Jackson a few names—*sap* one of the kinder ones. Jackson gave as good as he got.

There was respect in the banter between the two men, transporting Fitz back to their days at Harvard College. Back when his father was still his father. Calvin Fitzgerald had taught his son a love of competition, which had led, in part, to meeting these men.

Overly serious, not especially social, Fitz had tried out for the Harvard crew as much out of a love for sport as to make friends. A year ahead of Luke and Jackson, he'd earned the role of captain for their eight-man boat. Luke and Jackson had been strong rowers, and so Fitz had put them in the engine room, oar positions four and five.

Jackson sank two balls in a row, earning a groan from Luke. "You're cheating, I just can't figure out how."

"Watch and learn, my friend." Jackson gave him a goading grin. "Watch and learn."

Shaking his head in mock disgust, Luke moved to stand by Fitz. They spoke of nothing important, mostly their college days, which turned to their time on the boat. "I'm still bitter over losing the Regatta," Luke admitted.

Fitz snorted his agreement. The annual Harvard-Yale Regatta was always the culmination of the rowing season. Yale had won every year during Fitz's tenure, much to his scowling displeasure.

He eyed the man he once called friend, taking in the changes, wondering at them. "I heard you married this year."

"I did. Once I exchanged vows with my beautiful bride, we immediately embarked on a far too short honeymoon."

It was Jackson's turn to snort. "You were gone a month."

Luke cut him a glare. "Scoff all you want. But one month alone with my wife wasn't nearly enough. It should have been two. No, make that three."

As he said this, everything about Luke, his eyes, his demeanor, his voice, spoke of pleasure.

"You're happy."

"Elizabeth makes me a better man."

The dull clack of yet another ball dropping in a pocket rang out. Still leaning over the table, Jackson looked up, his pool cue between his curved fingers. "And that, old boys, is how it's done."

"You planning to gloat all morning or line up your next shot?"

Standing tall, Jackson pointed the tip of his pool cue at Luke. "You're a poor loser."

This, as Fitz could attest to, was true.

"Just get on with it." Luke ground out the words.

Jackson chuckled.

The men had always been good friends, easy with one another, but clearly both were even more relaxed and content than when they'd been young. Was that what marriage did to a man? Did it make him satisfied with his lot in life, comfortable in his own skin? It wasn't just about getting a woman to the altar, after all, but securing a life after the ceremony. A life, Fitz reminded himself, that could never be his. Not unless he found a cure for his father's condition.

"I highly recommend taking the marital plunge."

Fitz jerked, realizing Luke had continued talking while his mind had wandered. He reached for a calm that didn't exist. "The marital plunge?"

"I seem to remember something about you getting engaged to Harcourt Wentworth's daughter?" Luke eyed him closely. "Have you set a date?"

"No, we have not."

"Ah. I've conducted a few transactions with Wentworth. He's a ruthless negotiator."

Time seemed to bend and shift, taking Fitz to another room much like this one, when he'd been in discussions with Gigi's father for her hand in marriage. Harcourt Wentworth was a man who knew what he wanted, laid it out in precise language, and rarely relented on the terms of an agreement.

That trait had made him one of the most successful businessmen in the country, but probably not the best of parents. Fitz remembered now how Gigi had begged him not to go to her father with his suspicions about Nathanial.

Guilt swept through him.

Had he made matters worse? Had he all but delivered her into Dixon's waiting arms?

"Right corner pocket," Jackson called out, then, as promised, shot the last ball in the right corner pocket. The table was empty but for the white cue ball, game over.

While Jackson returned the cue stick to the mahogany stand, Luke slapped Fitz on the back. "Unless you have an objection, I'd like Jackson to sit in on our meeting as he's representing Richard St. James's interest."

The request made sense. Jackson would be standing in for the man who owned the share in Luke's company that Fitz wanted to purchase. Jackson was also an attorney. If Fitz and Luke came to an agreement, Jackson would probably be the one to draw up the contract transferring the shares from St. James to Fitz.

"I have no objection."

"Excellent."

They agreed to conduct their business in the club's library. The room was spacious. But the furniture had been arranged in such a way as to partition off smaller sections, creating just enough of a lived-in feel to issue a silent invitation to relax. Fitz suspected the staff had worked long and hard to perfect this level of elegant comfort in such a large area.

Once they were settled in chairs facing the fire, Luke broke his silence. "I understand you are in talks to purchase the Summer Garden Theater."

Fitz nodded, pleased to discover Luke had been gathering information about a potential investor. If their roles were reversed, Fitz would do the same. "I have my eye on several New York–based companies."

"Why New York?"

"I find most businessmen in this city think beyond America. International expansion is the gateway to the future."

Luke leaned back in his chair. "Good answer."

They shared a smile.

For nearly thirty minutes, they discussed Luke's current and future plans for his automobile company. When his friend wound down, Fitz said, "The idea of hosting a series of races across the country is sheer genius."

Jackson took over from there. "We're thinking of bringing in Brian Chesterfield to organize the inaugural Griffin Tour on Long Island."

Fitz knew the man well. Brian had been another rower in the engine room. Oar six. "I was under the impression he'd moved to Europe."

"He's back from two years of racing motorcars in France."

Which explained why Luke wanted Brian involved. The next few minutes were spent going over the various ideas for the Griffin Tours, many from Fitz.

"You're very knowledgeable," Luke said.

"Motorcars have become a recent hobby of mine." Fitz had needed something to take his mind off his father's health. Racing had provided that outlet and was what had brought Luke's company to his attention.

"You should come out to the factory on Long Island. I'll give you a tour and then you can test-drive one of our prototypes."

Satisfied with what he'd heard so far, Fitz thought this a splendid idea. "Set the date and I'll be there. I'll also want to take a look at the financial projections, speak to your chief engineer, and discuss your plans for expansion."

They negotiated a time to meet the next week. The conversation came full circle, and they were back on the Summer Garden.

"Have you met the incomparable Esmeralda Cappelletti?" Luke asked with a guarded look in his eyes.

No wonder. The opera singer's relationship with the man's father had to be a sore spot. "She is everything the papers claim her to be."

This earned him a small—very small—smile from Luke. "Have you met her daughter Sophie?"

"I have made her acquaintance."

Clearly waiting for more, Luke held Fitz's stare.

"She is a charming girl." Actually, Sophie was a woman, but Fitz wanted to make it clear to her brother that he had no intention of pursuing her romantically.

In the role of protective big brother, Luke continued staring at Fitz, hard. Fitz didn't waver under the close inspection.

"I take it you know of my personal connection with the . . . *girl*?"

"I did my homework," Fitz said. "You and Sophie Cappelletti are half siblings. You share the same father, different mother."

"Well," Jackson said on a low whistle. "That was certainly succinct."

It never occurred to Fitz to be anything but straightforward. If Luke was expecting some sort of judgment from him, he had a long wait ahead.

"What are your thoughts on a six-cylinder engine?" Fitz asked.

The question had the intended effect. The tension in Luke's shoulders visibly reduced. The discussion soon segued into a lengthy dissertation on automobile manufacturing, including costs.

When the topic was exhausted at last, Fitz stood. "Until Monday?"

Luke shook his hand. "Until Monday."

Fitz exited the Harvard Club with a lighter heart. If half of what Luke had claimed turned out to be accurate, Fitz would be in the automobile business by the end of the year.

* * *

Back at the Summer Garden Theater, Gigi was feeling rather satisfied with herself. What had begun as a temporary solution for Jessica's child-care problem had become a godsend for two other dancers with small children. Gigi was now in charge of watching three little girls: Fern, Lilly, and Amelia, ages three, four, and five, respectively.

Not only did Gigi enjoy her time with the children, but she would earn a significant amount of money toward the fifty dollars she owed for the necklace.

Best of all, tucked away with the children in a small, forgotten room on the northeast corner of the building, Gigi had managed to avoid running into Fitz for two full days, going on three.

This was in large part due to Esmeralda. Although Gigi suspected the diva wanted to keep her from interfering with her attempts to throw Sophie and Fitz together, she'd been surprisingly sympathetic to the plight of the young mothers.

Pleased that Esmeralda hadn't produced a fuss, Gigi had created a makeshift nursery far away from the stage. The room was some sort of holding cell for forgotten set pieces. Large trunks overflowed with torn costumes and small trinkets. An ancient piano that was surprisingly in tune sat in the farthest corner from the door.

"Miss Sally." Fern tugged on her skirt, her big blue eyes full of childlike hope and an eager smile on her pretty little face. "Will you read a story to us?"

"Please?" Amelia begged. "Will you, will you, please?"

Not to be left out, Lilly added, "Oh, please, please, pleeeease?"

Lips twitching, Gigi glanced from one little girl to the next. Fern held a well-worn copy of *Grimm's Fairy Tales* in her hand, the same one Gigi had read from every day so far.

She reached for the book. "I can't think of anything I'd like more."

Squeals of delight ensued.

Later, she told herself, she would take the children up to the roof garden to enjoy a bit of fresh air. For now, she would read from Fern's treasured storybook.

She laid out a threadbare blanket, sat, and then gathered the children around her. Opening the book, she found her personal favorite, "Briar Rose." She read slowly, in the soft, lyrical voice her own mother had adopted exclusively for fairy tales.

"'A king and queen once upon a time reigned in a country a great way off, where there were in those days fairies.'"

"Oh." Fern clapped her hands in glee. "I love fairies."

The other little girls agreed with fast head-bobbing.

Gigi smiled at each child before glancing back at the book. "'Now this king and queen had plenty of money, and plenty of fine clothes to wear, and plenty of good things to eat' . . ."

The children listened intently, eyes wide, riveted to the story much as Gigi had been at their age.

"'They had no children, and this grieved them very much indeed.'"

Amelia sighed dramatically, proving she'd been raised around theater folk. "Mommy says children are a blessing and should be adored."

Gigi's own mother had said something similar to Gigi and her younger sisters. She felt a powerful wish for something . . . more, something enduring and lasting. An unrealized dream that could never come from watching other women's children.

I want a baby of my own.

She would be happy with a boy or a girl. She, or he, would have dark hair and green eyes and sit on Gigi's lap while she read. A ripple of intense longing surfaced before she resolutely shut it down.

"Your mommy is correct," she said, her voice quivering. "Children are a blessing."

Amelia beamed at her.

Fern tapped her arm. "What happened to the king and queen? Did they ever have a child?"

"You'll have to wait and see."

Glad to get back to the story, Gigi lowered her gaze and continued reading about how the king and queen held a feast to celebrate the birth of their daughter, inviting all the people in the land. "'But the queen said, *I will have the fairies also, that they might be kind and good to our little daughter.'*"

"I want to invite fairies to my next birthday party."

Gigi suspected Lilly might change her mind once she heard the rest of the story.

"'Now there were thirteen fairies in the kingdom; but as the king and queen had only twelve golden dishes for them to eat out of, they were forced to leave one of the fairies without asking her.'"

"Why gold dishes?" Fern asked.

Gigi had no idea. "I suppose it's because they're fairies."

"Oh."

Gigi read on, telling the girls how the twelve fairies arrived, each with their gifts for the princess. "And then," she said, pausing for dramatic effect. "The thirteenth fairy arrived."

All three little girls gasped. "Was she very angry?"

"She scolded the king and queen." Gigi explained about the curse and that on Briar Rose's fifteenth birthday, she would prick her finger on a spindle and fall down dead.

Tears filled Amelia's eyes. "Did she die?"

"No. One of the twelve friendly fairies hadn't given her gift yet. She couldn't reverse the curse, but she was able to soften it." Gigi found her place in the story and read from the book. "'When the spindle wounded her, she should not really die, but should only fall asleep for a hundred years.'"

"I guess that's not sooooo bad."

"So, she fell asleep for a hundred years. And the entire kingdom slept as well. But then a handsome prince came to the old tower—"

"What did he look like?"

Gigi answered without thinking. "He was tall, with nearly unbearably good looks. His hair was the blackest of black, the color of a raven's wing. He had a strong jaw, often showing a bit of dark stubble by midafternoon. His eyes were the green of summer leaves, and he had very broad shoulders." Too late, Gigi realized she'd just described Fitz.

"I like him."

Gigi did, too, more and more each day that he stayed in New York. *Hopeless.* It was all so utterly hopeless. She shook away the thought and read how the prince opened the door to Briar Rose's little room.

As if transported to the story world, Gigi could practically hear the door creaking open as she read.

She cleared her throat.

"'And there she lay, fast asleep on a couch by the window. She looked so beautiful that he could not take his eyes off her, so he stooped down and gave her a kiss . . . she opened her eyes and awoke . . . and soon the king and queen also awoke, and all the court.'" She shut the book with a snap. "And everyone lived—"

"—happily ever after."

The breath in Gigi's lungs iced over. The ending words hadn't come from one of the children but a familiar baritone. A shiver crossed the base of Gigi's skull.

Slowly, she swiveled her head, glanced toward the now open doorway and straight into Fitz's handsome face.

Gigi felt it again, that powerful wish for something *more*. Once again, she pushed the sensation away. Ignored it. Denied it. To no avail. No more than she could go on avoiding Fitz.

She remained frozen in his stare, curling her fingers around the book so hard her knuckles turned white. She hated this anxious, almost panicky sensation spreading through her.

Unfortunately, it couldn't be helped. Simply staring into Fitz's moss-green eyes caused her anxiety.

He should not be here.

She wanted him nowhere else.

The moment grew thick with tension, the silence between them so heavy that Gigi could hear her own breathing.

"Look," shouted Lilly, her finger pointing to the door. "It's the handsome prince. He's come to rescue Briar Rose."

The three little girls rushed to Fitz. They spoke over one another in their attempt to gain his attention.

"I'm Fern, and I'm three years old," the smallest announced before she went on to introduce the other two girls. "This is Lilly. She's four, just like I'll be at my next birthday."

"I'm Amelia, and I'm five."

A rich tumble of laughter spilled out of Fitz, mingling harmoniously with little-girl giggles. He skillfully divided his attention equally between the children, which produced wide, happy smiles on each of their faces.

Gigi had never seen him this relaxed and easy. *This is the kind of father he'll be.* Patient, attentive, and kind.

"Miss Sally was reading us a story."

With Fitz's gaze locked on hers, Gigi's lungs forgot how to breathe. "Which one?" he asked.

The ability to communicate failed her, though she couldn't think why. She knew Fitz came to the theater daily, yet, somehow, his presence in this room, her very own sanctuary, felt different. Not at all intrusive but as if they shared a secret. A good one this time, something special and only between the two of them.

"She was reading about Briar Rose and her handsome prince," Lilly said. "He came to save her."

"It's what all good princes do." There was so much emotion in Fitz's eyes, which were still locked with Gigi's. She recognized that shattered look, the hint of vulnerability in his stance. As though he, too, wanted something that could never be his.

She wanted to go to him, to comfort and soothe whatever might ail him, as one kindred soul to another.

She didn't dare.

Regardless of their history, they were barely more than acquaintances. He was too good and she was spoiled goods.

The room suddenly felt too small, too hot. Gigi pushed a strand of hair off her face with the back of her hand.

Fitz shifted to his left, splintering the tense moment and their disturbing connection.

Clearing her throat, Gigi rolled her shoulders, set the book aside, and jumped to her feet. She swayed, unable to find her balance. But Fitz was by her side at once, holding her steady as his strong hands clutched her waist.

Chapter Thirteen

Ever since leaving the Harvard Club and his two nauseatingly happy former schoolmates, Fitz couldn't stop thinking about missed opportunities. When he'd listened to Luke and Jackson expound on their marriages, Fitz had thought he understood the source of their happiness.

Yet he hadn't, not fully, not until he'd stood in the doorway of this overstuffed, messy room and watched Gigi read to three little girls. He'd seen a mother with her children. He'd seen the future he might have had, had he acted sooner. Had he been smarter.

Gigi could have been his wife already, if only he'd been less mechanical in his pursuit of her.

Now, it was too late.

He inhaled sharply. She did the same, the movement reminding him he still had a hold on her waist. He released her and stepped back.

An unexpected bout of longing captured him, longing for a home and a family of his own, for a comfortable, settled life with a good woman by his side. With *this* woman by his side, their children gathered around her while she read.

The sensation came fast and hard, digging deep. For a painful moment, the loneliness in his soul spilled into his heart.

One of the children moved in next to her. "Can we sing our song for the prince?"

He heard a soft, throaty laugh before Gigi glanced at him with a question in her eyes.

Fitz nodded.

While Gigi lined up the children, small to smallest, the storm brewing in him calmed. His senses were still unnaturally heightened, though, and he became aware of giggles from the young, girlish voices.

The sound of family.

A sense of inevitability pushed him forward. Toward Gigi. He had one coherent thought: *her.*

She's the one.

He shoved the disturbing notion aside before it could take root. Even if, by the grace of God, Gigi fell for him and miraculously agreed to marry him, Fitz cared for her too much to condemn her to an uncertain future in his home. Not one of the specialists he'd consulted could give him a guarantee that he wouldn't become ill like his father. If he knew for certain, then perhaps, maybe—possibly—Fitz would consider pursuing Gigi in earnest.

As matters stood, his time to woo her had come and gone. He'd failed miserably to win her heart, treating her like another business transaction rather than a woman with genuine hopes and dreams. No wonder she'd found Dixon's attention so appealing. She'd probably felt neglected, or perhaps Fitz had simply bored her and that had been enough to send her into another man's arms.

Even now at the thought of the resulting tragedy, anger and guilt burned deep, not at Gigi, but at himself and the man who'd ruined her. Fitz's breath came in quick, hard snatches.

He'd waited too long to fetch her.

Why hadn't he searched harder?

He knew, of course. Pride.

"All right, girls, you know what to do." Gigi took her place at the piano and began to play a favorite hymn from his childhood.

"Jesus loves me—this I know."

Fitz stood frozen, struck immobile by the familiar melody wafting over him. Then he noticed the laughter. It was high-pitched and full of pure childish joy. He'd never really understood that sound.

Until now.

For a moment, he simply allowed the music to wash over him.

Hopes and dreams flooded into him, the kind he'd suppressed for a full year, ever since Gigi had run off with another man.

"For the Bible tells me so. Little ones to Him belong . . ."

Sensation after sensation seemed to come at Fitz at an alarming rate these days. Most of his fondest memories of Gigi were of her playing a piano. Her father had invited him to his home nearly three times a week, often more, under the guise of discussing business. But Harcourt Wentworth had had another agenda in mind.

Fitz had been smitten long before Gigi's father had pushed for the match. Gigi had been young, fresh and beautiful, talented, and the most confounding woman he'd ever met. And she'd played the piano with flair, indicating a passionate nature that should have warned him that winning her heart wouldn't be easy.

The attraction had not been one-sided, no matter what Gigi claimed. Their one kiss was a blur in his memory, however, replaced with their more recent meetings, when suspicions and accusations had stolen their smiles. His inability to open up hadn't helped his cause, though he was only just beginning to realize that.

Ironic that he found himself wanting to share his secrets with Gigi now that he couldn't.

Standing on the edge of this overcrowded room, listening to the sounds of children singing while she played the piano, Fitz realized something else. He'd missed her.

He wanted to be a part of the joy. He prayed the memories of his failure, or at least the worst of them, would stay away so he could simply enjoy this moment with Gigi and these precious, innocent little girls.

"They are weak, but He is strong."

Bracing himself, Fitz swallowed past a lump in his throat.

Not wanting to interrupt just yet, he held perfectly still, listening. He'd forgotten that Gigi could sing as well as she played the piano. He remembered standing in the pew behind her on Sunday mornings. Her sweet, melodic tone had been made for singing church hymns.

He mouthed the words along with them. "Yes, Jesus loves me. Yes, Jesus loves me."

The smallest of the little girls was pretty shaky on the verses, but she had the refrain down pat. Her sweet baby voice rose to a near shout as she sang, "The Bible tells me so!"

The music stopped, only to be replaced by clapping. "Oh, well done," Gigi declared.

She alternated between kissing each little head and praising their singing. A portion of a long-forgotten verse from Isaiah came to Fitz's mind: *The redeemed of the Lord shall return, and come with singing.*

Fitz would see her restored to her family. Nothing would stop him, not even the stubborn woman herself.

Gigi lifted her head, and their gazes met. Her eyes shone with emotion, and then . . .

She smiled. At him.

Fitz lost the ability to breathe. He felt himself suffocating until he managed to drag in a quick pull of air.

He'd once thought this woman beautiful when her hair was perfectly coiffed and she was clothed in fashionable attire. But Gigi had never been more appealing than in this moment. The sight of that ridiculous mobcap resting at an awkward angle atop her head and the long, poorly dyed strands of hair escaping to curl around her cheek was the most mesmerizing he'd ever seen.

As he continued staring into Gigi's pretty eyes, he felt a sudden sense of release. For that single moment, he was free. Free of his burdens and thoughts of what might have been.

Gigi smiled down at the children. "We've been inside entirely too long. Who wants to go to the roof garden and get some fresh air?"

All three chimed in at once. "Me!"

Gigi laughed.

The smallest of the little girls ran to Fitz and took his hand. "Will you come with us, Prince? Say yes."

He hesitated, not sure he wanted to extend this torture.

"Please? Oh, please, will you?"

How was he supposed to refuse such an ardent request? He bent over to speak to the child eye to eye. "I wouldn't miss it for the world."

The child twirled away in a series of dizzying spins. "Prince is coming with us."

"Perhaps *Prince*"—Gigi shot Fitz a wry look—"would be so kind as to help you into your coat."

"Prince would be delighted."

He caught Gigi's smile before she turned to assist the other little girls into their coats.

As they wound their way through the darkened auditorium and up the carpeted stairs to the roof garden, Fitz's chest felt odd. His pulse quickened in his veins. His throat tightened. All because this woman, whom he'd known most his life, had morphed into a stranger. One who fascinated him beyond reason.

The transformation had nothing to do with the clothes she wore, or the change in her hair color, and everything to do with the woman herself.

No longer proud and defiant, she was softer, kinder, and more Gigi than Georgina Wentworth had ever been.

Had her experience with Dixon changed her so completely?

Or was the transformation something that had occurred in Fitz?

He took Fern's hand and guided her through the doorway. Gigi escorted the other two children. The wind had died down since Fitz had left the Harvard Club, but the air still had a bite to it. The sky was a hard, brittle blue, the fat orange sun halfway toward the western horizon.

The children didn't seem to mind the cold. They hurried off to play a game of hide-and-go-seek. He and Gigi watched the game in companionable silence. The moment was strangely easy, almost tender. Fitz decided to keep silent in hopes of extending the glorious experience.

Fern rushed up to Gigi. "Did you see where they went?"

Gigi laughed, the sound almost musical. "You know I can't tell you. You have to find them on your own."

Undeterred by the gentle scolding, the child came to stand directly in front of Fitz. "What about you, Prince?" She planted her hands firmly on her hips in a display of profound little-girl frustration. "Did you see where they went?"

He shook his head.

"But you're the handsome *Prince*. You're supposed to know everything."

Charmed by the little girl, he nearly told her what she wanted to know. But he caught Gigi shaking her head at him.

"I'll give you a hint."

Ignoring Gigi's impatient snort, he leaned over and met the child at eye level. "They're hiding somewhere on the roof."

Fern stared at him for several long moments, then grinned. "You're funny, Prince."

A second later, she ran off to search for her friends.

"You have an admirer, *Prince*." Gigi angled her body toward his. "Imagine I said that last part without sarcasm."

"I'm trying."

"You're being very kind to the girls."

"They're adorable and sweet and think I'm a handsome prince. I don't know any man who wouldn't find himself charmed."

"There are some." She sounded sad and beaten.

Just how badly had Dixon treated her?

A protective instinct shuddered through Fitz, and one thought rose above the others warring in his mind. *I want to fight Gigi's battles.*

It was too late to protect her from Dixon. The damage had been done. But it wasn't too late to secure a better future for her. An odd sensation filled Fitz's chest, something good and noble. But he was no prince. And he certainly couldn't ride in on a white steed and save Gigi from her dragons. *You have reasons for keeping your distance,* he reminded himself.

Ignoring the silent warning, he moved closer, a mere inch, no more.

The wind kicked up, tugging a tendril of her hair free from its knot. Fitz reached up and tucked the strand behind her ear.

She drew in a shaky breath.

The world paused, and then . . .

Squeals and shrieks of happiness filled the air as Fern found the first of her two friends. Still, Fitz stared at Gigi. Her beauty was stronger, purer in the bold sunlight.

Her eyes, those amazing silver-blue eyes, stole his breath. *She* stole his breath. She always would, Fitz realized with a sudden jolt.

Alarmed at the direction of his thoughts, Fitz knew he needed to gain some perspective. It would help if he could look away from her startling face.

He continued holding her gaze.

Her very presence soothed him. She made the weight of his burdens seem . . . somehow . . . less.

Something wonderful and lasting was gathering in his heart, something life altering. He wanted—needed—to pull Gigi into his arms. He wanted to tell her his plan to restore her to her family. But not here. Not now.

"Will you allow me to escort you home, once the children's mothers come for them and your time is once again your own?"

He spoke the question with perfect politeness. Where had the fun *Prince* gone? Lost, Fitz decided, in this woman's gaze.

"I don't know if that's such a good idea. We don't have anything more to say—"

"I have something new I wish to discuss."

"We can talk here."

"It requires privacy."

Puzzlement sprang into her gaze, followed by a healthy dose of suspicion. "What are you up to now?"

"Nothing nefarious, I promise." He nearly reached for her hand but thought better of it. "I have an idea for a business venture I'd like to run by you."

"You wish to consult me on a . . . business matter?"

Coming out of her mouth, it did sound odd. "You'll understand once I explain the essential elements of my plan."

He had her. He saw her capitulation in the way she leaned slightly forward.

"Let me walk you home," he said.

"I suppose if we headed out in the same direction around the same time, it would be quite natural to speak to one another."

He grinned. "Quite natural."

"Prince!" A hard yank on his pant leg accompanied the new nickname. "*Prince*, you are not listening to me."

Duly chastised, he looked down at the little girl attempting to gain his attention. Fern's face was scrunched into an adorable scowl. Affection enveloped him at the sweet picture she made.

"I apologize." He crouched down to her height. "I'm listening now."

"You and Miss Sally have to take a turn."

Not sure what the child meant, Fitz angled his head.

The little girl shook her head at him, as if he was a big, dumb man who needed female guidance. "Miss Sally has to hide from you. And you"—she poked him in the center of his chest—"have to go seek her."

No, Fitz thought, Gigi would not hide from him. Never again.

Never.

Again.

* * *

Up to the point of sending Fern and the other two girls back into their mothers' care, Gigi had successfully put Fitz's request to walk her home out of her mind.

She had not thought of it when she'd "hidden" from him on the roof garden.

She had not thought of it when he'd "found" her behind a large potted plant.

She definitely hadn't thought about it when he'd leaned in to kiss her gently on the cheek, and took a moment to whisper, "I've found you."

Fitz had given her a very fierce look, silently daring her to try—just try—to get away from him.

The world had swung away then, everything suddenly out of focus.

Caught completely off guard by his ferocity—when was Fitz ever that *passionate* about anything outside a boardroom?—Gigi had been unable to tear her gaze from his. She'd been unable to move at all. She'd been overwhelmed and short of breath, and her heart had pounded as though she'd been running very hard for a very, very long time.

But now that she was back in her makeshift nursery, she couldn't think of anything else but Fitz and their upcoming walk.

The man himself soon arrived. Gigi fought to steady her heartbeat. But . . . *oh, my.*

There he stood, in all his handsome, prince-like glory, hat literally in hand, overcoat slung over his arm, shoulder propped against the doorjamb. He didn't look boring or unemotional or bland. He looked a little dangerous, and so different from Christopher Fitzpatrick the financier. Gigi didn't know what to do with him. Except a part of her knew exactly what to do with this man.

She soaked up the sight of him, drank in every glorious inch of his tall, lean, muscular body.

He gave her a long appraising look in return.

Gigi's mind raced back to the roof garden, to the moment when his lips had pressed against her cheek.

Her heart stumbled. She tried to remain cool and unaffected under his bold scrutiny. She really, really tried. But the lump in her throat was as big as a baseball, and her heart pounded out an erratic staccato against her ribs.

"Ready to go home?"

Fitz's tone, though quiet, carried an unmistakable hint of intimacy. His words held far more meaning than anyone listening would realize. *Ready to go home?* Yes. *Yes*, she wanted to go home. With him. She wanted to leave right now.

She couldn't, of course, not yet.

"I'm nearly ready. I just have to tidy up a bit."

And yet, she remained frozen to the spot.

Why did this new Fitz affect her so?

She knew why. *Of course* she knew.

The way he carried himself—calm, relaxed, full of confidence mixed with a hint of stoicism. And loneliness. The loneliness was what called to her.

A wry chuckle tumbled out of him. "So, we're back to awkward pauses and staring."

She laughed. "Apparently, it's what we do in each other's company these days."

"So it would seem."

Smiling broadly—oh, what a smile—he pushed away from the door and paced toward her.

Her mouth went dry as dust. She couldn't seem to move her feet. Why couldn't she move? Not more than a few days ago, Gigi and Fitz had hovered in a similar life-altering moment. She hadn't been ready for a change in their relationship then. Was she now?

A series of flutters took flight in her stomach. Yet in a nice, calm, rational voice she said, "I'll only be a moment."

Oh, look at her. So cool, so in control, a woman who knew her own mind. It was quite the act. Esmeralda would approve of her performance.

"Let me help." When she started to argue, he insisted, "We'll get the job done in half the time."

Efficient. The man was efficient to a fault.

They tackled the task in silence. Oddly attuned to one another, they moved in flawless harmony, as if they could read each other's next move.

Gigi told herself it didn't matter that they worked so well together. But it did matter. Their effortless camaraderie made her think of the future, of happy endings and princes rescuing damsels in distress.

There was no use denying the truth any longer. Gigi still wanted the fairy tale, and it was all because of Fitz.

Once they were outside the theater and heading in the direction of Esmeralda's town house, Gigi risked a glance in the man's direction. Her thoughts scrambled, circling one another like a cast of hawks swooping in for the same prey. She longed for so much, unable to define exactly what she wanted. The man strolling beside her was at the heart of the shocking sensation.

He wanted her advice. He wasn't here to tell her what to do or how to do it.

"You wished to run a business concern by me?"

"I'm seriously thinking about purchasing the theater."

His confession surprised her. "I can't imagine why."

He lifted his face to the sky. "It's a small, risky venture, I admit. But sometimes those end up the most profitable."

Somehow, Gigi doubted making a profit was behind his decision. Something else was driving him. As she waited for him to continue, the grind of wagon wheels rang in the distance. A baby wailed. A dog barked. A vendor shouted out about his wares.

"Do you hear that?" she asked when he continued to stare up at the sky.

Fitz cut a glance in her direction. "Hear what?"

"The sounds of the city." She swept her hand in a wide arc. "It's almost musical how each mingles with the other."

He slowed his pace and then stopped altogether. He looked down at her. The man had quite a piercing stare. "There she is."

"Who?"

"The woman with the heart of a composer and the romantic ideals of a poet."

"You're mocking me."

"On the contrary. I find the way you see the world charming." Eyes filled with quiet affection, he reached out and brought her hand to his lips.

The gesture was so unexpected, so sweet and gentle that Gigi's stomach dipped. She sighed, wanting this moment to last forever.

"It's one of the things I admire most about you," he said, continuing to cradle her hand in his.

Fitz admired her?

Gigi couldn't ask for more. *Wouldn't* ask for more than this one perfect moment with a man who admired her. *Fitz admired her.* Gigi didn't quite know how to respond.

She thought of her love of music, of poetry, of the Psalms, especially the ones penned by King David, and how she'd felt closest to the Lord when lost in the arts. Nathanial had stolen that from her. He'd wrecked her appreciation for what she'd once loved. She could no longer enjoy Shakespeare's sonnets, any of Byron's work or Emily Dickinson's, and that was . . .

Her own fault.

Nathanial hadn't stolen anything from Gigi that she hadn't willingly handed over.

The woman Fitz admired was in the past. An innocent. Gigi wasn't that person anymore. Letting herself forget that point, even for a second, was a mistake.

Nonetheless, whereas Nathanial had only taken, Fitz had given her something back.

"Thank you, Fitz. Thank you for reminding me of a part of my former self I'd nearly let die."

Tenderness moved in his gaze. "You're welcome."

They resumed walking.

Gigi slipped a covert glance at him from beneath her lowered lashes. Fitz's strong profile brought complicated emotions blazing to the surface. She forgot to wear her hard-earned outward control. Something had to be terribly wrong, because she wasn't supposed to feel this comfortable.

This connected.

She'd lost her balance. All because Fitz had reminded her of the woman she'd once been.

What is this? What's happening between us?

Gigi had to get back on even footing with this man. She searched her brain for something to say. "Tell me why you want to buy the Summer Garden."

Still holding her hand, he guided her down an unfamiliar lane. The path led to a small public park. Fitz directed her toward a thicket of evergreens. The ring of trees shut out the rest of the world.

As Fitz led her to the secluded area, their feet left indentations in the wet, muddy ground.

He stopped beneath a leafy pine tree with several low-hanging branches. He let go of her hand, reached up and plucked a stem free. His gaze turned dark and turbulent as he twirled the twig in his gloved palm.

"You do realize, Fitz, that you have *the look*."

He cast her a sidelong glance. "What look?"

"Whenever something is troubling you, a groove shows up right . . . there." She pointed to a spot in the middle of his forehead. "It's been a quirk of yours since we were children."

A strangled laugh rumbled out of his chest. "You always did know me better than I knew myself."

A mild glumness took hold of her. Gigi didn't know Fitz, not nearly as well as she wished.

"Let's sit. Over there." She gestured to the bench on the edge of the isolated copse.

For an endless moment, he stared down at her. He stood frozen for so long that Gigi thought he might turn down her offer and stalk off.

But then, in one furious burst of motion, he threw down the twig and headed toward the bench. She had to break into a trot to keep up with him. Much to her relief, he slowed and then sat. With his gloved hand, he patted the empty space beside him.

She sat as well, falling into a companionable silence as they both stared up at the sky. Thick clouds had moved in since their time on the roof with the children, turning the sky a dingy gray. The afternoon air was scented with a hint of pine and snow.

Gigi treasured brisk walks in the city. Her favorite time of year was when fat, languid flakes of snow tumbled from the sky. Sometimes, when she was feeling especially comfortable in her new life, she loved the blanketed anonymity, loved living in a city where no one knew her as Gigi Wentworth.

"Do you really wish to purchase the theater?"

"Yes, no. Yes." He shrugged. "Possibly."

"That's incredibly unclear."

"I can't stop thinking about the children. Or, more accurately"—he reached up and caught a wisp of Gigi's hair, wound it around his finger, then let it go—"about their mothers and the situation they have found themselves in, with no one to watch their daughters on a regular basis."

Gigi laid a hand on his arm, looked into his eyes. "It's only been a few days, a very busy few days at that, what with opening night less than a week away. It's no wonder they haven't found a more permanent solution."

"I was speaking of the larger problem."

Gigi removed her hand.

"They are raising their little girls alone, without the benefit of a husband or help from family." His turbulent gaze held hers. "That could have been you. You could have found yourself—"

He broke off abruptly, the lines of worry around his eyes cutting deeper.

Was he silently judging her? How could he not? She judged herself nearly every second of every day.

"Tell me something, Gigi. What if matters had turned out differently? What would you have done if he'd left you with child?"

The question was one she'd asked herself a thousand times since Nathanial had run off. The back of her throat stung with disgrace. Her eyes filled with tears—hot and instant and unwelcome.

"I would have survived." She looked down at her gloved hands. "Like Jessica and the other women at the theater, I would have considered the baby a blessing."

"Your strength awes me."

The respect in his voice had her lifting her head. She'd never seen Fitz look at her like that. It wasn't just respect she saw staring back at her, but something deeper, something a woman could build a life on if she dared to believe again.

A strong pulse of blood rushed in her veins. She desperately wanted to be worthy of that look. Of him.

His head came down over hers, stopping when their lips nearly touched. "Push me away, Gigi."

How could she when he treated her with such kindness, such understanding and caring? Things she thought never to experience from a man again. She was too weak to push him away, and far too desperate for this moment to be real. Her only answer was to slip her hands up his chest, across his shoulders, around his neck, and then . . .

His mouth moved over hers carefully, courteously, until he found the perfect angle.

She sighed against him.

The sound must have brought him to his senses, because he jerked away from her. "I apologize. I took advantage of the moment."

He had, yes. His spontaneity had been glorious and wonderful and so out of character for Fitz that Gigi could only smile. For the first time in eleven months, she felt worthy of a man's attention.

His shocked gaze moved to her lips. He seemed to be waging an internal battle with himself. "It won't happen again."

"Of course not."

"It can't."

"No."

They were back in each other's arms, their lips pressed tightly together, hearts pounding in a wild, shared rhythm.

Gigi tasted home. It was an illusion. A woman like her could never regain what she'd lost. But for this one moment, she allowed herself to believe her future could be more than a lonely existence with a cat as her only companion.

All too soon, Fitz pulled his head away. A shaken breath escaped him. Or was that her?

Doing her best not to do something ridiculously stupid, like climbing on his lap, Gigi laughed. It was either that or cry. She forced herself to speak calmly. "You were saying something about the children at the theater?"

He blinked. "Right. The children. But first"—he blinked again—"we should probably address what just happened."

Please, Lord, anything but that. "Nothing happened."

"We kissed. Twice."

Leave it to Fitz to make the situation a thousand times more awkward. He'd kissed her. She'd kissed him back. And for the life of her, Gigi couldn't figure out why either of them had done it. "We don't even like each other," she whispered.

"Apparently, we do. Rather a lot."

Hearing the amusement in his voice, Gigi whipped her gaze to his. The words of censure died on her lips. Fitz's smile was full of tender affection. He used to look at her like that when they'd been friends. Much had changed since then, too much to hope that a few kisses could bridge the divide that stood between them.

Gigi let another sigh move through her, let it flow from her lips this time in a sad, pathetic whoosh. "I don't want to talk about this, Fitz. Not right now."

"Yes, Gigi. Now."

She drew in several fast breaths. "Stop making such a big deal out of this." She shoved at the stubborn tendril of hair that kept falling over her left eye. "It was just a stupid kiss."

"We both know it was more than that."

"All right, *two* kisses."

"Talk to me, Gigi." Taking her hand, he cupped it affectionately in his, pulled it to his chest. "Tell me what's on your mind. I want to know what you're thinking."

"Oh, Fitz." She lowered her head, stared at their joined hands. "I'm not avoiding a difficult conversation"—*precisely*—"I simply need time to figure out"—*how things got so quickly out of hand*—"where we go from here."

"I'd like to think we could become friends again."

"I'd like to think that, too." She squeezed his hand, feeling as though they might actually be able to forge a real friendship. "Can we please leave it at that?"

He stared at her for several long seconds. He opened his mouth. Shut it again. Then, finally, he let go of her hand. "If that's what you want."

"It is. Yes. Thank you." Giving him no time to change his mind, she returned to their previous topic of discussion. "If I recall, we were speaking about the situation with the children at the theater."

A beat passed, then another. Eyes never leaving her face, he shook his head, then said, "It seems unfair that their mothers, all of them so young, have to constantly worry about their care. I can only imagine the strain of carrying that daily burden."

He spoke of burdens and strain as if he had intimate experience with both. Gigi wondered again what secrets Fitz harbored.

"At least they have a solution for now."

"It's temporary, at best." He rubbed a hand over his jaw. "They need a more permanent situation."

"You mean . . . at the theater?"

He nodded. "Something similar to what you're providing now, but with a woman in charge who would stay indefinitely in the position."

The intensity of his words highlighted his concern, one that Gigi shared. "If you purchased the theater, you could set something like that up."

Fitz nodded again, but the tension in his shoulders didn't release. If anything, they bunched tighter. "Suppose I put my idea in motion— would you be willing to offer me some thoughts on the matter?"

Gigi stared into his eyes and saw the man beneath the stern, overly polite exterior. She saw the man who'd kissed her, the one capable of great feeling, with a hatred for injustice, a heart for forgiveness, and the capacity to care for children that weren't his own.

In that moment, she fell a little in love with him. "I would be honored."

Chapter Fourteen

An hour after sharing her thoughts about a permanent nursery at the theater, Gigi entered Esmeralda's town house through the back door. At Mrs. Garrison's curt order, she quickly shut out the cold.

Time had gotten away from her, and now Gigi would have to move quickly if she wanted to help Sophie prepare for the ball this evening. Tonight would be the young woman's official debut into New York society. She must look perfect.

Gigi took the stairs two at a time, trying unsuccessfully to focus on the task that lay ahead, rather than her encounter with Fitz. He'd claimed they could become friends again. She wanted that, truly she did, but Gigi wasn't sure they could regain what they'd once had. Her fingertips went to her lips, locking in the sigh that wanted release.

Fitz had kissed her. He'd kissed her!

She'd adored the feel of his mouth on hers. The sensation had nothing to do with friendship. Gigi would have never imagined such a simple meeting of lips could throw her assumptions of everything she knew into confusion. The kisses—both of them—had been brief and yet far more real than any of the countless moments she'd shared with Nathanial.

She continued climbing the stairs with something more powerful than embarrassment. Anger. Anger at herself for what she'd done with Nathanial. For believing him. For trusting him.

Fitz was proving five times the man Nathanial had ever been. He wasn't one to ask for help, yet he'd requested Gigi's. To turn to her for advice was unprecedented. She'd wanted to jump into his arms and kiss him square on the lips again and again, and thank him for his extraordinary faith in her.

Fitz was shattering every preconceived notion she'd ever had about him. He was full of surprises, and that scared her.

Was she falling for him?

Hadn't she learned her lesson about men?

How much easier it would have been to think of Fitz as the villain in her story. Was he, like Nathanial, a bad man pretending to be good? Or a good man appearing to be bad?

On the third-story landing, she paused, tugged her still-tingling bottom lip between her teeth. She wanted very badly to believe Fitz was who he seemed to be. But she'd been fooled once. She couldn't allow it to happen again. And she couldn't fool him, either, that she was more virtuous than she was. At all deserving of his regard.

Gigi must keep her distance from Fitz. If she grew too close, too intimate in her feelings for him, she might do something massively daft, like become his friend and end up hurting them both. There was still so much she didn't know about him—and so much he didn't know about her. All the sordid details surrounding Nathanial. And her situation with the pearls.

If she fully confessed to him, he would never look at her with tenderness in his eyes. She couldn't bear that.

She hurried into her room and cringed at her reflection. Her hair was a mess, her dress wrinkled beyond repair, and, most telling of all, her cheeks were shaded a bright pink.

She switched the wrinkled uniform for a cleaner version and removed her mobcap. At the mirror, she reworked each strand, twisting and tucking and calling upon every trick she'd learned as a lady's maid. But no matter what she did, more red showed than blonde, and no longer just at the roots.

Sighing, Gigi ran her fingers along her hairline. Bleaching the strands so soon after the last time would result in irreparable damage. Why hadn't she chosen to go black instead of blonde? Because she hadn't had the expertise to know better, at least not enough to realize the darker color would have been gentler on her hair.

Taking a breath, she made her way to the second floor, gave a cursory knock, and walked into Sophie's room. The young lady was sitting at the small table by the bay window overlooking the street below. She had a dreamy look in her eyes, one that put Gigi immediately on guard.

She'd seen that look before. In her own eyes a year ago. Had Sophie met someone? A man?

With the eyes of a woman who'd fallen too hard, too fast, Gigi ran her gaze over her friend. What she saw frightened her.

Gigi recalled the young woman's wish to rebel against her mother. Sophie loved Esmeralda, but she hated drama. Esmeralda was the very essence of drama. The diva had her stormy days, when nothing went right or could be made right. She would turn her critical eye to Sophie then, finding fault with everything. But Esmeralda was also generous and welcoming of people from all walks of life. She was childlike in her affection for those she considered part of her inner circle. She especially adored those who adored her.

"Sophie, it's time for you to dress for the ball."

Nodding, the young woman stood. The look in her eyes turned from dreamy to wistful, a slight distinction but noticeable to a woman who'd worn both expressions after meeting Nathanial.

A man had put that look on Sophie's face.

Gigi's heart pounded in a fast tattoo against her ribs.

"I think I shall wear the lavender-and-silver gown." Silence met the pronouncement, until Sophie prodded, "Would you like to know *why* I wish to wear the lavender-and-silver gown?"

Gigi was afraid to respond. "I would think because the cut and color are the most flattering of all your dresses."

"Well, yes. But there is another reason."

Yes, Gigi figured as much. "If we don't get to it, you shall be unfashionably late. And since this ball is being thrown with you in mind, that simply won't do."

Sophie took a deep breath. "Gigi, my friend, it is not as though the good people of New York will reject me because I am a few minutes late."

The words showed how much she still had to learn about society. "One small misstep is all it will take to cause whispered speculation of your suitability."

And then all their hard work of the previous months would be destroyed. Sophie's life would be ruined, her heart crushed under her detractors' perfectly sewn slippers.

"At some point, I will have to accept that some people will never accept me."

"But others will."

"There are some who are extraordinarily polite. Very gracious. Impeccably kind. But I am the Daughter of Scandal." She jerked her chin at a defiant angle. "I am the child of an affair between an opera singer and her married lover."

"It's still possible you will make a good match."

Sophie turned her head in Gigi's direction. "The well-bred ladies of society consider me too much of a disgrace to be a wife to their sons. Perhaps it's time I settle for something less."

"Don't do anything rash, I urge you."

"I want a man to look at me the way Luke looks at Elizabeth, and Simon looks at Penelope, but I am no longer naïve enough to think I will find him among the New York elite. I ruined my chances when I confronted my father in front of the most influential members of his privileged world."

"You don't know that for certain."

"Oh, but I do." She gave a secretive smile. "And suddenly, it doesn't matter so much."

Gigi opened her mouth to refute the point, but Sophie continued talking.

"I have set my sights a few rungs lower than the very top of the ladder."

"There are good men at the top." Gigi thought of Fitz, and how very different he was proving from Nathanial. "And some very bad men every step in between."

Sophie gave a little huff of laughter. "Who knows?" The reflective look came back into her eyes, but this time there was a hint of daring, too. "Perhaps my search is over."

"Have you met someone, Sophie?"

"I'm not telling." Moving to her closet, she flung open the doors. "Let's get me dressed."

"Please, Sophie. Listen to me." Gigi hurried to stand beside the young woman. "Do not settle for a man unworthy of you. Wait for one who will treat you well."

"You are being a bit severe, don't you think? Simply because a man doesn't earn his living in the noble pursuit of banking or high finance doesn't make him less worthy."

"Of course it doesn't. But tread carefully. Do not be fooled by pretty words and false confessions of love."

Sophie entered the closet. "I no longer care what people think of me. From this night forward, I will make my own way in their world, on my own terms. And I will fall in love with the man of my choosing."

Gigi felt a spike of dread. She couldn't hold back one last piece of advice. "Whatever man you set your sights on, make sure that he is who *and what* he seems."

Sophie rewarded her words with a dismissive wave. "Don't worry, my friend. I will adopt great caution going forward. And"—she plucked the lavender-and-silver dress from its hanger—"I will do so while looking magnificent."

In that moment, Sophie had far too much Esmeralda in her, and Gigi's dread turned into outright fear. It was as if she was watching the sweet, innocent girl she'd come to know melt away, layer by layer, morphing into someone else entirely.

"Sophie, please be careful."

The young woman dismissed her with another flick of her wrist. "I brought something home for you."

Taken aback by the swift change of subject, Gigi absently took the silk gown from Sophie and followed the young woman out of the closet.

"It's there." Sophie pointed a finger to the far corner of the room. "On my writing desk."

Gigi eyed the envelope from where she stood. *Sally Smith* was scrawled across the front. Recognizing the neat, looping handwriting, she cocked her head in confusion.

Why was Elizabeth Griffin sending her a letter?

"Go on," Sophie urged, taking the dress from Gigi and nudging her forward with her shoulder. "Open it."

Gigi moved to the writing desk and stared at the ivory parchment paper. Her first instinct was to tuck the envelope in her pocket and read it when she was alone.

But Sophie looked at her with anticipation.

"Do you know what she wrote?"

Sophie merely smiled, lazily, catlike. "Why don't you open it and find out for yourself?"

Gigi tore into the envelope and read the handwritten request. "It's an invitation to luncheon at Elizabeth's residence."

"Yes, I know." Sophie moved in behind her and studied the invitation over Gigi's shoulder. "There's no need to respond. I told her you would be more than happy to attend."

Scowling at this, Gigi tucked the card back inside the envelope. She was surprised to see her hands shake. "I can't go."

"Why not?"

"It's simply not done." The burst of regret clogged her throat. Gigi would have adored having luncheon with the woman she considered a close friend. "I am a domestic, and domestics do not dine with the women they serve."

"Elizabeth warned me you would protest. I am to tell you that it will be a small private affair."

"How small?"

"Only five women are invited. You and me, of course, as well as Caroline, Elizabeth, and Penelope."

Gigi was tempted to accept the invitation. Though she didn't know Penelope very well, this would be the perfect opportunity to watch the woman with Sophie and determine if her sisterly affection was genuine.

Gigi knew Caroline and Elizabeth better. She'd worked for both of them, and they'd bonded in a friendship beyond employer and employee. Despite each of their rough roads to happiness, Elizabeth and her cousin, Caroline, were settled in their new lives. They'd married well, joined in life to men who adored and doted on them.

"Gigi." Sophie took Gigi's shoulders and gently guided her to the bench at the foot of her bed. "You are not a domestic. You are masquerading as a domestic. There's a difference."

"You are the only person who knows I'm not really a servant."

"I very much doubt that. The women you once served are intelligent and quite observant." She knelt down and pressed her palms on Gigi's knees. "I would wager both Caroline and Elizabeth already suspect the truth."

Gigi thought back over her time with each woman. Yes, they'd suspected she wasn't what she seemed. Their questions had been careful and discreet, and they'd let off when Gigi had refused to talk. But she'd left her positions with them because the questions had gotten too close to the truth, the risk of exposure too great.

"Please, Gigi, come to lunch with me at Elizabeth's house."

The urge to spend an afternoon in the company of women she admired was too strong to resist. She'd spent too many months poised between two worlds, belonging to neither, unable to find her place. Perhaps, for a few hours, in the company of women she liked and trusted, Gigi could be herself.

"All right, I'll go."

"Wonderful." Sophie clapped her hands together. Gaining her feet, she studied Gigi a long, silent moment. "You cannot wear your uniform."

"I have another dress."

"That hideous brown rag?" Sophie made a face. "No. If there is any part of that you didn't understand, let me repeat myself. *No.*"

"I don't have the money to buy a new dress." She needed every penny for the pearls.

"We are nearly the same size." Sophie circled her. "Yes, very nearly. You will wear one of mine."

Gigi's mouth opened, then closed. She felt something odd in her chest. Was that hope? An awakening?

She felt nearly like her old self.

A small victory and one she gladly accepted. Later, when she was alone, she'd worry about what to wear to the luncheon.

* * *

The ballroom overflowed with three hundred of New York's social elite. The ball would last well into the evening hours. Fitz would stay an hour, no more than two. He'd rather be anywhere but in the Waldorf-Astoria's famous ballroom. However, he knew the value of mingling with future investors. He also needed a distraction from thoughts of Gigi. Ever since he'd come upon her with the children, she'd taken up residence in his mind, and certainly in his heart.

Fitz had seen a side of the woman he'd never known existed. She'd looked like a mother, a woman he could see himself growing old with. He shouldn't have pulled her into his arms. He definitely shouldn't have kissed her.

Nothing could have stopped him.

Fitz was willing to admit, if only in the private recesses of his mind, that he wanted Gigi in his life. But friendship was the most he could hope for, the most he dared pursue.

Shoulder propped against the wall, he was, as usual, content to watch the celebration from a distance. He forced himself to pay attention to his surroundings.

The strains of a waltz floated on the air, while a rainbow of dancers whirled past him. It seemed the entire population of New York's upper crust had been invited to this affair. The men wore formal black suits, with white vests and matching white ties. The women were dressed far more colorfully in formal gowns. They wore long white gloves up their arms. Jewels adorned their hair, necks, and wrists.

Gigi should be among them, laughing, dancing, and using her charm to win the heart of every man in attendance.

She was probably holed up on the third floor of Esmeralda's town house, removing stains from a dress not her own. A pity, Fitz thought, and yet he knew the changes in her were because of her low position. She had more depth. But also more sadness.

Fitz wanted to erase the pain that lived in her eyes. He wanted to be the man who—

He cut off the rest of the thought.

Nothing could come of his growing attraction. He would never marry her, or any woman. He would not father any children. He would not destroy a woman for his own selfish gain. The investment firm would become his legacy, a tangible way to leave his mark on the world.

Clasping his hands behind his back, he looked out across the ballroom in time to see Luke walk in from the terrace, guiding his wife to the dance floor. The way the pretty blonde moved effortlessly on her husband's arm spoke of easy familiarity and connection.

I will never have that with a woman.

Fitz was sorry for that, more so now that he and Gigi were no longer at odds. Their kiss had sealed his affection for her. He felt more alive in her company, more awake, as if he were emerging from an unpleasant dream that had held him in its dark grip for far too long.

When Gigi was near, the world made sense. Fitz's footsteps were lighter and—

My footsteps are lighter?

He shook his head. Any more of this sappy introspection and he would find himself putting pen to paper to write poetic verse in Gigi's honor. Him, the man she herself had claimed had no imagination or sense of what constituted a romantic gesture, now reduced to poetic musings.

Mouth tight, jaw clenched, Fitz tried to calm his raging pulse. A frown knitted his eyebrows together.

"Now that's the sight of a man wishing to be anywhere but here."

Welcoming the interruption, Fitz pushed away from the wall and settled his gaze on his friend. Luke's eyes were full of humor.

"I prefer boardrooms to ballrooms."

"Don't we all?"

As he shook hands with his friend, Fitz got his first glimpse of Luke's wife up close. She was a beautiful woman. She had a petite frame and blue eyes, and her hair was the palest of blondes. With Luke's hair a shade darker than hers, the two made the quintessential golden pair.

"He sounds like you, Luke." A soft tinkle of laughter followed the statement, the sound complementing the woman's sculpted, elegant beauty. "Now do your duty, husband, and introduce me to your friend."

"I am at your service, my love." Luke took his wife's hand, swept an intimate smile over her face, then said, "Elizabeth Griffin, I would like you to meet Christopher Fitzpatrick. We attended Harvard together."

"It's a pleasure to meet you, Mr. Fitzpatrick."

"Please, Mrs. Griffin, call me Fitz."

"Only if you agree to call me Elizabeth."

He inclined his head.

"Wait, you're Fitz? From Harvard? Of course." She looked to her husband, then back again. "You're the friend who may be investing in Luke's automobile company."

"That would be me."

"How wonderful. But why are you hovering in the shadows instead of joining in the party?"

He decided to be truthful. "The ballroom is hot, overcrowded, and I am a bit—"

"Overwhelmed by the vast quantities of unfamiliar New Yorkers?"

"In a word, yes."

"Tell me about Boston," she said, clearly attempting to put him at ease. "I have only visited your city once, and it was a very long time ago."

Fitz welcomed the opportunity to expound on the city he called home. He told her about boating on Boston Harbor and picnicking on one of the islands, then added, "It's a city full of history."

This seemed to delight Luke's wife. "I adore history. If I can coax my husband into taking me for a visit, what should we see first?"

Fitz and Luke answered simultaneously. "Harvard's campus."

Elizabeth laughed. "I see my husband was right about you."

"How so?"

"You two are of a like mind." She patted Luke's cheek. "Now, it's time I leave you two to speak business."

"You wound me, Little Bit." Luke gave his best imitation of a man affronted. "I would never talk business in a ballroom."

With a display of amused indulgence, she kissed his cheek. "Then use the opportunity to speak about the 'good old days' at Harvard. It was a pleasure meeting you, Fitz."

"And you as well, Elizabeth."

"Oh, look, Penelope has arrived. I must speak with her about the luncheon next week." A whimsical smile on her face, Luke's wife wandered away.

Both men watched her go.

Once she was out of earshot, Fitz said, "I always suspected you were a man of sound judgment. Now that I have met your wife, I realize you are also a man of excellent taste."

Luke smiled with unabashed joy, as if he'd been laid low by love and couldn't be happier. "Elizabeth is the very heart of me."

"She's lovely."

"I'll be sure to pass along the compliment."

"Please do."

There wasn't time to say more, as a small commotion had broken out near the ballroom's entrance. Excited murmurs filled the air, followed by a quick straightening of shoulders, a widening of eyes.

All heads turned.

A beat passed. And another. And then . . .

Esmeralda made her entrance.

Dressed in a red silk dress with layers of matching lace and intricate embroidery, the infamous diva sauntered into the ballroom like a queen lording over her realm.

She took her time sashaying through the room, stopping every fifth or sixth step in order to strike a dramatic pose. With an assortment of feathers bobbing on her head, she waited for assembled guests to admire and adore her. Only then did she continue her journey through the room.

Sophie trailed after her mother, falling farther and farther behind, her eyes riveted on a spot where three young men stood watching the dance floor. Had one in particular caught her eye? Or was Sophie attempting to distance herself from Esmeralda's dramatic entrance?

Esmeralda caught sight of Fitz and altered her course. Hips swaying and her face arranged in a calculating smile, she stopped her pursuit inches shy of running into him, close enough for him to get a whiff of her cloying perfume. She struck a final pose—one hand on her hip, the other poised gracefully in the air at shoulder level.

"Fitz, *tesoro*." She squeezed in between him and Luke, the move forcing Luke to step aside or risk coming away with a mouth full of feathers from the hat she wore. "What a surprise to see you here."

Somehow, Fitz doubted anything surprised this woman.

"Sophie, come, say good evening to our friend." Esmeralda waved her daughter closer. One problem. Sophie had fallen so far behind that she'd been swallowed up in the crowd. There was no sight of the young woman. Much to Esmeralda's obvious displeasure. "Where is that girl?"

The words were spoken in a flat Midwestern accent, far truer than any Esmeralda had used before. Fitz tried not to smile, but the diva put on quite a show.

"I believe Sophie is conversing with my wife and sister over by that large potted plant." Luke supplied this oh-so-helpful piece of information with an ironic twist of his lips as he gestured toward the other side of the ballroom.

Esmeralda ignored him.

"You dance with me, *mi amore*." She held out her hand to Fitz, her Italian accent firmly back in place. "Come. We go now."

Fitz couldn't think of anything he'd rather do less.

Unfortunately, he'd failed to make his preference known quickly enough. Esmeralda had already hooked her arm through his and was looking up at him expectantly.

That, he supposed, was what he got for hesitating.

Fitz had a precious half second to assure Luke they would talk later before he was twirling around the dance floor.

Placing his hand at Esmeralda's back, he guided her through the steps of a waltz. They pushed and threaded their way through the crowded parquet floor in a semblance of dancing.

"You will ask my daughter to dance before the evening is through, yes?"

Fitz saw the hope in Esmeralda's eyes, along with the calculation and eagerness for him to agree. Then the diva quickly masked her expression with a bland smile.

So much pride in this woman, so much bravado. Fitz understood both emotions and thought it was time for a frank discussion.

"Esmeralda," he began, keeping his voice at an octave only she could hear. "I am not interested in courting your daughter."

"I insist to know why."

He'd upset her. He heard it in her sharp gasp, saw it in the angry tilt of her lips. "Sophie and I don't suit."

It was really that simple.

The dark eyes that swept over him held a hawk-like sharpness. "You like her, do you not?"

"She is a lovely girl."

Esmeralda dropped all pretense of charm. The diva disappeared. In her place was the mother wishing to see her daughter settled.

It would not be with Fitz. The sooner Esmeralda understood that, the better for everyone involved.

Out of the corner of his eye, he caught a flash of lavender silk heading toward a partially secluded alcove just off the right side of the dance floor. Sophie wasn't alone. The young woman's escort seemed familiar, but Fitz couldn't place where he might have seen him before, if he had at all. Then he remembered the group of young men that had captured Sophie's attention earlier.

Even from this distance, the look of adoration in her expression was unmistakable. For his part, the man beside her had a look of quiet affection. There was an obvious attraction there, one that didn't look completely new.

Fitz said nothing to Esmeralda. His only wish was that the man would turn out to be far more worthy of Sophie than Dixon had been of Gigi. Putting the two young women out of his mind, he switched his attention to the diva.

"I would think," he began, choosing his words carefully, "that you would want more for your daughter than marriage to a man she hardly knows."

The anger was back in Esmeralda's eyes. "You dare to suppose you know what I want?"

Before responding, he took them through a series of complicated turns, glancing out onto the terrace. Sophie and her mystery man had moved into the shadows of a shallow alcove. They were still in view but appeared to be in deep conversation.

Not your concern.

"I have insulted you," he said to Esmeralda. "That was not my intent."

"You think Sophie isn't good enough for you because she is my daughter."

Though she spoke in a low hiss, the diva's outrage was evident in the strain tightening around her eyes and lips.

"Sophie is perfectly suitable." *For some other man.* "She is not—"

"Suitable enough for you."

Esmeralda looked unsure of herself, Fitz thought, realizing he'd never seen her in anything resembling a vulnerable state. Until now. "She is not the woman for me."

He did not expand on his reasons.

A brief battle of wills ensued, where Esmeralda scowled and Fitz held the woman's gaze without flinching.

"Why do you refuse to consider courting my daughter?"

She's not Gigi. "It's not possible."

"You are married?"

"I am not married."

"Engaged, then?"

"I am not engaged." He knew he was being tediously redundant in his answers and not revealing anything specific. With women like Esmeralda, it never hurt to be overly careful.

"Then you are free to court my daughter."

Nothing could mask the hope in Esmeralda's eyes. Fitz almost pitied her predicament, the helplessness she must feel. Her daughter was suffering the consequences of her actions.

Esmeralda would be appalled if she knew the direction of his thoughts. And so Fitz gave her yet another vaguely accurate response. "I am not free."

He would never be free.

The reasons were his own and not her concern.

Fitz could, however, give her a portion of the truth.

Executing a perfect spin, he commanded the diva's stare and said, "My heart belongs to another."

Chapter Fifteen

Gigi hadn't always preferred quiet evenings at home. In truth, she'd hated being left alone, especially when there was a party or ball or theater event going on somewhere in the city without her.

Much had changed in her life. *She* had changed.

She relished her solitude now. And took pride in her life of service, craving her evenings alone whenever Esmeralda and Sophie went out and the other servants were enjoying their own time off.

As she did most nights, Gigi took the opportunity to play the piano. Sheltered from the world that had once been so much a part of her, she could allow her emotions free rein. She could let her tumultuous feelings flow through her fingers.

Gigi had one goal this night. Forget her problems, if only for an hour. She tucked the invitation to luncheon at Elizabeth's house in the pocket of her dress and went to the music room.

Battling unwanted sensations, she sank onto the piano bench. The Steinway was a new addition to the town house. It was smaller by a few feet than the concert grand Gigi had played in Harvest House but no less wonderfully crafted.

The instrument was perfection itself. Gigi ran her fingers across the gleaming ivory keys, sighed heavily, and played a few melodic notes, first with her right hand, then with her left, then with both. The rich sounds had the ideal balance of harmonics. *Only the best for Esmeralda.*

Gigi shut her eyes and played a piece from memory. She let her heart lead the way, choosing an adagio. The tempo marking suited her mood. Unfortunately, after the first bar, the slow, melancholy melody gave her mind a chance to wander.

She forced out all other thought and let the music fill her head. Images of Fitz came seconds later. He'd kissed her, twice. She'd wanted more. She'd nearly begged for more.

Have I not changed at all?

The first press of their lips had been sweet, tentative, two people meeting after a long time apart. The second kiss had been deeper, more emotional and urgent. Gigi had instinctively reached for Fitz, her hands clutching his shoulders, the movement as natural as breathing.

For those brief moments, Gigi and Fitz were closer than they'd been in years, at least physically.

Forgotten memories reared up, twining through the present, calling to mind that long-ago kiss that had come on the tail of a heated argument. That one had taken Gigi a full week to get out of her mind. She predicted an equal challenge forgetting Fitz's recent kisses.

Even now, his lingering scent of sandalwood and shaving soap teased her senses, making her yearn to speak with him again, to heal their rift, to start anew, to—

Gigi opened her eyes.

Play a different song, she ordered herself, lifting her hands away from the keys.

Rolling her shoulders, Gigi repositioned her fingers on the keys and switched to a livelier piece composed by Chopin in C-sharp minor. The descending octaves soon gave way to a fiery allegro appassionato, and Gigi lost herself in the music.

She played the polonaise with her heart leading the way once again. Her fingers took over. The diversity in textures, dynamics, and varying moods made this her favorite piece by Chopin.

But then the music gave way to a tender melody, and Gigi's mind filled with too many thoughts.

This time, it wasn't Fitz that plagued her.

Gigi couldn't help but think that Sophie was heading down the dangerous road she'd gone down herself. The young woman was not rebellious by nature, but neither had Gigi been prior to meeting Nathanial.

A lot had changed for Sophie since she'd stood in her father's private theater and demanded he acknowledge her as his daughter. The scandal should have been tremendous. But matters hadn't played out that way. With Mrs. Burrows setting the tone, most of her friends had rallied around Sophie. The younger woman had seemed eager to please her new allies. She'd practiced for weeks for the luncheon.

Something had happened to alter Sophie's desire to earn her way into New York society. If only Gigi knew for certain the cause wasn't a man.

She had to trust her.

She's not alone in this world, Gigi reminded herself. *She has her half siblings and their spouses supporting her.* The thought didn't soothe away her worry. A liaison with the wrong person—*a man*—could destroy Sophie's chance at a secure future.

Still, Gigi could not be with the young woman every second of the day. At some point, her friend had to make her own decisions.

Gigi put Sophie out of her head, along with all the other distractions battling for her attention, and switched to another piece by Chopin. *Grande valse brillante* in E-flat major, Opus 18. The waltz had been specifically composed for a solo piano.

Gigi played the piece, banishing all thought and letting the music woo her. She pulled her focus in tight, filtered out all other sounds in the house. Gigi liked being alone. She liked having only herself to count on—and to blame when she made missteps.

Play, she ordered her nomadic mind.

And she did, absorbing the piece as if it were as fundamental as air. The opus was mathematically perfect in its timing, and she gave herself over to the meticulous tempo. This was when she felt most like herself, and why she preferred playing the piano alone, without an audience.

Or so she told herself.

But that wasn't completely true. She missed playing for her family and close friends.

She missed playing for Fitz.

Every time she thought of her life in Boston, he was there in the memory. How had she forgotten that? *When* had she forgotten? Sometime after Nathanial had shown up, that much she knew.

Focus on the music, Gigi.

Eyes closed, she played from memory and let the song consume her.

* * *

For a long moment, Fitz stood in the doorway, caught up in the sensations coursing through him. He didn't move, didn't blink, hardly dared to breathe.

Gigi was hurting. He could hear it in her music. She'd always played with passion, but this was different. Fitz actually felt Gigi's anguish in the haunting melody.

Each note dripped with unspeakable pain. Fitz hurt for her, yet also found himself admiring her. She'd suffered but hadn't let the tragic events break her. She was strong and beautiful, and he couldn't stop staring at her.

He swallowed a few times, wanting to ease her discomfort. He wanted to help her find healing and forgiveness. He wanted to stand by her side, always, no matter the challenges the world threw at them.

In that moment, he understood his mother's devotion to his father on a whole new level.

Maybe Fitz should tell Gigi how he felt. Maybe he should *show* her. The overwhelming urge to take her in his arms seemed to crash in on him from all sides.

He was across the room before he could talk himself out of the absurd notion.

"Gigi."

Her fingers stilled over the piano keys, and the music stopped. She turned her head. Blinked. Blinked again. Her gaze fell over him, down to his toes, her eyes pausing on the way back up, lingering on the bow tie at his neck. "You were at a party."

"A ball," he corrected, his voice a shade too thick. "At the Waldorf-Astoria."

She flinched at the name of the hotel where Dixon had abandoned her, but rallied quickly enough. "You hate balls."

"This one was especially trying. Esmeralda made a grand entrance and then insisted I dance with her."

Gigi laughed softly, the sound full of commiseration. "I can only imagine how uncomfortable that must have been. But . . . wait. If you saw Esmeralda at the ball, I presume you also crossed paths with Sophie?"

"I did." He thought of the young woman and her mystery companion escaping onto the terrace. "In a manner of speaking," he amended.

"So . . ." Gigi spun around on the bench, the move placing her back to the piano keys. "If you left Esmeralda and Sophie at the ball, that must mean you came to see—"

"You, Gigi. I came to see you. Irving let me in the house. The music drew me here." He shouldn't have come. With what he knew about the disease ravaging his father's mind, Fitz couldn't in good conscience pursue anything beyond friendship with Gigi. But he wanted more.

He wanted a lifetime.

Because he also wanted her in his arms, now, this instant, he kept his hands clenched by his sides and settled for drinking her in with his eyes. She wasn't wearing that ridiculous mobcap he'd grown to hate. Her hair was disheveled and messy, falling in scattered waves around her pink cheeks. The glorious red competed with the bleached strands. The contrast should look ridiculous, but Gigi looked . . . breathtaking. Maybe in fifty years he'd grow used to her beauty.

Maybe in a hundred.

"You're sad. Won't you tell me why?"

She started to shake her head, but Fitz sat beside her on the piano bench. He did his best to keep his distance, but couldn't stop himself from cupping her hand in his.

"I heard your obvious distress in the song. You always did put your emotions into your music."

For several seconds, she stared at their joined hands. "I forget how well you know me."

Not so well. Or he would know what to say to erase her melancholy. He couldn't find the words to get her talking. "I shouldn't be here."

"Probably not."

He released her hand. "I should leave."

"Probably."

He didn't budge from his position beside her on the bench. He couldn't leave her in this state.

Emotions swirled in his gut. Deep and confusing, wrapping around him in a way that sent a bone-deep urgency to protect her, always—to take care of her, always.

He took a hard breath.

She rose from the bench with his name on her lips. "Why are you here, Fitz?"

How many times had she asked him that question in the past week? How many times had he skirted around the truth? No more. Perhaps it was seeing Sophie Cappelletti, dressed in all her finery, standing too close to a man in the shadows.

Torn between alerting Esmeralda to the budding romance and keeping out of a matter that didn't concern him, Fitz had had a revelation. And so he'd come to Gigi. "I missed you."

Her eyebrows rose. "You . . . what?"

"I have missed you for some time. I was a rotten friend and an even worse suitor. I let you down long before Dixon appeared in your life."

She didn't argue the point. "What changed, Fitz? What made you withdraw from me, from us?"

He badly wanted to give her the truth. But he'd made a promise to his mother and couldn't—wouldn't—break his word. Not even to keep Gigi from thinking ill of him. "I can't tell you."

"Why not?"

"It's not my secret to share." He reached for her, thought better of it, and let his hand fall away. "I apologize for hurting you, Gigi. That was never my intention."

"But you did hurt me. More than you know. More than even I knew at the time."

She didn't need to say more, didn't need to remind him of his neglect. "I'm sorry."

The silence that followed his words seemed to last a very long time. Moving to the window overlooking the street, she gave a little shudder.

"Gigi, if we had remained friends . . ." He drew in a harsh breath, hating the hot sensation of grief building in his chest. "Would you have run off with Dixon?"

She glanced at him over her shoulder. There was something haunted in her eyes. "I've asked myself that question a hundred times."

"You ran away with him because of me," Fitz pressed, needing her to say the words, needing to hear the truth from her lips. "Admit it. I am to blame."

"No. You're not." She shook her head. "I made my own choices. The consequences of my actions are mine alone to bear. But if it's complete honesty you want from me—"

"It is."

"Part of the reason I let Nathanial court me was to push you to react with something more than smug superiority. I wanted you to treat me as a woman, Fitz, not as one of your business deals."

How had he missed that? Why had he been so obtuse? Because he'd been consumed with his father's deteriorating health.

No excuse.

She showed her back to him again, pressed her head to the windowpane, then gripped the wood casing with trembling fingers. "Though I would never have admitted this at the time, and I'm not proud doing so now, I wanted you to regret losing me to another man."

"You can't know how true you hit your mark."

His voice was low and fierce, and he was by her side in three long, furious strides. His anger was directed at himself, not Gigi. Never Gigi. Even when he'd confronted her about her growing attachment to Nathanial, Fitz had been frustrated with his own inability to make his feelings clear.

By then, he'd known he had lost her. He'd accepted that she could never be his. But he hadn't been able to stand by and watch her destroy her future for a fortune hunter.

"Gigi." He took her shoulders and gently turned her around to face him.

Tears swam into her eyes, shimmered beautifully against the deep blue of her irises. "I have to know the truth, Fitz. Did you abandon our friendship because you saw a flaw in my character, something that made you think less of me?"

"No."

He opened his mouth to expand on that, but she was already talking again. "Then what was it? What is this secret you supposedly can't tell me?"

"I've told you all I can." He tugged her to him. With her pressed close, he felt each of her heartbeats with a raw intensity.

She said something low and unintelligible, the words muffled against his chest. He didn't need to hear the words to know she was asking him to reveal the one thing he had to bear alone.

"If I could share my burden with anyone, it would be you." He waited for her to look at him, then pressed his forehead to hers.

Sheltered in the moment, cocooned from the past and the impossibility of the future, Fitz did the one thing he knew he shouldn't. He pressed his lips gently to hers.

This kiss was like none they'd shared before. It was tender and poignant, full of promises neither would be able to keep. Gigi's heart didn't belong to him, and he couldn't give his to her.

His breath came short and thick. She was sweet, unbearably sweet, soft, and warm—and not for him.

A clock chimed from somewhere in the house, announcing the hour. Midnight. They were fully into the next day. A new day.

A new beginning, a new—

He tore his lips away and stepped back. Nothing but air stood between him and Gigi. And a whole lot of turbulent history.

The innocence that had called to him was still in her. Dixon had only stolen her dignity—and her good name. Fitz, too, had played his part in her disgrace. The least he could do was help her find her way home.

Setting his jaw, Fitz straightened his vest. "I will see you in the morning at nine o'clock."

"What . . . what happens at nine?"

"I'm escorting you to church." Realizing how that sounded, he amended, "If you'll let me."

"I don't attend church anymore. I haven't for a very long time."

Fitz couldn't have been more surprised had Gigi told him she was joining the circus. He struggled to reconcile the impossible with reality. "But you adore going to church. You find great joy in lifting up your voice in praise."

It was the one thing they'd had in common. Even when they'd been at odds, hardly speaking to one another, they'd shared the pleasure that came from worshipping the Lord in song.

When he reminded her of this, she shook her head. "No matter what church, no matter where, I can't seem to make myself walk up the front steps and enter the sanctuary."

"How long has it been since you tried?"

Her gaze chased around the room, landing everywhere but on him. "Months."

Fitz braced against the burning ache in his chest. Dixon had stolen so much from her, this probably the worst of all.

"I can't help thinking my shame is too great to be forgiven." Her bent posture made her look isolated and defenseless.

"No sin is too great to be forgiven."

His words sounded as clichéd as he feared they would. But this was too important for Fitz to take the time to develop a proper argument. "Gigi, the Lord's mercy is endless and always available, like waves breaking on the shore."

"You think it's easy for me? I hate being separated from the Father." She wrapped her arms tightly around her. "I feel so unworthy and inadequate. I have no idea how to ask Him for forgiveness."

She sounded defeated.

Fitz didn't know how to convince her of the Truth. He was out of his element and didn't read the Bible regularly enough to combat a crisis in faith this profound.

That didn't mean he was willing to give up on Gigi. She would never be free of the past if she didn't learn how to ask for God's forgiveness.

"Come to church with me." Fitz would get her inside the building and leave the rest to the Lord. "Please. If you feel uncomfortable, we'll leave."

The longing in her gaze gave him hope. "I will agree on one condition."

"Name it, anything."

"We have to attend a church in Brooklyn."

"Why Brooklyn?"

"It's the only place I'm sure no one will recognize me, or you, or know of our past connection."

"Then Brooklyn it is."

She smiled.

That smile, it reached inside his heart and squeezed. Fitz left the room with the image of Gigi branded in his memory.

Chapter Sixteen

Once outside Esmeralda's town house, Fitz moved quickly. The urgency that raced through him sounded in the hard strike of his heels. He crossed the street, slipped into the shadows, and waited for Mr. Offutt to show his face.

He didn't have long to wait.

The investigator joined him in the darkness seconds later. As he did at each of their meetings, Offutt asked, "You want me to keep following her?"

This time, Fitz gave a different answer. "No."

He'd made the decision days ago, but his change of heart was solidified the moment he'd walked into the music room and heard Gigi playing the piano. "I'm no longer in need of your services, Mr. Offutt."

There was enough light from the streetlamp for Fitz to see the other man's eyebrows lift. "You sure about this?"

"Completely." Fitz reached inside his coat, pulled out his wallet, and extracted a handful of bills. "That should settle our account."

The investigator moved closer to the light and began counting the money.

"It's all there."

Head lowered, the other man continued filing through the bills, his mouth moving as he counted. "So it is. And then some."

"A bonus for your diligence." And the man's silence.

Folding over the stack of bills, Offutt stuffed the wad in his jacket. "You want to know what I learned about her little trip to Herald Square?"

If Fitz and Gigi had any hope of becoming friends, he must let her tell him the truth in her own time.

Like you told her yours?

The situations were vastly different. "Thank you, no. I don't want to hear what you discovered."

This time, the investigator didn't argue. "Suit yourself."

"I'll bid you good night."

"It's been a pleasure working for you."

Fitz watched the man slink away, glad he'd cut him loose. He should have done so before now. Fitz didn't need to know what the investigator had uncovered about Gigi or her business in Herald Square. He already had a good idea what had led her to that area of the city.

What he didn't know was why.

She would tell him eventually. Fitz was sure of it.

He was definitely, almost, sure of it.

* * *

The moment Fitz left Esmeralda's town house, Gigi knew she would tell him about her great-grandmother's pearls when next they met. He deserved to know they weren't in her possession anymore. If he was beginning to care for her again, even if only as a friend, he must know how low she'd sunk.

Gigi owed him that much. Even if it meant losing him, she wanted nothing but honesty between them. And maybe if she opened up to him, he would open up to her. Friends shared confidences, didn't they? They turned to one another in times of need.

Is that what you really want from Fitz, friendship?

An image of his handsome, decent face played in her mind. Only moments ago, he'd held her in his arms as though his life depended upon it and had kissed her as though his world would end if he didn't.

Gigi had held on to him with just as much desperation. She could lose him if she told him the truth. She could lose him if she didn't.

She knew that now, accepted it.

Once Fitz knew about the pearls, about *everything*, he would never look at Gigi the same way. He would never kiss her, passionately or otherwise. He would find someone else to love, someone pure and innocent. He would be happy, and that was enough for Gigi.

Her heart bled for what might have been had she let her infatuation with Nathanial run its course and fade away with time.

Too late. The thought swept through her mind. *Too, too late.*

The hardest part about being a Christian, Gigi reflected, was the call for accepting blame where blame was due. If she hoped to achieve atonement, she must face up to what she'd done, not only in her own mind, but to her loved ones.

She would start with Fitz, tomorrow. It would not be easy. She would write out her confession tonight and practice the speech until she had the words just right in her mind.

Lips pressed tightly together, she dragged a fingertip across the piano keys with only the barest whisper of a touch, making no sound as she moved along the octaves, lowest to highest. The feel of the cool ivory beneath her skin was the final push she needed to leave the music room and get to work on her confession.

Almost the same instant she entered the hallway, as if on cue, she heard a muffled noise coming from the kitchen, then a crash, then a muttered curse that was decidedly female. She recognized the voice.

Why was Sophie entering the house through the back door? And why was she arriving home alone when she'd left the house with Esmeralda?

Gigi had a bad feeling. She went into the kitchen.

"Sophie?"

The young woman spun around, hand to her heart, eyes wide and a little spooked. "Oh, Gigi. It's only you. I thought for a minute you were my mother."

"Where is she?"

A mutinous expression spread across the young woman's face.

"I left her at the ball." A soft snort accompanied the statement. "Mama may not be an acknowledged member of society, but they seem to enjoy her company well enough."

Which told Gigi very little, and yet so very much. Members of New York society enjoyed having famous people on their guest lists. It was considered quite a coup to have several actors, singers, and artists in attendance at their parties, so long as they knew their place. Despite the recent scandal connecting Esmeralda to Warren Griffin, the diva was considered quite a prize for any hostess. She always brought a certain flair to an event. No wonder Sophie looked so miserable. She loved her mother but not the notoriety that came with her.

That still didn't explain why Sophie was sneaking in the house. "Was there a reason you entered through the back door instead of the front?"

The young woman looked helplessly around and up to the ceiling, as if inspiration would come from the room itself. "Not especially."

"You're shivering."

"It's cold outside."

Gigi took her friend's arm and guided her up the back stairwell. Once they were in her room, she tugged her to a chair by the fire, sat her down, and pulled off her sodden boots while Sophie divested herself of her outer garments.

A series of sighs leaked from the woman's mouth.

Thinking she was cold, Gigi quickly worked off the wet silk stockings.

"Sophie, you are soaking wet."

"I sort of . . . fell in a pond." Another sigh slipped from the woman's lips, softer than the others.

Now that they were in the light, Gigi realized it wasn't misery she saw on Sophie's face. It was happiness. The woman was happy. And in love.

Gigi's heart plummeted to her toes. "How does one *sort of* fall into a pond?"

"I wasn't watching where I was going." She giggled, then covered her mouth with her hand. "It was an accident, of course. My fault entirely. Oh, Gigi, he was so adorably remorseful that he hadn't moved quickly enough to save me from a proper dunking."

"He?"

"Robert Dain, *Doctor* Robert Dain. He recently arrived from England."

Nathanial had claimed to be from England. "What part of England?"

"He didn't say. Or maybe he did and I forgot." She shut her eyes and pressed a hand to her forehead. The move rivaled any of Esmeralda's emotional moments on the stage. "He has the most gorgeous face and a wonderful smile."

Gigi helped the young woman stand, then stripped off the rest of the wet garments. Sophie offered very little assistance, seemingly incapable of doing much else besides babbling about the brilliant young doctor with gray eyes and black hair and something about a medical clinic in the Bowery.

The Bowery? That was the most dangerous part of New York, known for its dilapidated rooming houses, riotous saloons, and bawdy theaters.

For several heartbeats, Gigi could do nothing but blink at the woman she'd come to consider a friend. She recalled a recent conversation they'd shared, when Sophie had been so certain she would find love. To discover that she had already met a man and was smitten came as a shock. It was very difficult for Gigi to keep her thoughts to herself. She wanted—needed—to warn her friend of the dangerous road she was heading down.

Gigi had attempted to guide her previous employer, Elizabeth, from making a similar mistake and had been thoroughly ignored. Yet that had ended well, and now Elizabeth was happily married to a man of impeccable character.

But Gigi couldn't be sure things would progress the same way for Sophie. She broached the subject with great care. "Have you ever been to the Bowery?"

"Robert said I wasn't to go there, ever."

"I suppose that's something," Gigi muttered, wrapping Sophie in a dressing gown and then planting her in the chair by the fire again.

"He's quite the philanthropist. He doesn't just support the needy with his wallet but with his mind and hands. I would so like to see where he works."

"Tread carefully, Sophie."

Sophie's eyes narrowed. "You don't approve of my new friend."

"I don't know your new friend, nor is it my place to approve or disapprove."

"Robert is a good man."

It was as if she'd been transported back in time to a year ago and the conversation she'd had with Fitz, when Gigi had claimed the same of Nathanial. "You don't know that, Sophie. You can't. You just met him this evening."

"I have known him for three days." The young woman gave her a distracted, starry-eyed look. "I know he would never hurt me."

Gigi thought she might be sick. She'd said those very same words to Fitz about Nathanial. *I know he would never hurt me.*

"Sophie, I urge you to take matters slowly. Get to know this young man. Take the time to make sure he is exactly who he appears to be."

"I refuse to believe Robert is anything but a good and true man."

No, Gigi thought, this couldn't be happening. To hear Sophie repeat, nearly verbatim, the words Gigi had used to defend Nathanial was the worst sort of blow. "May I offer a piece of advice?"

Sophie gave her a fond smile. "Can I stop you?"

"I would hate to see you fooled by a handsome face and pretty words."

"You mean fooled like you were?"

Gigi nodded. "Falling in love with the wrong man makes a woman go small and quiet."

"But, Gigi, falling in love with the right man makes her a better woman all around."

"I'm not suggesting you walk away from Robert Dain." Although Gigi would be relieved if the young woman would do just that. "I am merely urging you to show a bit of caution."

For several moments, Sophie stared at the fire. Her gaze was distant. "I can think of at least two examples to prove my point over yours."

Beyond her own experience, Gigi could think of at least one to prove hers—Sophie's mother. Though Esmeralda hadn't been defeated because of her affair with a married man, having a child out of wedlock could not have been easy for the young opera singer hoping to become a star.

Before Gigi could say as much, Sophie spoke again. "Elizabeth hasn't lost herself in her marriage, quite the opposite. Loving my half brother has enriched her life. The same is true of Penny. Her union with Simon has given her the sort of confidence I never thought possible. She had a terrible stammer as a child, did you know that?"

"I did not."

"It's true. Simon has been the best thing to ever happen to her."

"Elizabeth and Penny are exceptions."

"Oh, I just thought of another one. Caroline Montgomery."

Gigi acknowledged this with a half smile. Caroline and Jackson were, indeed, very happy. "For the rest of us, love is nothing but an invitation to pain."

"Oh, Gigi." Sophie gained her feet and placed her hands on her shoulders. "Don't let him turn you bitter."

Tears pooled in Gigi's eyes. "I'm worried about you, Sophie."

"I will try to say this as kindly as I can." Sophie dropped her hands from Gigi's shoulders. "Just because you made a bad choice doesn't mean that I will."

She wasn't listening. As Gigi had ignored Fitz's warnings, Sophie was ignoring hers. "Regret is a terrible bedfellow."

Sophie returned to her seat by the fire. Her hands reached for each other, twisted in her lap. "You have always been spot-on with your advice. This time, you are wrong."

The conversation was proving beyond frustrating. Was this how Fitz had felt speaking with her? Had Gigi been this stubborn?

No, she'd been more so.

"Life is all about choices, Sophie. One bad decision is all it will take to lead you down a path from which you cannot return."

"I'm sorry a man hurt you, Gigi. Truly I am. But you have to trust me when I say I know what I'm doing."

Gigi had claimed the same. She opened her mouth to say as much, but Sophie cut her off with a slash of her hand in the air.

"I wish to be alone now. You may go."

She'd been dismissed. Sophie would not listen to reason, at least not tonight. Gigi did the only thing she could under the circumstances. She left the young woman alone with her thoughts.

* * *

Fitz spotted Gigi waiting for him on the street corner a block away from Esmeralda's town house. She'd pulled the hood of her cloak down to cover her face. She probably thought she was in disguise. He swallowed a smile. Gigi could never hide from him.

After descending from the carriage, he approached her with confident strides. The closer he came to her, the more he could feel her nerves.

Hand outstretched, he offered her a smile, hoping to settle her agitation. "Good morning, Gigi."

"Hello, Fitz." She lifted her chin, the move sending the cloak's hood to the back of her head. The delicate sculpted bones of her cheeks and the extraordinary wealth of blue that were her eyes took his breath away.

He became oblivious to all else but her. A good way to start the day, he decided.

He took her hand and looped it through his arm. "I asked at the front desk for church suggestions in Brooklyn. I was pointed to the Brooklyn Tabernacle on Clinton Avenue and Greene Street."

"I've heard of it. The music is supposed to be world-class."

"Then the Brooklyn Tabernacle it is."

She smiled then, and suddenly everything was right in Fitz's world. *You've got it bad, my good man.*

In that moment, as he helped Gigi into the carriage, he understood the desire to run away from the world. Fitz wanted to run. He wanted to escape a future imprisoned in his own mind. He wanted a life where he could choose a wife, knowing she wouldn't be trapped with an invalid.

Heart bleak, he rapped on the roof of the carriage. They set off with a hard jerk. The move nearly sent Gigi tumbling into his lap from the seat across. He reached out to her, but she was already righting herself on her own.

So independent, he thought. Small wonder, that. She'd been taking care of herself for nearly a year.

With a flick of her wrist, she shoved the hood off her head. "Now that we're sufficiently alone, I want to tell you about my time with Nathanial and what I had to do to survive after he left."

A weight settled in Fitz's gut. He didn't want to hear the story. He wanted, if only for this one day, to enjoy Gigi's company without the past standing between them. "You can tell me after Sunday service."

She flexed her fingers in her lap, curled them into two tight fists. "I'd rather not wait that long."

"You don't owe me any explanations."

"Actually, I do. But if you don't care to hear them now . . ." She rolled her shoulders, brought her hands together and braided her fingers through one another. "Sophie has met a man."

Since he'd been a witness to this, Fitz decided to skip any pretense of not knowing where this was going. "You think this is a bad thing."

"I don't know." She shook her head. "Maybe. She's over the moon for him. I tried to warn her to be careful. She wouldn't listen to me."

How well Fitz understood the helplessness he heard in Gigi's voice. "I trust you didn't let it go at that."

He hadn't.

"She doesn't know the first thing about the man. She would hear none of my warnings. I was extremely adamant, and it was like speaking to a blank sheet of paper for all the attention she gave me." Gigi glanced up, her eyes full of emotion. "It was all so very frustrating."

"I imagine it was."

"Yes." She gave him an uneasy glance. "I suppose you know exactly what I mean."

He laid a hand over hers and said nothing. There was nothing to say. They'd already made their apologies.

Gigi started to speak, then stopped. She moved to sit beside him on his side of the carriage. "Will you let me tell you about Nathanial now?"

"If you must."

"I'm afraid I must."

The gentle rocking of the carriage was at odds with the tension that hung between them.

Fitz could see the beating of Gigi's pulse on her neck. Her face was sheet white, the muscles in her jaw tight. Her struggle to catch her breath made his heart trip. He wanted to make this easy for her. The extent of that longing humbled him.

He gently lifted her chin with his fingertip, holding it there until she looked him directly in the eyes. He ran his gaze over her face, taking careful inventory of the tiny lines of anxiety fanning out from her eyes and mouth.

A bone-deep urgency to protect this woman overwhelmed all other thought.

"What did Dixon do to you, Gigi?" Fitz was surprised by the rage in his voice. "How did he hurt you?"

She lowered her head. "I don't think I can tell you after all."

He could see she would rather keep her secret safely hidden. How well he knew the need to conceal bits of himself, to suffer through the tormenting pain of carrying his burdens alone. But if Fitz didn't encourage Gigi to unburden herself with him, would she turn to someone else? Was there anyone else? In whom could she confide?

A frown tugged at his brow as he contemplated how alone Gigi was in the world.

She didn't have family or friends. She didn't even have the benefit of going through life with her own name. Her only support was the woman who employed her. And him.

Gigi had him.

Fitz badly wanted to give her his unwavering support, his unconditional acceptance. The trick would be convincing her to let him.

She sat there, so strong and brave, her spine perfectly erect. Regardless of her stiff posture, Fitz was struck by the graceful way she entwined her fingers together in her lap. There was nothing hard about this woman, nothing coarse or brazen. Despite all that had happened to her, she still personified the elegance that had been bred in her from birth.

"Tell me what happened with Dixon."

Slowly, she looked back up. "You'll think differently of me once I do."

"You'll get no judgment from me, no condemnation."

"I don't know quite where to start." Her voice was very quiet. "I fell for him almost immediately." She smiled ruefully. "I was dazzled. He said all the right things to turn my head. I believed I was special. I began meeting him secretly within days of our initial meeting."

With slow, deliberate movements, Fitz sat back. "You let him court you in private that soon?"

"He was very persistent, very convincing with his attentions. I was blinded to his faults and allowed him certain . . . liberties from the very beginning of our acquaintance."

Fitz had never been prone to violence, but he felt his temper rise with vicious force. If Dixon were to show up now, Fitz would likely beat the man to a pulp.

"Go on," he urged.

There was another moment of hesitation before she continued. "When Nathanial asked me to run away with him, I thought he meant to marry me. He convinced me that once we married, my father would be forced to accept him."

He tried not to show his reaction, but with each new piece of evidence pointing to the man's despicable lies, anger stormed through Fitz.

She carried on, explaining in a halting tone how she'd managed to sneak out of Harvest House. "I took the pearls from the safe in my father's study."

"He told you the combination?"

"I figured it out. My father was never very creative. He chose my mother's birthday. It took me less than five minutes to guess the sequence of numbers." She sighed. "That wasn't my finest hour, I know.

The only thing I can say in my defense is that I had every intention of returning them."

Questions skittered in Fitz's mind, one taking priority over all others. If Gigi intended to return the valuable heirloom, why hadn't she done so by now?

Fitz suspected he knew the answer. Her various side jobs at the theater were starting to make sense.

"Nathanial wanted me to look my very best on my wedding day."

"Was it his idea you take the necklace?"

"No, it was . . ." Her face scrunched into a frown. "I always *thought* it was my idea. But now . . ."

She fell silent, her eyebrows pinched together in confusion.

"But now?" he prompted.

"I'm not so sure." The look on her face could only be described as stricken. "Nathanial often made a point of complimenting my jewelry. He said I had impeccable taste and frequently mentioned how beautifully I coordinated my accessories with my gowns."

Fitz's hands balled into fists. Dixon must be made to answer for his treachery. Perhaps Fitz had been hasty in releasing the private investigator. Unlike his predecessor, Mr. Offutt had been thorough, efficient, and, most of all, circumspect. He could locate the missing fortune hunter with the least amount of difficulty and fuss.

Something worth considering, but first, Fitz needed more information. "Did Dixon know about your great-grandmother's pearls?"

"I must have told him about them. I'm sure I did, when we discussed our wedding. I mentioned that every Wentworth woman wore them. How could I have been so foolish?"

Fitz recognized the shame in her quiet tone and what it boded. A part of his brain screamed, *Tell her to stop her tale.* But the rest of his mind was a black haze of fury. This time, at himself, for not trying harder to rescue Gigi from Dixon's clutches. "You were in love."

Her gaze connected with a spot at her feet. "And now I am a fallen woman. You said so yourself."

Fitz's heart thumped like the hammer on a clock. There was a depth of despair in Gigi's countenance that he recognized. This was a woman who'd lost a part of herself, but only because she'd trusted the wrong man. "You were the target of a master manipulator."

Leaning her head back, Gigi closed her eyes. "At least I didn't tell him I took the pearls."

"Why didn't you?"

A silent sigh lifted her shoulders, set them back again. "I'd like to say it was wisdom, but I wanted to surprise him on our wedding day, by looking my very best, just as he wanted. The pearls would have been the perfect adornment."

"I'm sure you were beautiful," Fitz said in a low tone, so low that he wasn't sure she heard him.

"Oh, Fitz." His name came out on a choked sob. "The part of me raised by godly, Christian parents should have known not to run away with Nathanial. I should have *known* not to believe his lies."

"You were dazzled, Gigi. Dixon preyed on your innocence."

"And I let him." She dropped her gaze. Then, as if determined to conquer her embarrassment, she boldly lifted her chin. Grief shone in her eyes.

The need to soothe away her pain had Fitz reaching for her. She shifted to her left and his hand met empty air.

"I should have never taken the necklace. But I wanted so badly to wear it on my wedding day, just as every Wentworth woman before me." She smoothed a shaking hand over her hair. "I know that's no excuse, but it's the truth."

The eyes that swung up to meet his were gray in the dim morning light, the color of fog under a full moon. How bitterly alone she looked.

Fitz's clamped jaw began to ache. He desperately wanted to pull her into his arms and tell her he would make everything right. But he couldn't do that without knowing all the facts. There was one large piece of the puzzle still missing.

"Where are the pearls now?"

She went still for a heartbeat. Her glassy-eyed gaze shifted around the interior of the carriage, landing on several spots in no particular order. "I thought this would be easier. I told myself I wanted only truth between us."

"Gigi, look at me."

He waited for her to comply. It took her a moment, but she finally lifted her head and stared into his face.

His eyes locked with hers, and Fitz asked the question again, softer this time, without an ounce of judgment in his voice. "Where are the pearls?"

A shudder moved through her. "When Nathanial never showed up at the church, I returned to the hotel room, thinking something terrible must have happened. I discovered all his belongings were missing, and he hadn't even bothered leaving a note, not one word of explanation."

A burning throb knotted in Fitz's throat.

"He'd taken all my money and left a large hotel bill to settle. The only thing of value I still had in my possession was the pearl necklace. The hotel manager vowed to turn me over to the police if I didn't pay."

Fitz had threatened the same and now understood why she'd gone a little wild at the warning. "You pawned the necklace to avoid going to jail."

"Yes. But the money I got for it wasn't enough to cover the bill."

That had to have been some hotel bill, Fitz thought.

"I took a job as a maid there to pay off the rest."

The weary resignation in her voice was Fitz's undoing.

He'd heard enough.

He drew her into his arms and whispered soothingly in her ear. "You aren't alone," he said over and over until she nodded and then slowly pulled away.

"Now you know my secrets, all of them." She met his gaze, the echo of defeat trembling on her lips. "And the full extent of my shame."

Cupping her face in his hands, Fitz brushed his mouth briefly across the slope of her cheek. "You were lied to and betrayed in the worst way possible. That doesn't make you dishonorable—it makes you incredibly human and brave."

"I'm not brave."

He brought her hands to his lips, kissed both sets of knuckles. "You are the bravest person I know."

"I'm not. I don't have the courage to put the past behind me, not completely. I don't think I will ever find it in my heart to forgive Nathanial."

"You don't need to forgive Nathanial. Gigi, you need to forgive yourself."

She made a soft sound of protest in her throat and tried to pull her hands away. He wouldn't let her.

"Forgive yourself, Gigi. Then go home and ask for forgiveness from your family."

Dismissing his suggestion with a sniff, she said, "I can't go home. Not without the pearls."

Fitz was no theologian, but he read the Bible. He was pretty sure forgiveness wasn't that simple, or that complicated. The cost was a contrite heart, not a pearl necklace.

"The pawnshop still has them," she said. "We made an arrangement so I would have a chance to reclaim them. But I only have three weeks to come up with the remaining balance, or the owner will sell them to another."

If buying back the pearls was all that prevented Gigi from going home, then, finally, Fitz could make one of her problems go away. "I'll give you the money."

She was shaking her head before he'd finished speaking. "No."

"Gigi, let me do this for you. There's no shame in accepting help from a friend."

Everything about her tensed at his words—her posture, her expression. "I have gotten myself into this predicament. I must be the one to get myself out. I nearly have the money I need."

"That's good. Really good." He set his hand on her shoulder lightly, carefully, because there was something in her response that didn't sit well with him. The word *nearly*. "How short are you?"

Instead of answering the question directly, she lowered her gaze and said, "I would have been able to purchase them before now if the pawnbroker hadn't charged additional interest at the last minute."

Fitz took his hand from her shoulder. "What do you mean, *additional* interest?"

Mouth grim, she told him about her recent visit to the pawnshop. The pawnbroker had taken advantage of her as surely as Nathanial had. "The man is a crook."

"You are not wrong."

The resignation in Gigi's tone spoke of the battles she'd had to fight on her own. Well, she wasn't alone anymore. "How much more is he asking?"

"Fifty dollars."

The carriage drew to a stop. As if welcoming a chance to escape, she reached for the door handle. He stopped her movement with a touch to her hand. "How short are you?"

"I have half."

Twenty-five dollars. Fitz spent more than that on his weekly supply of handkerchiefs. A ridiculously small sum to a man with his wealth. But to a lady's maid who probably didn't earn that much money in a month, the amount might as well be millions.

Fitz hadn't truly considered what Gigi's day-to-day existence was like. He was humbled by the woman she'd become. So strong, so brave, never letting circumstances break her. Well, her days of struggle were over. Fitz couldn't be with her, but he could help her.

He *would* help her. "We'll go to the pawnshop after service and redeem the pearls. You can pay me back once you have the money."

"While I appreciate the sentiment behind your offer, I cannot allow you to rescue me, Fitz. My way is the only way."

"The only way for . . . what?"

"The only way for me to"—she drew her bottom lip between her teeth, looked everywhere but at him—"atone for my sins."

In one fluid motion, Gigi twisted the door handle and alighted from the carriage.

That, Fitz supposed, was the end of their conversation.

For now.

Chapter Seventeen

Gigi was grateful she'd chosen a seat next to the center aisle, in the very last pew in the back of the church. If at any moment the service became too much, she could leave without having to disturb the other churchgoers, including Fitz.

He stood next to her, holding a hymnal open. Looking at her without quite looking at her, he angled the book until she could see the page. As if on cue, the first strains of organ music wafted through the sanctuary.

Although Fitz concentrated on the book, Gigi could feel his attention on her. She couldn't look at him. His behavior in the carriage had left her reeling. Instead of judging her, he'd offered tremendous sympathy and reassurance, once again proving he was a good and decent man. Gigi should be dancing for joy.

She felt nothing but regret.

How could she ever measure up to a man like Fitz? He was full of integrity and honor, while she was a fallen woman. His words, and something she must never let herself forget.

Unable to resist, she shot a covert glance in his direction. Her heart began drumming a wild, chaotic beat. Was she . . .

Could she be . . .

Was she *in love* with Fitz? She'd always thought love required a certain amount of pain. What she felt for Fitz was easy, full of peace, and yet more powerful than anything she'd ever experienced.

She closed her eyes and breathed him in. He smelled of soap and sandalwood and happier times. Gigi took another breath, leaned closer to the man, then promptly stood straight again.

The initial strains of a popular hymn filled the church. *Sing,* she told herself. *Don't think. Sing.*

As she launched into the hymn, peace enveloped her. How she'd missed singing in church. The melody rolled off Fitz's tongue, too, but in a clear, perfectly pitched baritone. Gigi had forgotten what a good singer he was, or had she never known? What else hadn't she learned about the man at her side? In this moment, she wished to know everything.

Their voices joined in flawless harmony, as though they'd been singing together all their lives. Which, in retrospect, she realized they had. Against her best efforts to stay focused on the song, Gigi's thoughts sped toward the future. She imagined a life with Fitz, attending church together, relaxing at home by the fire, teaching their children their favorite hymns.

They would . . . they would . . .

She shook away the image. *You are a fallen woman.*

Out of the corner of her eye, she glanced at him, only to discover he was watching her in the same veiled manner. Something quite pleasant passed between them, a feeling that instilled utter contentment. Perhaps attending church was exactly what she'd needed.

The singing came to an end, and Gigi sat next to Fitz while he returned the hymnal to the slot on the pew in front of them. It took considerable willpower not to lean into him. She could feel his heat. Capability all but radiated off of him.

Now that the music portion of the service was over, her nerves returned. She felt like the ultimate imposter. What right did she have stepping inside a church, sitting beside godly men and women as if she deserved to be in the same building with them?

She shifted uncomfortably in her seat.

Hand on her knee, Fitz whispered, "Relax, Gigi."

"I don't belong here."

"This is God's House." He took her hand, strength and assurance in his grip, and Gigi thought she might cry at the tenderness she saw in his eyes. "Everyone belongs here."

Why did Fitz have to be so good?

Why did he have to behave in a way that proved every one of her preconceived notions wrong, not only the ones she'd had about him, but the ones she had about herself?

Pretty, popular Gigi was a fraud. Plain, dedicated Sally was a pretender. *Who am I, Lord?*

She didn't know anymore. She'd never really known, not any better than she'd thought she'd known Fitz. She'd gone through her days as a silly, self-indulgent heiress, living in the moment, never thinking about anyone but herself. That lack in her character had been vulnerable to Nathanial.

The preacher took his place behind the pulpit with steady strides. He looked like no man of God Gigi had ever met.

Big and muscular, he resembled a blacksmith or perhaps a factory worker rather than a preacher of the Word. Tall, broad through the shoulders and chest, he had a penetrating stare, sandy-brown hair, and a piercing presence that put Gigi ill at ease. Fire and brimstone came to mind.

She nearly left the church.

But then the man swept a wide, welcoming smile over the assembled group, and she felt a little less out of place, a little less tense. *This is God's House,* Fitz had said. *Everyone belongs.*

The preacher greeted the congregation with a few words of welcome, then started with prayer, asking the Lord to open the hearts and minds of the people in attendance. "Heavenly Father, You are a good and gracious God. I thank You for each of Your children in attendance here today. I am but Your humble vessel. I pray You speak Your Word through me."

His voice was as rough as gravel, yet also soothing. Gigi closed her eyes and felt the corners of her mouth lift. Somehow she'd known he would speak in a deep, resonating tone.

"Some here may believe they don't belong in Your House."

Gigi cracked open an eye.

"I pray You give those individuals peace and the knowledge that they are loved and accepted as Your beloved children."

Gigi swallowed back the well of emotion rising in her throat. How could this preacher know what was in her heart? She looked covertly around, wondering if others shared her overwhelming sense of inadequacy and shame.

"I ask this in Your Son's name, Amen."

The preacher waited a beat, then looked out over the congregation. "God loves the lost."

Unable to hold back a gasp of surprise, Gigi shifted in her seat. Fitz gave her hand a reassuring squeeze.

"I am reminded of the parable of the Lost Sheep." The preacher paused again, caught several eyes near the front of the church, then added, "And the Prodigal Son."

Gigi shifted in her seat again, glanced down at her lap, back up again. Out of the corner of her eye, she saw Fitz sit up straighter as well, his lips pressed tightly together. She had no idea what struck him in the sermon, only that he was listening intently now. Would Gigi ever solve the mystery that was so much a part of the man?

"Both parables carry the themes of loss, searching, and rejoicing. The image of our Lord celebrating the recovery of just one lost sinner speaks of the fundamental nature of our loving God."

Though his smile remained in place, the preacher's expression turned serious. "Through the years, I have witnessed many fall away from the Lord, never to return. While others, like the Prodigal Son, come home after a season of rebellion with contrition in their hearts."

He paused, drew in a slow breath, waited for the congregation to lean in.

"What turns one heart hard and another full of regret? What makes one sinner repent, while another wallows in shame and self-pity?"

Gigi's blood roared in her veins. Was he about to give her the formula for redemption?

Looking down, he opened his Bible and read from the fifteenth chapter of Luke. "'What man of you, having an hundred sheep, if he lose one of them, doth not leave the ninety and nine in the wilderness, and go after that which is lost, until he find it? And when he hath found it, he layeth it on his shoulders, rejoicing.'"

He looked up, spoke of repentance, then read the story of the Prodigal Son. "I point you to the son's contrite heart. That was all it took for his father to forgive him. Many of us, like the older son in this story, falsely believe forgiveness must be earned."

Gigi sighed. A lovely sentiment, but not all earthly fathers were like the one in the Bible. Not all forgave so easily. Not all forgave without some token to prove change had occurred.

"The story of the Prodigal Son teaches us that no sin is too great, no transgression too terrible, for the Lord to forgive."

Gigi remained unconvinced.

"We all fall short. Making mistakes is part of living. God's love is stronger than our shame. We only have to ask for forgiveness, and then receive it."

Gigi wanted to believe she could be forgiven. She wanted to believe her earthly father was waiting for her return.

But Harcourt Wentworth had made his position clear. She was convinced now more than ever that if she had any chance of earning her father's forgiveness, she must show up with the pearls.

"Do not allow your past sins to define your future."

Gigi swallowed against the burning sensation in her throat. The interior of the church seemed to close in on her. Heat radiated from deep within her soul.

She needed fresh air. She needed it now, this very minute. "I have to get out of here."

Without a moment of hesitation, Fitz stood, reached for her hand. "We'll leave at once."

Gigi thought her heart couldn't get any gloomier, but Fitz's instant support nearly broke her. As they made their way out of the building, the preacher's voice lifted, and Gigi's feet ground to a halt. "If forgiveness has to be earned, then it isn't forgiveness at all."

Bitterness filled her, followed by an unbearable churning of the most terrifying emotion of all. Hope. That dangerous, slippery emotion that made her believe all would turn out well.

A year of struggle had taught her differently.

And yet, *and yet*, Gigi felt a tiny, minuscule, sliver of hope building inside her. Hope for the future, hope that she could return to being the godly woman she'd once been. And maybe capture some stability along the way.

Heavy footed, she stepped in the direction of the carriage Fitz had hired. The physical act of moving brought the rest of the world into focus. Sights, sounds, and the damp, earthy smells of autumn yielding to winter swamped her senses.

Heart in her throat, pulse beating wildly through her veins, Gigi made a decision. She was through running.

No more excuses. No more stalling.

She would give herself three weeks to settle matters in New York. Then, *then*, Gigi would board a train to Boston.

* * *

Fitz helped a pensive Gigi into the carriage. She was silent on the ride back to Manhattan, giving one-word responses to his futile attempts at conversation.

Apparently, the thought-provoking sermon had provoked, well, thought. Fitz had experienced his own share of revelations. His cousin had sent another telegram this morning. Though there was nothing new in the missive, Fitz sensed Connor's impatience. His cousin had urged him to *Complete your business and come home.*

Fitz knew he'd stayed away too long. It was time to leave.

Nothing had turned out as he'd planned, and he wasn't wholly sorry for it. He was falling in love with Gigi.

No, he wasn't falling in love with her.

He was already there.

How had he let this happen *again*?

There could be nothing between them. Even if she returned his feelings, which he believed she might, Fitz would never put her through what he'd seen his mother endure over the past two years. He cared for Gigi too much.

While they bounced and bumped along the pocked road, Fitz worked out the sequence of events that had led to this impossible situation. He admitted, if only to himself, that Gigi was the one that got away. He was not a man who took losing well, as the members on his rowing team could attest.

Pride was a lonely companion.

Fitz was used to being lonely.

When he'd arrived in New York, he'd told himself he'd come for the pearls. But he'd have never given in to Gigi's request to return the necklace herself if that had truly been the case. From the beginning, he'd known she would find a way to get the necklace to Annie. Fitz had known, *he'd known*, she hadn't meant to keep them for herself. He could have left town after their conversation in the alley behind Esmeralda's town house.

Instead, he'd stayed in New York, close to Gigi, making up excuses to seek her out instead of finishing up his business and going home.

He loved Gigi. Always had, always would. But the emotion was now built on more than infatuation. Fitz had gotten to know the woman she was at the core, the one she'd hidden beneath her pretty smiles and carefree manner.

Perhaps even Gigi didn't know her true depths.

She was no longer the frivolous, spoiled heiress, but a woman of substance and compassion. She was good and kind and sat on the dirty floor so she could read stories to little girls.

His father had always liked her. Would he even remember Gigi?

Frowning at the thought, Fitz retrieved his watch from the small pocket in his vest, the one his father had given him as a graduation present. The driver chose that moment to hit a large pothole.

The watch went flying to the floor.

Gigi tumbled forward.

Straight into Fitz's arms.

Ignoring the watch at his feet, he closed her in his embrace, reveling in the feel of her. A bit too much. "Stop wriggling."

"I'm trying to return to my side of the carriage."

"I want you here." He plunked her on the seat beside him.

Her breath caught on a gasp.

His did as well.

There was a long pause.

And then they were both talking at once.

"Gigi—"

"Fitz—"

They fell silent.

Fitz let out a slow, silent push of air. The gesture reduced the tension between his shoulders not one bit.

Gigi's eyes skidded up to his, their blue darkened to a rich sapphire. Words formed on his tongue, tender, heartfelt promises that would last a lifetime. He spoke none of them aloud.

She remained as silent as he. How he hated the awkwardness that had returned to their relationship. "Gigi—"

"Fitz—"

They both heaved a sigh.

Spinning away from him, she looked out the window, sufficiently ending the uncomfortable moment. At least she remained on the seat beside him.

Fitz's gut churned with a sensation stronger than affection, deeper than fondness, and more than a little complicated for his peace of mind.

"Gigi?"

She turned back around.

He reached for her hand, paused inches from making contact. Touching her again would be a bad idea.

The worst of all bad ideas.

As they stared at each other, Fitz noted, somewhat inappropriately, that Gigi's eyelashes were utterly enchanting, a pretty auburn shade similar to her real hair color. A smile of deep affection slid across his lips.

"I think I'd be more comfortable sitting on my side of the carriage." She glided across the short distance with exaggerated dignity, her movements graceful yet carefully controlled. Her posture perfectly precise, she leaned back against the squabs and proceeded to study the interior of the carriage.

With every bit of emotion stripped from her face, she nearly fooled Fitz into thinking she was completely self-possessed. But her gaze didn't quite meet his, landing instead on a spot just above his right eye.

Good to know he wasn't the only one feeling disconcerted.

This was his chance to broach the subject that had been nagging at him since their conversation on the way to church. Fitz admired Gigi's determination to redeem her great-grandmother's pearls on her own. But what if she was unable to earn the twenty-five dollars before the deadline?

Would she accept his help then?

One way to find out . . .

"Gigi, now that we are friends—"

"Are we friends, Fitz? Are we really?"

"Of course we are." He placed his elbows on his knees and leaned forward. "We have shared many confidences."

"You mean *I* have shared many confidences." She gave him a sad half smile. "I know nothing of your life in Boston beyond the basic facts. I know where you live, where you work, and the names of your family members but not much else."

She had him there. But even the smallest details of his day ultimately led back to his father. His lips remained firmly shut.

Gigi was not so easily daunted. She scooted forward, halting only once their knees touched. "I have shared so much of myself with you. Won't you share something of yourself with me?"

Gigi couldn't know how badly Fitz wanted to do exactly what she asked. But once he started, he feared he wouldn't be able to stop.

And so he took the easy way out. "I'm thinking of investing in an automobile company."

Chapter Eighteen

Gigi and Fitz had reached a stalemate in their relationship.

As she lay in her bed Monday morning, staring up at the ceiling in the gloomy pre-dawn light, she accepted that they would never be more than something between friends and passing acquaintances. Especially if he remained distant, speaking only of business matters.

An automobile company, indeed. Her eyes had glazed over as soon as he'd expounded on the virtues of multi-cylinder engines, which Gigi suspected had been the point.

She flipped onto her stomach and sighed. She couldn't help but think Fitz's reticence to share anything personal was because of her past. He might claim she was Nathanial's victim, he might even sympathize with her plight, but that didn't mean he saw her as a potential mate.

There'd been no talk of anything beyond friendship, no attempt at another kiss. All the proof Gigi needed that Fitz thought her unworthy of something deeper.

At least he'd agreed to let her redeem the pearls on her own. But not before he'd extracted her promise to accept his help if she failed to raise the money by the deadline Mr. Ryerson had set.

The man is a crook, he'd said with unmistakable indignation.

Fitz's reaction had warmed Gigi to her toes. She wanted to bask in his strength. She wanted to rely on him. But Nathanial had taught her well.

Gigi trusted no man.

You trusted Fitz with the truth about Nathanial and the pearls.

And where had that gotten her?

Fitz hadn't opened up in return. Though he'd softened toward her, there was still something he wasn't telling her. Something, Gigi suspected, having to do with his cousin or his family or perhaps both.

Crawling out from beneath the bedcovers, she dressed quickly and went downstairs to begin her day. Once her chores were complete, she would have to get herself, and then Sophie, ready for the luncheon at Elizabeth Griffin's.

Hours later, after she'd mended not one but two rips in the gown Sophie had worn to the ball, Gigi checked the clock on the wall and yelped. She'd lost track of time. She blamed Fitz. She couldn't get the man out of her head.

I'd rather moon over him than attend a luncheon any day.

Gigi used to look forward to such events. Sally, however, felt scandalous spending a large part of the afternoon doing nothing but sipping tea and eating fancy sandwiches. At least she wasn't shirking her duties at the theater. Maestro Grimaldi had called off the day's rehearsal because Esmeralda was giving a private performance for several donors with deep pockets.

Gigi entered her room and moved to her closet, hesitating when she saw a flash of peach silk on the bed. Sophie had followed through with her threat to provide Gigi a more suitable dress for the luncheon. Picking up the gown with tentative fingers, she studied it from every angle. The dress was exquisite, the color a perfect foil for her hair in its natural state.

Why, why did Sophie have to be so persistent? Why, *why* did Gigi long to wear this lovely creation?

She wasn't having it. She would wear the brown dress as planned.

She went to her closet and discovered the garment was gone. As if predicting Gigi's reaction, Sophie had taken away her only option besides her maid's uniform. Gigi moved aside the row of black dresses in a final, desperate attempt to search for something less pretty to wear. With profound reluctance—and resentment—she stepped back and shut the closet door.

Sophie had no right to make this decision for her. Gigi would wear her uniform. It was her *only* choice thanks to Sophie's meddling.

She blinked at the peach dress, sighed heavily. Yesterday's sermon came back to her. If forgiveness couldn't be earned, as the pastor claimed, then she was truly lost.

Sighing again, she moved to the mirror and stared at her reflection, honing in on her two-tone hair. What an awkward picture she made. One foot in the past, one foot in the present, with no idea what lay in the future.

Who am I?

Rebellion shot through her, digging deep, taking root. She was tired of concealing her true self inside this pale, nondescript version of a woman. Gigi wasn't clothing herself in righteousness, as she'd tried to tell herself. She was hiding.

It was time to stop living in this unhappy state of limbo.

If not now, when?

Decision made, she dug out her sewing kit, grabbed the scissors, and went to work. When she finished, she'd cut off nearly six inches of faded, dull, straw-like hair. Setting down the scissors, she studied her handiwork.

The remaining hair was thick, shiny, and red. Even better, Gigi had been able to leave just enough length to twist the strands into a modern style atop her head.

Next, Gigi changed into the dress Sophie had left on her bed and returned to the mirror. There. The woman smiling back at her was no longer Sally, but not Gigi Wentworth, either. She was a new creation and looked more herself than ever before. She was ready to step into the uncertain future.

Or else she wouldn't be this pleased Sophie had stolen her dress. But still. "Nosy, meddlesome, pushy young woman."

"Who do you mean, dear friend?"

Gigi whirled around. Sophie stood in the open doorway, eyebrows arched at an attractive angle, eyes twinkling with satisfaction.

"Your hair, it's, why it's really quite fetching." The young woman moved toward her, hand outstretched as if she meant to touch the strands. "I knew you were pretty, but I hadn't realized just how stunning you are until now, with your hair its proper color."

"I'm going to try to take that as a compliment."

"You should. It was meant as one."

"Sophie." Gigi took in her friend's appearance. "You're dressed already."

"How observant of you."

They shared a laugh.

"Well?" The young woman gave a slow, elegant spin. "What do you think?"

"I think that you are"—Gigi took in the green silk gown with the intricate flower embroidery on the bodice—"perfect. The dress presents just the right amount of innocence and maturity. Well done, Sophie."

"I am rather pleased with myself." She twirled around the room, somehow managing to miss the bed and dresser. "Though you may not believe this, especially after our discussion two evenings ago, I do listen to what you say, Gigi. I really, truly do."

"I'm glad."

Sophie laughed again. The sound was richer this time, full of delight and happiness. The signs were unmistakable. Sophie was infatuated with Robert Dain, possibly even in love.

Was the English doctor worthy of her?

Spinning across the threshold, Sophie halted in the darkened hallway and gave Gigi an expectant look. "Are you coming?"

Gigi hurried after her.

* * *

Outside, the sun shone bright. The air was crisp and refreshing. The town house Elizabeth shared with her husband was but a quick walk uptown.

Two blocks short of their destination, Gigi and Sophie came upon a well-dressed woman and her two teenage daughters. All three wore garments made from various shades of blue. Their beautiful, expensive overcoats were cut in a popular style.

The three halted when they saw Sophie. Clearly, they recognized her. Sophie smiled. None returned the gesture.

Proving she was Esmeralda's daughter with a spine of steel, Sophie refused to be daunted. "Good morning, Mrs. Pembroke." She glanced from the older woman to the two girls. "These pretty young ladies must be your daughters. I'm Sophie Cappelletti." She made a motion with her hand. "And this is my friend—"

"Girls." Mrs. Pembroke sniffed in disdain. "Do not respond to that woman."

She looked down her nose at Sophie, while completely ignoring Gigi, then herded her daughters a few steps to the left, giving Sophie a ridiculously wide berth to make a point that didn't need making. "We do not acknowledge women like her."

Gigi bit back a nasty retort. It was difficult not to speak in Sophie's defense. But she feared standing up for her friend would only bring more criticism.

Did Mrs. Pembroke think Sophie had no feelings? Did the woman not care that her snub caused unnecessary hurt? Gigi couldn't help but think about what this woman was teaching her daughters, that they were somehow better than Sophie, simply because they'd been born into a proper home.

Gigi's thoughts turned to her fellow servants in the various homes where she'd worked. They were good, hardworking men and women who earned their living by serving people like Mrs. Pembroke and her daughters.

Poor Sophie.

How long would New York society punish her for her parents' misdeeds?

"Come away, Sophie."

The young woman stood her ground, holding Mrs. Pembroke's stare without flinching.

Admirable, to be sure, but Gigi knew it could not be easy. She hurt for her friend. No wonder Esmeralda was matchmaking in earnest. Once Sophie was married to a man of good standing, much of this criticism would disappear.

But some would never go away. Something Gigi should keep in mind.

The three Pembroke women stalked off.

There wasn't much Gigi could say in the aftermath. She could, however, offer a bit of encouragement.

"Pay no attention to that woman and her hurtful words." Casting a frown at Mrs. Pembroke's retreating back, Gigi hooked her arm through Sophie's, and they continued on their way. "Hold your head high, Sophie. You are worth a thousand times more than closed-minded women like that."

"Indeed, I am."

Gigi heard new confidence in the young woman's voice. She glanced over at her friend. Sophie was smiling. Smiling! Broadly. As if she hadn't a care in the world.

"Sophie? Are you not bothered by Mrs. Pembroke's censure?"

"Not in the least." The young woman's smile turned into a smirk. "What a ridiculous way to behave, and in front of her daughters. Shocking, really."

Well, yes, it had been. "I'm glad you're not upset. You're not upset, are you?"

"Not even a little." Releasing a light laugh, she added, "I can't wait to tell Robert. He'll find the incident quite humorous, I'm sure. He dislikes New York society nearly as much as I do."

Gigi reminded her of the months she'd been desperate to fit into this very society.

Sophie gave a heartfelt sigh. "I find in matters such as these that a poor memory works best."

"Indeed."

"Oh, Gigi, be happy for me. I have discovered a new perspective." She gave another tinkling laugh. "A change in focus changes everything."

These weren't Sophie's words. Gigi felt a spike of dread. "When, precisely, did your perspective change?"

"When I met Robert, of course." She unhooked her arm from Gigi's. "He's very wise."

Sophie had only met him a handful of days ago. How much wisdom could one man impart in such a limited period of time?

"Have you seen Robert recently?"

"Perhaps I have and"—she winked—"perhaps I haven't."

The coy answer did not sit well with Gigi. In a matter of days, a stranger had influenced Sophie in ways Gigi hadn't been able to do in months.

She attempted to voice her concerns, but Sophie was already climbing the stairs to Elizabeth's town house. She lifted the knocker, let it fall with a loud bang.

A man of indeterminate age, dressed in the universal butler's uniform of black coat, black pants, and crisp white shirt, welcomed them with a sufficiently proper bow. "Good day, ladies."

"Good day," they said in unison.

Sophie gave him their names, then asked, "Are we the first to arrive?"

"You are the last. The others are awaiting your arrival in the parlor." He stepped aside to let them pass.

At their confused stares, he added, "At the top of the stairs, down the hallway, second door on your right."

As they made their way to the parlor, Gigi took a quick inventory of Elizabeth's new home. She noted details she would have missed a year ago. The runner on the steps had a soft burgundy pattern of colorful flowers and birds. The banisters gleamed with a fresh coat of polish. The scent of lemon oil meant someone had recently cleaned the wood.

In the parlor, her eyes went to the window treatments. Burgundy draperies with gold-corded trim hung from ceiling to floor. They, too, had been cleaned recently, with pressed pleats at even intervals. The porcelain figurines on the end tables were free of dust. They were dainty and feminine, and so very Elizabeth. The stack of books and basket full of embroidery added a homey feel to the room.

Gigi turned her attention to the three women huddled together. She held back and studied them much as she had the décor.

They greeted Sophie with hugs and kisses. The warm welcome spoke of their fondness for the young woman.

Sophie's half sister seemed the most excited to see her. The newly-wed was a classic beauty, her face a perfect oval shape. She had light-brown hair, and the family resemblance with Sophie was definitely there in those remarkable amber eyes. Their mutual affection and easy manner with each other gave Gigi a sense of great relief. When she left New York, she would be leaving Sophie in capable hands.

Gigi's gaze bounced from the siblings to Caroline and Elizabeth St. James, now Caroline Montgomery and Elizabeth Griffin. The two stood near the fireplace. Wrapped in the golden light, Caroline glowed.

Elizabeth looked equally beautiful. The two women had found their place in the world.

Gigi sighed with pleasure for them.

As if hearing the sound, Elizabeth glanced over. She angled her head, blinked. Then, her eyes widened and she gave a delighted squeal. "Sally, you came."

The woman hurried over, her cousin hard on her heels. The two made quite a stunning pair. Caroline's dark hair posed a startling contrast to Elizabeth's pale-blonde locks, and though one had green eyes and the other blue, they shared the same oval face and bow-shaped lips.

"Oh, Sally, I almost didn't recognize you." Giving her no chance to respond, Elizabeth dragged her into a quick hug.

Caroline took her turn next. Keeping her hands on Gigi's shoulders, she stepped back and gazed at her intently. Under the close inspection, a swarm of nerves took flight in Gigi's stomach.

"Your hair is striking," Caroline said in her carefully cultured British accent. "That shade suits your coloring to perfection."

Gigi fidgeted from foot to foot. She hadn't received this much attention since running away from Boston.

"It's not just the hair." Elizabeth peered over her cousin's shoulder. "Something else has changed, but I can't quite put my finger on it. You've always been pretty, but there's strength in you now. Yes, that's just the word. You're stronger."

"You do seem more confident," Caroline agreed, lowering her hands. "I declare you quite transformed."

"I'm the same person."

"Well, whatever has caused this lovely change, I'm glad you came today. I was just telling Caroline how much I have missed you." Elizabeth moved in and gave Gigi another fast hug. "Welcome, my friend."

"Thank you."

"Come, let's sit." Caroline reached out, laying a hand on Gigi's arm in an innate show of comfort. "I want to hear what you've been doing with yourself these past few months."

Gigi's heart drummed as she followed the two women to an elegant settee.

This moment felt like more than a reunion with former employers, more than a chance to catch up with friends. Gigi was a guest today, not a servant. Was this luncheon the next step to whatever awaited her in Boston? Or was the encounter with Mrs. Pembroke and her daughters a prelude of things to come?

One step at a time, she told herself, as she'd once counseled Elizabeth. No need to borrow trouble where there was none.

"Well," Elizabeth began. "Won't you tell us what you've been up to since we last met?"

Positioned between the cousins, Gigi tried to remember the last time she'd seen either woman. It had been at Elizabeth's wedding. "I've been enjoying serving as Sophie's maid."

Both sets of eyes swept over the woman in question. "How is that going?"

Gigi glanced over to Sophie as well. She and Penelope were caught up in their own animated conversation. "She is settling into her new life as well as can be expected."

Elizabeth let out a small push of air. "Luke will be happy to hear that. Let me take this opportunity to say thank you. We've been worried about her."

Gigi wasn't sure if she should tell Elizabeth about Robert Dain or not.

"You have guided Sophie through the labyrinth of New York society quite successfully. Many homes have opened for her, though not all, but we knew that would be the case."

"I did nothing out of the ordinary. I am merely her maid."

"You are more than that," Caroline said. "I pray one day soon you will trust Elizabeth and me enough to share the truth of who you really are."

They knew.

These women knew she was a fraud.

As she studied the compassion in each of their faces, a white-hot ball of remorse burned in her chest. She nearly jumped up and rushed out of the room.

But Elizabeth's soft voice stole her ability to move, to think. "Whatever you are hiding, you will get no judgment from us, Sally."

Sally. These kind women who'd taken her into their homes didn't even know her real name. She'd told so many half-truths and lies. Too many to know how to ask for forgiveness.

But then she remembered Caroline had told her share of falsehoods. She'd come seeking revenge on the grandfather she'd thought had abandoned her and her mother, only to discover the family she'd always desired.

If Caroline could find forgiveness, could Gigi?

She locked her panic deep inside a dark place in her soul, wrapped her arms around her waist, and waged an internal battle. The fight melted out of her with every tick of her heartbeat. The need to tell these women the truth was too strong to dismiss.

If only she knew where to begin.

As if she'd been waiting for this moment, Sophie moved to a spot directly in front of Gigi. She knelt in front of her, took her hands, and squeezed them gently. "It's time to tell them who you are."

Gigi's heart wobbled.

"At least tell them your real name."

Her name. Yes, that was the place to start. She glanced from Caroline to Elizabeth and then to Penelope, a woman she hardly knew.

The soft smile she gave Gigi was identical to the one on Sophie's face. "Your secret will be safe with me. But, if you would prefer, I will leave the room."

Because she believed the young woman's sincerity, Gigi insisted, "I would like you to stay."

"Then I will stay." Penelope moved closer, still smiling kindly.

The remaining scraps of Gigi's resistance dissolved. "I was born Georgina Wentworth, but I have been called Gigi for as long as I can remember."

"Gigi." Caroline turned thoughtful. "It suits you."

"I hail from Boston." She gave Sophie a meaningful look.

"So you *do* know Mr. Fitzpatrick."

She nodded.

Now that she'd begun, Gigi dropped the Midwestern accent she'd adopted as part of her disguise and spoke in her real voice. "Fitz and I grew up together. Our families have always been close."

"He came for you."

"Yes."

"How . . . romantic."

It was hardly that. Gigi opened her mouth to disabuse Sophie of her misconceptions when Caroline asked, "Who, precisely, is this Mr. Fitzpatrick?"

The question unleashed the rest of Gigi's story. Once she began, she was helpless to stop the words from coming in a rush, tumbling over one another.

Gigi told them about her long-ago friendship with Fitz. "I'm not sure when everything went wrong, but he changed almost overnight. The man I had always considered a friend became a cold stranger, one my father was determined I marry."

"Did you marry him?"

She shook her head. "I tried to express my concerns about the match, first to Fitz, then to my father. Neither man would listen."

She cringed at the memory of her father's refusal to bend on the matter.

"So you ran away from an arranged marriage," Caroline decided. "This Mr. Fitzpatrick must be a truly terrible person."

"I've met him. I like him." Sophie's cheeks colored to a becoming shade of pink when all eyes turned to her. "Not in *that* way. He's been nothing but kind to me. He seems to know how to handle my mother, which says a lot about the man."

"I've met him as well. He seemed quite nice," Elizabeth said, frowning. "Luke is considering going into business with him. Is there something I should tell my husband before the contracts are signed?"

Gigi shook her head. "Fitz is the best man I know."

As soon as she said the words, she realized they were true.

"Then why didn't you want to marry him?" Caroline asked, her confusion evident.

Gigi explained about her friend Verity and her arranged marriage to a man of her father's choosing. The volatile life she'd led ever since her wedding day. "I didn't want to be trapped in a marriage like hers. With the change in Fitz, I feared we would both be unhappy."

"So you ran away."

"Yes. But . . ." Now came the hard part. "I didn't run off alone."

She held Sophie's gaze, praying the young woman listened very closely to the next part of her story.

With very little inflection, Gigi explained how she met and fell in love with Nathanial. She left no detail out. She told of Fitz's warnings, of her father's threats, and of her own refusal to see reason.

"I was in love." Again, she looked at Sophie. "Nothing and no one could persuade me to take matters slowly."

Eyebrows drawn together, Sophie moved to a chair opposite Gigi.

Gigi continued with her story, describing their time in New York, spending wildly and denying themselves nothing until the day

Nathanial left. "He sent me to the church ahead of him. He claimed he had a special wedding gift planned. He never showed up."

Sophie gasped. "Was he hurt?" Her eyes looked large and round in her face. "Was it something truly terrible that kept him away?"

Gigi hunched in her seat. Sophie's romantic sensibilities were so much like hers had once been. And so very much off the mark.

The horrors of that awful moment when she'd realized Nathanial was never coming played through Gigi's mind. "He left me with nothing but a large hotel bill to pay. That was when I met you," she said to Caroline.

"Oh, you poor, poor dear." Caroline dragged Gigi into her arms and held her for several seconds. "To be betrayed so completely by a man you trusted. What you must have suffered. It's quite unconscionable."

The others agreed with various degrees of sympathy and agony on their faces.

"Don't feel sorry for me. I brought shame and misery on myself." Barely trusting herself to speak any longer, Gigi quickly added, "Now that you know the full nature of my disgrace, I wouldn't blame you if you thought less of me."

"Less of you? Not at all." Elizabeth gave one firm shake of her head. "I have nothing but admiration. Nathanial tried to break you, but you survived."

Gigi glanced from one woman to the next, seeing the truth of their acceptance in their gazes. "You don't think me a—"

"Now, Sally. I mean, Gigi. I just adore that name." Elizabeth gave her a soft, affectionate smile. "Anyway, *Gigi*, you will receive no judgment from us. No condemnation. You were treated horribly and you made the best of a disastrous situation."

"You are to be admired," Penelope said, speaking for the first time. "If it were me, I don't think I would have had the strength to carry on after what Nathanial did to you."

Sophie nodded, her troubled thoughts whirling in her gaze.

For Sophie's sake, Gigi admitted the truth of her life as Sally Smith. "There have been days when I haven't done so well." She gave a self-deprecating laugh. "Many nights I have wrapped myself in a blanket to sit and lament over all that I have lost because of my own foolishness."

A servant appeared in the doorway, gave a short nod at Elizabeth, then disappeared again.

Just as Caroline muttered something very unladylike about fortune hunters, Elizabeth stood and reached to Gigi. "We'll finish this in the dining room."

Once she was in her seat at the dining room table, Gigi took a sip of tea and eyed Sophie over the cup's rim. The young woman was unusually quiet and thoughtful. Had she taken Gigi's sad tale to heart?

Tired of talking about herself, Gigi turned her attention to the woman beside her. "Marriage suits you, Caroline."

The other woman laughed, clearly delighted by the compliment. "I never expected to find such joy, not with my sordid past. But Jackson is the best thing that ever happened to me. I fall in love with him more and more every day."

Oh, to love that completely. "It shows."

"While we're here among friends, Caroline"—Elizabeth smiled at her cousin—"why don't you share your happy news."

A delicate frown marred Caroline's pretty face as she cast Gigi a quick glance from beneath her lashes. "Not now."

"Please, Caroline," Gigi urged. "Tell us your news."

"Only if Elizabeth tells hers first."

Wondering at the secretive smiles the cousins shared, Gigi looked from one to the other. "What's going on with you two?"

"I'm with child. Jackson and I are going to have a baby."

A baby. Gigi stared at her friend. *A baby.* Caroline and Jackson were officially starting their family.

"I'm in the same condition," Elizabeth announced next. "Luke and I will welcome a baby boy or girl into our home nearly a year from the day we were married."

Gigi blinked as the news settled over her, as reality gripped her heart and squeezed. *Will I ever be that blessed? Will I ever have news such as this to share?*

For a terrible, awful moment, she didn't know what to say, how to feel. Happy. She was supposed to be happy for her friends. *Of course* she was happy for them. She'd been with them on their journey to love and rejoiced that they would soon be mothers.

Gigi found her voice. "This is marvelous news."

Penelope reached over and squeezed her sister-in-law's hand. "You're going to make a wonderful mother."

"You, too, Caroline," Gigi added.

Happy tears sprang into everyone's eyes.

Gigi's filled as well, though she felt a surge of crippling jealousy. If only she hadn't rushed matters. If only she'd trusted the Lord to guide her to the right man. If only . . .

No. She'd made her choices and must live with them, even if that meant entering her dotage as a spinster.

Gigi's vision blurred as her eyes turned misty, and she thought she might blubber into her soup.

As if sensing her shift in mood, Caroline patted her hand. "I'm confident you'll find a good man, one worthy of you and far better than that terrible, awful Nathanial."

"You're right, of course." Gigi said the words for her friend's benefit. But she could barely hold back her grief. One rogue tear wiggled to the edge of her lashes and slipped down the side of her face. *No.* No more crying. She would not give Nathanial that much power over her, not anymore. No. More.

Despite her best efforts, Gigi couldn't hold back the tears after all. She let a few fall freely down her cheeks before swiping them away.

"Gigi?" Caroline's worry sounded in her voice.

"I'm all right. Truly. I'm just so pleased for you both."

Determined to make the words true, she allowed herself to get swept away in her friends' joy. By the time dessert was served, her happiness was real.

Sophie and Penelope soon left for an appointment at an upscale department store. Caroline made her exit a few minutes later. Gigi made to leave as well.

Elizabeth stopped her with a hand to her arm. "Please, stay a bit longer. Now that I have you all to myself, I so want to enjoy our time together."

"I've missed you, Elizabeth."

"And I have missed you, so very much." Questions swirled in her friend's eyes. "I'd like to hear about your life in Boston, if you'll tell me."

Instead of putting her off, Gigi felt a moment of great relief. "I'd like to tell you about my life in Boston. I have two sisters, did you know that?"

"I always thought you were alone in the world."

I'm not alone, Gigi realized. She never had been.

Pride had kept her separated from her family, her friends, and God. Had she been the one to move away from the Lord and not the other way around?

Determined to start anew, Gigi settled in for a good, long talk with her friend.

Chapter Nineteen

"What a spectacular piece of driving." Luke climbed out of his motorcar and, goggles still in place, sauntered over to shake Fitz's hand. "And may I remind you, gloating is rude and unseemly."

Fitz accepted Luke's congratulations with a self-satisfied grin. It had been a hard-won race, with Luke almost overtaking him at the finish line.

Almost, but not quite. "You'll get me next time."

"Count on it."

Fitz laughed at the gruff promise. "You always were a fierce competitor."

"Something we have in common."

"Too true." Barely able to see the other man through all the grime on his own goggles, Fitz shoved them to the back of his head.

Luke looked out over the track they'd raced around for the agreed-upon twelve laps. "I noticed how you chose the driving line and followed the same path each lap."

"Actually, it took me a few trips around to pick the best route," Fitz admitted, looking out over the muddy track, too. "I usually like to walk the course backward to figure out where I need to enter, travel through, and then exit a turn."

"Not a bad idea."

Fitz liked to take a slow-in, fast-out approach, which required a good understanding of the turn so he knew when to throttle and when to brake. "I thought if I did that today, I would show my hand."

Luke smirked. "Clever, and proof you are more than a hobbyist. You drove through the corners like an expert."

"I wouldn't go that far." Driving had become his sanctuary, an outlet from the stress of his father's illness. "When it comes to investments, I do my homework."

"Sure, let's go with that."

Smiling, Fitz ran his hand over the steering wheel, clutching the polished wood in the nine and three o'clock positions as he had in the race. "You've engineered a remarkable machine."

"We have several more prototypes in production, including a six-cylinder engine, but the four-cylinder is the one I believe will take the company into the future."

"We're in agreement there."

"Ah, here comes my chief engineer now."

Luke motioned over to a man dressed in coveralls as dirty as the ones he and Fitz wore. But whereas Fitz's and Luke's were coated with mud from the racetrack, the engineer's sported oil stains.

"I'll let Dietrich explain our plans. I hired him away from a German automobile company and gave him autonomy to choose his team of engineers and mechanics. He poached them from across Europe, mostly England, since, on the whole, British designs are far superior to our American counterparts."

Fitz's research had told him the same thing. Two hours later, after touring the rest of the facilities, he had a good understanding of petroleum-powered engines and how they worked. Once the engineer went back to work, Luke took over the conversation, which turned out to be one of the best sales pitches Fitz had encountered in a long time, maybe ever.

"You do nothing by half measures," Fitz said.

"A job worth doing is worth doing well."

Fitz nodded. "What's next?"

"As Jackson mentioned at the club, I've hired Brian Chesterfield to coordinate a series of races to increase Griffin Motors' profile. We'll invite automobile clubs from across the country to compete against our motorcars."

"Thereby proving yours are the best in the world?"

"That's the plan." Luke's grin was full of confidence. "I originally asked Brian to join us today, but he's stuck in Manhattan until later this afternoon."

Pity. Fitz would have relished hearing Brian's thoughts. If Fitz remembered correctly, Luke had mentioned that Brian had been racing in Europe for several years now. His experience would make the inaugural Griffin Cup a success.

"If you're available, Brian has agreed to meet us at my home around four o'clock."

Fitz checked his watch. If he left Long Island within the next half hour, he would have just enough time to return to his hotel room for a much-needed bath and change of clothing. "I should be able to make that happen."

"Excellent." Luke gave Fitz his home address. "My wife is hosting a private luncheon, but the ladies should be gone by the time you arrive."

As it turned out, one of the ladies was still at the Griffin home. That was how Fitz found himself standing in a parlor, on the second floor of Luke's town house, staring at a familiar figure moving quickly toward the edge of the room.

It took precious few seconds to make the connection between Gigi and Luke's wife. Fitz mentally filed through the private investigator's report. Gigi had been Elizabeth Griffin's lady's maid and had obviously maintained a friendship since.

As always, she moved with a natural grace, like a delicate flower that had found a way to bloom in the dead of winter. She paused at a painting. Presenting her back to the room, she pretended grave interest in the artist's handiwork.

The woman was intentionally avoiding him.

He couldn't blame her. They hadn't ended yesterday's outing on the best of terms. Fitz had returned to his old ways, withdrawing into the safety of talking business. After several attempts to steer the conversation back to the personal, Gigi had given up trying and let him explain the intricacies of multi-cylinder engines.

He narrowed his eyes and angled his head. Something about her was different today.

Her hair. The stringy blonde ends were gone. Although her complicated hairstyle made it hard to tell how much of her hair she'd cut off, just that one simple change had completely altered her appearance.

A smiling Luke reacquainted Fitz with his pretty wife. "You remember Elizabeth?"

"Indeed, I do." Fitz took her offered hand.

She glanced briefly at Gigi, then back to him. "What a pleasure to see you again and so soon after our last meeting."

"The pleasure is all mine."

Something thoughtful came and went in her eyes. "I believe you are also acquainted with my friend."

She called out to Gigi. "Come say hello to Mr. Fitzpatrick."

Unable to hide from him any longer, Gigi turned away from the painting and made her way over to him with reluctance in every step.

The moment she emerged from the shadows, Fitz's heart kicked an extra-hard beat. He knew he was staring. How could he not?

Fitz could no longer ignore the truth. Gigi had worked her way past his defenses and brought light to the darkest portions of his soul.

She made him think of forever, of happy endings and possibilities he'd thought out of his reach.

He wanted a future with her. The battle had been decided long before she'd run off.

She stopped in front of him. Fitz couldn't make his mind work properly. When had he gotten lost in her gaze?

"Hello, Fitz."

"Hello, Gigi." His voice sounded like sandpaper scraping over gravel.

What a picture she made. So pretty and perfectly controlled. Not a single wrinkle in her composure.

"You changed your hair since last we met."

Her hand went to the red tresses, dropped just as quickly. "It was time."

Tender affection filled him. "I couldn't agree more."

"Now wait just a minute. I feel like I've stepped into the middle of a play halfway through the second act." Luke looked from Fitz to Gigi and back again. "You two know each other?"

They nodded.

"Well, then. Right. Out with it, Fitz." Luke's eyebrows traveled toward his hairline. "How do you know my wife's former maid? And more to the point, why are you calling her Gigi?"

Fitz was formulating his response, sorting through how much to reveal, when the Griffins' butler entered the room and addressed Luke directly. "Mr. Brian Chesterfield has arrived for your four o'clock meeting."

A look of utter horror crossed Gigi's face.

Fitz went immediately to her. He took her hand and squeezed. But the attempt to comfort her did nothing to alleviate the terror in her eyes.

"It's going to be all right," he said for her ears only.

"You can't know that."

No, he couldn't. Brian had attended Harvard with him, Luke, and Jackson. And, like Fitz, the man came from a long line of Harvard graduates from Boston. Most concerning of all, Brian's father was Harcourt Wentworth's personal attorney.

Gigi knew Brian.

And Brian knew Gigi.

Fitz had but one goal now. Protect her from discovery. Several routes would serve his purpose.

"Tell Brian we'll meet him downstairs," he urged Luke.

Unfortunately, Fitz spoke a shade too late. Luke had already sent the butler back down, and Fitz could hear the man direct Brian to where he could find Mr. Griffin upstairs.

He searched for a quick escape route. "Do you have another way out of this house?"

"There's a back stairwell the servants use."

"Gigi, what's the matter? What's happened?" Elizabeth touched her arm. "You're trembling."

Gigi stared blindly at Luke's wife. She opened her mouth to respond. No sound came out.

"I'm going to get you out of here," Fitz promised.

She managed a nod. "I . . . yes, please."

Fitz glanced at Luke. "How do we find the back stairwell?"

"Exit that way." He pointed to the door they'd entered earlier. "Take a right and continue down the hallway to the end. Go left and you'll see where to go from there."

The sound of footsteps spurred Fitz into action.

Once again, he'd reacted a split second too late.

Brian Chesterfield sauntered into the room, his easy gait indicating he had no idea of the drama his arrival created. Smiling broadly, his gaze landed first on Fitz, then on Gigi. Until that moment, Fitz had forgotten just how closely Brian and Gigi were acquainted.

How many times had he watched the two interact, their manners relaxed and easy, their heads bent at similar angles? He found himself stewing in an unpleasant rush of . . .

He refused to name the emotion.

"Well, as I live and breathe." Brian grinned far too intimately for Fitz's peace of mind. "Gigi Wentworth, home from Europe at last."

* * *

The thoughts racing through Gigi's mind were similar to those she'd had when Fitz had first shown up at the Summer Garden.

She was caught.

Her plans were thwarted. Her hope for redemption crushed.

The threat was equally real, perhaps more so, because Brian's father worked closely with hers. Gigi had lost her chance to go home on her timetable, on her own terms. News of her *return* would travel to Boston with Brian.

"Welcome back to America, pretty lady." Brian shoved around Fitz, who did his best to stand between Gigi and the other man. "I must say, Vienna hasn't changed you one bit. You are as utterly captivating as ever."

"Vienna?" Elizabeth's eyes cut from Brian to Gigi, a tiny frown pleating the small space between her eyebrows. "When were you in Vienna?"

"She's been there for nearly a year." Brian took Gigi's hand, pressed his lips to her gloved knuckles. "Eleven months too long, as far as I'm concerned. You belong in America, where the real men live."

Her face burned at the outrageous flirting. She belonged in America, did she? Where real men lived? If she recalled correctly, Brian had been in Europe himself. She'd forgotten what a silver tongue he had, so similar to Nathanial's.

Although he was a well-regarded gentleman among his peers, Brian had always been too forward, expressing more than simple interest with a look or lingering touch. As she had in the past, Gigi felt a little soiled after spending five minutes in his company.

She made her muscles relax, though her stomach remained a frantic flurry of nerves. "What a kind thing to say."

"Only the truth, my dear." His dark eyes smoldered. "Only the truth."

Gigi wasn't ready for this conversation. Any number of things could slip out of her mouth that would throw her character into question. She'd always known someone might recognize her. Why hadn't she prepared better for a moment such as this?

Aware of the stretching silence, Gigi adjusted her smile to one of polite indifference and attempted to engage Brian in the sort of inane banter she'd once prided herself in. "Tell me, what brings you to New York?"

"Funny, I was about to ask the same of you."

Fitz touched her arm, lifted his eyebrows. Grateful for his presence and the silent offer of rescue, she gave a short, nearly imperceptible nod.

With surprising alacrity, he stepped into the conversation. "I don't believe you've met Luke's wife."

With Brian's attention now on Elizabeth, Gigi forced her mind to work through what to say next. She wanted to retreat into her alter ego, even felt her shoulders hunching forward. The habit of making herself unremarkable was hard to break. But even that slight misstep would raise questions.

Shoulders squared, Gigi flicked her gaze to Fitz, then dropped it away at his ready smile. He was rescuing her, the big, sweet, dear, dear man.

After so many lies, she would have to tell more. And once again, Fitz would have to join her in the deception. A symphony of shame blossomed in her chest.

"Chesterfield." Fitz enunciated the man's name with a hint of impatience. "I understand you completed the inaugural Gordon Bennett Cup from Paris to Lyon."

Brian took up the switch in topic with enthusiasm. "Came close to winning. Lost to a French Panhard."

This sparked a rather detailed dissertation on the various European motorcar races in which Brian had participated and the types of automobiles he admired most.

Perhaps all was not lost, Gigi thought. It appeared Brian wasn't returning to Boston straightaway but would be settling in New York to work with Luke. Something about organizing an automobile race similar to the ones he'd participated in across Europe.

Brian seemed to have forgotten Gigi completely, with no small help from Fitz. The wonderful man kept repositioning his stance, moving inch by tiny inch, until he eventually shielded Gigi from Brian's direct line of vision.

Gigi used the momentary reprieve to shoot an apologetic grimace at Elizabeth. Tenderness and understanding mingled in her friend's returned smile. The deliberate show of support was more than Gigi deserved.

Linking her arm through Gigi's, Elizabeth said, "Where are my manners? I am neglecting my duties as a hostess. Come, Gigi. Let's leave the men to finish their discussion while I show you the painting Luke bought me for our two-month anniversary."

Her breath shallow, her heart full of gratitude, Gigi allowed her friend to guide her to the opposite end of the room.

Once they were out of the men's hearing, Elizabeth pulled to a stop near a picture painted in the American Impressionist style.

Standing shoulder to shoulder with her friend, Gigi ignored the embarrassed heat crawling toward her cheeks and pretended avid interest in the painting. She'd really gotten herself into a fix this time, simply because she'd stayed at this town house too long. But it had felt marvelous talking about her past, without shame and only a very little bit of sadness when she'd told Elizabeth about her sisters and how much she missed them.

Elizabeth pointed to the top right-hand corner of the painting. Rather than make an observation about it, though, she lowered her voice and asked, "I gather Mr. Chesterfield thinks you've been in Vienna this past year?"

Stepping forward as if to study the spot Elizabeth had just indicated, Gigi nodded.

"That's the story my family told to explain my sudden disappearance. I'm supposed to be expanding my music education at the Conservatory in Vienna." Aware she sounded a little angry, she attempted to soften her tone. "I learned of this by reading the Boston society pages."

"I understand."

Gigi didn't know how Elizabeth could comprehend a situation she didn't fully understand herself. Eyebrows lifted, she looked at her friend. "Do you?"

"It's all very clear, really." Elizabeth's expression warmed. "Your family wanted to protect your reputation."

Behind Gigi's eyes came the hot prick of tears. "I'm sure they told the story more to protect my younger sisters and the family name than for me."

Elizabeth considered this a moment. "I suppose you won't know for certain until you return."

"I suppose you're right." Gigi had told Elizabeth of her plans to attend Annie's wedding, though she'd left out the part about her great-grandmother's pearls.

Her friend had been full of encouragement, and for a few precious hours, Gigi had allowed the sparks of hope in her heart free rein. Fitz's arrival had only enhanced the feeling. But then Brian had appeared.

Glancing briefly over her shoulder, Elizabeth lowered her voice to a mere whisper. "Mr. Chesterfield has no idea you ran away with a man?"

The ice in Gigi's belly turned into a ball of dread. "None whatsoever."

"But Fitz knows the truth."

Gigi's only reply was a quick nod of her head.

"And he's over there attempting to protect your secret?"

"It would appear so."

A sigh slipped out of Elizabeth. "He must care for you a great deal."

For an instant, Gigi allowed herself to consider the possibility. Yet she felt an unpleasant pinch in her chest because she knew a future with Fitz was an unattainable wish on her part. She was spoiled for a proper marriage.

Oh, sure, Fitz had spoken of forgiveness and God's grace. He'd listened to her secrets without judgment, but he hadn't shared any of his. She'd given him every opportunity to open up to her. Yet he continued to keep her at a distance.

Nothing had changed between them. Fitz was as withdrawn as ever. Even if he truly accepted her past, and she could believe herself worthy of a man like him, what chance did they have if he refused to open up even just a little?

Gigi glanced at him from beneath her lashes. Her heartbeat went a little crazy, thudding hard and unevenly against her ribs.

She quickly looked away.

Elizabeth grimaced. "It would appear Mr. Chesterfield has returned to the subject of your presence here in New York and is asking questions."

"He must be stopped." Gigi turned.

Elizabeth stilled her progress with a hand on her arm. "Fitz seems to have the situation under control."

That's what concerned Gigi most. Brian had left Boston at a time when their family and friends had been expecting the announcement of her engagement to Fitz.

She was on the move in the next instant.

This is what comes from telling lies.

The truth always came to light eventually and rarely in a convenient manner.

Gigi's mind worked furiously for an answer to Brian's queries that didn't include a close connection to Fitz. She was in New York to visit old friends, to see the sights, to attend the opera or perhaps a performance at Carnegie Hall. A million reasons came to mind, any of which would do.

Gigi heard Elizabeth say her name, but she didn't slow her approach.

"She recently made the acquaintance of Esmeralda Cappelletti," she heard Fitz say. Thankfully, he left the specifics vague.

It was the perfect moment for her to join the conversation.

"I've always been a fan. Esmeralda is a marvelous talent." Gigi drew to a stop beside Fitz. "Her rendition of *Carmen* has no rival."

Luke snorted. Elizabeth gave him a sharp glance.

Missing the silent interchange between husband and wife, Brian took to the new topic with aplomb. "I heard Esmeralda sing the lead role of that particular operetta in London last year. She was marvelous. I understand her American debut is coming soon."

"In two short days." Her nerves suddenly making her talkative, Gigi proceeded to expound on the preparations under way and let herself get carried away, closing with, "The Summer Garden Theater is the perfect setting for Esmeralda's return to the stage."

Brian smiled. "Fitz said nearly the same thing."

Too late, Gigi realized she'd revealed details that even someone of Esmeralda's "acquaintance" should have no way of knowing. Unless she'd been given a tour backstage by, oh say, a potential investor wanting to impress his future fiancée?

What have I done?

Black tinged the edges of her vision. For a dangerous moment, she thought she might faint.

Her legs would have given out from under her if Fitz hadn't wrapped his arm around her waist and pulled her in close to his side. The move robbed her of thought, and all she could do was blink up at him.

For a second, she got lost in his gaze.

He seemed equally unable to look away.

"Well, well. You lucky sap." Brian clasped Fitz on the shoulder. "Now I understand why you want to purchase the Summer Garden Theater. It's to be a present for your future bride."

"Perhaps." Fitz's smile remained in place, but Gigi saw the strain at the edges. "I wished it to be a surprise."

"Right, right." Brian dropped his hand, grinned. "About time you made it official."

Luke found his voice. "Made what official?"

"Their engagement. It's been rumored for years. To be honest, I thought you'd never get up the courage to ask her. Well done, my friend." Brian slugged Fitz good-naturedly in the arm. "Well done."

"You're . . . engaged?" Luke's tone was understandably incredulous.

Gigi attempted to speak, but words simply wouldn't form in her mind.

"It's new," she heard Fitz say.

She glanced up at him. He gave her a meaningful look that said, *Don't utter a word. Let me handle this.*

"Our families don't even know." Eyes never leaving her face, Fitz dropped a brief, achingly tender kiss to Gigi's forehead. "We want to wait to tell them until after her sister's wedding."

Brian aimed a beaming smile at Gigi. "Mum's the word."

"We appreciate your silence," she said in a small voice.

"Well," Elizabeth whispered into Gigi's ear. "That's certainly one way to solve the problem."

Chapter Twenty

Afraid he would make matters worse if he tried to talk his way out of the debacle he'd created in the Griffins' parlor, Fitz left Gigi in her friend's capable hands and returned to his room in the Waldorf-Astoria. He'd done what he could to ensure Brian's silence.

There would be plenty of time to repair the damage. He would seek out Gigi and discuss their next step later tonight or first thing in the morning.

For now, Fitz needed to think. To do that properly, he needed privacy.

He slammed the door behind him with a bang and yanked open the top drawer of the small writing desk.

With swift flicks of his wrist, he laid out several sheets of paper on the desk and began reviewing the notes he'd scribbled after each consultation with the medical experts.

Now, with his future at stake, Fitz searched for something, anything, to give him hope. He'd asked each of the doctors if his father's condition was hereditary. None had been definitive in their answer, but not a single one of the four had ruled out the possibility, either.

The last of the four physicians had been the most optimistic. The man had at least three patients with symptoms similar to Calvin Fitzpatrick's who were also the first in their families to contract the brain disease.

Fitz continued searching for evidence that would allow him to go forth with the plan formulating in his mind. He would need to return to Boston immediately. The sooner he left New York, the sooner he could return and make things right with Gigi.

His future happiness hinged on incomplete medical research. He'd made risky investments before. Was this just another leap of faith?

He shut his eyes and prayed. *Lord, show me the way. Give me a spark of hope, just one; that's all I need.*

He reviewed his notes on brain diseases again, losing himself in the process, managing to focus for fifteen uninterrupted minutes before his thoughts wandered back to the parlor in Luke's town house.

And to the moment he'd all but declared Gigi as his fiancée.

What had he been thinking? Telling Brian Chesterfield that he and Gigi were engaged? He'd added to her family's lie, embellishing a shared past that had only been real for him.

Why hadn't Gigi stopped him? If only she'd said *something*. Her silence had sealed her doom.

Fitz wanted to claim her for his wife.

The tender kiss he'd pressed to her forehead had been out of reflex, not for show. And the look in her eyes when he'd pulled her close had not been revulsion, far from it. The way she'd stared up at him, with trust and gratitude and something more, had made him want to conquer the world, slay her every dragon, and keep her close by his side, forever. She'd made him believe.

Fitz would not saddle Gigi with a lifetime of misery for the sake of his own happiness.

Find a solution, he told himself.

He returned his attention to his notes, bending over to study them with squinted eyes. He wanted to make his words true, hence this desperate attempt to find some piece of surety that he could have a future with her. But there simply wasn't enough research; there was no concrete proof that Fitz wouldn't end up just like his father. The risk of contracting the brain disease would always loom on the horizon.

The prognosis was bleak. He felt a happy future with Gigi slipping away like water through splayed fingers.

Reading through his notes one more time, *just one more time*, he searched for something he'd missed. A tentative knock jolted him upright from the desk. His heart gave a few thick beats in his chest.

He crossed the sitting room and opened the door with a yank.

Gigi stood in the hallway, head high, spine erect, chin at a perfect ninety-degree angle with the floor.

At the sight of her, Fitz went hot all over. His brain was trying to tell him something, but he couldn't decipher the message. Gigi was the same woman she'd always been. Yet . . . not.

The last few hours in the company of her trusted friend had produced a remarkable transformation. Her cheeks had gained color. Her eyes sparkled.

The effect was devastating. Disconcerting.

Any words of greeting vanished from his mind.

"Are you going to just stand there staring at me?"

"Gigi, I . . ." His brain emptied. "I wasn't expecting you."

"I realize that. The look of horror gave you away. But I thought we should discuss how to proceed, now that we are, that is"—her lips curved in a sad smile—"now that Brian Chesterfield believes us engaged."

"You're right, of course. Come in." He stepped aside to let her pass.

Her scent hit him, hard, tearing his resolve to shreds. *Tell her how you feel.* "I'm sorry."

"I know." She sighed. "You have put us in an impossible situation. The news of our engagement will surely reach our families."

Would that be such a bad thing? Fitz didn't have a definitive answer. "Brian will keep silent until after your sister's wedding."

"You can't know that."

"He doesn't plan to return to Boston for months. And he's not the kind to write home."

She angled her head. "You know this for certain?"

"He told me after we left the town house together." Fitz had followed the man out, and on the way to their individual hotels, he'd pumped Brian for information about his future plans.

"You trust his word?"

"Implicitly."

Instead of calming, she seemed to grow more agitated.

Fitz hated seeing her upset. Especially knowing he was the cause.

"Don't worry, Gigi." He reached to her, took both her hands, and pulled her close. He wanted to kiss her. *Mine.* No other man could have her. The urge to claim her was primitive and nearly brought him to his knees.

He should not be touching her.

He'd done enough damage.

Reluctantly, he set her away from him. "I have a plan to make this right."

"What sort of . . . plan?"

"A good one."

Her eyes narrowed. "I don't know if I can believe you. You're being awfully vague."

"Hear me out. That's all I ask."

Seven seconds of silence passed. Fitz counted each one in his head.

At last, she relented. "All right. Tell me what you have in mind."

* * *

Fitz took Gigi's cloak and showed her to a chair beneath a pool of soft, golden light cast by a tall lamp. The setting was too intimate, too personal, with an inviting mood that put Gigi in mind of quiet nights at home with loved ones.

Oh, this is bad, she thought, staring up at Fitz's lean, aristocratic face. His strong sculpted mouth was beautiful in the weak tendrils of lamplight. The tender expression in his remarkable green eyes called to her, making her want to believe he would take care of matters.

He smiled at her then, his eyes turning serious and full of intent.

Oh, Fitz.

She knew what *that* look meant.

He was going to propose to her, formally, for all the wrong reasons. Why did he have to be so noble?

Why did he have to be so . . . good? Where was the distant, unfeeling man he'd been in the carriage yesterday? At least she knew what to expect with that particular Fitz. This one? She was at a loss. And her heart was too full of hope to think clearly.

Ever since he'd declared them engaged, Gigi's mind had traveled down countless roads, all of them leading to the same destination. Marriage to Fitz. A houseful of children. Growing old together.

Gigi wasn't sure they could be happy, though, at least not for any length of time. Fitz didn't trust her with his secrets. He might be full of acceptance at the moment, but he would withdraw from her eventually. Especially once he'd fully reflected on the kind of woman he married. She was flawed and broken, ruined in every sense of the word. No amount of serving others would absolve her from her past. No amount of saying she was sorry could erase the harm she'd caused.

Worse still, they would always live in fear of discovery. Lies would have to keep the world from knowing what she'd done. Fitz would grow tired of keeping her secrets. And then he would grow to regret marrying her. Regret would turn into resentment. And . . . no.

Gigi couldn't bear to watch him grow cold and detached again. For his sake, she should refuse his offer of marriage. She should give him no chance to ask the question. It was the one thing she could do for him.

And yet, she found herself saying, "Let's hear your plan."

"We tell our families we're engaged."

Something wonderful filled her heart. "Are you saying you want to marry me?"

"Forgive me." He rubbed a hand across his forehead. "I'm making a hash of this. I've spent the last thirty minutes reviewing a series of . . . calculations, and my mind is still half on the pages."

His confession softened her guard, and Gigi found herself feeling a moment of deep affection for this man. How desperately she wanted to marry him.

"My father is much the same way." She found the similarity endearing, which made her more than a little homesick and determined to mend all her relationships. "After a long day of reviewing contracts, my mother claims he is the worst conversationalist imaginable."

"Then you understand."

"Completely." A horrible, awful spark of hope ignited. Perhaps they could be together. Perhaps Fitz wouldn't grow to despise her. Perhaps they could make a go of marriage.

Stop lying to yourself, Gigi.

"I don't think it's wise to enter a pretend engagement," she said, mostly for herself. "We both know what comes from lying."

"Let me finish spelling out my plan."

What more could he possibly have to say?

"We'll keep the story simple and stick as close to the truth as possible." He relaxed into a smile, the one she loved, the one he reserved just for her. "I came to meet you in New York and we fell in love."

Those four words, *we fell in love*, touched the deepest chambers of her heart. A sob rose in her throat. She would remember this moment forever. She would tuck the memory in a quiet corner of her heart, along with images of Fitz looking at her with tenderness, affection. Love.

Hope tried to get the better of her. She ruthlessly battled it back. "You know that won't be enough for my father."

"We'll tell him more, of course." He smiled, though a hint of regret showed in his eyes. "I'll admit that I've been searching for you since you disappeared, which happens to be the truth. Then, when I got word you were in New York, I came to fetch you and bring you home."

Gigi pressed her fingertips to her temples and rubbed. "You are missing one key component in your story. What will we tell my father about the pearls?"

"I'll leave that portion of the story up to you." He gave her a sweet smile. She saw no judgment in him, only the solid support he'd shown when she'd admitted the truth, which somehow made her feel worse. "Whatever you decide to tell your father, I won't contradict you."

Oh, Fitz. "I won't ask you to lie for me."

But, of course, he would have to lie for her. He'd already done so with Brian Chesterfield.

"I'm afraid it's too late for that. We're in this together, Gigi. We stand as one."

How long she'd waited for him to say those words, longer than she'd realized.

"I won't abandon you." The sincerity in his promise stole her breath. Gigi wasn't sure she could love Fitz any more than she did at this moment.

Perhaps there was a chance for them after all.

"Of course, we won't stay engaged for long."

And there it was. The end of all hope.

She would not cry. She would not cry.

She. Would. Not. Cry.

"What reason will we give for our"—she choked back a sob— "change of mind?"

"Not *our* change of mind, *yours*." He hit her with the full force of his stare. "We'll say you broke off the engagement because I proved to be as coldhearted as everyone claims."

She looked at him blankly, absently noting how the lighting in the room emphasized the nearly blue-black of his hair. "But it's not true. When you let down your guard, you are kind and compassionate and—"

"I insist you walk away from this free and clear, Gigi. A fresh start, that's what I wish for you." His tone was both gentle and firm.

"Your reputation will suffer."

"Hang my reputation."

The monumental sacrifice he was willing to make on her behalf was staggering. "We must share the blame."

"No, Gigi. You must be the injured party. I insist upon it."

There he went, being noble again. Knowing that he would risk his reputation for hers gave her the courage to say, "If I refuse to go along with this plan of yours, what then?"

He said nothing.

"What if . . . what if I refuse to break things off?"

He closed his eyes and gave a slight shudder. "We cannot marry, Gigi."

His tone brooked no argument. There was such finality in the words, as if he couldn't think of a worse fate than linking his life with hers. But when he opened his eyes, she saw the flash of longing in their depths. It was the same emotion that shot through her.

Maybe, just maybe, he thought her worthy enough to marry.

Then why push her away? *Again?* She knew, of course. The answer was all too painfully clear. Still, she needed him to say the words. Gaining her feet, she held his gaze and asked, "Is your reluctance to be with me because of my past?"

She was in his arms before she finished speaking. He buried his face in her hair, murmuring her name over and over again. She clung to him with as much fervor.

"No, Gigi, never think that. Not even for a moment. You are brave and strong and I can't think of anyone I admire more. You have endured hardships and have done more than survive. You have thrived. You have become a woman of honor and integrity. I am humbled to know you."

The words she'd longed to hear, said with such sincerity. But also with such . . . regret. "Then why don't you want to marry me?"

He set her away from him and moved to the center of the room, his arms stiff at his sides, his back ramrod straight. "Every man of your acquaintance will race to assure you that you deserve better than a life shackled to me."

Why, oh why, had Fitz once again put up the invisible wall between them? She circled back to the beginning of their argument. "What if I don't want to call off our engagement?"

There. She saw it again. The spark in his eyes that told her he wanted to take her as his wife. Or perhaps it was simply wishful thinking on her part.

Aware of the risk she was taking, she progressed across the room until she was within inches of him. Though he remained unmoving, she heard his breath catch. It was all the encouragement she needed.

"Admit it, Fitz. You care for me."

Another shudder moved through him. "Of course I care for you. I have always cared."

Most marriages in their world were based on far less.

"Would it be so bad, then, if we married?"

"It would be . . ." He swallowed. Shaking his head, he clamped his mouth shut and said nothing more. He looked absolutely miserable.

She saw the truth in his eyes. The love. Though he hadn't said the words, Gigi knew that Christopher Nolan Fitzpatrick loved her.

There was no joy in the knowledge.

Finally, she knew what stood between them. If they had any chance of being together, Fitz must trust her, as she trusted him.

"Fitz." His name came from low in her throat and sounded really quite wonderful, as if she'd been meant to say his name, just that way, all her life. "Tell me one thing I don't know about you. Just one. Something no one else knows."

He went still as a statue. "You know more than most."

His vague response slammed into her like a punch. "You have a secret, something you're not telling me."

"You are very persistent."

"Part of my charm."

A shadow of a smile played across his lips.

Gigi responded in kind.

For that one moment, everything felt right between them, comfortable even, a solidarity that went beyond words.

But then . . .

Fitz's brow creased. Somehow, Gigi knew the source of that look wasn't her. She wanted him to . . . no, she *needed* him to share his burdens with her.

Without thinking too hard about what she was doing, she reached out to him. "Tell me what troubles you, Fitz."

His eyes went dark and turbulent, then shuttered closed. When they opened again, Gigi saw the withdrawn man she'd left in Boston. "I'm merely worried about you. I put you in a tough spot this afternoon, and it's tearing me apart."

Just like that, the progress they'd made in the past few weeks was gone. But why? "Is it something to do with your family?"

A muscle shifted at his jawline. For a moment, she thought he would tell her the truth. Gigi waited, the world seeming to slow down and wait with her.

Fitz glanced at his desk, frowned.

She followed the direction of his gaze but saw only several slips of paper spread across the surface, a cup of writing utensils, and an inkpot.

He rolled his shoulders as if to relieve the weight there. "We were talking about our engagement."

"You mean our *fake* engagement."

His brow was furrowed once again, making him appear more confused than thoughtful. "The timing of our breakup will have to be carefully thought through."

He wasn't going to open up to her.

Gigi tried to shrug off her sorrow, but this moment was bigger than her, and she simply couldn't find a way to get past the agony of losing Fitz. When she'd only just found him.

Pushed past her endurance, she gave up all pretense of control and glared at the confounding man. If she were wise, she would turn around and walk out the door. After, of course, she issued a dazzling set-down.

Or . . .

She could be a little more daring. She could tap into the woman she'd been long ago, the woman who knew how to attract a man's interest—before one secret, scandalous act had changed her from the inside out.

"You are hiding something painful within your heart, Fitz. No, don't deny it." She drew even closer, giving him one last chance to confide. "Keeping it to yourself is hurting you. You need to unload your burdens with someone who cares. Let that someone be me."

A single winged eyebrow lifted in surprise.

She gave him a soft smile. "You listened to me. It's my turn to listen to you."

Now both eyebrows rose.

It was a very intimidating look, dark, brooding, slightly dangerous. Most women would be cowed.

Gigi was not. This was Fitz. The man she loved. "Let me be the one you share your secret with. Let me be your helpmate."

"I don't have a secret."

"Oh, but you do." She placed her palm flat on his chest. The muscles beneath her hand were coiled tightly as a spring. "You told me so yourself, so it's beneath both of us to argue otherwise."

He looked so weary. Fatigued by whatever he kept buried in his heart. "Did you just accuse me of lying? *Sally?*"

Mutiny swept through her, making her bolder than she'd been in a very long time. "Don't turn this back on me."

It was his turn to glare.

"Go ahead. Stand there all silent and broody. But I'm not leaving this room until you tell me what's going on with you, Fitz." She poked him in the chest. "I mean it."

"We've had this discussion before. I . . . cannot."

"You mean, you will not."

His expression didn't change at the accusation.

"Please, Fitz, give me your trust."

Making a sound deep in his throat, he moved to the small writing desk. He placed his hand over the stack of papers and took a long, rough pull of air.

Lifting his hand, he muttered something under his breath.

Gigi didn't catch all of what he said, but she thought she might have heard *perhaps it's possible.*

Not sure what he meant, she whispered his name. "Fitz?"

He drummed his fingers atop the stack. "I have to go to Boston."

"You're leaving? When?"

He drew in another careful breath. "Tonight."

He couldn't mean to . . .

"You're going to speak to my father? Tonight?"

"Not your father. Mine."

"But why?"

"I can't—"

"—tell me. Yes, I know." She bit back a sigh. "Will you return for opening night at the Summer Garden?"

For a span of three breaths, he said nothing, merely frowned down at the floor. "I will try."

He looked back down at his desk, reached out, and stuffed the small stack of papers into an inner pocket of his suit jacket. His gaze shifted to Gigi. A moment's hesitation, and then, in the next heartbeat, she was back in his arms. She didn't know who'd moved first, her or him, but did it matter?

His lips pressed to hers tentatively, pulled away, pressed again. Fitz was telling her good-bye.

She thought she might be sick.

"I have to go."

Her mouth went dry. Every muscle in her body tensed.

She'd just lost him, before she'd ever really won him. "You'll want to pack. I'll leave you to it."

She walked to the door, reached for the handle, stopped when he called her name. "Gigi, wait."

Her hand froze. Unable to find the courage to turn around and look at him, she pressed her forehead to the door.

Purposeful footsteps struck the floor as he approached. Closer. Closer. He reached around her, pressed his palm on the door as if to keep her from opening it, then quickly dropped his hand. "I prefer not to speak to your back."

It was the desperation in his voice that had her turning. His expression was fierce, his eyes hot enough to burn. "Gigi, I vow I will do everything in my power to—"

She launched herself at him, all but burrowing when he pulled her close and called her his love. His love. Not a declaration, but close. Gigi had to struggle not to lose herself in the moment. "Don't go."

"I can't stay."

With those three words, all hope was gone. "Good-bye, Fitz."

Chapter Twenty-One

Fitz didn't make it back to New York in time for opening night. Gigi hadn't held out much hope that he would.

Who was she kidding?

Of course she'd held out hope.

For every hour he was gone, all forty-five and three quarters of them, she'd waited anxiously for his return.

He'd sent no word. Not a telegram, not a note by special courier, nothing.

His silence hurt.

And the longer he stayed away, the more certain she became that he would never return.

To make matters worse, Gigi had another, equally troubling situation to deal with. Sophie had disappeared. The young woman had gone missing the same night Fitz had left town.

At least Sophie had left word. Nothing more than a hastily scribbled note, but that was better than no communication at all.

Now, as Gigi unfolded the piece of parchment paper for what must have been the seventieth time in two days, she admitted the truth to herself.

She'd failed Sophie. As surely as if she'd personally helped the young woman escape the town house with her lover. Gigi prayed her friend's tale would end better than her own.

She lowered her head and read the runaway's words.

My Dearest Gigi,
Your brave story has given me the daring to take my own
leap of faith. Robert has asked me to marry him, and I
have said yes. By the time you read this, I will be away.
> *Please. Do not worry for me. Robert is a good man. He*
is no Nathanial. He is my Fitz. And I am blissfully happy.
> *With all my love,*
> *Sophie*

"Oh, Sophie, what have you done?" Gigi pressed the note to her heart.

Her friend had listened to her story and somehow used it to rationalize running off with the man she loved. *He is no Nathanial. He is my Fitz.* Well, that was certainly unexpected.

Gigi's one consolation was Esmeralda's reaction to Sophie's act of defiance. In a surprising twist that rivaled any fictional plot, when Gigi has screwed up the nerve to tell the opera singer about Sophie's note, Esmeralda hadn't blamed Gigi for her daughter's rash behavior.

She'd blamed herself. "I should have realized Sophie's resentment toward me ran deep."

"I'm sorry, ma'am."

"Yes, yes." She'd brushed off Gigi's sorrow with a dismissive wave. "I know you are, my dear."

They'd come to an understanding that day, one that transcended their age difference. They were two women with regrets and a strong desire to see their loved ones protected from the consequences of their mistakes.

Heart heavy, Gigi placed Sophie's note on her dresser, her eyes catching on a single sentence.

He is my Fitz.

Oh, how Gigi hoped that was true. If Robert Dain turned out to be half the man that Fitz was, then there was no cause for concern.

Please, Lord, let it be so.

It wasn't the first prayer Gigi had uttered in the past two days. Each time she lifted up a request to the Lord, her burdens seemed to grow lighter. She was starting to feel restored, not quite the old Gigi, but not Sally, either.

In an effort to renew her spirit, she'd spent hours reading her Bible and was coming to understand two profound realizations: God's plan often incorporated His people's mistakes, and He was actively involved in the intricate design of His children's lives.

For the first time in a year, Gigi looked at herself through God's eyes and felt whole again.

She went in search of Esmeralda so they could set the time for their departure to the theater. To her surprise, the singer was ready to leave.

"This early?"

"I prefer to arrive ahead of the others. Walking through each scene is part of my opening-night ritual."

With the entire household staff waving from the doorway, they climbed into Esmeralda's private carriage. Once they were settled on opposite seats, the singer dug around in her reticule. "Before I forget, this is for you."

She passed Gigi an envelope. "What is it?"

Proving she truly didn't hold Sophie's behavior against Gigi, she said, "Consider it a token of my appreciation."

"For?"

"For skillfully guiding my daughter through these difficult months."

Feeling like a fraud, Gigi tried to return the envelope.

Esmeralda would have none of it. "You taught Sophie how to move successfully in her father's world. She had her chance to rise above the condition of her birth."

Regret whirled in Gigi's stomach. "She ran off with a man."

"A man who happens to be an educated doctor. It is more than I hoped."

The churning in Gigi's stomach eased. Still, she made another attempt to return whatever Esmeralda had stuffed in the thick envelope.

"Do not insult me."

Gigi stuffed the envelope in the pocket of her skirt. "Thank you."

"You are most welcome."

Esmeralda proceeded to shift around, stretching out her legs, pulling them back in, repeating the process over and over again. It was the first time Gigi had seen the diva nervous. "Tell me what I can do."

"Your calming presence is enough."

How ironic that Esmeralda was the Cappelletti woman who required Gigi's *calming presence*. At least someone needed her, Gigi thought with a spurt of gratitude.

Her pleasure was short-lived.

As soon as they arrived at the theater, Esmeralda banished Gigi from her sight with a little shove. "Go away, now. I wish to walk through my scenes minus any distractions, your company included."

Well then. With extra time on her hands, Gigi decided to set up the makeshift nursery for later that evening. She'd promised Jessica and the other single mothers that she would watch their children during the performance.

One more in a long line of surprises awaited her there. "Oh, I . . ." Her eyes narrowed. "Who are you?"

"I'm Mrs. Tupper. And you must be Sally." The plump elderly woman had a mane of long white hair, smiling eyes, and a grandmotherly air about her.

"Uh . . . yes, I'm Sally." How odd to hear that name in reference to herself. In two short days, despite carrying out her household and theater duties, she'd become Gigi again.

She chanced a peek around the other woman and felt her eyes widen. The room actually looked like a real nursery.

The floors gleamed from a recent polishing. New rugs had been moved in and the excess furniture out. The piano was situated against one wall, a small bookcase on another. There were several trunks overflowing with toys, while child-sized cots lined the farthest wall.

"You seem confused, dear."

That was a magnificent understatement. "Who did you say you were?"

"I am Mrs. Tupper. I have been hired to watch the children."

Hired? "By whom?"

"Mr. Everett, of course."

Fitz had followed through with his plan for the children. He'd managed to convince the theater owner to turn this room into a permanent nursery. "When did he hire you?"

"Yesterday afternoon. Apparently, a generous patron is underwriting my salary."

That was so . . . Fitz. The dear, wonderful, thoughtful man.

Gigi hardly trusted herself to speak. She let out a breath. "You've been busy."

"I suppose I have been, with the stage manager's assistance. Mr. McClain was quite adamant that his men help me put the nursery in order." The older woman took a moment to glance around the room. "There is still more I wish to do, but I'm pleased with the start I've made." Satisfaction swirled in her gaze.

"Is there anything I can do to help?"

Mrs. Tupper suggested that Gigi ask the wardrobe mistress if she needed any assistance.

Mere seconds later, Gigi stood in the dark hallway, staring at a firmly shut door. "That certainly put me in my place."

She wandered around to the wardrobe closet and was met with a similar lack of desire for her services. With no one requiring her help, Gigi found herself at loose ends. *I want to go home.*

What was stopping her?

Twenty-five dollars. Gigi was still twenty-five dollars short of being able to redeem her great-grandmother's pearls.

Members of the orchestra had begun to arrive. She could listen to them tune their instruments. Or perhaps not. The disjointed musical notes would only serve to agitate her further.

Her ears caught the subtle sound of female conversation. Gigi moved in that direction. She hesitated on the fringes of the group, engaging herself in silent debate. She didn't really want to talk with anyone. Turning, she gathered her skirts away from her ankles and froze. The sound of paper crinkling reminded her of the envelope Esmeralda had given her.

Consider it a token of my appreciation.

Curious at the meaning behind the cryptic words, Gigi dipped her hand in her pocket and fished out the envelope. Slipping her fingertip beneath the flap, she flicked it open and peered at the contents inside.

"Oh, my." Her fingers skimmed over the bills. Counting the denominations silently in her head, she came up with an impossible sum.

She counted again.

Shock had her collapsing against a nearby wall.

In her hand, Gigi held more than enough money to redeem her great-grandmother's pearls.

It's over. I can go home.

All that stood in her way was ten city blocks and one final transaction with a shady pawnbroker.

Tomorrow, Gigi promised herself. First thing in the morning, she would buy back the necklace.

She didn't want to wait, but the afternoon had gotten away from her. With empty hours stretching before her, she tapped her foot in impatience. If she packed her suitcase tonight, she could leave for Boston as soon as her business at the pawnshop was complete.

Unable to contain her excitement, Gigi shoved away from the wall and hurried toward the exit.

A hand on her arm stalled her progress.

"Sally, where are you going in such a rush?"

"Home," she told the wardrobe mistress. "Oh, Mrs. Llewellyn, I am going home."

* * *

Fitz leaned against the wall opposite the door he'd just exited, heart in his throat. The last two days had been harrowing to say the least, tonight the worst yet. After working at the office tying up loose ends on several contracts, he'd arrived at his parents' home far later than planned and had been confronted with utter chaos.

His father had been in the middle of an *episode*, according to his mother. *Night terrors* was the more technical term. One of the specialists Fitz had consulted in New York had warned him what to expect. The doctor had claimed that Calvin Fitzpatrick might be capable of performing violent acts during a course of five to twenty minutes and then, when it was over, not remember a thing.

Fitz wouldn't have believed it if he hadn't witnessed it for himself.

Hand shaking, he speared his fingers through his hair. Matters were far worse than he'd realized.

Unable to stand still, Fitz pushed away from the wall and paced back and forth down the long corridor. His father had come at him, eyes burning with rage, accusing Fitz of stealing his golf clubs. Fitz hadn't played a single game of golf in his life.

No amount of reasoning had calmed his father. Taller by three inches and with thirty pounds of additional muscle, it had still taken Fitz considerable effort to physically subdue the older man. When he was finally calm, Calvin Fitzpatrick hadn't remembered any of his anger, or the reason for his fury, or that he'd accidentally landed a blow on his son's face.

Flexing his fingers, Fitz went back to alternating between pacing and praying. Praying and pacing.

Pacing and praying.

He'd come home for clarity. He'd certainly gotten that.

The door to his father's bedroom swung open, and his mother stepped out into the hallway.

Fitz strode over to her. Taking note of the worry creasing her brow and the pale color of her complexion, he opened his arms in silent invitation.

She entered his embrace without hesitation.

"Oh, Fitz," she said in a low, pain-filled tone. "I'm sorry you had to see him that way."

"Does he have these episodes often?"

"Hardly ever. Only when his sleep is interrupted." She pressed her cheek into his shoulder. "He must have heard you arrive."

Fitz inhaled his mother's scent, a soft mix of iris and mint. "I'm sorry."

"You didn't know." She stepped back. Within her eyes resided all the fatigue and sorrow she endured. "His night nurse gave him a seda-tive. He'll sleep through the night now."

"Praise God for that." Fitz studied his mother's face. She looked exhausted, her dull, lifeless skin showing every bit of her sixty-five years. "Why didn't you tell me he was having night terrors?"

"They're rare, and I didn't want you to think poorly of your father."

More secrets. More lies.

Fitz breathed through his frustration. With each breath, a hot ball of dread expanded in his throat. His eyes throbbed, his heart ached, and a dozen simultaneous thoughts shuffled through his mind, pinpointing one frightening concern. "Has Father ever attacked you?"

"Never." She must have seen his skepticism, because she added, "I promise. Tonight was the first time he's become inconsolable."

Fitz still wasn't sure he believed her. When he persisted, Mary Fitzpatrick stuck to her story. "All I can think is that he didn't recognize you."

That had been excruciatingly evident. His father had called him Sebastian. They had no Sebastian in the family.

The truth could no longer be denied. Calvin Fitzpatrick was losing his mind.

"Oh, dear. Look at your eye." His mother reached up and touched an especially tender spot.

Fitz winced.

She immediately went into her role as caregiver. "Come with me." She hooked her arm through his. "We'll put some ice on it to stop the swelling."

Minutes later, Fitz was sitting in his parents' enormous kitchen while his mother searched for a clean cloth to wrap around the chunk of ice quickly melting in her hand. She opened and closed drawers, coming up empty.

Fitz stopped her before she could mount a search through the entire house. Standing, he took the ice and set it in the sink. "My eye is fine."

"It's already turning purple."

"It's fine," he repeated, then softened his volume when she flinched at his harsh tone. "Truly. Please, Mother. Sit. Now that we're alone, I want to discuss something with you."

After another round of opening and closing a series of drawers, she finally admitted defeat and did as Fitz requested. He sat beside her.

With her no longer in constant motion, he was better able to take in her features. She'd aged considerably in the past year and had lost weight, too much. Her clothes practically hung on her thin frame. Her coal-black hair was streaked with thick strands of gray, and the once wrinkle-free face was lined and haggard from worry.

As much as he hated saying the words, Fitz couldn't help but voice what was in his heart. "You can't go on like this."

"He is my husband." She said this as though it were explanation enough.

"He's not the man you married."

"Of course he is." Faded blue eyes rolled up to his, distress written all over the still-pretty face. "I pledged to love him in sickness and health, till death do us part. It is my greatest joy to care for the man I love."

There was honor in that kind of devotion, Fitz knew, but he still found himself saying, "Even if caring for him is killing you?"

"I'm fine, really."

"You could put him in an institution." There, he'd said the words that had been on his tongue for weeks.

Instead of feeling better, Fitz felt worse, shameful even, as if he didn't love his father enough.

But he *did* love him. He grieved for the man who was slowly disappearing into a dark place, locked away somewhere in his own mind. And his mother was trapped right there with him. By choice. "You don't have to carry this burden alone."

"I'm not alone. You and your cousin have made sure of that. I have a team of nurses at my disposal."

"That's not what I meant."

"Fitz, try to understand." His mother offered him a soft smile. "Your father and I have been married for over thirty years. I have loved him in the happy times, the trying ones, and the terrifying moments like what you witnessed tonight. I have no regrets, other than to say I wish he wasn't suffering so."

There was a lesson in her words, Fitz thought grimly, but he couldn't seem to process exactly what it was he should be learning.

"Where do you get the strength?" he wondered aloud.

"It's not my strength that gets me through, but the strength the Lord provides in my times of weakness."

Fitz looked into his mother's face and saw the very definition of sacrificial love shining back at him. She wasn't a religious woman. Or, rather, she hadn't been before his father took ill. "You don't regret marrying Father?"

"Not for a single minute." Her eyes filled with tears. "The Lord brought Calvin Fitzpatrick into my life, and I cherish every moment I have with him."

An image of Gigi flashed in Fitz's mind. He thought of her delicate beauty. She was strong and capable, more now for the hardships she'd endured.

He loved her. Too much to ask her to live through what his mother suffered. "I spoke with some specialists in New York."

"That wasn't necessary. We have excellent doctors here in Boston. Some of the best in the world."

"I wanted anonymity for the questions I had."

"What sort of questions did you have that you couldn't ask his doctor here?"

Fitz told her about his concern that his father's condition was hereditary, ending with, "The research is inconclusive."

She digested this information in silence.

"Mother, may I ask you something?"

Still thoughtful, his mother reached out and patted his hand. "Anything, dear."

"If you had known about Father's illness before the wedding, would you have married him anyway?"

"Absolutely, I would."

She'd said it without hesitation. "You don't want to take a moment and think about your answer?"

"I don't need a moment. Fitz, darling." She laid her hand over his. "What's this really about?"

"I've found the woman I want to marry, but I . . ." He didn't know how to finish the thought.

"Ah. You're afraid you'll turn out like your father and don't want this young woman to turn out like . . . me."

"When you put it that way, it sounds like I'm trying—"

"To play God?"

"I was going to say, trying to rationalize my decision to protect the woman I love."

"Fitz. Let me ask *you* a question. If your roles were reversed, and this woman was the one destined to become ill, would you still want to marry her?"

His answer came as quickly as his mother's had. "Absolutely, I would."

"You don't want to take a moment and think about your answer?"

A low chuckle rumbled in his chest. "Point taken."

"Since neither of us is going to sleep tonight, why don't you tell me about this woman you want to marry."

In the low light of the kitchen, Fitz told his mother about searching for and subsequently finding Gigi. He didn't reveal anything about the pearls or Gigi's time spent with Nathanial, but instead focused on the way his own feelings had morphed from infatuation to a deep, abiding love. "I always cared for her, but now, when I think of the woman she's become, I'm honored to know her. My heart aches for her. It literally aches."

His mother went to the door and swung it open with a flourish. The beginnings of a new day were evident on the pink-tinged sky beyond the backyard.

"Well?" she asked. "What are you waiting for, son? Go get the woman you love."

Chapter Twenty-Two

"I'm sorry, Miss Smith. I'm afraid the pearls are no longer in my possession."

Stunned speechless, Gigi blinked at the pawnbroker. She must have misunderstood. He couldn't have said her great-grandmother's pearls were gone. "You . . . *what?*" she croaked.

"I sold the necklace."

No, it wasn't possible. Mr. Ryerson couldn't be this cruel. "We had an agreement."

The eyes that looked at her were sharp and measuring. "What can I say? The client made me an offer I couldn't refuse."

"But you . . ." Fury surged, prowling through her blood, seeking release like a wild animal straining at its leash. "You put your promise in writing."

Surely, he would honor their agreement.

Forcing down her panic, Gigi fumbled inside the velvet satchel on her lap, pulled out the piece of paper, and slid it across the desk.

"Ah, yes, that." He studied the promissory note with a satisfied smirk. "There are only two signatures here, yours and mine. You failed to secure witnesses to our transaction."

"What does that mean?"

"Our agreement was never legally binding." He spoke casually, as if he were discussing a change in the weather. Then, with a wicked grin, he proceeded to shred the paper into tiny pieces.

"Stop." Gigi jumped to her feet. "You . . . you can't do that."

"I just did." He dropped the remaining scraps of their agreement in the trash bin at his feet. "Our business is concluded, Miss Smith. My clerk will see you out."

Finished with her now, he picked up his pencil, lowered his head, and proceeded to make random marks on the ledger beneath his hand.

The rising temper inside Gigi writhed and kicked for release. The muscles in her stomach tightened. She was out of her league. She'd known this for some time, but had pretended she held a portion of the control.

The air in her lungs grew hot, so hot she feared she would faint. Oh, but her fingers were ice. She might be out of her league, but she was not out of dignity.

She lost her fragile grip on her composure and released her anger. "You are a swindler and a thief."

Mr. Ryerson ignored her. The scratching of his pencil across the page tore at her attempt to remain calm.

"You prey on people in desperate need of your help. How do you sleep at night?"

"You'll have to excuse me if I'm not overwhelmed with remorse." He set down his pencil and sat back in his chair. "I am a man of commerce, Miss . . . Smith. Whatever trouble led you to my shop is not my concern."

Gigi thought of the compassion he'd shown her that day she'd entered his *shop*. It had all been a lie. All along, this man had held the control. He probably wanted her to beg, to cry. Dry eyes were her only defense.

"Have you no shame?"

He regarded her with blank, patient eyes, giving the impression he considered her daft. "You fell short of the money you needed to redeem the necklace. I had an eager buyer willing to make up the difference and then some."

"When did you sell it?"

"Two days after your previous visit. The man was leaving the country and, as I said before, he made me an offer I couldn't refuse."

That, Gigi decided, was the very last straw.

All the money in the world couldn't bring the pearls back. They were gone. Sold. But to whom?

Please, Lord, let it not be over. "What did the man look like?"

"I beg your pardon?"

Wild with hope, she clutched the velvet satchel tightly to her. Perhaps the heirloom that had been in her family for generations wasn't lost after all. "The man who purchased the pearls, what did he look like?"

Please, Lord, please let him describe Fitz.

"Short, middle-aged, slightly overweight, receding hairline, British accent."

It was no use. Her great-grandmother's pearls were gone forever. Concealing her grief, Gigi crossed to the exit. She didn't look back. There was nothing left for her in this building.

Out on the street, the light hurt her eyes. The air roared with the noise of her defeat.

It's over.

She would have to go home empty-handed. Just like the Prodigal Son, she would have to face her father with nothing but a contrite heart.

* * *

It took Gigi a full hour to gather up her suitcase and bid farewell to the rest of the household staff. She was going to miss this group of former actors turned servants. They'd been good to her, accepting her without question.

Gigi took her time telling them each what they'd meant to her, finishing her words with a fierce hug. Mrs. Garrison hugged her the hardest in return. "You will be terribly missed, Sally."

Gigi would miss Sally as well.

The young maid had taught the frivolous heiress how to work hard, take care of herself, and love with a servant's heart.

"Thank you, Mrs. Garrison, for everything." Blinking back yet another bout of tears, Gigi kissed the weathered cheek. "I have one final favor to ask of you."

"Whatever you need."

"Will you give these to Sophie and Esmeralda?" She handed the housekeeper two envelopes.

Gigi would have preferred to say good-bye in person. But Esmeralda was still abed and Sophie had yet to return from her honeymoon. In her letter to the younger woman, Gigi had urged her friend to write and let her know she was safe.

Gigi gave Mrs. Garrison her forwarding address and, with nothing else to say, made her way to Grand Central Station.

* * *

Fitz jumped off the train while it was still pulling to a stop. His feet barely hit the platform before he took off at a brisk pace. He wove through the throngs of other travelers with purposeful intent. He'd had a lot of time to think on the journey from Boston to New York and had come to several conclusions about himself, none of them flattering.

For an intelligent man, Fitz had been exceedingly foolish and stubbornly prideful. *Can't forget prideful.* He'd convinced himself that pushing Gigi away was for her sake. Keeping her at a distance hadn't protected her.

It had protected him.

Fitz had a lot of groveling to do. He just hoped it would be enough to win her heart.

A movement out of the corner of his eye had his feet grinding to a halt. His breath stalled in his chest.

Set apart from the milling crowd, there stood Gigi, a small battered suitcase at her feet.

Fitz switched directions. *Let the groveling begin.*

Coming to a stop beside her, he drank in the sight of her.

"Fitz?" As if coming out of a trance, she slowly turned her head. A range of emotions raced across her face, shock the most dominant. "You came back."

"I couldn't stay away."

The skin beneath her eyes was dark with fatigue, but the eyes themselves were bright and full of happiness. She was happy to see him.

"Oh. Oh, Fitz." A gasp slipped out of her. "What happened to your eye?"

"It's a long story. I'll tell you all about it, every detail." He held her gaze, willing her to hear the unspoken message in his words. "I promise you that, Gigi, and I always keep my promises."

Her entire bearing softened. "I know. It's one of the things I love most about you."

She loved him. He saw it in her eyes, heard it in her voice.

His heart stopped beating too fast. With affection and without caring who saw them, he bent to place a tender kiss on her forehead, her nose, her lips.

A pretty blush spread across her cheeks. "I'm very happy to see you."

"And I, you." He couldn't get enough of looking at her.

The soft curve of her lips, the light in her eyes, and the slight tilt of her head all called to him. Stunning from every angle, she'd always been beautiful.

Now, she made him yearn.

Lost in the moment, in the girl from his past who'd become the woman he loved, he paused a while and simply stared.

Big, expressive eyes looked back at him. For a moment, unspoken promises flowed between them. Fitz would spend a lifetime following through with every one of them.

"Gigi, I want—"

The blast of a high-pitched train whistle interrupted the rest of his speech.

Swallowing back his frustration, Fitz looked down at the suitcase sitting at her feet. "Did I catch you leaving New York?"

Her eyes slid past him, brushed over the train pulling into the station, then slid back. "I'm going home."

One side of his mouth kicked up. "You redeemed the pearls."

"No, I, that is . . . the pawnbroker . . ." She caught her bottom lip between her teeth. "He sold them."

"They weren't his to sell."

Fury flashed in her blue eyes. "No, they were not."

Fitz angled his head. "I thought you had a written agreement."

"We did." In short, clipped sentences, Gigi told him about the promissory note lacking the signatures of two witnesses.

Fitz had experienced a host of disagreeable emotions in the past three days, but nothing compared to the rage that scorched through him now. He drew in a hard breath. Let it out. His fury only deepened. "That crook."

"Mortifying as it is to admit, I trusted the wrong man. Again." She gave a short laugh devoid of all humor. "There's nothing to be done. The pearls are gone."

If only Fitz had acted when she'd first told him about the necklace. He should have gone to the pawnshop in Herald Square as soon as he'd known. "Did the pawnbroker say when he sold them?"

"A week ago, to a man with a British accent who was leaving the country."

Fitz wanted to hit something. No, he wanted to hit *someone*. The desire left him shaken to the bone. He'd been unable to make Nathanial Dixon pay for what he'd done to Gigi. This corrupt pawnbroker would not be so lucky.

"Tell me he at least told you the name of the man."

"He only gave me a description."

Fitz made a mental note to contact Mr. Offutt. With the help of the private investigator, he would make this right for Gigi. Somehow, someway, though the odds were stacked against him finding success. He started to tell her what he planned but was interrupted by a blast of steam and another ear-splitting train whistle.

As he tugged Gigi away from the tracks, Fitz reached down for her suitcase. Only when his hand closed over the handle did the magnitude of her presence at the train station hit him. "You're going home without the pearls."

Tears swam into her eyes. "I have no other choice."

"I'll go with you." He reached for her, cupped her cheek. "When you face your father, I will be right there, standing next to you."

Closing her hand over his wrist, she smiled tenderly. "It's a tempting offer. But I have to face him alone."

"You don't, Gigi. You really don't."

A cold wind swept off the tracks.

Gigi didn't seem to notice. "Do you remember when we went to church together?"

He nodded.

"And the sermon? Do you also remember that?"

Again, he nodded.

"I have read the story about the Prodigal Son at least twenty times since, but it wasn't until this morning, after I walked out of the pawnshop, that I had something of a revelation."

Her voice held raw vulnerability. Only a sense of propriety kept Fitz from pulling her into his arms and soothing away her pain. "What did you discover?"

"The Prodigal Son didn't repent until he lost everything. Only then, when he was at his lowest, did he go home. Don't you see? He returned home empty-handed." She lifted her hands, fingers splayed, to emphasize her point. "All he had to offer in exchange for his sins was a remorseful heart. That's how I will return to my father's house, with nothing but a remorseful heart."

Fitz didn't think he could love this woman any more than he did in that moment. "You are a courageous woman, Gigi Wentworth."

Her lips twisted at a wry angle. "I am also a very slow learner."

"We have that trait in common."

"How do you mean?"

The fast-moving crowd seemed to close in on them. Fitz was jostled from behind. He let out a weighty push of air.

"Let's sit." He looked around for a suitable place out of the main traffic. "There. On that bench beneath the blue awning."

With her suitcase in hand, he guided her across the crowded platform.

Fitz set down the luggage and joined Gigi on the bench. "On more than one occasion, you've asked me to confide in you."

Her fingers curled around his. "I remember."

"You were right. I should have opened up to you long ago."

Before she could do more than sigh, he told her about his father's illness. He left nothing out, baring his soul, giving her every detail of his fear and anger and frustration.

Her face drained of color. "That's awful. Why didn't you tell me he was that sick?"

Emotion clogged his throat, tightened his chest. "My mother swore me to secrecy. Besides her and me, the only other person who knows is my cousin Connor."

"That's why you feel indebted to him."

"He's told no one of my father's illness, which hasn't been easy. Especially"—Fitz's voice went hoarse—"at the office, where his symptoms were magnified."

"I can only imagine."

"The rumors are true about Connor and me. We pushed my father out of the company. We had to, for his sake, or risk exposing his condition."

Gigi squeezed his hand. "There are no words to express how sad I am about your father."

Now that he'd begun, Fitz held nothing back. He told Gigi about his father's night terrors, including the most recent episode that had resulted in his black eye.

Gigi placed a soft touch to his bruised skin. "Your poor mother. What a terrifying moment that must have been, watching her son forced to subdue her husband."

"The burden of my father's care is taking a heavy toll. She's aged considerably in the past year. But she is determined to ride out his illness with him, even to the grave. Her devotion leaves me in awe."

"Sounds like your parents have a solid, loving marriage."

Now that the topic of marriage had been broached, Fitz turned the conversation to the final piece of the tale, the part that directly affected their future together. "I have consulted several physicians, including specialists in brain diseases. My father's prognosis is grim."

"I'm so sorry." Gigi blinked rapidly but was unable to prevent a few tears from trailing down her cheeks. She swiped at them impatiently.

"It's so unfair. Your father is a good man, Fitz, one of the best I know. I've always liked him."

"He's always liked you."

They shared a sad, gut-wrenching smile.

"There's something else you should know. My father's disease could be hereditary." He commanded her gaze. "Now you know why we can't stay engaged."

"Oh, no you don't." She bounded to her feet, jammed her hands on her hips, and glared down at him. "Don't you dare use your father's illness as an excuse to push me away."

He stood, drawing himself up to his full height. "Gigi, you don't want to marry a man like me. Trust me on this. I've seen—"

"Do not make up my mind for me." She waved her finger in his face in a scolding manner that would put any schoolteacher to shame. "I am a grown woman. I know what I want and who. I love you, you big idiot."

"I love you, too, Gigi, too much to chain you to a man who may one day lose his mind."

"You're afraid."

He gave a short, bitter laugh. "You're right, I'm afraid. I'm afraid for you."

"You think that little of me?"

"I think that much of you. I won't sentence you to a lifetime of servitude to an invalid."

"That's not your decision to make. I love you, Fitz. In the same way your mother loves your father. And as you have already promised to stand by my side, I shall stand by yours. No matter what comes our way, we will weather it together. Do you hear what I'm saying?"

A smile tugged at his lips. She was offering him the precious gift of her heart. Her trust. Her future. "I hear you."

"At this point, any self-respecting gentleman with a modicum of sense would sweep me into his arms and whisper soft, affectionate words in my ear."

How he adored this woman. "He would, would he?"

"He would then tell me he loves me, has always loved me, and will love me until his last dying breath."

It sounded like the perfect way to start the rest of their lives together. Fitz stretched out his hand.

Gigi shifted out of reach. "I'm not through."

"My mistake."

Keeping her expression bland, she tilted her head at a haughty angle. "After he professes his love, he should promise to marry me as quickly as humanly possible."

Fitz liked that last part. A lot.

"Well?" Her foot started tapping out a rapid tattoo on the platform. "I'm waiting."

Had he truly thought he could live without her? No more. Not a second more.

He yanked her into his embrace. "I am completely and utterly unworthy of you, Gigi Wentworth. You make me want to be a better man. It would be my honor and privilege to stand by your side until we're old and gray."

She softened in his arms. "And?"

"I love you. I have always loved you, since I was in short pants and you wore girlish pinafores." He pressed his lips to her ear. "I will love you until my last dying breath."

"And . . . ?"

The woman was ruthless. Fitz wouldn't want her any other way.

"And . . . I promise to marry you as quickly as humanly possible. Say yes, my love." He pressed his mouth to her temple before pulling back far enough to stare into her lovely eyes. "Say you'll marry me."

"Yes, Fitz. I'll marry you."

He smiled down at her. *"And . . . ?"*

She laughed, a sweet tinkling sound that warmed his heart. "I want to marry you immediately, this week, no later than next. Our families will adjust to the shock."

"I'll make you a good husband."

"I'll make you a better wife."

Fitz had no doubt. They had a future to plan, hopes and dreams to share. He took Gigi's hand, lifted her suitcase, and said, "Let's go home."

Chapter Twenty-Three

Her father had agreed to see her. The thought gave Gigi small comfort as the family's stiff-backed butler led her to Harcourt Wentworth's private study on the first floor of Harvest House.

"You are to make yourself comfortable." He opened the door without fully securing eye contact. "Your father will be along shortly."

"Please tell him not to rush on my account. I don't mind waiting."

"I will relay your message." He turned to go, then paused and glanced back over his shoulder. His gaze filled with compassion. "If I may be so bold as to say, it's good to have you home, Miss Gigi."

"Thank you, Joseph. It's good to be home."

They shared a brief smile before he continued on his way. The moment he disappeared around the corner, Gigi stepped inside the cavernous room.

With nerves fluttering in her stomach, she roamed aimlessly. She barely glanced at the masculine décor, hardly noticed the rich wood paneling or bookshelves lining three of the four walls. The only sound she heard over the beat of her heart was her heels clicking across the polished floorboards.

This would be the hardest meeting of her life, far harder than that last time she'd entered her father's inner sanctum to defy his plans for her.

Please, Lord, let his anger have softened over time.

Unpleasant memories assailed her. Gigi let them come. She had no regrets, save one—her great-grandmother's pearls.

The sound of footsteps echoed from the vast hallway. Gigi recognized those hard strikes of heels to wood, like hammers to nails. Each step brought her father closer. Gigi would tell him about the pearls and then confess her other sins. No matter his reaction, she would be free.

This was it, then.

Her chance to stand firm.

A quick burst of fear stole her breath. The resulting pain in her chest was massive, like sharp, needle-thin icicles stabbing her heart.

Lord, please fill me with Your courage.

The footsteps grew louder.

Pasting a smile on her lips, Gigi pivoted to face the doorway. A shadow fell across the threshold, elongated, and then . . .

Harcourt Wentworth appeared.

Gigi's smile slipped.

Her father looked agonized. And older. His hair, once the same color as hers, now held more silver strands than red. Though his frame was still lean, he seemed to have shrunk an inch or two. His gray eyes, the color of morning fog, were red-rimmed and tired. He'd never looked more dear to her.

From his body language, Gigi could tell the shock of her sudden return had left him reeling. Even from this distance, she could see the muscles in his neck shift and tighten.

Silence hung between them, growing thick and heavy and uncomfortable.

Gigi braced for the moment when her father would throw her out of the house. Any minute, he would demand she leave his sight.

The command never came. And then she knew. He wasn't angry with her. He was hurt. Sad. And a little broken.

She had done that to him.

Everything in her shattered into tiny, jagged pieces. Her head grew dizzy from the effort to hold his gaze. So much strength there. And yet so much pain.

Pain I caused.

"Oh, Father, I'm so sorry."

"Gigi?" His shoulders flexed, then went still again. "Is it really you?"

She rushed forward, came to an abrupt halt. She nearly wobbled but forced her knees to lock. "I have come home. If . . . if you'll have me."

"My precious daughter." His arms were around her with the speed of a single blink. "My beautiful, stubborn, willful girl. Your mother and I have been so worried."

The sobs came then, big, loud, uncontrollable sobs that rocked her to the core.

"Please forgive me. Please . . ." Her voice strangled on the rest of the words.

"I forgave you the moment you disappeared." He set her away from him and studied her face with intensity. "We despaired of ever seeing you again."

The horror of what she'd put her family through brought back the shame. "I sent word that I was alive and well. You received the letters, didn't you?"

His head bobbed up and down, but the concern stayed in his gaze. "Were you truly well?"

"I . . ." She paused, thought over the past year. "I became a lady's maid. I was treated with respect and dignity and learned the value of hard work."

Relief entered his eyes. "I imagined the worst."

"I'm sorry."

He turned to pace and, running a hand through his hair, added, "Your letters gave little detail of your life. Your mother decided that meant you were well. Not I. I feared you were stuck in some hovel, frightened, alone, left to fend for yourself, with no money or skills to speak of. And there was nothing I could do. Nothing."

He was blaming himself. The remorse in his voice was so unexpected her stomach dipped.

"I cannot tell you how many times I wanted to go back and relive our last conversation." His hand raked through his hair again. "I would have never issued those threats. I would have attempted harder to reason with you."

"I'm not sure I would have listened."

"Perhaps not. You have too much of your father in you." His tone was not unkind but rather a bit wistful, maybe even a little ironic, and full of love.

"I should have come home and asked for your forgiveness sooner."

His face tightened. "Why didn't you?"

"I couldn't." Her voice broke as she told him about Nathanial's abandonment.

"So, it was as bad as I feared."

She told of her despair and shock. As she spoke, her father never once interrupted, but he looked at her with devastated eyes.

"I was desperate." The words came out on a gasp. Even to her own ears, there was such regret in the sound. So. Much. Regret. "I could think of no way out. I didn't dare turn to you."

"Why would you?" His voice cracked. "You must have been afraid."

"Terrified. But I wasn't completely without resources." She took a hard breath. "And so, I did the only thing I could think to save myself."

A pall of silence fell over them, broken only by the sound of a clock ticking somewhere in the distance.

"What did you do, Gigi?"

"I sold your grandmother's pearls." The confession did nothing to soothe her nerves.

A muscle twitched in her father's jaw, a sure sign of his irritation. More than irritation, she thought.

Anger.

Fury.

But no, none of those emotions were in her father's gaze. He looked at her with tears in his eyes.

At the obvious sign of his sorrow, sorrow for her, a fist of ice clutched Gigi's heart and squeezed. She didn't know what to do with such undeserved understanding. Her father had always been so hard, an unforgiving rock in the face of iniquity.

With awkward movements, Gigi reached out and touched his hand. "Father? Did you hear me?"

He shut his eyes and released a shudder. "Thank God you had the pearls."

Words backed up in Gigi's throat. "Yes, but . . . I sold them. I'm sorry, Father."

She couldn't stop saying the words, no more than she could stop the tears from spilling out of her eyes. A crack in her heart opened, begging this man to fill it with acceptance and fatherly love. "Can you forgive me for the pain I have caused you and the family?"

He reached out and gripped her hand. "We were both wrong. I forgive you, my darling girl, and I ask that you forgive me in return." For the first time in Gigi's memory, he focused that hard tone of censure on himself. "I abandoned you, as surely as that fortune hunter did. For that, I owe you my own apology."

What an odd turn of events. Gigi had come seeking forgiveness, only to discover her father had his own share of regrets. "Of course I forgive you."

At last, he smiled. It was the smile from her youth. "Welcome home, Gigi. It's good to have you back."

"It's good to be back."

They shared another, longer hug, this one full of love and healing.

She stepped out of his embrace. "There's one more thing I need to tell you."

His brows drew together in a heavy frown. "I think there've been enough revelations for one day."

"I'm engaged to be married," she said. "I believe you will approve. He is everything admirable and worthy."

"High praise, indeed." But the worry returned to his expression.

"I greatly admire him. I love him with my whole heart, the heart of a woman, not the infatuated girl you once knew." The power of her certainty hitched the breath in her lungs. "I wish to pledge my life to his as soon as possible."

Her father's silver eyes became like smoldered glass, completely concealing his thoughts. He stared up at the ceiling, his expression so focused and intense that Gigi found herself looking up as well.

"Dare I ask the name of your fiancé?"

"Christopher Fitzpatrick."

Wide eyes stared back at her. "You want to marry Fitz?"

"We'd like your blessing, sir," Fitz said from the doorway.

Throat suddenly dry, Gigi turned to the man she loved. Words failed her. Coherent thought disappeared. So . . . she simply . . . stared.

Fitz responded in kind.

"You didn't have to come," she told him. But, oh, she was glad to see him.

"I needed to make sure you were all right." He cut a quick look at her father. "Are you all right, Gigi?"

How could she not be? Fitz had come to stand by her, no matter the reception she received. But he'd also given her the chance to state her case first.

Fitz trusted and respected her, and yet he loved her enough to want to protect her.

She reached out to him.

He took her hand.

"How, exactly"—her father divided a look between them—"did this come about?"

With uncharacteristic passion and verve, Fitz explained his yearlong search for Gigi and how, once he'd found her, he had worked to win her heart.

"I love your daughter, sir."

Hard to argue, when the proof was in his romantic retelling of the past weeks.

"I want to marry her."

And then, with a smile for Gigi and a slap on Fitz's back, her father said four of the most beautiful words in the English language. "You have my blessing."

* * *

Fitz proved, as always, to be a man of his word.

Gigi was impressed with how he'd removed all obstacles standing in the way of a quick wedding. He'd called in favors, secured the marriage license, and had even spoken personally with the minister of the church.

Apparently, it had taken considerable debate to convince the man of God that the reason for their haste was primarily due to Fitz's eagerness to make Gigi his wife and nothing more sordid.

The minister must have believed Fitz, because he'd agreed to perform the ceremony at their earliest convenience.

And so it was precisely one week and three days after Gigi had arrived home that she stood in her childhood room, preparing for the ceremony.

She'd requested they marry at Harvest House. Fitz had happily agreed.

They'd wanted a small ceremony. But once her sisters and mother had taken over, the simple wedding in her father's study had turned into an elaborate affair in the ballroom.

"You must give me this," her mother had said with no small amount of pleading. "I have always wanted one of my daughters to wed at home."

Annie was marrying Connor in three weeks at Trinity Church. So, after what Gigi had put her family through, she'd been more than willing to agree.

Fitz, being Fitz, hadn't cared where they married, so long as they said their vows as soon as humanly possible.

How she loved that man.

Gigi had risen early the morning of her wedding. Determined to impress her groom, she took special care dressing, paying particular attention to her hair. Her mother had sent in a maid to assist her in the preparations, but Gigi had looked the girl straight in the eye and then given her the rest of the day off.

Confident her hairstyle was some of her best work, Gigi pinned the last ribbon in place, brushed a wrinkle from her skirt, and picked up the letter that had arrived earlier that morning.

Smiling, she scanned Sophie's words with deep fondness for the young woman she considered a dear friend. Apparently, the elopement had been the bride's idea, a way for Sophie to prove to herself—as well as to her groom—that she no longer cared what New York society thought of her.

Gigi paused over the letter long enough to whisper, "Good for you, Sophie," then continued reading.

We honeymooned in Washington, DC. Robert wanted to visit the capital of his newly adopted country, and I had no objections. We spent two glorious days and nights touring the sites. We would have stayed longer, but Robert had to return to his job at New York Hospital. I am happy to report that he is already a favorite with the chief of surgeons. His volunteer work at the clinic in the Bowery is especially admired. I predict a promotion for my handsome groom in the near future.

The pride in Sophie's words all but jumped off the page. One more cause for relief, Gigi thought.

I can scarcely believe my good fortune in husbands. Even Mama adores him, which was as much of a surprise to her as it was to me.

Gigi laughed softly. She could just imagine Esmeralda bestowing her favor on the newlyweds with dramatic flair, as if she were a queen and they her loyal subjects.

I am not the least bit ashamed to admit that Robert spoils me beyond measure. He recently purchased a town house on the same block where Penelope and Simon live, which is barely a half mile from Luke and Elizabeth's home. Our children will grow up playing with their cousins. I cannot ask for a better situation, or a happier ending to my story.

"Nor could I," Gigi whispered, setting aside the letter with a grateful heart. Her prayers had been answered. All had turned out well for Sophie.

Smiling, Gigi strolled to the window overlooking Harvest House's backyard and took in the view. The sun shone in a cloudless sky, soaring over a world washed white with snow. It was a perfect day for a wedding.

A soft knock heralded her sister's entrance.

"Oh, *Gigi*." Annie gasped, her words coming out in a rush of pleasure. "You're beautiful."

A breath later, she was pulled into Annie's embrace.

She clung to her sister. *I should have come home sooner.* The thought was becoming an hourly refrain. And yet, had Gigi left New York before now, she wouldn't have learned the lessons Sally Smith had taught her.

One more squeeze and Annie released her.

In the clear light of day, Gigi studied her sister. It was like looking in a mirror. They were of a similar height and had the same red hair, face shape, and delicate features.

"I'm so happy you're marrying Fitz. I always thought he was your perfect match."

An overwhelming rush of affection filled Gigi. This wasn't the first time her sister had said this in the past week. Nor was it the first time she'd admitted just how right Annie was.

She and Fitz *were* perfectly suited. Her penchant for impulse tempered his tendency toward rigidness. Her love of the dramatic complemented his love of speed.

She'd once thought the man boring? How wrong she'd been. One ride in his motorcar had dispelled any lingering doubts. Fitz had the heart of a rebel beneath his starched exterior, much like her own. He just did a better job of hiding it.

"I wish I had seen the truth sooner," she said now to Annie.

"Yes, well, the past is the past."

"I've made so many mistakes."

"We all have." Annie linked their arms. "It's what we do in the aftermath of our mistakes that determines our character."

"When did you get so wise?"

Annie shot her a grin from over her shoulder. "Blame Connor. He's always saying things like that."

The mention of her sister's fiancé was the perfect opening for Gigi to ask one more time, "Annie, are you certain you aren't upset about Great-grandmother's pearls?"

"Oh, Gigi, please stop worrying. You have to believe me when I say I would much prefer having my sister back home and in my life than a silly old necklace that I would have worn once."

Sounds of happiness moved up Gigi's throat. "I love you, Annabeth Wentworth."

"Of course you do. Everyone does."

They shared a watery smile.

"Oh, no. No crying. I was sent to fetch you. Mother will have my head if you arrive downstairs with red eyes and a runny nose."

This time, Gigi did laugh.

"The guests are assembled." Annie unlinked their arms, then reached out a hand. "It's time to get married, dear sister."

Smiling, Gigi reached out as well, but a low-pitched clearing of a throat had her dropping her hand and peering toward the masculine sound.

"Father," she said in surprise. "I thought you were waiting with Mother downstairs."

He moved deeper into the room with his usual air of authority. "I would like to speak with you first."

He sounded so formal. So distant. So like the father who'd given her the ultimatum that had sent her running.

But then he smiled, revealing a dimple in his left cheek, and Gigi immediately relaxed.

"I'll leave you two to talk." Annie squeezed Gigi's hand, kissed her father's cheek, then left the room humming the wedding march.

Alone with her father, Gigi stood very still, very attentive.

Seeming in no hurry to speak, he scanned the room and then flicked a glance out the window. After moving closer, he rocked back on his heels and studied the scenery below.

Gigi held her breath as he turned to face her again. When their eyes met, she saw fatherly love staring back at her.

"You make a beautiful bride, my dear." Tears formed in his eyes. "You look so much like your mother on our wedding day."

Love and hope blossomed in her heart. "That's the best compliment you could have given me."

"I have something for you." He stuck his hand into one of the inner pockets of his coat and pulled out a small velvet box.

Gigi willed her own tears into submission with a hard swallow.

"Oh, Father," she said, curling her fingers around the gift.

"Go on. Open it."

She flipped back the lid and gasped at a beautiful emerald-and-diamond pendant on a gold chain.

"It belonged to my mother," he said, his voice storming with emotion.

Blinking rapidly, Gigi concentrated on the necklace. On the black velvet box. On anything but the fresh ache in her chest.

"I remember her wearing this," she whispered. "At all the important family gatherings."

"Your mother and I want you to wear it today, the start of a new family tradition."

The muscles in her throat quivered, making a coherent response impossible. In silence, she handed him the necklace, turned to face the mirror.

"Will you help me with the clasp?" she choked out.

Epilogue

The wedding reception lasted two hours. Gigi and Fitz had a train to catch for New York City, where they would spend their wedding night and two additional days. With Calvin Fitzpatrick's illness, and Gigi still in the early phases of restoring her relationships with her family, neither the bride nor the groom wanted to stay away any longer.

Due to the modern convenience of railroads, and Fitz's newfound penchant for calling in favors, the newlyweds were settled in their suite at the Park Avenue Hotel by the end of the day.

While her husband ran a mysterious errand, Gigi stood at the window overlooking the bustling streets below. She watched the sun dip below the horizon, turning a strip of low-riding clouds a kaleidoscope of pinks, purples, and golds.

Fitz entered the suite, calling out her name.

Gigi glanced over her shoulder. "Yes?"

"You will be happy to know I have secured us a private box for the performance tonight."

Her brows shot up. According to the hotel manager, Esmeralda's play was sold out for the next three weeks. "How on earth did you manage that?"

"Simple, really." He drew alongside her and gave her a tender kiss on the lips. "All I had to do was purchase the theater."

"You bought the Summer Garden? But I thought you said it was a bad investment."

He groaned at the reminder. "I have learned that some investments can't be quantified properly, not where sentiment is concerned."

That sounded nothing like the man who'd made a name for himself in corporate finance. "Is that so?"

"I have something for you." He slipped his hand inside his coat, pulled out what looked like an official document. "Your wedding gift."

Gigi's eyes went wide with pleasure, reading eagerly. It didn't take long for her to realize she held the deed to the Summer Garden in her hand.

"You really, truly purchased the theater. And . . . and . . ." She read to the end. "Oh, Fitz, you wonderful, thoughtful, romantic fool. You put the theater in my name."

"Happy wedding day, my love."

"It's the best gift anyone has ever given me." She wrapped her arms around his neck. "You are an amazing, perfect—"

He kissed the rest of her words away.

Lost in the glorious moment, they kissed for a long time before they pulled apart, both gasping for air, grinning like romantic fools.

She kissed him again, shorter, but with equal passion and dedication to the task. "Thank you," she whispered against his mouth.

"I have one more surprise for you."

Arms still wrapped around him, she twined her fingers into the hair at the nape of his neck. "I don't think I can bear much more excitement."

"You'll like this one."

"I liked the first one." She dropped her hands. "Actually, I loved it, nearly as much as I love you."

He kissed her on the right temple, then the left. "Sophie and her new husband are joining us tonight."

"Truly?"

"Luke and Elizabeth will be there as well."

Gigi couldn't wish for better company. The couples weren't considered the most popular among New York society and were denied access to certain homes, but they were some of the finest people Gigi knew. She was proud to call them friends. "Oh, Fitz. Would it be too much if I kissed you again?"

"You have to ask?"

Moments later, both breathless, Fitz made a grand show of stepping back and putting distance between them. "Unfortunately, Caroline and Jackson are unable to attend. Your friend is suffering from severe morning sickness."

"Poor Caroline."

"I have more bad news."

Gigi frowned. "I'm afraid to ask."

"It appears your great-grandmother's pearls are, indeed, lost forever. Mr. Ryerson has proven himself a skunk of the first order. Not only did he sell the necklace, he destroyed all evidence that it was ever in his possession."

Though disappointed, Gigi wasn't surprised by this turn of events. When Fitz had told her of his plan to approach the pawnbroker, she'd hoped for the best but had prepared for the worst. Mr. Ryerson was one of the shadiest men she'd ever met.

"I'm sorry I wasn't able to buy back the pearls."

"Oh, Fitz." She cupped his cheek, humbled by his love. "What a good man you are. I'm grateful you attempted to recover them at all."

He pressed his lips to her palm, then released her hand. "I suppose now would be a good time to share happier news."

"The very best."

"You'll have many chances to see your friends in the future. I invested in Luke's automobile company. I am a full partner and plan to oversee my interest personally."

"You want to move to New York?" Gigi didn't want that. She didn't think Fitz did, either. Were they about to have their first argument as a married couple?

"I would never ask you to leave your family." His gaze darkened, and he grew very serious. "And I can't abandon my father, not for long spans of time. I thought we could have two houses, one in Boston, one in New York."

Gigi liked that idea.

"We'll live mostly in Boston, of course, but come to New York as often as we can. And . . . I'm making decisions without you." He shoved a hand through his hair. "What do you think of my idea?"

"I think"—she took his impossibly handsome face in her hands—"it's a brilliant plan."

There was more kissing after that, and still more, and then a considerable bit more. They arrived late at the theater. No one said a word. The owner, after all, was allowed a bit of leeway.

Esmeralda put on the performance of a lifetime.

Some speculated this was due to Sophie and Robert Dain's presence in the audience. Others suspected it was because of the new owner's unexpected arrival. Gigi figured it was a combination of both.

After the final curtain call, Gigi and Fitz said good-bye to their friends, then went backstage to congratulate the cast on a stellar performance. Barely twenty minutes later, Fitz pulled Gigi into a shadowed corner behind a piece of scenery from the second act.

"I find I am a selfish man at heart." He said this against her ear, his breath sending pleasant shivers down her back. "I want you all to myself."

"I like the sound of that." She nuzzled against him, then pressed a kiss to his clean-shaven jaw, another to his lips. "But there's one last stop I'd like to make before we leave the building."

"I had a feeling you might say that. Come along, then." He hooked her arm through his and tugged her toward the nursery. "Let's say hello to the children."

Mrs. Tupper welcomed them with a broad smile. Lilly and Amelia showed their delight in a series of ear-splitting squeals, while Fern got straight down to business. She tugged on Gigi's skirt and asked, "Will you read us a story?"

"What a wonderful idea," Fitz declared, joining the little girls on the floor without hesitation.

Happy to oblige her captive audience, Gigi took her place in the rocking chair. "Which story should I read?"

"Briar Rose," all three children said in unison.

"Because Prince is here," Amelia explained as she climbed onto Fitz's lap. He laughed fondly when she proceeded to tell him every major plot point of the story before Gigi had a chance to open the book.

One day that will be one of our children chattering away with Fitz. And he'll listen with that same affectionate grin on his handsome face.

Gigi lost herself in the image for a moment. Then, with the help of an impatient prompting from Lilly, she turned to the proper page and began reading. "'A king and queen once upon a time reigned in a country a great way off' . . .'"

It was the perfect ending to a perfect day, and the perfect beginning to a future Gigi would live well with the man she loved.

Discussion Questions

1. Why is Gigi visiting the pawnshop in Herald Square? What happens during the meeting with the owner that leaves her upset? How long does she have to come up with a solution?

2. What is Gigi hiding from? Why has she changed her name to Sally Smith and taken on the role of lady's maid? Who is she serving now?

3. Who does Gigi encounter at the Summer Garden Theater? What does his appearance mean? Have you ever had a plan that was thwarted before you could put it into motion? Explain.

4. Describe Fitz and Gigi's history. How did Fitz find Gigi? Why has he come now? Does his reason for seeking her out change over the course of the book? If so, how?

5. What does Esmeralda want Gigi to do for her concerning her daughter? How does Gigi feel about this? How does Sophie feel?

6. Why does Fitz seek out a medical professional? What comes of this meeting?

7. What happens the first time Gigi asks Fitz to let her return the pearls? What happens the second time she asks? Why has Fitz had a change of heart? Have you ever

been determined to follow through with a plan only to decide to let it go? What happened?

8. Why does Fitz meet with Lucian Griffin? What comes of that meeting?

9. What happens at the church service? Why is Gigi so distraught? Does the message of forgiveness ring true? Have you ever had to forgive yourself for something? How did that turn out?

10. What is in the envelope that Sophie gives Gigi? Why does Gigi agree to go to the luncheon?

11. What happens at the luncheon? Who shows up afterward? How does Fitz "fix" the problem?

12. Why does Fitz leave New York? What happens during his visit home? What advice does his mother give him?

13. When Gigi returns to the pawnshop, what happens? What does she decide to do?

14. Where does Fitz find Gigi? What is her reaction when he tries to give her a way out of marrying him?

15. What happens when Gigi confronts her father? What does he give her on her wedding day? What wedding gift does Fitz give her? Why is this special?

About the Author

Photo © 2012 Caroline Akins / One Six Photography

Renee Ryan is the author of over twenty inspirational, faith-based romance novels. She received the Daphne du Maurier Award for Excellence in Mystery/Suspense in the Inspirational category for her novels *Dangerous Allies* and *Courting the Enemy*. She is an active member on the board of the Romance Writers of America. Ryan currently lives in Lincoln, Nebraska, with her husband. For more information on the author and her work, visit www.reneeryan.com.